**BRAND NEW!**
**Special Triple Western Edition!**
**Three action-packed western adventures**
**by Lee Floren**
**in this low-cost collector's volume.**

# RENEGADE RIFLES

"Put down that rifle, you ol' fool!"

Jim Overcast's thin lips sported a tight little smile. When he shook his head, the flaps of his muskrat-skin cap wobbled.

"Not until this young bucko is safe in his saddle do I put down the rifle." Bill felt the imprint of the oldster's eyes. "When you feel ready, young man, climb into leather, an' we'll sashay out of these diggin's."

"Thanks," Bill said, his voice almost natural.

Al Ganns suddenly sat up, sanity full on him. He wiped blood from his nose and he glared at Bill Dupree. Bill got to his feet, eyes on the man. He expected the Rawson man to explode with oaths.

Jim Overcast said, "You'll live, Ganns."

Ganns said, "None of your jokes, you old reprobated hunk of leather." He looked at Bill. "You might have won the first hand, fella, but we might deal out some more cards some other day, savvy?"

# BUCKSKIN CHALLENGE

He came to a stairway and went down it, knife in his hand. His eyes searched the darkness. He stopped at its base and squatted, knife between his teeth. He heard nothing out of the ordinary. The hull squeaked occasionally as it lifted and fell and rubbed against a fir piling. His eyes probed the darkness and became somewhat accustomed to the blackness.

Suddenly, he heard a strange noise.

He stiffened against the wall of the cabin behind the door. He heard a man coming. He was whistling a gay tune. His boots came along the walkway and stopped in front of the cabin door. Then the door opened. It did not open to its full width, though; this told Ed the man was not entering. He had his knife in his hand. The guard never knew how close he was to death.

# GUN QUICK

Jocko Smith blocked the doorway. He was crouched and his right hand hung over his pistol. His long face was twisted, his eyes narrowed slits.

"You gunned me down," Smith said shortly. "An' now I'm paying you back, Harrison—and with interest! You've got a gun. So use it here and now—"

Smith had not noticed that Wad Martin had come in behind him—even now, Jocko Smith was pulling. Matt rolled to one side, gun rising—he put everything he owned into his draw but sick coldness told him Smith had him bested. Jocko Smith was lightning fast.

Smith shot once.

The bullet plowed into the floor at Smith's own boots, shooting up splinters. Wad Martin had hammered a hard fist down on Smith's head from behind, sending him reeling.

# RENEGADE RIFLES/
# BUCKSKIN CHALLENGE/
# GUN QUICK

## LEE FLOREN

LEISURE BOOKS   NEW YORK CITY

A LEISURE BOOK®

December 1990

Published by

Dorchester Publishing Co., Inc.
276 Fifth Avenue
New York, NY 10001

# RENEGADE RIFLES

# ONE

This was one of the coldest winters northern Montana had ever seen. Snow fell early. Howling blizzard after blizzard roared across the Milk River rangelands. Always the thermometer was low in its bulb.

Usually, Montana winters had periods when the wind did not blow, and the sun was blue and distant and metallic in the cold, cloudless sky, but this winter no Chinook warm winds came.

Livestock died by the thousands, carcasses soon covered by the driving snow. Wolves and coyotes dined on dead cattle and horses and sheep, and were sleek and fat.

Mountain lions and bobcats moved through the timber, bellies distended and full. Saucy black and white magpies landed on the dead animals, and their sharp, long bills began pecking.

Here, during these early stirrings of Montana's history, were two types of men, those white of skin and those red of skin. And though the driving successions of blizzards took deadly toll in cattle and sheep, they also reached their icy fingers into the ranks of the men, both white and red. Down along the Milk River and along Beaver Creek, up in the lodges of the Little Rockies, the redman huddled in his teepee, body warm on one side from the fire and the other side cold. Squaws died and papooses died, and the buck sometimes died, too. They wailed and prayed to their Manitou, and all the time the great Arctic owl circled overhead on clear days, harbinger of harsher weather yet to come. For he had been driven out of his Arctic home, and had come south.

One morning in December, after an exceptionally tough blizzard, game warden Bill Dupree sat his pinto gelding on a hill, his breath hanging in the cold winter air air now silent and registering about forty below zero. Below him was a coulee about two hundred feet wide. Down there Ed Rawson and his hands were skinning out dead sheep—sheep that had been trapped in this draw and had frozen to death. Now the men and the teams of Ed Rawson were stamping the snow flat as they moved back and forth about their grisly task.

The dark eyes of game warden Bill Dupree were narrowed in thoughtful speculation. Occasionally his pinto stirred, fighting the cold, but the horse was tired, for he had bucked the snowdrifts out to this point here on the ridge. He was a tough horse, this pinto, just as his rider was a tough man—although mild-spoken Bill Dupree would have been the last person on earth to boast of toughness. He was a wiry man of about twenty-five, but his age, at this moment, was hard to determine. Frost had bit into his high-cheekboned face, and the skin was peeling a little from his high nose—a nose somewhat hawkish in appearance.

A muskrat-skin cap, made by a Mandan Sioux squaw, was on his head, the flaps tied under his square jaw. A long sheepskin overcoat hid the muscles of his hard young body, and he wore a thick flannel shirt and heavy long woollen underwear. His pants were California pants, thick and made of wool, also. He did not wear high-heeled riding boots. Riding boots were never used by a horseman here in this rough winter climate. He wore overshoes, and under these were felt slippers and woollen socks. His feet were warm this way; a man could freeze his feet fast in riding-boots.

Sitting there, he watched the men and teams working below him, and his mind went back a few hours to the conversation he had heard in Dodson, the Montana town some eight miles or so to the north, huddled along Milk River. For the blizzard had howled for three days, but had died down toward morning. But it had turned the coulee into a death-trap for the woollies. The sheep had drifted with the howling sleet-thick wind—drifted to topple over the cutbank into the coulee and there die, bleating in pain against their cold lot.

That morning the owner of the sheep had found the frozen body of the Basque sheepherder out there in the snow-covered sagebrush. Now Bill remembered how the body had been taken into Dodson, the dead man lying stiff as a plank in the back of a bobsled pulled by two big gray horses.

The driver had pulled up in front of the Town House and had come inside. Bill had been eating breakfast— eggs, ham, toast and gallons of coffee. The driver—a roustabout for a big sheep-outfit—was filled with importance, his scrawny chest bulging.

"Got a dead man in my bobsled outside," he told the entire house. "Oh, there you are, marshal, over at the far table. The boss told me to report his death to you, 'cause you sit as county coroner too, he done told me."

The marshal had got to his feet. "Who is the dead man, and how did he die?"

The man rattled off the dead sheepherder's name. "Us Circle F fellows lost our whole Beaver Crick herd to the blizzard. After the sheepherder froze to death, the whole band—must have been a thousand head—must've started to wander with the storm. They went over a cutbank and there they are on the flat, dead as they'll ever be. What'll I do with the corpse?"

The marshal had grudgingly gone to work. They had toted the dead sheepherder into a little log building used as a town morgue. They did not need a stretcher to carry him for he was frozen stiff as a two-by-four lumber. The driver did not help the lawman and the other man, but he remained in the hotel dining room close to the pot-bellied stove, rubbing his hands for circulation. Bill Dupree had sat about ten feet away and the man's eyes ligthed on him.

"Ed Rawson done bought every head of them dead woollies from the boss," the man said. "Two cents of pelt, but Rawson and his crew has to do the skinnin'. You ought to ride out there, stranger, and hit Rawson up for a job. He'll need some hands with that many head to skin."

"You seem anxious to get me to work." Bill Dupree had shown a tight smile. The arrogance of the man irritated him sowewhat, and he did not know exactly why. Then he laid his finger on the sore spot. He did not like overbearing, self-important people, and this man acted as though he had just brought in great news, which he had definitely not done.

Bill had come into this area the week before. He had a job to do . . . and he was out to do it, and nobody but himself on this range knew he was a game warden, and he wanted this information kept secret. He had pretended he had been looking for work. He had said he would work on either spread, sheep or cattle. This put him somewhat apart. For no cowpuncher, decent and upright, would work with sheep and no sheepherder, likewise loyal, would work with cattle. And then another thing also set Bill Dupree apart, and he was keenly aware of this, also.

He was a halfbreed.

His white father, who was now dead, had come into the Dakota territory as a Hudson Bay trapper, and he had met Quick Dove, the Mandan Sioux squaw. They had been married by the father in the Black Hills and the children had come. Bill was the last of fourteen, all miraculously alive, and he had been educated in the school on the Rosebud Reservation, to the east in the Dakotas. He had gone into government service, and here he was—a federal game warden.

But still, he was a halfbreed. Educated or not educated, he was marked by the times, by his breeding, by his dusky skin. He tried not to let it bother him but it did bother him, for he wanted, like all humans, to belong to the great legion of man, and to him the colour of skin meant nothing. It was what was inside a man or woman that counted, and the blackness or redness or whiteness of their skin meant, to him, little or nothing.

At this time, with the terrible Indian Wars so close behind in history, a halfbreed there belonged to neither the red or the white—he was in between, lodged in neither niche. The whites referred to him as an *Injun*; the Indians referred to him as a *damned white*.

Bill was aware of this, too.

He stirred in his saddle, the cold biting through his buckskin mittens with their woollen liners. And his memory moved back to the scene in the hotel dining room.

"Here's a chance for a job," the man had said, importance still on him. You would think from the way he talked and acted he was about to hire Bill himself. "You're lookin' for work, so here it is."

Bill had said, "I'll ride out to see Rawson, and many thanks."

"Don't thank me, fella. Skinnin' them frozen woollies with the thermometer at thirty odd below ain't no nice job."

"A man has to eat," Bill had said.

Bill had saddled his horse and had headed south toward the snow-covered foothills. The day was ice-sharp with metallic coldness. Occasionally there would be bursts of wind that moved the salt-like granules of snow, but for the most part the day was calm—coldness hung on the air and his breath was steam-white, a cloud ahead of him. He had bucked some snowdrifts that had taken the energy out of his horse in a hurry, but then he had found the trail left by Rawson and his hands as they had headed for the draw to skin the sheep. They had moved in with bobsleds and teams, and the hoofs of the horses and the runners of the bobsleds had made a rather hard trail. For this trail the horse had apparently been grateful, for he had picked up his pace, not having to break his own trail through the snow. To the south the Little Rocky Mountains were snow-swept peaks, and occasionally a person, despite the distance, could see the crags, high and wind-blown. This was a wide and gigantic land, slumbering in stubborn cold-silence under the snow. But when Spring came the snow would melt, some of its moisture would soak into the ground and some would run into streams, making them reach the flood-stage. The crocuses would come out of the soil in miraculous beauty, spreading their fragile thin-blue petals, and the grass would leap behind the flowers, bringing a clean green carpet to the rangelands. But Spring was still some days away, Bill realized; by the coming of Spring, he would have to have this mystery solved, for when warm weather finally came, fur would be no good, for the fur-bearing animal—especially the beaver—would have slipped his winter fur, thereby rendering his pelt useless.

Now Bill watched the men working below him. He had his thoughts, and they stirred across his high-cheek-boned face, giving him, for a moment, a predatory hardness. Then he rode down the slope toward the men and the teams there in the coulee with its carcasses of dead woollies.

The hardness had departed from his face, giving his brown-red skin a deceptive smoothness.

Bill was quick to notice that Ed Rawson's men knew how

to skin the dead sheep. They had had much practice lately, he realized. Thousands of sheep and cattle had died because of the blizzards and the cold weather. The skinners, he saw, worked in pairs, two men to each pelt. The sheep had died in a pile about three sheep deep. Snow had been driven over their carcasses and therefore they had to be pulled out of the drifts. After dragging a frozen sheep from the pile, the skinners dexterously cut the pelt down the belly and their sharp knives skinned out the hind legs. The pelt was then cut loose around the front ankles and the neck. This left the hind-legs bare and around these were passed two small chains attached to a single-tree. This kept the legs spread wide. Then another chain was attached around the loose hide hanging from the hind legs. This was then run out and tied onto the double-trees of a team of horses. Meanwhile, the chain running to the single-tree, holding apart the frozen hind legs, had been attached to another team of horses.

From then on it was simple. Each team went in opposite directions, the dead sheep between them. They literally ripped the pelt loose from the dead woollie. The carcass went with one team, the pelt with the other. In a few seconds the sheep had lost his overcoat.

Then the chains were taken off the carcass and the pelt. The pelt was tossed onto a bobsled and the carcass was left in the snow. Then another woollie was dragged from the pile, he was slit open from jaw to under his tail, the hind legs were skinned out, the teams moved in—the process was repeated.

By pulling the pelts loose, much knife-work was eliminated. The work went faster—much faster—than if the sheep had been skinned in the usual manner with a knife. At two cents a pelt, a man and team had to keep moving.

The carcasses of the skinned sheep were all around. Coyotes and wolves would devour some of these, but they could not eat them all. When Spring came and they thawed out, flies by the millions would swarm over the stinking hunks of flesh. Bill looked at the man who was piling the hides flat in a bobsled. He was throwing a little salt on each pelt, the rocksalt landing on the flesh-side. The pelts would be hauled to Dodson and loaded onto a Great Northern boxcar. There would be more salt applied to them as they were stacked in the boxcar, Bill knew. Suddenly a harsh voice cut into the game-warden's thoughts, the voice coming from behind him.

"What do you want, fella?"

Bill had been so interested in watching the skinners he had not heard Ed Rawson come behind him in the silent snow. Now he stood on his stirrups and turned a little in his saddle, with surprise momentarily moving across his wind-beaten face.

He looked at the man below him. "You're Mr Rawson, aren't you?"

"I'm Ed Rawson."

Bill Dupree was looking at a man who was not too tall, but who was very, very broad. Of course, his thick sheepskin coat, going to his knees, made him look more squat than he actually was, and it also helped build out shoulders and torso already bulky and thick with muscles. Bill figured the man was somewhere around thirty years of age—give or take a year or so. Rawson also wore a muskrat-skin cap, but the flaps hung loose on each side of his big face, the strings dangling. He looked up at Bill, eyes narrowed a little to fight off the reflection of cold sun on cold snow—his eyes were a dull brown, Bill saw. His face was square where Bill's face was lean, his nose was flat and wide where Bill's was Indian and hawkish, his lips were thick where Bill Dupree's lips were thin. A week of stubble covered the heavy jowls and made his face look even wider.

"What do you want?" Rawson asked, and his voice was not cordial.

Bill smiled despite his irritation. "I want a job," he said evenly.

The narrowed eyes studied him momentarily. "Ain't you the bum that has been hanging around Dodson for the last week or so?"

Bill overlooked the word *bum*. He was not looking for trouble. "I rode out from Dodson to ask you for a job, Rawson. I was in town when the fellow brought in the dead sheepherder. Fellow mentioned you might be hiring a hand or two to help with the skinning."

"You're an Injun, ain't you?"

Bill Dupree felt hardness take over. But he kept his anger down. "If it is any of your business, I'm a halfbreed. But I came out here to ask for a job, Rawson, and not to discuss the human race."

"I ain't hirin' no Injuns."

Bill apparently overlooked that jibe, too. He seemed to speak almost lazily. "I'm from the Black Hills. I trapped there last winter. I'm a good trapper, Rawson." Presumably he was watching the crew doing the skinning. Actually, from the corner of his eye, he was watching Ed Rawson.

"I ain't hirin' nobody, even if he used to be a trapper." Rawson kept his brown eyes on Bill. "I got a farm down in the valley. Farmin' is a tough way to make a livin', 'specially since last summer was so dry."

Bill nodded.

"Seein' sheep was freezin' to death, and the sheepmen never wanted to skin them, I bought these pelts to make a few honest dollars. But I can't hire another hand, be he a trapper or a skinner, Injun."

There it was again . . . *Injun.*

# TWO

Anger ran its ugly distance across Bill Dupree's face, but clear-headedness came in and shoved it to one side. The thought came that he had a job to perform here on Milk River—an important job—and this job required he keep a clear head. The thought came that maybe he had made the wrong statement when he had mentioned being a trapper.

He had been feeling out Ed Rawson. Maybe no damage had been done. He hoped so. He murmured, "A long cold ride out from Dodson for nothing."

"For nothing."

There was a moment when no words were spoken. The teams moved back and forth, ripping hides from the dead woollies. Tug chains jangled, men spoke in voices that the cold air carried easily; there was the sound of hide tearing loose from frozen flesh, the pound of shod horsehoofs against the snow that was already becoming packed and solid.

Bill was quick to notice that a man named Al Ganns stood a few feet away and was listening to them talk. Al Ganns, from what Bill had heard, was Rawson's straw-boss. Ganns was not too tall and he, also, was very wide. He looked momentarily at Bill and the impression of his small eyes was strong on the game-warden. Bill glanced at him and Al Ganns looked away.

He had heard tell that Al Ganns was a tough customer in a rough-and-tumble fight. From what he had been told, Ganns had had a number of saloon brawls down in Dodson, and had come out winner every time. Bill had come into this Milk River country two years ago, and they had proved-up on adjoining homesteads. But Ganns had sold his property to Rawson and now worked for him. Rawson had bought out other farmers, and now he controlled some of the finest land on the river bottom.

Bill had listened carefully. He knew that a man could learn a lot if he kept his mouth shut most of the time and had his ears peeled back. Farmers had come into the basin and the drought had broken them, and Rawson had stepped in and bought them out. He had beat two local cow-outfits to the punch, for they also had wanted the land on which the farmers had filed homestead entries.

Two big cow-outfits ran cattle here on Milk River. The north side of the river was controlled by the Bar S, an outfit that ran cattle north to the Canadian line, about fifty miles across the snow. The Box 7 ran its stock on the south side of the muddy river that had been named some eighty odd years ago by the Lewis and Clark expedition. Milk River, the explorers had named it, because its brown waters were the colour of coffee with cream in it. The Box 7 ran its cattle south to the Missouri—the Big Muddy—which was about sixty miles away. They were big, powerful outfits, the Bar S and the Box 7. They had trekked in cattle after the Civil War, coming up the Powder River trail out of Texas. From what Bill had heard, each outfit had expected the farmers to settle, then find that the river-bottom was no good for farming without irrigation. Then the two cow-outfits had expected the disappointed farmers to move on, and the range would go back to normal after the cattlemen had jerked down the barbwire left by the hoemen.

But Ed Rawson had fooled both the Box 7 and the Bar S. Before either outfit was fully aware of what was happening, Rawson had bought the deeds from the farmers. Now he controlled much acreage down on the river's bottomlands. Before the Box 7 and the Bar S had become aware of it, a new cattle king was sprouting right under their proud and stern noses.

Many people wondered where Ed Rawson got the money to swing these deals, to purchase the deeds. Of course, the farmers, being broke and hard-up for cash, had sold out at a low price, Bill had heard. But Rawson had bought quite a few of them out, so therefore he had spent quite a sum of money, despite the fact each had sold at a low price. The local people were not the only ones who wondered where Rawson got the money. Bill Dupree also had his conjectures. Because of these, he was on this Milk River range . . .

Now Bill Dupree's mind flicked back two weeks to the time when he had sat in the main office in Miles City, which was also in Montana but some two hundred miles or so to the southeast. And he remembered the words of the boss, head game-warden Matt Driscoll.

"Bill, I have a bit of work for you."

"Good, Matt."

Matt Driscoll had walked to the big map on the wall. The office was warm, the pot-bellied heater red with Montana lignite coal, but outside the storm rapped on the windows with cold knuckles. Driscoll picked up a pointer, much as a schoolteacher does, and let the tip of the pointer rest on Dodson, Montana.

"What's the trouble?" Bill had asked.

"Beaver pelts."

Bill had nodded. Beaver pelts were worth money. Hats were made out of beaver, and hats went all over the world from the New England mills. Beaver pelts were becoming scarce, too. The federal government had stepped in a few years before and laws—federal laws—were made protecting the beaver clan. Inroads of trappers had almost exterminated the beaver—the animal with the sleek pelt that lived in burrows along the banks of streams, who cut down willows and trees, and slapped mud against them with his broad tail to make his dams. Despite government regulation, beaver pelts were getting out of Montana, being smuggled to dealers back in the midwest and east. Bill walked to the map and stood beside his boss.

"Coming out of the Milk River country, huh, Matt?"

"That they are doing, Bill. We have worked back from St. Louis, trying to find the origin of the pelts. They are being bought in St. Louis."

"Any arrests?"

"Not yet."

"Why not?"

"We don't want the dealers who are buying the pelts as bad as we want to know who is trapping the beaver. The men doing the trapping are the ones to stop. The only way to kill a snake is to cut off his head."

Bill studied the map. "And the pelts come from around Dodson and Malta, huh?"

"We know that much."

"When do I start, boss?"

"Today, if you want to."

Bill looked now at the skinners and had his thoughts. Matt Driscoll had told him other essential points. Sign pointed to a man named Ed Rawson. And the voice of the head game-warden had been thick with warning.

"They tell me this Rawson's a tough gent. Some claim he has a prison record, but so far we have not located it. He has a sidekick named Al Ganns. We know one thing about Ganns: he has had trouble with the law back east. This is mostly hearsay, except for Ganns' record. We have had a little information out of the capital in Helena, but not much."

"Nobody else—no other game-warden—has done any work up there, huh?"

"That's right, Bill."

"I have to start from scratch, I take it?"

"That's the deal, Bill."

So Bill had headed north toward the Milk River country, and here he was. And so far he had discovered little . . . if anything. Three nights ago a stranger, plainly a trapper, had come into Dodson, had made discreet inquiries about the whereabouts of Ed Rawson, and then had left town on snowshoes, pack on his back. Bill had trailed him to Rawson's farm. That man, he knew now, was trapping on upper Beaver Creek, presumably trapping muskrats, skunks, an occasional mink, and maybe he would catch a marten or two before Spring came to make wilding shed their hair.

Bill did not know whether this newcomer trapped for himself or for Rawson. He had trailed the man two days ago, right after he had moved in on his trapping grounds. From his hiding-spots Bill had seen the man set traps for muskrats and mink, but had seen him make nothing that looked like beaver sets. And Beaver Creek had many beaver. The signs pointed that way—dams covered by ice and snow, the signs of their dens back in the creek banks.

Past experience had shown Bill that it was difficult to catch a man in the act of making beaver sets or pulling a beaver out of his traps. These beaver poachers set their traps in the dark and took them out of the water before daylight. And in this country it snowed almost every night and the poachers' tracks would be covered in a few minutes. And when it was not snowing, the poachers would not make their sets. Also, the snow was their friend in another manner—it limited visibility that the night did not kill.

So in this past week, Bill Dupree had gotten exactly nowhere, and he was aware of this as he looked at the skinners, with Al Ganns watching him covertly, and with Ed Rawson standing beside the pinto.

"No job," Rawson repeated.

Bill said, "I need work bad, man. I got to eat, Rawson."

"No work here."

"Think it over a few minutes?" Bill said, putting a pleading note in his voice. Evidently this pleased the big red-faced man, for he smiled. Bill knew what prompted that smile. Rawson hated Indians and a halfbreed, to him, was an Indian; he had one on his knees, begging for bread. This irked Bill, but he said nothing. And his mind went back to the problem at hand.

Government game-wardens in St. Louis had managed to get hold of a pelt that had been smuggled in, so Matt Driscoll had told him. From the hair-growth on this pelt and from its colour, they had identified the locale from which the pelt had come. The length of the hair-growth told them the beaver pelt had come from a very cold country. The colour was identified as the shade of colour belonging to beaver grown in Milk River valley around Dodson.

To the experts, this was an easy thing to do. They were trained to their jobs. A good skin was dragging down fifty bucks on the St. Louis market. A good trapper, working a new section of a creek at night, could pull out twenty pelts if the catch was normal. That meant a thousand dollars for a night's work.

Good money for a few hours of work, of danger. Now Bill's attention was jerked to Al Ganns, who came shuffling forward, big overshoes dragging on the snow. He spoke to Ed Rawson, but his eyes were on Bill Dupree.

"What does this Injun want, Ed?"

"A job."

Al Ganns kept his eyes on Bill. His eyes were sharp as a skinning-blade's edge, and Bill wondered if the man had not been drinking. He knew, from what he had heard in Dodson, that Al Ganns was a heavy drinker.

Now Ganns said, "A job, huh? You got a job for him, Ed?"

"No job."

Ganns grinned and nodded. "We got a good crew. A Injun is no good. Good for nothin', a Injun is. We don't need no Injuns on our crew." His eyes became colder now. "You might just as well ride on, fellow. Maybe you ain't all Injun blood, but we don't need no damned halfbreed, either. Now get to hell down the road, Injun!"

The others had heard. They stopped their work and watched. The challenge, mean an ugly, lay on the thin, cold air.

Bill had to take it, or get out of this Milk River country.

Bill had been in the act of turning his pinto. He did not want trouble. But if he sidestepped this he knew he was done on this snow-covered range. A coward did not last long here. Word would get around he had backed down in front of Al Ganns and he would be the laughing-stock of the community.

The skinners stood and watched. For a moment the thing was a frozen tableau—the horses standing still, loafing in their tugs; the frozen sheep, piled under the loose snow; the skinners watching like vultures—pointed and vigilant, eagerly anticipating trouble. Then this was gone, broken and shattered in the snow—and reality was facing him.

Bill said, "I don't want any trouble, Ganns."

Al Ganns said, so all could hear, "Another yellow 'breed, eh? Well, Injuns are that way, and a 'breed is mostly redman. Get one white man alone in six 'breeds, and the 'breeds are full of courage—they'll beat the hell out of the white man. But get one 'breed and one white man—the 'breed runs. Jes' like this Injun on the fancy pinto hoss is doin'!"

A skinner laughed at this moment. He laughed with a grating sound, like the knotty branches of an old cottonwood tree rubbing together in a slow, cold wind. His laugh had a grating effect on Bill Dupree, rubbing against him as rough as pumice.

Bill said, "You might have pegged this 'breed wrong, Ganns."

Ganns had a rough smile on his whiskery lips. "Can you get off that pinto and prove I've judged wrong, Injun?"

Bill saw right away that he had said the wrong thing. For that matter, anything he said would be twisted around by Al Ganns, he figured. He glanced at Ed Rawson. The man watched with a smiling face. Despite the smile, though, his face was tough, almost evil-looking.

Rawson said one word: "Yellow."

Bill looked back at Al Ganns. "I came out here looking for a job," he said. "I never came out here looking for trouble." He had a disturbing thought. Did this pair know he was a federal game-warden? There was something fishy about this. He got the impression that maybe he was walking into a trap set by these two. This seemed too patent, too set-up, too sure. Ganns wanted trouble . . . and he wanted it right now. And why should he want trouble with him, Bill Dupree, who was almost a stranger to Ganns?

Did he hate him just because he was a halfbreed? Head game-warden Matt Driscoll had promised him that his trip into the Milk River country—the reason behind it—would be kept in utmost secrecy, for Bill's life might depend on secrecy. Bill found himself wondering if, somehow, word had got ahead to Al Ganns and Ed Rawson. Maybe the pair was aware of his true identity?

This thought made his blood cold. A number of federal game-wardens had gone out to trace down illegitimate trapping and had never returned to head-quarters. The bodies of some had been discovered by their fellow wardens; the bodies or whereabouts of others had never become known. Bill thought suddenly of a hole being chopped in the blue-white ice of the Milk River. And when the ice-cold waters were exposed, into this hole would be slipped the body of a man, shoulders wired to his legs, his wrists, and his neck. It wouldn't be nice to lie there in the mud and have the big catfish nose around.

But maybe his imagination was running riot. He had no reason to believe word had got out of Driscoll's office. Driscoll was an old hand at this game, having come up through the federal service. Bill decided he had to avoid trouble. This might be a trap to get him to fight so one of them—Ganns or Rawson—could have a chance to kill him.

"I want no trouble, Ganns."

Al Ganns moved forward, overshoes crunching the snow. His right hand went out and bunched the reins behind the bit and the pinto was frozen in his grip, held in a vice-hard rigidity.

"Get off thet pinto, you damned breed! No 'breed is getting' the best of Al Ganns, then ridin' off scotfree!"

"I don't want trouble—"

"It ain't what you want now," the big man said huskily, "but it is what you'll get, fella!"

Bill realized this had gone too far. He could not escape a fistfight now, he knew. Ganns would reach up and drag him from his saddle. This knowledge was sharp in him, keen and cutting. He did some quick thinking. He doubted if he could whip Al Ganns with his fists. Ganns outweighed him by many pounds. Ganns was on the right side of the pinto. Bill had a sudden plan.

He took his right foot out of the stirrup. "I'll get off this horse and beat the hell out of you," he gritted. A satanic grin split the big man's whiskery face. He expected Bill's right foot to risé and go over the saddle as the man dismounted. But Bill did not dismount.

His ruse had worked. Now his right boot was free of the stirrup. Anchored in the saddle, body deep between fork and cantle, left foot braced against the other stirrup, Bill Dupree kicked out with a savage suddenness and unexpected hardness.

And too late Al Ganns realized his error.

Bill heard Ed Rawson yell out in warning. Ganns saw the heavy overshoe coming at him. He let the reins go free and he flung up his forearm to block the blow. Bill's foot smashed the arm to one side. The tip of his wide overshoe landed full on Al Gann's blocky jaw.

"Watch that boot!"

Ed Rawson had screamed the words—too late. Bill felt the crunch of his toe on Ganns' jaw. He felt good with savage elation. He figured Ganns outweighed him by at least thirty pounds. Some of these pounds, though, were probably fat and loose. He was younger by a few years than Ganns, too. He had spent a term at Haskell Institute—two years, in fact—and his body was still tough from football. These were points on his side.

He had been on the Haskell boxing team, too. Ganns, of course, did not know this—he apparently classified all redmen and halfbreeds under two labels: cowards and sneak-thieves. Bill had liked to box. He knew how to box, too. Not rough-and-tumble fighting; scientific fisticuffs. And he figured this would help him now.

Ganns was knocked backwards. He went staggering backwards, hands trying to grab the cold air for a hand-hold. He found no aid in the air, of course, and the next thing he knew, he was sitting in the snow, gasping for his breath. He was big and wild and awkward.

By now, Bill had slid out of his saddle, and he stood with his fists ready. He had hurriedly taken his mittens off and dropped them in the snow.

"Come on, Ganns," he said huskily.

Ganns got his hands down, burying them in the snow, and he jacked his body upright, never taking his eyes off the game-warden. He came out of the snow with a great slowness, seeming not a bit hurried or worried.

"First Injun I ever met what would fight," he said jerkily. "But like all 'breeds and redskins, he fights dirty—he kicks a man when he ain't looking."

"You aimed to drag me out of my saddle! I just beat you to the draw, Ganns. Are you going to fight or are you just going to blow off your big mouth?"

"Don't rush me, 'breed."

Rawson snarled, "Go in and git him, Al!"

The skinning of the sheep was completely forgotten. The two teamsters dropped their lines and watched in gleeful anticipation. Ganns would kill this young half-breed. The teams stood and paid no attention. The horses were not concerned with the foibles and craziness of a thing called man. They were glad to have a rest.

Ganns said, "Here I come."

He moved forward. He was in a crouch. Bill moved to the right. He could not retreat. His pinto stood directly behind him and he did not want Ganns to pin him against the horse, which would have happened had he stepped backwards. He had his plan of battle clear in his mind. Ganns outweighed him too much to fight close-in. He would fight from a distance, making Ganns rush. He would wear him down and then pick him off.

They were circling now. Their overshoes were tramping flat the fresh snow. Each looked for an opening. Ganns was wicked and low and his arms made short vicious blows. They were too short—they missed. Bill thought, we're two wolves. Circling, fangs bared; waiting for an opening. There it comes, and in goes my left hand.

He went in over Ganns' guard. His knuckles crashed down on the man's mouth, bringing a spurt of blood. This made Ganns mad. He moved ahead rapidly. He was faster than Bill had figured. Much faster, Bill discovered. Again, Bill hit with his left; he felt his knuckles rip flesh. He got in two blows and Ganns got in one. Ganns hit him with a mauling and stunning right fist. He hit Bill on the left ribs. Bill had to gasp. The blow had hurt him bad, coming close to his heart. It was like being hit with a hard-thrown boulder.

Bill's chest burned. He had taken blows before,

straight and true, but this curving and mauling blow had been the hardest he had ever assimilated, he was sure. If this were a sample of Ganns' power, he wanted to taste no more samples. One taste had been plenty.

Bill hurriedly decided he wanted no more of that right fist. He decided to circle to his right and he would be travelling with the blow if it landed again, and he figured it would land sooner or later. He knew he had hit Ganns twice with all the power his left hand owned. The blows had slowed Al Ganns but they had not stopped him. He was tough.

Accordingly Bill moved in a circle. Ganns stood still. Ganns couldn't understand this type of fighting. Bill had hit him twice; he had connected only once. The other men he had fought had been proud of their bull-strength. They had rushed in with their fists working madly, their arms spread wide, and they had been glad to clinch in a contest of brute strength. They had used no science.

"Come on in an' fight, Injun!"

But Bill did not fall for the taunt. He kept shuffling, moving, hitting—his left went in and out. He was waiting for a chance to cross his right in a solid uppercut.

"Come after me," he growled.

"I'll do that—" Ganns' words were clipped short. The left had hit him again on the mouth.

Ganns then moved ahead. His right hand was working like a piston. Bill blocked it and then crossed his right and he hit Ganns hard and solid. Again Ganns took the blows. Took it with his head solid on his rock-thick neck. Took them and waded in, relishing the fight.

Bill had to retreat. He hit as he went backwards. He could hear the dim scream of the watching men. They were begging him to stand and make a fight of it. But he was not taking their advice. He wasn't even heeding their voices. The yells were dim and distant sounds, somewhere outside the throbbing of his ears. They were meaningless water washing against dead sand.

Gone now was Bill Dupree's hesitation. Ganns had hit him and hurt him, and now Bill really wanted to fight. He had a hard time controlling his desire to bring the battle to Ganns. Only the realization that this would be fatal to his hopes kept him in retreat.

He was sure Ganns wanted to kill him. Every movement, every grimace, told Bill Dupree this. Bill realized he was possibly fighting for his life, his right to breath God's good air. He was in the toughest fight of his life.

Another thought came, quick in the heat of battle. Every stranger on this range would be under the suspicions of Ganns and Rawson if the pair were, in reality, beaver poachers. Every stranger would be considered a menace to them until time and circumstances proved otherwise.

Ganns grabbed him by the sleeve. Bill tried to jerk away. But he could not and they both toppled down into the snow with Ganns on top. Bill felt the man's hot, panting breath. He heard Ganns' panted words, meaningless and filled with hate. Ganns had him where he wanted him.

But Bill had done a little wrestling in college, too. He knew he would have to regain his feet. He got his knees in Ganns' belly and straightened them. They hammered against the man, driving him backward and off Bill. Ganns landed sitting down a few feet away.

Bill thought, I was lucky to get out that way so fast . . . He was on his feet now. His nose was jetting blood. He realised they were both getting winded. The fight seemed to have lasted for hours. Ganns had expected him to launch himself on him, and he got to his feet as fast as he could, too. But his fastest movements were rather slow, Bill was quick to notice.

Bill sucked in ice-cold air, filling his lungs in heaving breaths. He said pantingly, "Come on in, you big scissor-bill. I'm still a 'damned 'breed', remember?"

"I'm comin!"

The brief rest had given Al Ganns added strength. But it had also delivered to Bill Dupree his second wind. Ganns did not rush. He stood still, turning when Bill turned, and his fists were up. His face was bloody. Now he was fighting the way Bill had wanted him to fight from the start.

Bill circled him, jabbing and cutting him down. He went into a crouch and fought out of it and then, when Ganns seemed to have solved this form of fighting, Bill shifted to standing straight, sending in his left fist. His left was what decided the issue of the fight. Ganns could not solve it. It was a hard wall, hitting him, beating him—a wall between him and Bill. He tried to go under it and it came down; he tried to go over it, and it rose with him. Bill saw a frown of puzzlement groove the wide, bloody forehead. Ganns had never fought a man with science before. He was taking a beating.

Bill's knuckles knocked the frown away. Ganns hit him in the ribs again, but the blow was a mauling blow—it was not decisive and stunning as it had been at the start of the fight. Ganns hit and missed. Bill stepped in. For a moment, Al Ganns was wide-open, guard down.

Bill used that moment.

He brought in a right uppercut that started from his knees. He twisted his fist as it came in and thus he made it a ripping hammer. Ganns' head went back. Bill was mad with elation. The end was in sight.

The men watched now in silence. Their idol was getting whipped. The second blow—another right uppercut—dropped Ganns to the snow.

"My god," a man said.

"He whipped—Ganns!"

"He's out cold," another gasped.

Their voices rang with disbelief. Bill's arms felt like hunks of lead and his fists weighed tons. His forearms ached. Suddenly he heard Rawson's voice say, "Turn around, fellow, and tangle with me, huh?"

Bill turned as fast as he could, but he was very slow. He saw Rawson's fist coming and he tried to fling up an arm but he was very, very late. Rawson hit him back of his left ear, knuckles digging into the soft spot there. Bill dimly remembered falling.

He landed on his side in the snow. Both he and Al Ganns were now on their backs and on the ground. But he was not unconscious, although his ears were buzzing. He had a foolish thought. They had accused him of being yellow. But Rawson had slugged him from the side, and he had been out on his feet at the time. Rawson was the yellow son, not he.

He saw that Rawson was coming toward him. He knew the man was only about five feet away, but in his dazed condition Rawson seemed to waver in and out and sometimes he was twenty feet away and the next clock-tick he was on him. Bill figured the man intended to boot him and he got to his feet and then he went to his knees again, for his legs had failed him.

Rawson said, "I'll give you the boots, you damned—"

Then, without warning, Rawson stopped. He stopped as though he had run head-first into a rock wall. The words had stopped him. The voice was harsh, laden with authority.

"Don't move toward that man, you damned killer, or I'll shoot you!"

# THREE

Bill Dupree could stand on his knees no longer. He sat down and looked toward the direction of the voice which had come from his right.

A man stood there and Bill had difficulty focusing his eyes. The glare of the sun on snow was blinding. But he saw a short man who was not much over five feet tall. He held a rifle in his wizened, unmittened hands. The rifle looked as big as a cannon, but Bill blamed it on his wavering eyesight.

The first thing Bill thought of was that this man was a stranger to him. He held the rifle on Ed Rawson, too, so that meant he had come to help him, Bill Dupree. And this was indeed strange—a stranger helping him out.

Bill had steadier vision now. He looked up at the man's face, his eyes leaving the rifle. He saw an aged face, for the man was well up in the years. His face was as homely as a bone-dry prune. Wrinkled like a prune, too, from the wind and rain and sun and snow.

Rawson snarled, "You stay out of this mess, Jim Overcast."

So that was this ancient's name . . . Jim Overcast. The name made no niche in Bill's memory. Evidently Ed Rawson knew the man, though. Bill got the idea the old man was a local resident. But why would he buck the powerful Rawson to help a stranger?

That did not make sense. But maybe the old man was for fair play. Some men were still honest around here, so Bill had heard. By now his vision was steady and the buzzing had left his ears. He glanced at Al Ganns, who was stirring a little. Ganns was coming out of it.

Behind Jim Overcast was a mule, a homely long-eared reprobate. The mule had on an old saddle. Bill found surprise in this—very seldom did men ride mules in this country. But maybe Overcast was a farmer and the mule was the only form of transportation he had? Bill had to be content with that for an answer, not that the matter was very important. But the oddity of it struck him.

Bill heard the oldster give out with a dry chuckle. Apparently he was amused, but Bill got the impression that this was just a pose and that the old boy was hard as railroad steel underneath.

"I'm takin' a hand in this, Rawson. Here I am, riding out to court a widder, an' I run into this fistfight. This young fella beat Al Ganns fair an' square. You jumped on him when he was winded and pooped-out, Rawson. An' in my book thet ain't fair play."

"Put down that rifle, you ol' fool!"

Jim Overcast's thin lips sported a tight little smile. When he shook his head, the flaps of his muskrat-skin cap wobbled.

"Not until this young bucko is safe in his saddle do I put down this rifle." Bill felt the imprint of the oldster's eyes. "When you feel ready, young man, climb into leather, an' we'll sashay out of these diggin's."

"Thanks," Bill said, voice almost natural.

Al Ganns suddenly sat up, sanity full on him. He wiped blood from his nose and he glared at Bill Dupree. Bill got to his feet, eyes on the man. He expected the Rawson man to explode with oaths. In fact, Ganns let his mouth sag open slightly, like a fish gasping for air, and Bill saw he was not all there yet upstairs. Then Ganns clipped shut his mouth and said nothing.

Jim Overcast said, "You'll live, Ganns."

Ganns said, "None of your jokes, you old reprobated hunk of leather." He looked at Bill. "You might have won the first hand, fella, but we might deal out some more cards some other day, savvy?"

"Whenever you're ready," Bill said.

A workhorse shifted, cold biting through his thick winter-coat of fur, and his tug-chains made a sharp and lonely sound. The skinners said nothing, poised like buzzards, black against the clean snow.

With difficulty, Bill mounted his pinto. His muscles were sore and he ached in every joint.

"Hand him his mittens," Jim Overcast told a Rawson hand.

The skinner handed Bill the mittens. Bill jammed them in a pocket and draw his .45 from under his coat. He looked at Jim Overcast.

"I don't trust this bunch any further than you could throw a skunk by his tail, fellow. I'll ride back a spell and hold my gun on them while you get on your mule and ride over toward me."

"Good idea."

Rawson said, "You two ain't makin' no fast and true friends, Overcast."

"Me," said Overcast, mocking surprise. "Shucks, and I so want to be your boosom friend, Rawson."

"You break my heart," Bill Dupree said. He turned the pinto and when he was about fifty yards away, he stopped him and let his short-gun cover the Rawson bunch. "Come on, Overcast."

"Be along pronto."

Jim Overcast got his stirrup and went up on his mule with agility. He loped over to where Bill Dupree sat the pinto. Bill was about ready to holster his weapon. He figured the precaution he had taken had been wasted energy. But still, he knew he could not trust Rawson or Ganns . . . or any of the Rawson hands. But he was danged glad old Jim Overcast had come on the scene. Rawson might have killed him had not the oldster interfered. Bill still remembered the cowardice of Rawson's attack, and his blood was hot with anger momentarily. But this was not finished, by a long shot.

Now the mule thundered by him, running low to the ground, his rider perched like a jockey in the old saddle—knees almost to his jaw. And he heard Overcast say, "Don't reckon they'll shoot, fellow. Not that Rawson ain't low enough to shoot a man in the back, but he'd do it from the brush when he was alone . . . not with a witness or two around that might belly-ache out on him."

Bill turned his pinto and galloped after the hard-charging mule. He figured that the oldster had guessed correctly. But still, there was a tight spot on his back, and this was there until a hill arose and hid the Rawson crew. Bill's pinto was fast, and the respite at the Rawson camp had rested him a little, but the mule was the fastest mule Bill Dupree had ever seen. His pinto had a hard time catching the mule. Jim Overcast rode upright now, pounding his mule with the ends of his reins, and yelling for all he was worth. His high-pitched yell brought a jackrabbit out of the snow-covered sagebrush. The snow-white jackrabbit jumped out in wild fear, and Jim's pinto shied at him—but the mule kept thundering on, shod hoofs cutting the snow.

Bill wondered if the man had his right senses. He was yelling like a drunk Sioux chasing a tomcat down an alley. Bill grinned and that hurt his bottom lip. He felt of his bottom lip. It was about twice its normal size and felt as thick as the tug on a harness. One eye was almost swollen shut. He was a real good-looking specimen of a game-warden, he thought wryly. He was glad his boss, Driscoll, could not see him now.

He was just about even with the mule when Jim

Overcast suddenly reared back, reins as tight as fiddle-strings, and brought the mule to a jarring, bucking stop. Bill Dupree pulled down his labouring pinto and they went at a walk. The mule could singlefoot, too. Curiosity became greater in Bill Dupree. Who was this frosty old rooster astraddle his hard-running mule?

"Your face is a mess," the oldster suddenly said. "Son, don't take no offence, but you look like you fell head-first into a big corn grinder. You'll never catch no women at the rate you're goin', young man."

Bill had to grin, despite the discomfort. "Bet you sure hit the spike on the head, Overcast." He took off his glove and stuck out his right hand. "My handle is Bill Dupree and I sure want to thank you for the boost. Rawson was aiming to beat the living hell out of me—maybe kill me. He was mighty mad."

"Bill, I'd do the same for one of my brothers."

Bill liked the old rooster. He had plenty of fight when he got his tail feathers pulled. "Which way you heading?"

"Toward Dodson."

"But you mentioned you was riding across country to court a widow. Does the lady live in Dodson?"

"Heck, thet widder story is an ol' joke of mine, Bill. Jes' said it to have somethin' to say." Jim Overcast struggled with a plug of Horse Shoe. He finally got a chew bit off. He handed the plug to Bill, who turned it down. "Haven't got the habit, Overcast."

"Good boy." The plug went back in the overcoat pocket. "What was you and this Ganns son strugglin' so valiantly about, Bill?"

Bill told about Ganns picking a fight with him.

"Why he want to waltz with you?" Jim Overcast wanted to know.

"Said he had no use for a halfbreed, and then he tied into me. Didn't seem much of a reason to me, but sometimes it's hard to think from where the other fellow stands—his boots all the time don't fit the other fellow."

"Some of these fellows hate Injuns," the old man said slowly. "Some of them has had a few of their ancestors scalped and they consider a halfbreed an Injun, and maybe that is the way Al Ganns done thinks."

"Must be," Bill had to admit. "That man can handle his dukes, but he lacks science. And Rawson—he's all dirt. Slugged me from the side, when I was winded—but shucks, you saw all that."

"I sure did." Jim Overcast masticated his chewing tobacco. "But how come you ride out to thet draw to start with?"

"Looking for a job with Rawson. No work on the cow-outfits now. The cowmen got the winter crews they need. Sheepmen are the same—they both laid off men when winter came. And a man has to eat, you know. How come you rode out there?"

A chuckle slipped around the chewing-tobacco. "Same reason you rode out there, son. Lookin' for a job skinnin'. But when I saw you get such a rough deal, I horned in—and after that, Brother Rawson would never hire me."

"You live around here?"

"Got a homestead, down on the river bottom."

"Settled down, huh?"

"I sure have. Roamed the whul United States and most of Canada and *Mejico*, but now ol' Jim Overcast and his mule has their boots on soil they own. Been here some over two months, I reckon—more'n than, come to think about it. Time sure flies. Figgered I'd squat down the rest of my few days and see how stayin' settled feels for a change."

"Did you file on your homestead?"

Bill found himself liking the oldster and his company. Overcast, in fact, was the first man he had really enjoyed talking to here in the Milk River country. Most of the local citizens were tight-of-lip for some reason. Maybe it was because of the trouble and the winter—the trouble between the farmers and the cowmen, between Rawson and the cowmen, and the horror and tragedy of this winter that was killing sheep and cattle and men.

"No, never filed on a homestead, Bill. Done bought the homestead entry off one of the sodmen that went broke and had to pull stakes. Made Rawson sort of mad, too. Ain't the first time him and Jim Overcast have tangled."

The old man told him the story. When he had bought the deed to the hundred-and-sixty acre homestead he had made Ed Rawson angry. Rawson had been dickering with the same farmer, intending to buy the homestead, but Jim Overcast had not known this fact, and he had offered the farmer more money than had Ed Rawson—therefore he had got the homestead.

"Rawson rode into the yard the day I was movin' into my new house. The farmer had done built a strong log house, he had. He never got off his hoss. He just sat there and looked down on me an' said I had paid too much for my land. At first, I never ketched onto what his words meant, but it soon dawned on me."

"Yeah?"

"He done told me I had set a bad example. Some of the other farmers—them he was dickerin' with—wanted more money now thet I had paid my farmer more than Rawson had wanted to pay."

"He was sort of sore, huh?"

"He was right mad, Bill. But I told him I didn't aim to buy any more land, 'cause I had all the land I wanted. Thet had a tendency to settle his tail feathers a little."

"He must have lots of money."

"Reckon he has some dough, at thet. He done bought out a farmer that the Bar S tried to buy—he went over the Bar S's price for a spring along the hills. And the Bar S ain't no poor outfit, by a long shot—even though this winter-kill has cut into their herds a lot, they tell me."

They talked about other things—the hard winter, the

dead sheep, the sheepherder who had frozen to death, how hard-up the farmers were. But the mind of Bill Dupree was not on their words. He wished he could find the answer to one question: did Rawson and Ganns know he was a game-warden? He still remembered the eagerness of Al Ganns to start a fistfight. there was another question, also: were they poaching beaver pelts?

He remembered the trapper who now trapped on upper Beaver. That man had contacted Ed Rawson out at Rawson's homestead. He felt sure that Rawson was behind this illegal beaver trapping. But how did the man get his pelts shipped out of Dodson? Bill did not know. His ride to the Rawson sheep-skinning camp had netted him not a bit of information. Now both Rawson and Ganns hated him. He was worse off than before making the cold ride to the camp. Things had surely gone wrong. But this, he decided, was water under the bridge, and his mind went ahead. But thinking was difficult for him. His head throbbed like a Sioux war drum. He had a cut back of his ear where Rawson had slugged him. The cold air had coagulated the blood, but he figured it should have a stitch or two in it. Jim Overcast leaned from his saddle, studying the wound, and Bill saw his lips purse.

"Yep, you need a stitch or two, young un." He straightened in his saddle. "There's a doc in Dodson. Name of Hamilton. He's got the purtiest little halfbreed nurse I've ever done seen. But I reckon you know that. Somebody done told me you squired her to the dance at the schoolhouse about the first or second night you was in town."

Bill smiled. "That was when I had some money to spend on the women," he lied. "But now I'm right broke. A little bit saved up, but it has to go for board and room, not for women."

"Thet Mary Red Robin is sure a nice little girl, son."

"You're telling me nothing new," Bill Dupree said.

They came into Dodson. The day was almost through

40

and the bitter coldness of night was coming slowly down from the Little Rocky Mountains. The world was lifeless, hidden by driven snow, and the world waited for the Chinook winds to come, but the winds did not come.

Bill understood that both the big cow-outfits were short on hay. Both the outfits cut native grass—bluejoint grass—on the flats on each side of the river. But the winter, with its great cold and miserable length, had cut into their stacks and both spreads, he had been told, were almost out of hay.

Blizzards had driven native steers and cows toward the south-east, and they had met the fences made by the farmers. They had piled up and frozen to death and some places, he had heard, a man could walk over the fences, walking on the frozen bodies of the cattle. Cattle stood in the willows along the river and the creeks, and died from cold and starvation. And when the cowpunchers had cut one open they had found a willow as big as a man's fist in her belly. Sheep were luckier—they had thicker coats; therefore they turned more cold. But they starved to death because the thick snow and sleet covered what little, if any, grass there had been left after the summer grazing.

While it was none of his business, Bill Dupree, being reared in the cow-country, could feel nothing but pity for the doomed cattle and, although he disliked sheep, he was sorry for the woollies, too. But his real job, he reminded himself, was to find out who was trapping beaver illegally, and how they were smuggling the pelts out of Milk River Valley.

"Where you heading for, Overcast?"

"Put my mule in the livery-barn."

Bill said, "I'm going into the doctor's office." He dismounted and tied his horse to the hitchrack. Dodson was sleepy and cold, buildings covered by snow. "Thanks again for the help."

"Don't mention it."

The old men rode down the street toward the livery-barn at the street's end. Bill gave him a glance before crossing the snow-covered board sidewalk. Hope the old man didn't get into too much trouble because of me, he thought. But it doesn't seem to worry him one bit, the old rascal. Bill crossed the sidewalk, overshoes grinding on the packed snow, and the sign on the door said enter without knocking. He went into a room warm with heat from the heating-stove that was filled with coal. There were some benches here and another door which opened before he could seat himself.

A girl entered the room. Bill Dupree felt something warm move into him, making the rough circumstances of the day fall back against time. Mary Red Robin was also a halfbreed. Her skin was smooth and olive-dark and her hair was jet black, but it was not the wiry black of her Cheyenne ancestors—it was soft and black, like the hair of her white father. The darkness of her clear skin offset the redness of her lips that were now open in surprise at seeing his battered face.

"Bill Dupree, you have been fighting!"

"I sure have, Mary."

"Oh, you men—you have a cut behind your ear. Oh, and Doctor Hamilton is out for a moment or two, and—well, come into the office and let me look at you, and who were you fighting with?"

Bill went into the main room and sat on a low table. He told her about his fight and how Jim Overcast had come along to help him. She daubed and worked and he liked the feel of her free hand on his shoulder. He had taken off his sheepskin coat and he could feel her fingers on his muscle. He liked the clean and good woman smell of her—sweet and nice and feminine. He thought, the fact is, I like her more than I'll admit, and I do hope she likes me.

He had been in Dodson but one day and he had heard about the dance to be held next night at the school-house, and he had screwed up his courage and had asked

Mary Red Robin to go to the shindig with him and, to his surprise, she had accepted, but she had warned him on one point.

"We'll probably be the only halfbreeds there, Bill. The others—well, they stay close to the Fort Belknap reservation."

"We'll live through it," he had said.

They had had a good time, in one respect—the respect of being together, both of the same caste, both young. Her premonitions had proven correct: they were the only halfbreeds at the dance. When they had entered, the whites had looked at them, but nothing had been said until Bill had asked a pretty white girl for a dance and had been turned down.

"I just don't feel well, sir."

Bill had bowed and had thought, why didn't she tell the truth? And he noticed the girl, although pleading illness, did not leave the dance-hall. She kept on dancing and chatting but her eyes never met his again. Once he caught her looking at him and he glanced at her, but she looked away, and then she was gone, in the arms of her white skinned partner.

A few of the lower-classed white men, the kind that hung around the saloons and bars, offered to dance with Mary, but she turned them down. None of the so-called *better* class asked her to dance, though.

So she and Bill had danced the evening together.

Mary had glanced up at him and had smiled—a womanly sweet smile. "Bill Dupree, don't take it so hard."

"It's tough not to belong."

She kept her eyes on him—soft and wise and pretty. She floated in his arms, but he felt her full body and the promise it held for the right man. And when she spoke, she was whispering.

"There is one thing to do, Bill, and you and I are doing it."

"And that, Mary?"

"Work hard and better ourselves, for in doing that we better our cast-off people. There is no use in sulking. History repeats itself, as the historian once said. Get a good education and be useful. We both have done that, you with your work in college, and I with my learning the nursing profession. Bill, don't be down-hearted."

He had tightened his grip on her thin waist. "You're a real sweetheart," he had murmured.

Later she told him about herself. Little things, mixed with laughter, with smiles. She had gone to the Sister's School in the Little Rocky Mountains in Mission Canyon. She had taken up nursing and obtained her certificate. She was still studying, with Doc Hamilton helping her.

She had tried to get jobs with other doctors in the various towns along the Great Northern Railroad, but none would hire her.

"Doc Hamilton is a great man, Bill. He went against lots of public opinion when he gave me a job. Some whites don't like to be treated by a halfbreed nurse."

Bill had grinned. "You can treat me any time, young lady."

"Oh, you joker."

He had spent an enjoyable evening, despite his being shunned by the white people. Now, sitting on the low table, feeling the imprint of her cool and capable fingers, his mind left the night of the dance and came to the present situation.

"Ouch!"

She smiled. "Big baby. Just a little iodine."

"It—burns."

"Wait until Doctor Hamilton sews your cut."

"Somebody just came into the office."

It was the doctor, a short elderly man. He went right to work. He made Bill have tears in his eyes. Bill clenched his hands. By luck or accident or design, one of Mary's hands slid between his. He smiled at her. Doctor Hamilton noticed it and thought, Lord, do I have to lose the best nurse I've ever had? But he said nothing.

"That's it," he said. "Come in tomorrow for a check-up. Mary, you can let go of his hands now."

"Oh."

Mary pulled her hand back, slightly red-faced. Doc Hamilton winked at Bill Dupree. Bill smiled, his aches and pains suddenly gone. The doctor went to the basin to wash. Bill and Mary went into the waiting room and Mary closed the door behind her softly. She looked up at him and smiled.

"What are you smiling about?"

"You sure are a tough-looking halfbreed, young man. Wonder what Al Ganns looks like."

"He isn't pretty," Bill said.

"You had best go to bed and take it easy." He saw her hesitate. "If you need money for a hotel room—"

"None of that," he interrupted. "Thanks a lot, young lady. But I got a few bucks left. I'm not flat yet."

She smiled. "No offence, Bill."

Evidently she really believed he was a drifting cow-puncher down on his luck and out of a job. This thought, in one sense, was not pleasant; yet in another sense, it held satisfaction. Even though she figured he was financially embarrassed, she was willing to be his friend. He found himself wishing he could tell her he was in reality a government game-warden. But he knew he dared not do that, much as he wanted to let her know he amounted to a little of something in life.

"You go to your hotel room," she said, "and get a little rest before eating. Then get a good night's sleep. Tomorrow you'll have a beautiful black eye." She giggled. "I know about black eyes. I got three brothers, you know."

"Take care of yourself," he said, and left.

# FOUR

After Bill Dupree and Jim Overcast were out of sight, Al Ganns lay on his back in the snow and Ed Rawson squatted beside him. Rawson said, "Close your eyes, you fool," and he wiped snow on the bloody, swollen face. Ganns was a sad-looking animal lying there with his eyes closed. His upper lip was split and his right cheek was badly swollen.

Rawson mopped the huge face with snow, taking away the blood and grime. The coldness of the snow also helped stop the bleeding. The men stood around and watched and talked about the fight. One said, "You sure split him back of the ear with that blow of yours, Rawson."

Rawson said nothing for a while. Then he said, "I thought he was turning faster than he did turn, otherwise I'd not have hit him from the side like that."

He was telling a lie. He knew it. So did his men. He had deliberately and cowardly slugged Bill Dupree. Rawson stood upright. He glared down at Ganns. He was angry because Bill Dupree had whipped Ganns. He wiped his hands on his pants, driving the coldness from his fingers.

"Can you see, Ganns?"

"Sure I can see, you fool."

Rawson grinned, but there was no mirth in the grin. "One eye might stay open. Other will swell shut, though—unless I'm plumb wrong. Man alive, that fellow sure gave you a hell of a whuppin'!"

"I handed plenty back to him, remember that."

Derision rimmed Ed Rawson's voice. "Oh, hell yes, you did—like hell! He whupped the jeepers outa you, Ganns. First time I've ever seen a man take you. That fella knows some science. That left fist of his must've hit you a dozen times while you was gettin' ready to haul-off with your right."

"I'm not whipped . . . yet."

Anger was now a livid, living force on Rawson's wide face. He boasted of having a tough bunch of men working for him on his homesteads. Now a man had whipped his top tough-hand, and that man had been a low-down halfbreed. Of all people, it had to be a halfbreed, which added insult onto injury. His mind went back to the scene. And old Jim Overcast, curse him, had thrown down on them, making them stop fighting. Old Jim Overcast had come out of nowhere on that damned mule and he had got the upper hand again, just like when he had bought out that nester when he, Ed Rawson, had been dickering for the nester's farm. Old Jim had jerked the rug out from under him then; now he had done it again. Word would sweep across this snow-filled range of death, and the prestige of Ed Rawson would fall a notch or two. Which made the pride of the man grow anger-heavy.

"You match fists with that 'breed again, Ganns, and he'll kick the daylights out of you. He's fought in the ring somewhere. I know that for sure."

"You didn't do yourself no good by hittin' him from behind," Ganns growled surlily, tired of being goaded. "Ol' Jim Overcast saw you hit him. Overcast will let the whole country know about it, he will."

Rawson grew dark with anger. But his foreman, he knew, spoke the truth. Overcast had a gossipy tongue. Had he known the old man on the mule had been behind him, he would not have slugged Bill Dupree from the back. But . . . it had been done, and there was no use re-hashing it here.

"Get to work," he told his men.

He watched his men resume their skinning chores. He watched them, but he did not see them; his thoughts were black. Because his mind was far away, dwelling on other matters, he had no eyes for things close at hand. The snow was blinding in its white glare. Soon the day would be drawing to its cold close. These northern days were short this time of the winter. The smell of wool, the stink of frozen death, these were in his nostrils—but he did not heed these, either.

Ganns had climbed up out of the snow. He had shaken himself free of snow, shaking like a big dog, and he had ambled away, walking slowly. The teams moved, tug chains made their dismal sounds, and there was the sound of hides being ripped from frozen flesh. Men cursed and worked and sharpened their already-sharp knives. The knives made swishing sounds on the hones. A light sound against the wilderness and its eternal silence.

Ganns moved over and said, "Not much daylight left, Ed."

Rawson said, quietly, "Follow me, Al."

He and Ganns walked to one side, out of earshot of any of the crew. Ganns shuffled, overshoes parting the snow; he was beaten and glum and sullen. The air was cold and biting on his swollen, bloated face.

Rawson walked out about two hundred feet and stopped, and Ganns stopped too, and Ganns looked at him and said nothing, letting his boss speak first. And Rawson's words were dry and dull.

"Maybe he ain't no game-warden, Ganns?"

"We don't know . . . for sure."

"Maybe we jumped the wrong man?"

Ganns shrugged. His sheepskin coat lifted and then fell. He touched his jaw. But it hurt, so he dropped his mittened hand.

"Why do you say that, Ed?"

"Do you reckon the gover'ment would send out a halfbreed to try to enforce trappin' laws?"

"The gover'ment," said Ganns, "will do some odd things. Maybe them bigwigs in Washington don't care what colour a man's hide is, eh?"

Ganns scowled fiercely. The sun was glaring in his eyes.

Rawson seemed to be talking to himself. "Still don't seem logical. Seems to me the gover'ment would send out a white man."

Ganns looked at his boss. "Don't fergit he follered that new trapper out to his grounds on upper Beaver Crick, Rawson. This 'breed follered thet trapper. Then he laid in the brush an' spied on the man. That means he's a gover'ment man, don't it?"

Rawson had to nod. "I reckon it does," he said thoughtfully. "But I wish we knew for sure."

"I'm sure he is a gover'ment warden, boss. From what I've heard, some Injuns and 'breeds are workin' for the gover'ment."

Rawson kicked the snow with one foot. His big overshoe made the snow geyser out in a small cone.

"Reckon you might be right, at that," Rawson said slowly. "But it was to our tough luck that you or me never got to kill him in thet fight."

"Blame it on Jim Overcast, Ed."

Ed Rawson nodded. "We could have kilt him, too, if thet ol' Jim Overcast hadn't horned it. We could have cut a hole in the ice down on Milk River an' shoved him into the hole with some boulders or hunks of scrap-iron wired to him, and if he is a game-warden his office would never get a report from him."

"Damn that Jim Overcast."

"We got to get rid of this 'breed, Ganns."

Ganns said, "I'll get a rifle sight lined against his back, with me hidin' in the brush."

"You didn't do good that night you trailed him to thet trapper's outfit, if I remembers rightly."

Al Ganns scowled. He raised his mitten to touch his jaw, then thought better and let his hand drop.

"The night came down too fast on us that evenin', I could have maybe got in a shot or two, but when I line a man on my sights I want to make damned sure I kill him. But there'll be another time. I'm out for sure to get him now. And into the river he goes."

Rawson rubbed his whiskers. The sound could be heard in the snowy stillness. "This Jim Overcast, Ganns . . . I don't savvy him."

"In what manner, Ed?"

"Oh, just a thought, maybe . . . might be more. He might be a game-warden, you know."

"I doubt that."

"Well, we got to play our cards close. We know there is a gover'ment game-dick in this area. Our headquarters in St. Louis told us that, and them big boys know what they are talking about."

"Odd thet the boys in St. Louis never got hold of this new man's name, Ed. Seems to me their inside information would tell the name of the game-warden sent to this locality."

Ed Rawson continued, talking in a low tone of voice. The big boys in St. Louis did not know, in fact, that for sure a game-warden had been sent out to this Milk River area. But a government inspector had found one of their poached beaver pelts, stumbling across it by luck.

"That all the big shots got to work on?"

"That's enough," Rawson said. "With that hide, they could tell where the hide came from—what locality it was shipped out of, and trapped in."

"How?"

"That's not hard to do. Beavers run in colonies, it seems. They all have different family characteristics, like the gover'ment books say." He elaborated, feeling proud he could impart information. The quality and colour and even the length of the fur differed from locality to locality. The same held true for gold, he said. A gold expert could look at a nugget and, if he knew his job, he could tell what goldfield in what part of the country the nugget came from by its weight and colour and shape.

"Well, I'll be hanged, Ed."

"Them gover'ment boys are smart, Al. They know beaver furs like we know the beaver runs in this locality. They know thet pelt come from this northern Montana area, as sure as I'm a foot high."

"So because of that the big shots think a game-warden will be sent out here, huh? And you think he is this 'breed."

"If he wasn't this 'breed, then why did the 'breed trail thet trapper?"

"He must be the man, no two ways about that."

"He's got to go under the ice," Rawson said. "But I would like to know more about this ol' Jim Overcast."

Ganns shrugged. He had no answer to that. His mental capacity was not too large, as Rawson knew. He was best when dealing with problems involving brute strength and extreme hate or anger. Just now his hate and his anger, his boss knew, were directed toward Bill Dupree. Ganns was being paid well. The trappers got a third and Rawson cut Ganns in on the other two-thirds. As a result, they all made good money—Ganns, Rawson and the trapper— for beaver pelts were plentiful and of top quality because of the coldness of the winter.

"We got a money-makin' deal here," Rawson said. "We got to watch this 'breed. We can't let a gover'ment man break up our deal. If they caught us red-handed, it would mean the federal pen for us."

"Wonder if them federal men found out how we smuggle them hides into St. Louis, boss?"

"Don't reckon they do."

"Why say that? You say one gover'ment man found one of our beaver pelts. Maybe he discovered the way we have of shippin' them out of Montana?"

Rawson shook his head. "Our last two shipments went through all right. Never lost a beaver pelt. So that tells me that the gover'ment men never found that pelt in a shipment—they've stumbled across it later on in some shed or back room, I'd say."

"This hard winter, with all these woollies dyin', has been luck for us," Ganns said.

"Sure has."

"In our business," said Ganns, "we need lots of sheep pelts. Well, I'll go and do some skinnin', Ed."

"Good."

Ganns ambled over to the skinning crew, took a skinning-knife out of a log where it had been impaled, and went to work. Rawson felt the raw push of impatience and he watched his men for a while, ugliness riding his squat and compact frame. Then he glanced at the sky and decided the day would soon be over. Accordingly he walked to where Ganns was working.

"Knock off in half an hour, Al. Haul the pelts to the spread and salt them down. I'm doin' some ridin' "

"Where to?"

"Dodson."

"Want me to go with you?"

"Old enough to take care of myself."

Ganns scowled. "That game-warden might try to get the law after you or me. And if you go to Dodson—"

"Forget it, Al."

Ed Rawson went to where his horse was tied in a clump of bullberry bushes. He untied the beast, with difficulty got his overshoe into the stirrups, and with more difficulty lifted his heavily-clothed body into the saddle. Then he gave his crew another glance, seemingly was satisfied, so he neck-reined his horse around, heading toward Dodson.

He hit the packed road and his horse lifted to a lope that would eat up the short distance. Around him stretched the wilderness of snow, running its whiteness across the prairie, marred by the dull cottonwoods, leafless and scrawny, along the river. Yes, and the diamond willows, too. Then the plains of snow ran on again, finally meeting the foothills north of the river. Beyond that his vision could not go, for the dusk was tiptoeing in.

But this snowy wilderness, primal in its white beauty, held no attraction for him, for his mind was on more mundane things. Behind him and behind Ganns lay the same things, and the prime point was that they had always moved in the pale of the law, not too far beyond the boundaries to be arrested, but always within the shadow of the boundary. Once or twice that border had come close, and each time they had had to move on—cattle rustling, robbery, and looting. Now they were in Montana, and the next step would have to be still further north—a dash across the Canadian line in the night, guns in their hands. This game, he realized, was tightening, but this was nothing new to him or to Ganns, for each game eventually drew itself to a conclusion. He was a sensible man, though, and he was afraid of danger, for danger became violence—and there was danger on this snow. He remembered one fall evening, the autumn just past, and he remembered Ganns riding in, his face studious and in thought.

"Sure a lot of beaver in Milk River an' in Beaver Crick, Ed."

"I've seen them beaver at sundown, comin' out of their holes."

"I scouted the river and the crick today, Ed. Some of

them beaver swum out of their holes along the bank and so help me hanner they looked like small dogs, they are so big."

"When winter comes and hair sets, them pelts will be worth money."

Ganns had dismounted, loosening his latigo-strap. "They should be easy to trap," he said. "Number four traps, double-springs. Man, we could make some money—big money, too."

"I've thought of that."

Ganns had pulled loose his saddle and had put it over the saddle-rack. His sweaty horse trotted to the watering trough and submerged his nose and drank.

"Number four traps, boss."

"No steel traps, Al."

Ganns watched his bronc roll. "What do you mean by that?"

"We use steel traps and somebody would see them in the beaver runs and holes. And in would move a federal man. A federal game-warden, Al. Some local citizen—even some kids skating on the river or crick—would notice the traps. You can't hide a steel trap, even if it is back in a beaver den. The chain always has to stick out. The chain gives it away."

"Then how could we get them beaver?"

"Remember that trapper we met in Wyoming? When we was stealing—I mean, borrowin'—them Circle X cattle?"

"That guy on the Wind River?"

"That's the fellow. Gink with all them whiskers. He trapped beaver without steel traps—but I reckon you weren't there the day he showed me how to trap beaver."

"No, and how did he do it?"

"We need some dogs, Al."

Ganns looked at Ed Rawson. His eyes held an amused look. "We was talking about trappin' beaver and not runnin' down wolves and coyoties with dogs, Ed."

Ed Rawson said, "Don't interrupt me, Al. We need dogs—short legged, tough dogs. Terriers and bulldogs. Fighters to the last breath. That fellow had dogs, and he took out beaver right fast, too. Had a stream cleared before the local citizens got wise."

"I still don't understand."

Squatting there, the evening sun warm and good as it sank in the west, Ed Rawson explained his plan—the plan divulged to him by the Wyoming trapper, the man who poached beaver for a living.

"Well, I'll be hanged, Ed."

"I don't know much about beaver," Ed Rawson had had to admit. "But I can learn something by watching them work evenings."

"How about gettin' rid of the pelts?"

"We can make connections, Al. We know men who can set us straight on that. This Wyomin' trapper shipped his to St. Louis. He told me to write to a fur company there if ever I seen a lot of beaver."

"You got the name of the company?"

"I wrote it down in my little book. The book is in the house. But we should get hold of a trapper."

"Why?"

"To spot our holes and runs."

"We'd have to cut him in on the take."

"He'll know his business, though. I'll get in touch with this fur company. They might know where we can hire a trapper."

The contact had been made. The fur company had even sent out a representative. They had made their plans. The fur company knew all the angles. What had started out as a ranching proposition had turned into a beaver-poaching deal. But there was money—thousands of dollars—to be made in this beaver smuggling.

They got their dogs, too. The company saw to that. The company shipped them in, but the dogs did not go to Dodson to be uncrated. That would have aroused suspicions. The dogs were shipped into a town on the railroad to the south, where they were received by Ganns and Rawson. With the dogs had come a trapper—an elderly man, stooped and round-shouldered, yet holding a willowy, tough strength. When winter had come, when the pelts had reached maturity and prime value, they had gone to work. But the trapper had not tarried long. He had made a good-sized stake and then one morning his bunk had been discovered empty.

"He's done flew the coop," Al Ganns had said, adding some choice curses. "You don't reckon he'll turn us over to the law?"

Rawson had chuckled. "He's involved in this, too. He squeal to the law and into the clink he goes along with us. No, he's got cold boots, and pulled out—stake-bound, with cold feet."

Ganns had looked out the frost-rimmed window. "True in more ways than one," he had joked. "The thermometer must stand at fifty below."

"Cold night."

The company sent out another trapper, the one Bill Dupree had trailed. This brought Ed Rawson's thoughts around to the tough halfbreed. Bill Dupree would have to go under the ice to be sure . . . Rawson's face was ice-cold, cheekbones white, lips merciless.

Fifty bucks for a prime beaver pelt. Fifty dollars and already over a hundred had been shipped to St. Louis. His mind did some figure juggling. So far, around five thousand bucks. Easy money. Easiest money he had ever made. And yet they had to work upper Beaver Creek. There would be easily another hundred pelts taken from the creek. That meant, then, the take would run to around ten thousand. Even with the cut to the trapper and to Ganns, it still was a lot of dough. Still a nice big gob of folding money . . .

Yes, this 'breed would have to go.

Now that his mind was definitely made-up, Ed Rawson

thought of Dupree no more. He made the horse lope faster. Dusk was inching across the snow and the night would be very cold. There was no wind, and he was thankful for that. Already the thermometer had fallen ten degrees or so since he had left the skinning camp.

He had ridden into Dodson to watch Bill Dupree. To hang around the saloon or the hotel, to listen and watch. Maybe he could get the halfbreed into another fight. But it would not be with fists, this time. He had seen Bill use his fists. He wanted no part of the halfbreed's knuckles. This time it would be with a gun or a knife, if he had his way. And when the fight was finished the halfbreed would be dead. He preferred guns, and the halfbreed carried a pistol. Maybe Bill Dupree would jump him because he, Ed Rawson, had slugged him from behind?

That would suit him just dandy.

When he reached Dodson, darkness was thick and lamps were lighted, throwing their yellow squares of light across the hoof-packed snow. He rode first to the depot, raw and new against the wilderness, for the raiload had gone through the summer before, and the depot had not yet been painted grey. The pot-bellied heater was red hot, and he warmed his hands and back as he talked to the operator. He would soon need a boxcar to ship out his sheepskins.

"Already got a car on sidin', Rawson. Been here for some time. Railroad business is slow because of the winter, so they sidetrack cars along the line. Say, done heard Al Ganns tangled with this halfbreed Dupree?"

"Who told you that?"

"Jim Overcast."

"They had a fight," Rawson said, and left before he had to answer other questions. He got his horse and rode to the courthouse. The marshal was in his office, for it had a light. He dismounted and knocked on the door and was called inside. He put a pious look on his face. Anyway, he thought the look was pious, but the marshal

57

did not, although the lawman did not mention this fact.

The office was warm. The lawman was in the act of putting on his coat to go home for the night. The door to the cell corridor behind the jail was open and Ed Rawson heard a couple of men singing in a strange weird tongue. He knew then that a few of the reservation Indians were in jail on some charge or other. Probably too much firewater.

"Marshal, I came to report a fight out at my skinnin' camp."

The lawman, a heavy man, buttoned his overcoat, bit fingers gnarled and strong. "You mean the fistfight between this halfbreed Dupree and Al Ganns?"

"The same. How did you know about it?"

"Jim Overcast came into town with Dupree. He's got a tongue like an old woman is supposed to have. If you're worried about Dupree swearing out a warrant for Ganns, just forget it."

"Did you talk to Dupree?"

"Down at the hotel, in his room. His face is a mess. He sure looks like Ganns won."

"He whipped Ganns."

"Don't seem logical."

"He must've fought in the ring. He's got science."

"What did they scrap over?"

"Nothin'. Just started throwing words at each other. Truth is, Marshal, that Ganns had a bottle, and he had been hitting this—I never knew about it. Fact is, I think too much barleycorn jarred his aim, and that is why he lost."

"Well, it's over, and that is that. My God, them Injuns—that same tune, all day. I'd turn them loose— they got drunk and tore up the saloon—but the county attorney wants to make an example outa them for the other bucks. Give them six months on the work gang, over to the state pen."

"Sure a terrible sound."

"Sounds to me like somebody tearing' a steel loco-motive apart," the marshal said. He studied Ed Rawson suddenly. "You didn't come here to get me to arrest the halfbreed, did you?"

"Hell, no."

"Always figured you was the type of man what fought your own battles. Well, the missus will have supper ready for me and the kids, and if one of us is a minute late trouble pops." They went outside into the cold-gathering darkness. The lawman said, "So long, Rawson," and tramped away through the snow. Rawson went to Dodson's main saloon, the Broken Bit. The place was big, and lighted by kerosene lamps that did not do a thorough job because of the huge vastness of the saloon. Three stoves were red hot, but they could not turn the cold.

Three old pensioners—broken-down cowboys from the neighbouring two ranches—played whist, sitting close to one stove. Two Bar S cowboys were at the bar. They gave him a glance, but offered no greetings and returned to their low-spoken conversation. Rawson knew they wanted no words with him, civil or otherwise. The cowmen and their cowpunchers held him and his skinning-crew in low degree. Just as they disliked the sheepmen who ran their woollies on the benchlands where there was little grass for cattle to graze on.

Rawson smiled inwardly. He had outsmarted both the Bar S and the Box 7. He had come in and bought up their grazing lands and he had done it legally, beating them to the draw. And he would buy more land from other farmers, and he would stake hired hands out on home-steads and then buy their rights from them. Within a year or so, he would control almost all of Milk River. The money from the poached beaver would pay for most of it, too. He had been running low on cash when he and Ganns had decided to trap beaver illegally.

The money obtained from beaver pelts would go into

the buying of more land and more cattle. Because of the hard winter, cows would be cheap in the spring, for they would be gaunt and weak. He already had five hundred head on his grazing area, and by summer he would have doubled that mark, he was sure.

He ordered a drink of bourbon and tossed it off, the whiskey raw in his throat. He was no whiskey drinker—beer was his drink. But it was too cold to drink beer. He looked at the two punchers again and this time they did not look at him. He put two-bits on the bar and went outside.

A woman came down the snow-covered sidewalk, moving toward him; he recognized the halfbreed nurse, Mary Red Robin. He felt something stir in him, a sort of vague longing, for he had been a long time without a woman, and this woman was everything a man desired—for one night. He only would want a woman for a night, no longer. They cluttered up a man's thinking and his desires by being with him all the time. This mental point reached, he moved forward and stopped.

"Good evening, Miss Red Robin."

"How do you do, Mr Rawson."

"And how is your patient, young lady?"

"I have a number of patients, Mr Rawson. Which one do you mean?"

Her voice was as cold as the night. He felt a touch of anger and he wanted to put the halfbreed in her place, but discretion came in and checked this and made his voice level.

"Bill Dupree."

"Oh, the *halfbreed*, huh?" The Arctic owl that had been driven south had settled figuratively in her voice. "Oh, Bill will be all right in a day or so—just beat-up some, not serious."

"Good."

"And how is Al Ganns?"

Now her voice was sweet. It dripped honey. It had been

rolled in sugar and syrup.

"Al Ganns," said Ed Rawson, "is so tough he doesn't need to see a doctor—or a nurse, either."

"Man of steel, huh?"

"That he is."

"Good for him."

She turned and moved away without another word. Suddenly Rawson became aware that he was angry and he had almost hissed his words. He looked at her and this anger went back, retreating to the secret recesses, and the logic moved in and took its place.

He went toward his horse. He untied the cold beast, the horse rubbing his bony nose against him, and he led the animal down the street to the town livery. The interior of the barn was so cold it killed the smell of manure. He turned the horse over to the barn-man.

Then he went to the hotel.

# FIVE

Mary Red Robin stayed at a private home but she ate her meals in the hotel's dining room. She went down the corridor and tried the knob on the door of Bill Dupree's room, but the door was locked. She knocked, but got no response. Then she realized it was before six in the morning and Bill might be a hard sleeper, so she returned to the dining room. Old Jim Overcast was sitting at a table talking to the waitress who was taking his order, and his eyes showed something when he saw her enter.

"Miss Mary," he said.

"Mr Overcast, how are you this morning?"

"Spent the night in my cabin but decided I'd eat somebody else's cookin', so rode into town. Cold night it was, Miss Mary."

She had doctored him for a thumb he had cut while stretching some barbwire, and between them had come a sort of understanding—the objective type of understanding that can easily exist between a man and a woman when the man is much older and out of the class as a possible suitor. He could talk about a cold night and cold blankets on a bed without the words bringing any ideas to her mind.

"Yes, I almost froze in bed, it seemed like."

"Sit down and eat with me?"

"Thank you, sir."

She gave the handwritten menu a quick glance and then said, "Jennie, the usual breakfast," and the waitress left, a heavy girl with a wide back and hips. She said, "Bill told me he had never seen you before until you pulled a gun on the Rawson bunch, Mr Overcast."

"Jim, not Mr."

"Well, Jim, so he told me." She smiled.

"You have a lovely smile," he said.

"You men" she said. "You'll court a woman until the day your eyes close for the last time."

"I'd seen him around town a time or so," Jim Overcast said, "but I reckon he never got to noticin' me, or somethin'. How is he this mornin', or ain't you done checked on him yet?"

She told about knocking and trying the doorknob. "I didn't knock too hard, though. Best he get all the sleep he can."

Old Jim Overcast allowed that sleep was indeed Nature's remedy. He got a little poetical and a trifle philosophical. He said that God was so thoughtful he even put out the sun each night so man could sleep in the dark. "But some danged men seem to figger God ain't got much brains, 'cause they operate at night and sleep in the bright daylight."

"I'm in no mood for philosophy."

"What are you in the mood for?"

She smiled. "Nothing this morning, I guess. I always am cranky in the morning. Well, here comes our breakfasts."

Jim Overcast ate a big breakfast. Two slices of thick red ham, a half-gallon of black coffee, some fried potatoes and some toast. Mary nibbled on her toast and sipped her coffee.

"That all you eatin', woman?"

"My usual breakfast."

"No wonder you're so fat. A man could hang a hat on various bones in your anatomy."

"Here comes a friend of yours," she said.

Ed Rawson came into the dining-room. He had spent the night at the hotel. He was clean-shaven and washed, and shiny with sin. He nodded at Mary, an impersonal nod, but he apparently did not see Jim Overcast, for no salutation went toward the old farmer. This brought a smile to Overcast's shaggy face.

"Jes' like a hoss what gets blind," he said. "First he can't see close to him, but kin see off a long distance."

"Not so loud, Jim."

"Them hosses what get blind like that also lose their hearin' in direct ratio to their blindness."

"Jim, please. No bar-room brawl in here with me around."

He grinned. "As you say, honey."

Rawson went to the far end of the dining room and took a chair at a table. Apparently he had not heard Jim Overcast's words. Or, if he had heard them, his face gave no indication of hearing—it was wide and smooth and expressionless, Mary Red Robin noticed.

A few others were coming in for breakfast—the two cowpunchers Ed Rawson had seen in the saloon the evening before, and even the marshal came in to eat. He said his wife was ailing and he ate without a worry, or so it seemed to the girl. Finally Jim Overcast had annihilated his repast.

"Let's amble down the hall and call on the heavyweight champ," he said.

"He might be out of his bunk by now."

They had to knock hard to get Bill Dupree to the door. They finally got him out of his deep slumber. He saw Mary and said, "Just a minute," and when they entered he had on his trousers, with his chest bare. His skin showed black and blue spots. His one eye was closed and his lips were not pretty.

"You're a sound sleeper," Mary said. "I tried a while ago to get you to wake. We almost hammered the hinges off the door."

Bill looked at himself in the mirror on the dresser. His face was distorted. He moved closer. The face danced, then stretched out the other direction. He moved back. The face shimmered, then the bulge moved to the right side. He walked back about four feet and the image was somewhere near normal. He looked at himself with critical thoughtfulness.

"I'm almighty pretty," he said.

Mary said, "Let me look at those stitches."

He sat down and she studied his wound. "You have good blood," she said. "You heal fast." She looked at his eye and smiled. "That eye is shiny black—like a crow's wing, Bill."

Bill Dupree smiled. "Bet I know of a gent who packs an eye just as black as mine, and his name is Al Ganns."

"Rawson is in the dining room," Mary said.

Bill Dupree nodded. "Probably stayed in town to keep his ear close to the ground," he said.

Jim Overcast chuckled. "On my way into town this mornin' I talked with one of Rawson's hands headin' for the skinnin' grounds. He said that Ganns was so well swoll up around the eyes he can hardly see. Boy said he reminded him of a bee-stung bear who had raided a hive."

"I should smile," Bill said, "but it hurts too much. I should laugh, but my teeth would fall out. Wonder if I can chew water?"

Mary said, "Well, I have to see some patients. When you get time, Bill, drop over to the office, and I'll wash you up a little bit."

"Thanks, Mama."

They heard her steps retreat down the hall. Old Jim Overcast sighed and said, "Oh, to be eighty again." And he said then, "she's got her cap set for you, Dupree."

"I'm not hard to catch."

"Them curves," Jim Overcast said, "are in the right places."

"Time will make them slip down and out," Bill Dupree said, and smiled. "Just like your chest. It's fallen down to your belt."

"Thanks, bucko."

The building crackled under the bite of the intense cold. There was no wind, though—just the bite of the intense cold. Wind made the cold seem even worse, because under its pressure the cold was pushed into houses and through clothing into a man's bones.

Jim Overcast said, "Reckon I'll head back to my shack. Braidin' a rawhide riata, which takes up my spare time. Have done fed my hosses and cows and chickens, and the dog sleeps beside the stove."

"Regular home-body," Bill said.

Bill pulled on his shirt and wined. He had some sore ribs. Jim Overcast stood with one hand on the doorknob, the other hand holding his old muskrat-skin cap. He was short and wiry, and his eyes were without thoughts. Bill got the impression that the oldster wanted to stay and talk for a while, and this was agreeable with Bill. But then the old man put on his cap and said, "See you later, Dupree," and he left.

Bill heard his overshoes shuffle away on the worn hall-runner. He buttoned his shirt and remembered the look in the oldster's faded eyes. Overcast had looked at him in a queer sort of way—a sort of appraisive way. Or was he just imagining things? Maybe his fist-hammered face was so swollen and looked so bad it sort of fascinated the old man? Well, his face would have looked worse . . . had not Jim Overcast stopped the fight.

The memory of the fight swung his thoughts over to Al Ganns and Ed Rawson. After sleeping on it for a night, Bill was more convinced than ever that the pair had wanted to kill him and that he had done them a favour by riding out to the skinning grounds. He wondered if the pair knew, for sure, he was a federal game-warden? There was a lot of guesswork and conjecture in this proposition, but he had run into others just as tricky and deceptive in his work for Uncle Sam. The main thing to do was play his cards close to his chest, and say little and not tip his hand. To keep working on the case, and doing his best. Beyond his best, he could not go. Maybe he was wrong on some points and right on others. But time would tell that, just as time revealed all things to all men.

He had definitely reached a mental conclusion on one point. From now on he would treat Rawson and Ganns as if they were aware of his true purpose here on Milk River. He might be wrong about them or he might be correct, but one thing was for sure—he would watch his backtrail . . . and the trail ahead and on both sides.

He went to the dining-room and ate a good breakfast. He was hungrier than he had figured. Eating was not too difficult. He then went to Doctor Hamilton's office, as much to see Mary as to get his wound examined. This done, he loafed the forenoon away in the hotel lobby reading the *Pillips County Journal*, the local weekly. He looked like a cowpuncher out looking for a job, nothing more. Everybody had heard about the fistfight at the skinning-camp, and by this time almost everybody in town had seen the damaging effects left by Al Ganns' sledge-hammer fists, so he was in the background again, and he was thankful for that.

About noon, Ed Rawson rode down the street, heading for his skinning-camp. Bill could see him through the hotel window and Rawson also could see him. Bill noticed Rawson glance toward him, see him, then look away. Soon the horse and rider were beyond the limited vision of the window.

Bill stretched and dozed for an hour in his chair, the lobby warm and good. Then he got out of the chair, stretched, looked at the clerk and said, "Got to look for a job, man," and went out the back door, going down the hallway to get there. Within a few minutes, he was in saddle. His pinto was full of hay and oats and wanted to do some travelling. There was still no wind. The cold hung over the snow, holding it in silent grip. He crossed the snow-covered ice of Milk River, the caulks of the pinto's shod hoofs crunching on the ice under the snow. Had anybody been watching him, that person would have figured he was heading out to the Bar S, looking for a job. He wondered if anybody did watch him.

He followed the Bar S road a short distance and then turned west among a clump of high diamond-willows. He rode up-stream a few miles and then recrossed the Milk, heading across the flat toward the southern foothills. Once he drew rein among the big sandstone rocks along the edge of the foothills. He gave the country a careful and thorough scrutiny.

Far to the north, across the Milk River, the smoke from the chimneys of the Bar S spread coiled upward against the blueness of the sky—they were dim gray ribbons suspended in the coldness. To the east, along the rim of the foothills, was other smoke, but this came from the Box 7. It, too, hung against the day, marring the blueness of the sky. There were other ribbons of smoke, too—but these came not from the stoves of cowmen but from the stoves of the farmer.

Apparently nobody was on his backtrail, but vigilance did not leave him, for long had it been a stern power in him. He knew he was in danger every minute he spent on this range, but that was old to him now for in his work with the government he had been in danger before. His eyes moved out and picked up the Rawson spread. The cabin and buildings was set closer to the Milk, being on the rim of the underbrush. He took his field glasses out of their case. To do this he had had to doff his mittens. The cold made his fingers numb within a few minutes. He adjusted the glasses on the Rawson oufit.

Two men were working in the feed-lot. They were shovelling hay out to Rawson's bawling cattle. One man drove the hayrack while the other doled out hay. Rawson's haystacks were in the distance—two long stacks of bluejoint hay. He had more hay per head, Bill figured, than had the two cow-outfits. Rawson had bought hay from the farmers before snow had come, so Bill had heard.

The hungry cattle followed the slow-moving hayrack with its team of black horses. They grabbed at the hay as it hit the snow-packed field-lot. Bill's glasses showed the scene with harsh clarity.

Again, he searched his surroundings, seeing no enemy. Then he rode toward the Rawson spread. He came in down-brush and tied his horse about a half-mile away from the outfit and went ahead on foot, rifle in his hand.

Behind the house, he stopped in the buckbrush and he crouched there, looking at the Rawson outfit. The house had about three rooms and was made of logs rolled into position and chinked with cement. The back door, he saw, was made of logs, skinned flat and bolted together. Two stovepipes stuck out of the roof and none had smoke coming out of them now, for evidently the house was empty and the fires in the stoves had died.

He wondered if Rawson kept any dogs. If a dog caught his scent—and started to bark—but he had to take that chance. He looked at another building, also made of native cottonwood logs, and he judged this to be the bunkhouse—it was longer than the house but it, too, had a sod roof. No smoke came from its chimneys, either. He figured the only two men on the spread were the pair out shovelling hay to the cattle. The rest of Rawson's crew, he figured, were at the skinning-grounds, tearing the hides off dead sheep.

The wind shifted a little, and a sudden odour—almost nauseating—came out of the barn, which was a building made of willows and mud, the willows being placed upright between poles and wired into place, the mud being heaved onto them and let freeze into position. This building did not have a sod roof, but it also had a willow roof. Bill thought, that stink came from sheep pelts piled in the barn, and then the wind died down and he lost the smell, for which he was thankful.

He sent his eyes carefully around the buildings and the area, and saw no trace of man or dog. There was a small shed—evidently a blacksmith shop—to the west of the house, and the door was open on this. He moved to his left and then darted across the overshoe-packed snow and ducked into this building. For a moment he flattened himself inside against the door jamb, and listened for danger. Had anybody seen him make his dash?

But he heard nothing that told him danger was abroad. He turned his attention to the inside of the blacksmith shop. He was looking for beaver-traps. Already the short Northern day was pulling to its close and shadows were creeping across the snow. He saw a forge and some blacksmith tools—tongs and hammers, and an anvil sitting on a stump—and he saw some harnesses on the pegs. But apparently there were no traps, for he saw none.

He had planned to mark traps, had he been able to find any. And this was the logical place to find the traps, he figured. He had marked traps before on other jobs. He had a small, sharp chisel in his overcoat pocket. With its point he had planned to run his initial—B—under the pan of the trap, lightly scratching it into the steel. Then, if the trap were discovered set in a beaver run, it could be traced back to Rawson.

Because the initial was always made under the pan of the trap, nobody would ever see it except the man who had put it there. But this blacksmith shop held no traps, so he was stumped on this point.

He looked at the house, wishing he knew for sure if

anybody were at home. He was nervous and uncertain. But if any person were on Rawson's homestead he was either asleep in the house or he was keeping out of sight. Bill glanced at the open door of the barn.

He decided next to look over the barn. He went around the corner of the blacksmith shop and then openly walked into the barn. He was nervous and his eyes roamed and searched, but he saw nobody. He was glad when he was in the barn. The place smelled of manure and hay and harnesses and gear. The roof was held up by cottonwood posts. Harnesses hung from spikes in these posts. A team stood in a stall and they wanted hay, for their manger was bare. They were sorrel horses, both geldings, and they were heavy, although they were not fat; they were good work horses. But he was not looking at horses; he was searching for traps.

And he found none here, either.

The barn had a haymow. He went up the ladder. There was some hay but nothing else. Luck was with him for he had hardly got into the mow when he heard a man enter the barn below.

Lying prone, Bill looked down between a crack. His breath caught, for the man was short and the man was Jim Overcast.

He wondered if his eyes were seeing right, and then he realized they were. Now what was Overcast doing here on the Rawson farm? He and Rawson were not good friends, Bill knew. But here the man was—

Bill watched him, hoping the oldster would not climb up to the mow. Overcast walked around the barn, giving the interior a long raking set of glances, and then his eyes settled on the haymow ladder. Bill held his breath. Was the short man looking for a man named Bill Dupree? Had Jim Overcast trailed him to this farm? This man was a puzzle—a riddle—a far cry in the harsh, cold wind. Overcast walked over to the ladder. He laid a hand on a rung. Bill thought for sure he intended to scale the ladder and climb into the mow. But then Overcast moved away, and Bill breathed easier. Overcast walked around the barn a few times and then left by the back door, the door he had entered.

Bill thought, what and why did he come into the barn? Was the oldster looking for something . . . or somebody?

Bill waited about twenty minutes, but nobody else came into the barn, so he went out of the haymow. He had again found no traps. By now the dusk had become thick and he saw that a kerosene lamp had been lighted in the house. He went through the shadows and moved close to a window. Frost covered the window for it had no storm-window; therefore he could not see inside. He heard a man grumble and he heard a stove-lid make a clang, and he figured the cook was getting supper for the Rawson crew, which should be hailing-in soon from the skinning-grounds.

Evidently the cook was the only Rawson hand on the farm. And he had been sleeping the afternoon away. Cooks were up early and sometimes they slept in the afternoon, he knew. But he knew now he could not get into the house. His feet were cold despite the protection of woollen socks and overshoes. His high cheekbones were white from the ice-cold air. He decided to return to Dodson. Later on he would scout the creeks, looking for beaver-traps. He would either do that or trail Rawson, hoping the man would lead him to the trapping-grounds.

He went toward his horse. To do so, he had to move around the corner of a log building, set close to the hen-house. The wind was idly blowing toward him and he got a strong scent—he halted, back against the logs, and smelled. Smells like a bunch of dogs, he thought. He had smelled the same smell once in a kennel in the home of one of his friends who was a veterinarian down in Denver. The lean-to had a door and he opened it and entered the room.

He slid into semi-darkness. He shut the door behind

him and looked about himself, waiting for his eyes to pick out objects. The smell was stronger in here—humid and close and strong. He heard ahead of him a low rumble—a dog growling softly. Then he saw the dogs.

Ahead of him was a wooden wall about three feet high, and from the top of this ceiling was chicken-wire. Chained to the opposite wall were six dogs. They watched him in silence. This in itself was an odd, odd thing. Usually dogs barked at a stranger. Or, for that matter, by all rights these dogs should have barked at a man entering their home, be that man a friend or a stranger. But these dogs had not barked. Even the growl had been very low and indistinct.

Bill Dupree was fascinated by the dogs. He took a chance and he lit a match and it showed them clearly in its flaring light. Each was chained to the wall, the chain snapped to each collar. And the odd thing was that the dogs were opening their mouths, as though they were barking—but no sounds came from their canine throats!

They pulled on their leashes. Their mouths opened and closed, but they made no sounds.

Bill thought, they have been operated on, and their voice-boxes have been taken out. He remembered that one had made a sound like a growl. Maybe he had not growled from his throat; maybe he had made the sound with his tongue against his palate. Now why had the dogs had their voice-boxes removed?

The answer to that was simple and it was the only answer logical. They had been rendered dumb so they could not bark, and for no other reason. And what good were they? The match showed them to be mongrels. They were very short of legs and thick of body. The shortness of their legs made their bodies seem heavier than they were in reality, he decided. He did this all in the flare of the match. Then the match had died down, and dusk was thick again in the small room.

He listened, wondering if the flare had been seen

outside, for the room had a few high small windows. The memory of the dogs, straining at their leashes, mouths opening and closing, fascinated him, and the ghoulishness of the scene—their straining leashes, their extended eyes, their drooling fangs—remained strong in him. Their presence here made little, if any, logic. But then he remembered old Jim Overcast sneaking into the barn and looking furtively around before ducking out the back door again. And that did not make logic, either.

Bill Dupree shivered, and it was not from the cold. They had stared at him, eyes glistening, and one had wagged his stubby tail. Evidently they had dachshund blood in them, for no other dog he had ever seen could breed such short legs into his offspring. Why did Rawson keep them?

He did not know.

Suddenly he stiffened, the tension driving the trembling from his body. From the yard outside came the sounds of bobsleds sliding over packed snow, the ring of steel shod hoofs on frozen ice, and the call of men. The skinning-crew had come home and was stopping wagons in front of the barn.

Somebody hollered, "Lots of hot coffee, Cook, or we'll slit your gullet open, fellow."

The cook did not answer. Bill slipped outside. He was close to the building, shadows hiding him. The crew was unhitching teams from the bobsleds. He smelled sheep pelts. They were piled on one sled. He wished it were darker. He had stayed too long on this spread. Now he had to get away—dash for the brush. The skinners were about three hundred feet away.

Bent over, a shadow, Bill ran for the brush, a distance of about fifty feet. He was almost in the protection of the buckrush when he heard a man's voice holler, "Somethin' movin' over by the brush, men."

He thought, Al Ganns' bull-like voice.

Then he was in the brush, among the trees. He was out

of sight, the barn between him and the men. Nobody had taken a shot at him. He knew he had been an indistinct blur moving through the gathering darkness.

"That looked like a man," one of the skinners hollered.

Another said, "Looked like a deer to me. A deer has come up to try to get some hay out of the stacks."

"Good luck we got a high woven-wire fence around the hay," another man said. "Looked like a buck to me."

Bill, hurrying for his horse, heard another voice—he recognized it as belonging to Ed Rawson.

"Cook, have you seen anybody pilferin' around the buildin's today?"

"Nobody been around that I've seen, Ed."

Bill thought, I made it, and then he stopped, breathing tense. He had heard the crunch of overshoes ahead of him. He stood there hidden by the night, back against the rough bole of a big cottonwood tree. The man was dog-trotting. He moved past Bill, and Bill saw he was short and wiry. Bill knew he could be only one man—and that man would be Jim Overcast.

Then Overcast was gone, the brush taking him. The man had been heading away from the Rawson spread. Bill got the impression that after Jim Overcast had left the barn he had hidden himself in the brush to watch the Rawson outfit. Maybe he was running toward his horse which was back against the hill somewhere?

Bill heard the sounds of another man moving toward him. He made noise as he went through the brush. This told Bill he was one of Rawson's men. Rawson had sent a man out, then, to look through the brush, just to make sure it had been a deer they had sighted, and not a man?

The man turned out to be Rawson himself. Bill could not see his face clearly, but he judged the man to be Rawson because of his wideness and solidness. A devilish thought pestered game-warden Bill Dupree. He smiled crookedly although it hurt his swollen lips.

He might be able to come in behind Rawson without the man hearing or seeing him. Then a downward sweep of his six-shooter's barrel on Rawson's skull. The man would then fall, knocked unconscious. But, if he heard Bill move in, or if he saw him—Bill decided to forego the sudden plan. Though he did this with reluctance, because he remembered the stitches in the cut on his jaw—a cut made by the cowardly fist of Rawson, who had come in behind him.

Bill could not afford to take chances. Sooner or later he would pay back Rawson for that cowardly attack, but he figured the time had not yet arrived. Rawson went out of sight and then Bill heard him say, "Must've been a deer. Never seen nobody in the brush."

The voice came from the clearing around the house and buildings. That meant that Rawson had abandoned the search. Bill went toward his horse. The animal was cold and he rubbed his bony nose against Bill, wanting his master to ride him to hay and to shelter.

Bill swung into his saddle with difficulty. He had so much clothing on, the act of mounting a horse was made difficult. He rode away at a walk, because if he had hit a stronger pace the sounds of the horse's hoofs would have gone back to the Rawson men.

Once out of hearing-range, he put the pinto to a lope. The horse pulled at the reins and wanted his head, and Bill let slack come into the rawhide-lines. The day's ride, he decided, had accomplished little, if anything. Or had he learned something? He was not sure.

First, his mind dwelled on Jim Overcast.

Overcast was a riddle. He thought long and he did some diligent thinking—but he could not see where Overcast fitted into this puzzle, if he did fit at all. He remembered how the oldster had sneaked into Rawson's barn. How he stood there and had given the barn a long and careful scrutiny. Was he working for Rawson?

when you trailed a man you didn't openly lope a mule down a trail, even if it were dark. Evidently Overcast was heading for Dodson, also.

"Get along, pinto."

This fellow Overcast, he again decided, was up to something, and Bill wondered again—with no results— as to why the old man rode out in such cold weather. He could have stayed home beside his hot stove. But instead he was hightailing it over the ridges of snow, and sneaking in on the Rawson spread. Bill dismissed the thoughts of the oldster.

When he rode into the livery-barn he saw that Overcast's mule was in a stall, saddle stripped from him, and the livery-barn man was rubbing the mule with an old gunny-sack, taking the sweat and saddle-marks off him. Bill dismounted and stripped his pinto, putting his saddle over the rack.

"That mule," Bill said, "looks like he's been rode hard."

"Sweaty, he is."

"Grain my horse good tonight and in the morning. Give him plenty of hay. I'm leaving this burg come daylight."

"Can't find no work, huh?"

"Only thing I have found so far," Bill said with a grin, "is a fight with Ganns. But no job. And without a job, a man's goin' starve to death unless he knows somewhere he can ride the grub-line, and I don't know of any such place."

"Jobs are scarce this time of the year."

"You tellin' me?"

Bill left the barn and went down the street, overshoes making crunching sounds on the frozen snow. The wind was gathering strength and it pushed cold fingers through his sheepskin coat. He glanced at the town and it looked cold and miserable, hunched there on the bleak Montana plains. He was hungry, and he wanted hot coffee and a good steak. When he was going past the saloon, old Jim Overcast stepped out and said, "Time for chuck, Bill. Have you done et yet?"

"Headin' toward the nosebag now."

"I'll put it on with you," the oldster said, and swung into stride beside him. Bill wondered if the old man had waylaid him to get to talk to him. He decided to play his cards close to his chest—very, very close. Sometimes a man played up to you, got your confidence, and then slit your throat. And he was trusting nobody on this range. Oh, maybe one person—Mary Red Robin.

Overcast said, "You bin out ridin' this afternoon, I take it? Saw you ride into the livery barn."

Bill nodded. "Rode out to the Bar S."

"Lookin' for a job?"

"I'm scrapin' the bottom of the money-sack, Overcast. I have to get work or move on where I can find some. Thought maybe I could get a job tossin' hay off a hayrack to cattle."

"I take it you had no luck?"

"No luck. Come daylight I'm leavin' Dodson. A man can't live on air an' water, you know. Or snow, either."

"Which way you ridin'?"

Bill thought, nosey old devil. He said, "Might head south for the Missouri River country. Much as I hate the sight of a homely sheep I wouldn't mind shovellin' hay to them this winter. And them Basque sheepmen over there run thousands of woollies along the Big Muddy."

"If the guy pitchin' the hay can stand the stink of them, Bill."

Bill said, "And I might head west toward Chinook or Havre. Bigger towns than Dodson, and there might be work." He glanced at his companion. "You been moseying around town all day?"

They were turning to go into the hotel. When they were crossing the porch, Jim Overcast answered the question.

"Went down and courted the Widder Jones this afternoon. She had a nice warm kitchen and plenty of vittles. Sometimes I think a man is a lost man unless he's married."

They were in the dining room. At this moment Mary Red Robin came from the kitchen, where she had been talking to the cook about a meal for one of her patients. Her dark hair was sleek on her pretty head and her eyes met Bill's.

"On that point," Bill Dupree assured, "I think you are plumb right, Jim Overcast."

"But I got to head out to my farm soon to do my chores. Milk my cow and feed the hog and grain the chickens— hey, young man, it shows in your eyes when you look at thet young heifer."

"She's almighty nice to look at," Bill agreed.

Jim Overcast's eyes twinkled. "I got a hunch thet young woman is goin' miss you when you drift out, Bill."

"She'll find another man right off the bat. They don't weep long at her age," Bill said, laden with the wisdom of his few years.

"Come and eat with us, Miss Mary?" the oldster asked.

Mary Red Robin gave Bill Dupree a look of scrutiny. "You seem to be getting along all right," she said. "Tomorrow, come over to the office and we'll take out the stitches."

"In the morning," Bill said.

"That's all right with me. Doc will be in about seven."

"I'll be his first patient."

"Have chuck with us?" old Jim Overcast repeated.

She declined with thanks. She had to go over and see the Watson family. Everybody was down with colds and one of the boys might have pneumonia. She wished the cold spell would break.

"We all wish that," Bill said.

She hurried out, pulling on her long coat. Old Jim

Overcast looked at her pretty straight back and her well-formed hips.

"Oh, Lord," he sighed.

# SIX

The field glasses were very powerful. The head office issued them to every game-warden and the head office bought only the best. They had been made in Germany and the lenses were ground to perfection. The glasses picked up the Ed Rawson crew in the draw below, about three miles away. They pulled the men and the bobsleds and the horses in close and made them separate things, not part of a picture.

The crew was finishing the sheep-skinning job. The snow had been tramped flat, hard as ice, and the carcasses of skinned sheep were scattered around in profusion, awaiting the arrival of the coyotes and the wolves and the bobcats. But there was more here than the scavengers could eat. When Spring came the stench of the carcasses would fill the air.

Bill Dupree realized the crew had, in a few days, skinned many, many sheep—they had the system down to perfection and they really stripped the hides off the dead woollies. His glasses came to a man he knew was Al Ganns. Ganns was driving one of the teams and was about ready to strip a woolly of his pelt. Bill wondered what the man's face looked like. As for himself, he had a beautiful black eye, and, having had shiners before, he knew it would be a week or so before the darkness left his eye.

He moved the glasses slightly to the east, which was his right, and they rested on the figure of Ed Rawson. Rawson was on one knee honing a knife with a carborundum stone. Bill watched him for want of something to do, and the game-warden's thoughts were miles away. When the knife was sharp enough to suit his fancy, Ed Rawson went to a dead sheep, rolled him over on his back, and went to work slitting the hide down the belly.

Bill watched the man work for a while, then he lowered his glasses. The halfbreed game-warden lay on his belly up there on the rimrock that overlooked the south wall of Milk River Valley. This was an area of huge sandstone boulders, some now covered by the drifting snow; the boulders cut the wind, though, leaving an area of calm behind them—and for this Bill was thankful. The wind was as sharp as Ed Rawson's hunting-knife.

The snow showed the tracks of cottontail rabbits. The cottontails lived under the boulders and came out occasionally to forage for food. One now sat close to the rock he lived under and he watched Bill Dupree, evidently wondering what form of animal life this constituted. Because Bill had lain so quietly for a period of time, the cottontail had lost his fear and was now apparently very curious.

He sat up, ears upright, and he sniffed, nose making wrinkles. Bill moved his hand a little and the rabbit scooted into his home under the boulder. Bill Dupree smiled softly. His cut lip had healed pretty well, the stitches had been pulled from the wound on his head, and he felt more like living now—but he did wish the cold weather would stop. Despite his woollen liners and heavy horsehide mittens, his fingers were cold. His feet were cold, too, in the heavy woollen socks and overshoes. He was, in fact, cold all over. For two days he had haunted these hills, watching the Rawson crew, watching Rawson, watching Al Ganns. There was one warm thought in him, though, and this was centred around a dark-haired half-breed girl—a nurse, in fact—and her name was Mary Red Robin. She was warm and soft, and nice to hold in his arms, and he had found that out the morning he had called in Doctor Hamilton's office to have his stitches removed.

Cold, miserable, an outcast, he lay there in the snow, the vast and tumbling northern ranges below him, and his thoughts swung readily over to the scene, there in the Dodson doctor's office.

The medico had made him yelp. He had been rough as a horse-doctor while pulling and cutting the stitches. He was evidently in a gruff mood and later Mary had told him the doctor had been working all night, for a little boy had pneumonia and the doctor had spent the night at the sick child's bedside.

Bill then decided the medico had not been as rough as he had been incompetent because of weariness. This was after he had paid the doctor and was alone in the waiting-room with Mary Red Robin.

"Well, Mary, I'm leaving Dodson today, I am."

The words, for some reason, had been hard to utter. His heart was pounding against his ribs, also.

"Leaving, Bill?"

"No work around here." He had shrugged and smiled. "Like the Chinaman says, 'No workee, no eatee!' "

Her dark eyes had searched his face. They had moved across his features slowly. He had not known that her heart, too, was doing strange things. To control herself she had walked to the window and looked out on Dodson's snowy mainstreet.

"This is sort of sudden, isn't it, Bill?"

"Well, I been thinking about it for a few days . . ."

The heater smiled and cast out warmth, one side of it red from the lignite coal in it. The room was warm and comfortable. Outside, the thermometer stood at twenty-three below zero, but there was no wind. One of the rafters suddenly creaked, contracting still further from the cold.

"I'm sorry I have to go, Mary."

"Why?"

"Because I'll have to leave you."

There it was—he had said it! The words had been spoken; she knew now how he felt about her—but he figured she had known this all the time. The language without words—the touch of a hand—the meeting of their eyes—they had told him this, just as they had also told her. He moved over closer to her. She still stood with her back to him, and she seemed watching something out of the window. The first thing Bill knew, he had his arms around her, and his chin was buried in her dark sweet-smelling hair.

"Oh, Bill, let me move away from the window. Everybody in town—they'll see us—tongues will go a hundred miles per hour . . ."

She moved to one side and faced him, and her arms went around his neck. "I was afraid, Bill, afraid," she whispered.

Bill had gone with other girls, of course, but, for some reason, he had not gotten serious about any of them, but he was serious about Mary. Her lips were warm and nice and her body was pressed against him, and the promise of it was there ready for him to eventually take.

"You'd better come back, you no-good cowpuncher," she had joked, tears in her eyes. "I'll—I'll miss you."

"I'll write."

"If you don't, I'll scalp you. I'll work at this end—save my money—I'll see if I can't get you a job on one of the outfits when Spring comes and they hire men."

"I'll be back," Bill said.

He had a picture of himself in his wallet—a little picture taken when he had gone to college—and he gave her this and she, in return, gave him a snap of herself, too, and now this was in his shirt-pocket, securely buttoned down. He had ridden out of Dodson, young and hot-blooded and in love, and he had not noticed the cold one bit. He had ridden down the mainstreet so the entire town would see him leave, for he had to give the impression he was leaving for good. He had been whistling off-key, for he never had learned to whistle good, and when he had ridden past Doc Hamilton's office, he had lifted his mittened hand to the girl who had watched from the window, and she had waved back. Then she was out of sight and he had had a hard lump in his throat and, without thinking of it, he had whispered into the cold Montana air, "I'll be back before Spring, young lady—if this works out all right." Then he remembered he was going on a cold and dangerous and deadly mission—there were thousands of dollars at stake and unscrupulous and deadly men to face—and he might not be back. But he had shoved this thought off the precipice. He had to stop thinking such terrible thoughts, he knew.

He *had* to come back . . . now.

The first night out had dulled his inner fire a little, for it had been intensely cold. He had made his camp back off the rimrock in the boulders, and the wind had been knife-ice sharp. He had had a buffalo robe and three thick Hudson Bay blankets tied across the back of his saddle, his cooking utensils and razor and other necessities securely wrapped in the bed roll, and he had laid the buffalo robe on the snow, back under a boulder, and had pulled the four heavy blankets over him. But he had still been cold, although he did not take off his clothing. It started to snow sometime after midnight. When he awakened, his bunk was warm; that was because he was snowed in. He was under the new clean white snow; a prisoner in his cocoon of downy whiteness. He thought, on first opening his eyes, that he was in prison—one of those odd thoughts that come to a person upon awakening suddenly in strange circumstances. He had struggled up out of the white prison and then he had seen the cold blue sky, and he sat there, covered with snow, and he had almost laughed at his fright. The earth had a new white blanket, and the sky was without a cloud—the sun was dull, with sun-dogs surrounding it. And the air was crystal-cold.

His horse was half-covered with snow, standing about a hundred feet away. Bill brushed the snow from the rump and withers of the animal. He had some oats in a sack and he fed part of this to the horse. He had a small collapsable pail he used for a nosebag for the animal. He wished he had some hay for the horse, but he had none—so, that was that. The oats had strength but it did not fill the horse. The horse was thirsty, too. Bill saw where he had licked the snow for moisture. Bill got a fire going, using twigs from the gnarled juniper-trees, and he melted snow in the pail, and the horse drank. This filled his flanks a little, but he still needed hay.

Bill had some canned goods—beans and some peas—and he lived on these. A meagre fare, but about all he could carry on horseback. He shot a cottontail and broiled him—he was tough and hard and like rubber. He must have been ten years old, at least, he figured. But he was filling, which made for energy.

Chewing on the tough rabbit-flesh, he had had a wry thought. Maybe his boss would give him a desk job where he could sit beside the hot stove come winter? But this, he knew, was wishful thinking; working inside, to him, was misery—he was an outdoor man, even if the thermometer was frozen down in the bulb. Well, when summer came, he would have it easy. His job then was to scout beaver-streams and count the beaver population. Beavers spent the day in their dens and came out to work in the dusk. All a warden had to do was sit still along the bank in the willows and count the beavers as they left their dens in the bank. Mary could sit with him, and he found drive in this thought.

Now he watched the Rawson men finish skinning the storm-killed sheep. He figured that at two cents a pelt the sheepman made nothing. He merely salvaged a few dollars from his already dead herd. Rawson then shipped the pelts east to market. He doubted if Rawson made much, either. Rawson had a crew to feed and pay-off, and the pelts were worth little on market, Bill knew. Somewhere these sheep pelts might be tied-in with the beaver hides? But where would this link be? He had a hunch that Rawson was skinning these woollies for another reason beside the few cents each hide would bring to him. Or was he wrong? For the life of him, he could not see a connection here—and he blamed it all on an overworked imagination that would grasp at any mental straw.

Bill looked at the sun. He had an hour or so more of daylight, he figured. He saddled his horse. The beast stood humped against the cold. Before he put the bit between the horse's jaws he warmed it with his hands, rubbing the coldness out of it, for a cold bit, suddenly inserted into a moist warm mouth, would take the skin off the horse's tongue and jaws, for the intense coldness of the steel would freeze the saliva. He rubbed the bit and then gingerly tested it with his own tongue, hoping his tongue would not stick to the steel. It did not and he put the bit between the grass-stained teeth.

The horse wanted to get moving, for movement brings warmth. Bill rode off the rimrock, keeping a hill between him and the Rawson men, and he headed for Beaver Creek, about four miles away. The horse found a trail made by wild range horses and he loped along this, the heat of the run loosening his long and tough muscles. Range horses had pawed snow to one side, there on the foothills. This way they got to what little dried grass there was that had been left from the summer-grazing and had become covered with snow. Gaunt cattle, ribs showing, followed the horses, for cows do not paw snow to one side

89

to get to grass, as does a range horse. These cattle did not get water or hay. They licked the snow and got their moisture that way, and they lived on what they could forage. The range horses were bony and with long shaggy coats of hair. Already the mares were getting heavy with unborn foals. One colt had already been dropped and he had frozen his ears down to little stubs. He was what is called in range parlance a *crop-eared* horse. He had selected the wrong month in which to be born. Bill hoped his mare had milk for the little fellow. The horses did not run, for they were too weak; they stood and watched him ride past, but made no movements toward flight.

Bill hid his horse in the brush along the creek and walked up and down the ice, making his inspections. He came to some riffles. Here was open water, for the creek flowed swiftly here; only on the coldest nights would this ever freeze over. He saw a muskrat set here, the trap in the riffles. He was hiding in the brush when the Rawson trapper went by with his day's catch. He had four muskrats and a mink, Bill saw from his concealment in the brush.

The man tramped along, snowshoes helping him walk. The wind had already covered Bill's tracks. The man carried his catch hanging from a hand, and he had no sack on his back. And he carried no beaver or beaver pelts, Bill was quick to notice. Then, the man was gone, tramping around a bend in the creek.

Bill wished it would stop snowing and the wind would cease. With snow falling each night and with the wind blowing most of the time a person couldn't follow tracks, for the snow soon covered all tracks. He squatted in the windbreak of a cottonwood tree and did a little thinking. But he had gone over the problem so many times before, there was nothing new.

Before going on this job, he had studied up on the habits of beavers. Other wardens, wiser than he, had also schooled him on the method of living the beaver employed. These beavers did not live in dens made in the middle of a stream, because this stream was too fast and too deep. Therefore they dug their dens in the banks of the creek, and they dug two holes to these dens. The den itself consisted of an area back in the bank, above the water-line, where the beaver family lived in dark comfort.

One entrance to the passageway leading to the den proper was level with the water in the creek. This entrance the beaver used in the summer time. Suddenly, out of the bank he would come, swimming swiftly and making the water ripple silently behind him. When the ice froze over and closed this entrance to his den, the beaver had another entrance which he used in the winter.

The beaver, being a canny creature, knew how thick the ice usually got, so he dug this entrance deep in the water, the passageway slanting upward toward his den. Thus, when the top entrance was frozen shut, the beaver and his family could enter the water through the bottom entrance. He could then come out under the ice. He could travel under ice, too. When his lungs got tired, when the air in his body became stale, he merely went to the bottom of the ice, expelled the air from his lungs, let it get fresh again, and then he again inhaled it and went down, swimming through the ice-cold water.

When the ice was clear and a man could see through it, Indians used to kill beaver by watching them swim under the ice. They would be dark, bulky shadows zipping through the water under the crystal-clear ice. But sooner or later the beaver would have to renew his breath, so he would lie for a minute or so under the ice, the bubble of air expelled from his lungs. At this juncture the redman would pound on the ice over him and drive him away from his air. The beaver, frightened, would dive, leaving his air-bubble behind him, and not in his lungs where it should have been. Thus he was literally choked to death. If he had any air in his lungs, he would soon stop and try to renew it; again, the redskin would pound on the ice, driving him on. As a result, the beaver—an animal who lived in water—would soon die of suffocation.

The Indian would then chop a hole in the ice and take the dead beaver out. His pelt would go into clothing, his flesh would be eaten, his long teeth—the teeth with which he hewed down trees—would go on a string and become a necklace or wrist ornament. And the string holding his teeth together would be made from his sinews. Other sinews would be used for thread. The scent box of him would be made into perfume.

So nothing was wasted.

But Bill Dupree was not thinking of these points at this time. He wanted to catch some beaver poachers, and he wanted to find out how they shipped their beaver pelts out of this Milk River country—and so far he had not even reached first base. He decided to keep on moving. He went upstream and came, within a few hundred yards, to a beaver dam.

He had visited this dam before. It was a big dam, built higher than most beaver dams, and he figured it backed up water about half a mile, at the least. The size of the dam meant one thing: there were lots of beavers here. For it took lots of the busy fellows to build a dam this large and solid.

During the hot summer time, this stream would almost cease to run, but with the dam holding back water, the beaver clan would have plenty of water in which to work and swim, for such was the purpose of the dam. Beavers were industrious people. With their long teeth they cut down small cottonwoods and box-elder trees and willows, and these were then cut into shorter lengths, being inserted into the mud and rocks, and thus, starting from the bottom of the stream, the dam was reared upward—now it held back quite a few acre-feet of water. Bill figured that the water depth directly ahead of the dam would be around twenty-five feet. The dens, of course, were behind the dam.

He had admired the sizes of some of the logs that had been interlocked into the mud and gravel. They were rather good-sized hunks of wood, and this told him it had taken big beaver to handle them, to put them into place. The bigger the beaver, the larger the pelt—therefore the greater the price paid for that particular pelt.

Bill walked along the bank, looking at the dim recesses that told him a beaver-den entrance was at this point. He saw no traps had been set. Had a tap been set in a den entrance, the chain would have extended out of the ice, for trappers let the chain freeze in, thereby anchoring the trap. The beaver upon being caught in the trap, would struggle, run out of air, and then die in the trap under the ice, for the chain, frozen into the ice, would keep the beaver from swimming off with the trap.

He saw no signs of the ice ever being chopped out, either. For, had this area been trapped, the ice would have had to be chopped out so the beaver carcass could be removed, and this would have left scars in the ice. He had even scraped snow to one side so he could better study the ice, but he had found no trace of axe-work. He was, in other words, stumped as to how the beaver were being snared.

He was doing no good along the creek, so he went to a high hill, and from here he could see the trapper, who was heading for his cabin.

The man stopped occasionally to check his sets, and out of one he took an animal he had caught; the distance was so far Bill could not tell what the animal was. But he knew it was not a beaver, for the man was not following Beaver Creek now—he was hiking across a flat area, thick with snow, heading for his cabin. Then he was out of sight, the dusk hiding him.

Bill Dupree was all alone in the northern Montana wilderness. The game-warden thought of Mary down in Dodson. She would be eating in the hotel about now, or she would be out checking some patients; he got terribly lonesome for her. He had just known her for a few days, but still it seemed as though he had known her for years. He decided not to think of her. But that was impossible, for she was always in the back of his mind.

Bill mounted and rode toward the skinning-grounds. There the snow was packed, dirty from the hoofs of horses, the overshoes of the skinners. There were still some unskinned sheep, half-covered by snow. He wondered if Rawson intended to come back after these pelts, or just forget them. Then he decided, with a wry smile, that Rawson's business was the business of Ed Rawson, not of one Bill Dupree. But the night was here, and Bill had to get back to his rimrock camp. Much as he dreaded it, he had to get in between cold blankets, and shiver the night away. And the night was getting colder.

He fed his horse a measure of oats and tied the animal back in the shelter of the boulders. Before getting to sleep, he lay there in the snow, doing some thinking. He wondered, first of all, if Rawson knew that he, Bill Dupree, was a game-warden. He had decided to go under a different name on this job, and to that the head office had concurred. That fact—the fact that he travelled under an alias—should have thrown Rawson off-trail, had Rawson received a tip that a game-warden was visiting this vicinity. But maybe his description had been sent to Rawson from his unknown informants; that is, if Rawson had been tipped off?

He chuckled.

Mary Red Robin would sure be surprised to find out, when they got married, that her married name would not be Dupree, but would be Smith. Good old common, stout Smith! He sank into a cold, jerky sleep. He came awake half a dozen times, but not so much on account of the cold as on account of his dreams.

His dreams were bad.

He kept dreaming of dogs. Short-legged, thick-barrelled—dogs without voice-boxes. Dogs that peered at

him and barked at him, but they made no sounds. Dogs that made the gesture of snarling, but yet made no noise.
  Dogs!

# SEVEN

Two days later he was still in the wilderness. This time he was on the rimrock, back of the Rawson spread, watching that outfit. The thermometer stood at thirty odd below zero. The land was frozen, the snow slanting off the hills, and the sun-dogs played around the sun—dark spots proclaiming further storms. The day before, Bill Dupree had again scouted, and out of his scouting came no conclusions that were solid—only more conjecture, nothing else.

He was gazing, so he reasoned, at a blank wall. He was sure of one thing, though—beaver pelts were leaving this section, going to St. Louis. He had watched carefully, but, to the best of his knowledge, no pack-horses, laden with pelts, had left the Rawson spread. The day before, he had focused his glasses on a rider, down along Beaver Creek, and the lenses had shown that the man had ridden a mule, and the rider had turned out to be old Jim Overcast.

Jim Overcast had come out of the brush along the creek. He had not been coming from his homestead, Bill knew. Bill had watched the mule-rider cross the valley toward Dodson, a dot in the cold-filled distance.

Bill let his thoughts dwell on the oldster. He rubbed his

face. His face had lost the effects of Al Ganns' stunning blows. Even the cut put on him by Rawson's cowardly attack had healed. But his thoughts were on old Jim Overcast. He doubted if Overcast were in the beaver-pelt smuggling. Beaver-pelts had been going out of this area before Overcast had come into this region, he reasoned. He had eliminated almost every man on this range with the exception of Rawson and Al Ganns. But Jim Overcast, he reasoned, had little, if any, reason for riding range this cold weather. He had no cattle on range. He had told him that. No horses, either, so why did he ride this Beaver Creek region? Bill did not know. But he decided he would keep an eye on the man who rode the mule.

Rawson and his hands had finished skinning out the blizzard-killed sheep. They had peeled off the last of the pelts and had thrown them on a bobsled and then had abandoned the skinning-area. Bill Dupree had watched their bobsleds glide away over the packed snow, heading for the Rawson spread. He had watched from the rimrock, field glasses showing the scene clearly. With the sheep all skinned, with the Rawson men gone, he was alone here in the wilderness. Again he had thought of Mary Red Robin. He had wanted to ride into Dodson and see her. To talk to her, to look at her, to be near her. But he could not do this, he knew. He had to give out the appearance that he had left this Milk River region. Then perhaps Rawson and Ganns would make a move in the open—a move that would betray them? He had to bet on some surprise element of this nature.

He wondered if some word had come out of the home office for him. He had made arrangements with the Big Boss to check the great Northern telegraph station in Malta, some miles to the east. He had not done this. He decided to make the ride into the cowtown, further east along Milk River. This he did, getting into the town at dusk of a cold, wintery day.

He got a room at a hotel, his horse going into the barn behind the hostelry, and he shaved and washed, the water warm and good to his skin. He bathed in the cast-iron tub after the Gros Ventres stable-boy had carried buckets of warm water up from the basement. He sent the boy out and he bought a suit of new clean underwear, some socks, some razor blades, and he wished the boy could have brought him back a haircut, too—he joked about this, saying the boy should disconnect his head and take his face and head downtown and get its hair cut. The boy did not understand this, and he regarded him for a moment with a long, slanting glance that clearly questioned Bill's sanity. Bill thought, no sense of humour, and let it go at that.

He watched the town through the hotel window. There were not many people stirring, despite the fact that this cowtown was the trading point for a bunch of big local cow-outfits—the Circle Diamond that ran north to Canada, the N Bar N that ran cattle along the river, and for the Little Rocky Mountain outfits—the Circle C and the Ben Phillips' TU spread. The weather was too cold. Hay hands doled out precious prairie hay to starving cattle. He did not want to be seen. He ate supper in his room, the meal being brought to him by another Gros Ventres buck. This redman was slow and suspicious, and Bill realized the hotel management probably figured that it had an outlaw hiding out in one of its rooms. But the sheriff or town marshal did not come to talk to him. When darkness had been on the earth a few hours he went to the telegraph station. The depot was new and raw against the snow that was dirty with cinders. Jim Hill had built the road through this wilderness a few years before, and with the exception of a drift-fence or the fences of a farmer there was no long string of barbwire on either side of the right-of-way fences. He asked, "Is there a message here for Bill Adams?" And there was. It was from the Big Boss. Pelts were still reaching St. Louis, but how were they getting there? His job was to find out. Get to work, Bill. Bill read it twice and then tore it up. It had been in Malta about five days, a glance at the calendar told him. The Big Boss had not mentioned the word 'beaver'. He had just mentioned the word 'pelts.' The operator would know nothing; he had just taken a message down over the wire. Nothing more.

"The red light district," said the operator, "is across the tracks, down along the river—down there in thet string of log cabins."

"Not for me," Bill said.

The man watched him under the green eyeshade. The key clicked, but not for this station; the man deciphered the code, though, his lips moving.

"Nice girls down there," he said. "Two new ones, last week. Came in on the evening train—Number 4."

"Broke," Bill said.

"Cowpuncher, down on your luck, eh?"

"Need a job."

The man shrugged. "None around here. Cowmen are feeling this. They've cut their payrolls down. Most every hand is working for room and grub. Ridin' the grubline, in fact."

"Don't know what the country is comin' to," Bill said.

The man was lonesome. He wanted to talk politics. Bill did not want to talk politics. He returned to his hotel room, coming in through the back door. He slept like he was dead. The clerk awakened him at five. He ate in the kitchen, for the cook was still asleep; Bill and the clerk fried bacon and eggs and made coffee. Then he paid his bill and pulled on his sheepskin coat. He hated to leave this warmth and this building. The rimrock was cold and foreboding. But he had to keep moving, and his eyes met those of the young clerk.

"Ride the straight and narrow," Bill said.

"I'll do that."

He paid and went into the night. Dawn was still hours

away. The wind was blowing, but the snow would not lift; the snow was hard and solid. The wind was cold. His horse did not want to leave the barn. Bill used his heels and his quirt and got the animal moving to the southwest.

The wind did not strike him with direct force, and for this he was grateful. For the wind was cold. He remembered the startled look on the face of the clerk when he had told the menial to "ride the straight and narrow." Surely the clerk had thought he had been talking with a wanted man, an outlaw. Bill got a lift out of this for some odd reason, and he analyzed it down and he found out this: every person liked to think himself important, and he had by his words set himself in a selective class—even though this class rode outside the pale of the law. This was childish, he knew, and he knew, also, that every man, no matter how mature, had some of the child in him, and he was always his father's son, regardless of his chronological age. But this move into philosophy brought him no beaver poachers. His mind went back to the short telegram. From its brevity he gathered that the federal government still did not know *who* was shipping the stolen pelts into St. Louis, nor did government agents know *how* they were coming into town. Two essential points, necessary points, had not been deciphered, been discovered. Had these two things been determined, all he would have had to do would be step in and solve the case. This brought his mind around to Ed Rawson and Al Ganns. Both would fight, he figured; that is, if they were the guilty persons, and he could get evidence against them to arrest them. *If, if, if.*

He decided to spy on the Rawson camp. There was no use riding back to the rimrock. He had his buffalo robe, his bedding, his supplies and utensils all on his saddle. His horse had had a few hours of necessary rest. He had been grained with oats and had filled his belly with good hay, and this showed in his toughness. He moved through the wind, and he had more strength now. The wind increased and it started to snow, and soon the range was covered by the white blanket. The horse went through it, and Bill, being range-born and bred, could determine directions, although the snow was a white wall, shutting in his vision.

Daylight came but it was not clear and bright; daylight sifted through the driven snow, giving the world a queer yellow colour. The thermometer was not falling, but it was about ten below, he guessed, and he realized there was no use riding toward the Rawson camp. He might, in fact, ride openly into the yard, the blizzard being so deceptive. He had to postpone watching the camp. He turned the horse more south than west, and thus he came to the rimrock area again. He rode unexpectedly into a group of big sandstone rocks. Range cattle and horses had moved in, letting the boulders break the brunt of the storm; they stood in the lee of the boulders. They had packed the snow down by their movements. When Bill rode into their midst, the horses did not run; they were weak and hungry and had no fear of man, for their lack of strength was greater than their fear. The cattle did nothing; they kept their heads down; they kept their rumps into the wind. Bill dismounted and took the bit out of his horse's mouth and tied his catchrope to the hackamore rope. He went back in between two boulders, where cattle or horses could not penetrate, the rope trailing behind him, his buffalo robe under his arm. He sat down there, back to a boulder, and pulled the robe over him. He tied the rope to his leg. His horse could not wander without making the rope tight and letting Bill know he was moving. He had to hang onto his horse. He got deadly cold, the cold seeping into his feet, creeping up his legs. He wondered if he were freezing. Occasionally he would more around, bringing back circulation. Inside of him was a harsh sense of futility, a rising against his luck. But he knew he had to wait, to work, to go ahead, that even if he apparently were making no progress, he was still on the ground and working. These thoughts did much to kill the feeling of futility. He had to play a waiting game.

He had no other choice.

The blizzard did not break until noon of the next day.

# EIGHT

Rough fingers dealt the cards. Despite the bigness of the fingers, the cards rippled out swiftly, landing on the table. Then Al Ganns cupped his cards and scowled. "Same damned hand I had the last time," he said. He threw his hand into the discard. He looked at Ed Rawson and then at the other man at the table. "Do your betting and name the number of cards you want."

Rawson scowled, studied his cards. "You sound riled, Al," he said.

"This damned blizzard," Al Ganns said. "Howlin' night and day. Gawd, man, will Spring ever come?"

"We don't want it to come too fast," Rawson said. "I'll take two." He tossed his cards into the discard.

Rawson won the hand. The other man stood up and said, "I'm broke. Flat to my arches. You boys are too fast for me." He pulled on his coat and pulled down the flaps of his muskrat-skin cap. "Wonder if I can find my way back to the bunkhouse in this blizzard."

"Follow the rope," Rawson said.

The man jerked on his mittens. "That I aim to do," he said. "Without a rope to foller, a man would lose his way inside of a minute. Once a fellow over in Dakota—a farmer—wandered all night between his place and the barn. Found him dead in the morning, right in his own yard. Snow and blizzard so thick he couldn't find his way to either the barn or the shack."

"Follow the rope," Rawson repeated.

The man nodded, then left. Snow came scurrying across the floor, then the door went shut and kept the wind away. Rawson took the cards and looked at Al Ganns. "Another hand?"

"No."

"Why not?"

"Don't want to play cards."

"You're behin'."

"Makes no never-mind to me."

"Your chance to break even . . . or win."

Ganns got to his feet. He paced across the floor to the window. Despite the storm-window, the window had frost on it. He got an open spot and he looked out into the swirling snow. The barrel-stove was hot with lignite coal. Ganns stood there for a moment, face grim and determined, and Rawson, still seated, watched his partner, his short fingers idly shuffling the cards.

"That Dupree fellow," Ganns said.

"What about him?"

"He's pulled out. Left Dodson."

"Good."

Ganns turned. His face still bore marks left by Bill Dupree's fists. "I don't like that fellow."

"He's gone, now."

"Maybe . . . maybe not."

Rawson said, "Solitaire for me." He spread out his cards. Without looking up, he said, "We might have had him pegged wrong. He might not have been a game-warden. Easy to make the error, you know."

"No other strangers in Dodson," Ganns pointed out.

Rawson played a king. "How do we know?" he countered.

"Small town. One hotel. We got our fingers on it.

104

We're keepin' track, Ed."

"Could be a slip . . . easy enough."

Ganns moved away from the window. He went to the stove and put his hands behind his back and warmed himself.

"Wish we knew for sure, Ed."

Rawson said, "Forget it, Al. Cross your bridges when you come to them and not before. We still got plenty of beaver to take out."

"Not many left on the Milk."

"Yeah, but Beaver Crick has plenty. Behind that big dam is many a big beaver, man. We've saved it until the last. We've waited for them pelts to get at their prime, and the time is now."

"We can't get them beaver with this blizzard on, Ed. Hell, a man couldn't see his hand in front of his face, let alone get beaver."

"It'll break."

Ganns rubbed his jaw. His jaw still hurt from Bill Dupree's fists. His mind moved out, searching this point, feeling of this one. He had moved beyond the rim of the law for all his life, and he had developed a strange sense of perception—a sort of wilding characteristic. This was pouring into him now and making him suspicious and ugly and alert. Accordingly, his mind settled upon another unknown factor and this found words.

"Overcast," he said. "That old man. He's got me thinkin', Ed."

"Just an old farmer."

"He outwitted you, remember?"

Ed Rawson had a dark and evil glance. Little lights of anger flicked and played momentarily across his narrowed eyes.

"You tryin' to rib me, Al?"

Ganns sensed the man's anger, and this in turn rubbed against him, for his nerves had felt the edge of this storm, this danger.

105

"Maybe I am."

"Well, don't . . . if you value your life."

Ganns caught himself. He said, "Hell, Ed, this storm is makin' us both jumpy. Forgit it, friend, forgit it. But still, I don't cotton to this Overcast gent. He throwed a rifle down on us, remember."

"He had his grounds for doin' that. We aimed to get that Dupree gent, and he came in and broke it up."

"Still don't like him."

Rawson shrugged. "We've watched him. We've spent hours watchin' him. But . . . nothin' suspicious, so far. You worry too much, Ganns. Far, far too much, man."

"This is a dangerous game."

"But a good game," Ed Rawson corrected. "Lots of money in it. Now, we got more sheep pelts, too. We'll salt them down and ship them out. Nobody will ever get wise to the way we ship out the beaver pelts. Nor how we get them without traps, Ganns. Ride a steadier horse, man."

"Well, maybe you're right."

Outside, the storm beat with new fury against the building. Down at the bunkhouse, men lay on bunks and read or played cards; they too listened to the new howl of the Montana blizzard. High on the slope of a peak in the Little Rocky Mountains, a cougar lay curled in his den; he too heard the roar of the wind, but it was dim and far away—his belly was full of white-tailed deer. A doe, and one leap, and she had gone down; now she was in him and feeding him. The pines bent, the spruce talked, and cottontail looked out of his den, then turned and scampered back into the opening in the snow. Down in Dodson, Mary Red Robin sat at the bedside of a sick little boy, and felt his pulse and judged his chances. Doc Hamilton worked across town, putting a mustard plaster on a man. Mary Red Robin thought of Bill Dupree. She knew she had fallen in love. She missed Bill Dupree. The next time she saw him, she decided she would not let him get away and out of her sight.

Then a sickening and dismal thought hit her. Bill might not return. Men were always making promises they never had any intention of keeping. Maybe Bill was a married man? She felt sick at heart at this thought. Maybe she had worn her heart on her sleeve?

She had to put such thoughts aside forever. Bill Dupree would come back—she knew that, she just felt he would.

So she contented herself with this deduction.

Bill Dupree was also thinking of Mary Red Robin. Above everything else he wanted to ride down to Dodson and talk to her, and be warm and eat some hot food and sleep in a good warm bed, instead of out in the rimrock in his blankets and his buffalo robe. But this he dared not do, of course. He even thought about changing his occupation. Besides being a dangerous job, this job called for cold rides, and cold nights spent not under a roof but under a stormy sky. But then he also put such thoughts to one side. He had a job to do here and he had to do it. But he did wish he could make some headway. It seemed as though everything he had done to date had backfired on him, and he was right where he had started—well, not right back that far, but close to it.

Even the weather, it seemed, was against him. Everything was in conspiracy against him. The wind was ice-cold, heavy with snow; the world was constricting, a white-snow barrier on all sides. Therefore he was glad when the blizzard finally blew itself out. It ended within an hour, first falling, then rising again, but each time the wind rose it seemed to have less power. Then the wind was gone and the earth was new with snow—white snow, clean and beautiful. Even in his cold state, Bill could not help but realize the world was fresh and beautiful. The wind had banked the snow against the hills and the cut-banks and trees. The valley stretched below him, with only the black spots that were houses visible; the rest of the world, it seemed, was covered with white. Even the barren cottonwoods and box-elder trees along the creek and the river were white.

That night the moon was very bright. There was no wind and the rangelands were shimmering white under the high moon. Bill watched the Rawson house and outbuildings until the lights went out. Then he went back to the rimrock camp. He was running low on grub. His supply of cans was sinking. He shot a cottontail rabbit—a big buck—and he was two meals. He had just a few more meals of oats left for his horse. The horse needed hay. Bill decided that if something did not break soon he would have to leave the rimrock camp. He would need grub for himself and hay for his horse. He would head into Malta. Days had stretched out and moved one into the other, and he was not sure how many nights he had spent on the rimrock. His field-glasses were busy all day. The trapper worked the Beaver Creek area. Bill watched him, but apparently he was not taking beaver from the ice. His only hope was to say close to the Rawson spread.

The second night after the blizzard he sneaked into the barn and got an armful of hay. He carried this out the back door and fed it to his horse hidden in the brush. Three times he came out with hay. That afternoon he had seen Rawson and Ganns go to the lean-to building back of the barn. They had come out with the short-legged dogs and they had exercised them. The dogs, glad to be out of their prison, ran and scampered, and Ganns loped down the lane, the dogs following. Here the hoofs of horses had packed the snow flat and the dogs had no difficulty in running. They leaped and ran to and fro and it seemed odd to hear no barking. Bill had watched through his glasses and had again marvelled at the presence of the dogs. They were so short of legs they had a hard time keeping up with the horse even at a slow lope. They reminded him of a dachshund he had once owned when a boy. The dog had bounced in his efforts to run, just as these short-legged mutts bounced up and down.

Ganns and the dogs returned. Now the dogs trotted and did not scamper, and their desire to run had been taken out of them. They were led back into the lean-to. Some did not want to be caught for evidently they hated their prison. Ganns had to rope one. He was a good hand with a rope. The dog was a hard, elusive target but Ganns, despite having cold fingers, caught him the first time, the catchrope whipping out to snare the dog. Within a few minutes, the animals were out of sight and, had not Bill actually seen the scene, he would have thought it a figment of his imagination—but this was not imagination, for this was the second time he had seen the short-legged voiceless dogs.

He was sure his horse was securely hidden, so he decided to spend the night in the haymow of the Rawson barn. He had two reasons for this act: he wanted a warm place to sleep, for a change, and he wanted to spy on the ranch. He was taking a chance, but he had to take it. He ate his next to the last can of beans and then he went on foot toward the ranch. He came in behind the barn, coming through the willows along the creek, and he darted around a haystack and came in through the building's back door. Moonlight was silver—molten silver—on the snow. There was no wind; not a trace of breeze. The night was cold, though—snappy cold, biting cold. He came into the barn. The interior was very dark. He caught the odour of horses and of manure, and of hay and of harnesses and saddles. He almost bumped into a centre post holding up the ceiling. He heard the crunching jaws of horses working on hay. With difficulty he found the stairway leading upward; he climbed this ladder, carrying his buffalo robe. He came out on all fours in the haymow. He went to one end, climbed over some hay, and dug a hole in the musty bluejoint hay. He figured he would be safe even if somebody came into the mow to shovel hay down through the hay holes, for he was at the far end of the hay and was hidden. He felt warm, for once, and he pulled the robe over him, and he went to sleep in a short time. Once he was awakened by the cracking of a rafter under the cold. He thought of the dogs in their lean-to and of their throats without voices.

They would be warm in the close building. Then he drifted back to sleep. He had to be awake and away from the ranch before anybody got out of bed, he knew. He hoped he would not oversleep. But he did, for he was dead-tired; he was tired to the sinews, and his body had demanded sleep. The sounds of voices below in the barn awakened him.

He awoke quickly, but he did not sit up; his mind brought him back to earth, and he remembered climbing into the haymow. He could hear the voices clearly. He did not recognize them, though.

"Boss says to grain his horse an' Ganns' horse extra good," a man said. "A extra measure of oats for them, Baldy."

"You shovel down the hay, huh, Ike?"

"Sure."

Bill Dupree lay very still. He heard the lid of the grain-bin open. Then he heard a man climb the ladder to the haymow. He heard the man climb into the loft, and he heard him grab a pitchfork. He hoped and prayed the man would not come to the far end of the loft. Bill lay there below the level of the hay and he had his six-shooter in his hand. He dared not breathe. He heard the fork dig into the hay, then, fork laden, the man went to the hay-holes, shoving the hay down into the mangers below. It did not take him long. Bill dared not raise his head and watch. He had to use his ears. The man moved to the top of the ladder to go down—or so Bill judged his position—and then he stopped. For a long moment there was a silence. Was he suspicious—had he seen him?

Bill was cold. Very, very cold. His hand, gripping his six-shooter's handle, was wet, despite the coldness. He had been a fool for sleeping here. He could see, in his mind's eye, the man standing there—looking around the darkened haymow. Bill expected to hear the man come toward his hiding-place any moment now. Well, he'd have to fight, to get him!

Then from below came the voice of Baldy. "You done go to sleep up there, Ike?"

"No."

"I'm done grainin' this bunch. If you ain't done fell asleep, what you doin' up there all this time?"

"Tryin' to fix a buckle on my overshoe."

Bill breathed easier at this news. He heard the rustle of the man's clothing—the rubbing of his sheepskin coat, the sound of his fingers working on the buckle on his overshoe.

"I'm headin' for the house, Ike."

"Wait a minute. The buckle done come loose. I'll fix it onto the overshoe in the bunkhouse—have to sew it on."

"Come along, Ike."

Bill heard the man go down the ladder. There was a little bit more of conversation, irrelevant and meaningless, and then the voices trailed into nothing, and he heard the barn door roll shut, the rollers making thin sounds of protest as they slid along the cold, oilless runners. Then there were no more voices; the danger was gone. And Bill sat up and sheathed his six-shooter, putting it in the leather holster. And he smiled to himself.

That had not been a close call. He had been securely hidden there in the dark. But his nerves, he realized, were jumpy. He had been on this dangerous assignment for some time now—too long, in fact. Next time he would ask the Big Boss to let him go after some farmboys trapping muskrats out of season, or some simple chore like that?

He thought of his horse. He had to get to the animal and give him some grain, and then he would head back into the hills to spend the day. From the rimrock he would watch this spread through his field glasses.

He crossed the haymow, boards under his weight, and

he looked first down at the horses below him, making sure no human was in the barn. He saw nobody, so he went down the ladder. He needed grain for his horse. He was hungry as a man could be, but he had to feed his horse first. He went to the grain-bill and filled the pockets of his pants and his sheepskin coat with oats. This done, he went out the back door, and, for a moment, he straightened against the door, keening the cold day for danger.

Somewhere he heard men talking. The sounds came from the west side of the barn, he reckoned. Evidently two hands were loading a hayrack with hay from the stacks, preparatory to taking it out and doling the hay to the cattle on the snow-covered feed-lot, back of the barn. He moved to the corner of the barn and peered around it. His guess had been correct. The men were on the haystack pitching the hay down on the rack, which was mounted on bobsled-runners and was therefore low to the ground.

He moved back, and did a little thinking. He had to get across the distance without them seeing him. He watched them again and, when they were both with their backs to him, he scooted across the strip—which was about forty feet—and he was behind another haystack. He stopped there and listened. But no voice raised itself in warning; he had not been seen. The next thing to do was skirt the feed lot and reach the willows. He decided to act like one of the Rawson hands. So he walked openly through the cattle, his back to the men pitching hay. He was about two hundred feet from them, now. Evidently his ruse was successful. All men on this range wore about the same garb this time of the year—a long sheepskin overcoat that went almost to their ankles, and muskrat caps. Nobody called to him. He felt shaky, for he expected a bullet through the spine; this did not come, though. He was glad when he had come to the creek bank. He dropped over this, the cattle between him and the men in the hayrack;

the bank was about ten feet high, and it hid him.

Here was underbrush and he started through it, following a trail made by cottontails and jackrabbits.

Behind him he heard a voice holler, "Hey, Joe, where you going?"

One of the men on the haystack had done the yelling. Bill wondered, does he think I am somebody named Joe, or is he calling to somebody else? His conjecture was settled when again the man hollered, "Bring back some fresh snowshoe rabbit, Joe."

"That man didn't tote a shotgun or rifle," another man said. He was the other hayhand; his voice carried clearly in the stillness. "That wasn't Joe, was it?"

"Then who the devil was it?"

Bill Dupree waited no longer. He came to his cold horse. He had left the saddle on the beast, with the cinch loose. He jerked the catchrope loose and mounted, riding the horse with a loop of rope around his bony nose, the bridle hanging over the horn.

The cold horse wanted to run, and Bill let him run. He rode along the creek bottom, on the ice; he was hidden securely. And as he rode he had a small grin on his whiskery face.

That had been a close call.

## NINE

The day was clear and it was not as cold as usual, Bill thought. He had no way to check the temperature, for he did not pack a thermometer. From the rimrock he watched the range; now that the storm was gone, he could see Dodson in the distance. Every time his glasses fell on the black dot that was the cow-town—it was about fourteen miles distant, at least—he thought of Mary. He had been bit hard, and at this thought he grinned boyishly.

He kept his field glasses on the Rawson spread. He saw men come and go, crossing the man-packed strip of snow between the barn, the corrals, the haystacks, the bunk-house, and the other outbuildings. Some of the men were packing sheep pelts on a bobsled. Evidently they would soon be shipped out of Dodson on the new railroad. They were tossing a handful of salt between the hides to preserve them. Or so it looked to game-warden Bill Dupree.

The thought came that Rawson had a lot of hands around the spread. But Bill knew he did not pay them money at this time of the year; because of hard financial times, and the cold winter that was breaking cattlemen and sheepmen alike, there were extra cowhands, and he figured these men worked only for their room and grub. Either that, or, if Rawson did pay wages, they had to be low; he had a lot of mouths to feed, in this crew.

That afternoon his field glasses picked out an object in the brush at about the point where he had tied his bronc the night before, in the brush along the creek. At first he had thought this object was a mule deer working his way toward one of Rawson's haystacks. Despite the high fences, the deer sometimes could leap them; they would then enjoy a repast of hay. This object moved through the brush slowly, working toward the haystacks. He came to a clearing and, because of his high altitude, Bill could look down on the moving object; he saw then it was not a deer—it was a man. He could not, at first, identify the man, for the distance was great—too far for accurate recognition.

But one thing was sure: a man was sneaking in on Rawson's outfit. Bill scowled and thought, who is he . . . and what is he doing there?

He moved his glasses to the east, the direction whence the man had walked, and there he saw an animal, tied in some brush. He recognized it as being a mule, a saddled mule. Only one man, to his knowledge, rode a mule on this range. His glasses went back to the man, and he was sure he was none other than old Jim Overcast.

Bill watched with fascination and wonder. What was the old farmer doing here on Rawson's front doorstep? Why was Overcast sneaking in on the Rawson spread? Was he tied up in this beaver poaching also? Maybe he didn't want to ride openly in to see Rawson and Ganns for fear suspicion would point a finger at him, so he was sneaking in to see his friends in crime?

Bill did not know, but he wished he had known. He watched the man move in, coming from behind the barn. Then Overcast was out of sight, for the barn was between him and Bill. Bill did not see him go to the house. Within an hour or so, the man left the back door of the barn, went across the feed-lot, and ducked down behind the creek bank, just as Bill had done that morning. Bill saw him go to his mule, and mount and ride away to the east. By riding east instead of west, Jim Overcast was riding away from, not toward, his homestead. And that, to Bill Dupree, did not make logic.

Bill kept the glasses on him. The thought touched him that there were many other movements of men on this range that also did not make sense. Overcast had toted a rifle. He had not put the Winchester in the saddle-holster but now he rode with it across the fork of his saddle ready for instant use. To utilize the rifle, all he would have to do would be to raise the weapon, swing it and aim it, and let the hammer fall. Plainly he was taking no chances.

Bill wondered if the man had crept into the barn to spy on the Rawson spread. Or had he met somebody there instead of in the house? He swung his glasses back to the barn, but saw nobody come out of it; he put them back on Overcast. But now, distance and the glimmering white reflection of the sun on the driven snow had claimed the old-timer, folding him into its mystic distance and absorbing him.

A thousand ideas, some utterly wild and utterly fantastic, ran across Bill Dupree's brain, seeking an answer.

Was old Jim Overcast nothing more than a petty thief? Had he sneaked into the Rawson barn to steal something? But he had carried nothing away in his hands except his rifle, Bill was sure. But he could have stolen something small and put in in a pocket? But what would a man steal from a barn?

This assumption did not make good sense, he realized. But one thing, then, did make logic? Overcast was watching Rawson and Ganns? Maybe Ed Rawson and Al Ganns were not poaching beaver . . . maybe Jim Overcast was the head of a gang that hid out back in the hills . . . and was working the country for its beaver?

But, if such were the case, why would he sneak into the

Rawson farm; why would he watch Rawson and Ganns?

Bill abandoned the many questions tormenting him. At this stage of the game, they seemed impossible to answer. He looked at the sun. The days were short, and the sun would soon be gone; he hated to see the sun go for although it rode the sky low in the south, it still held a measure of heat—not much heat, but a little bit. And the night would be cold, he was sure.

He glanced at his horse, standing patiently in the boulders, one bony hip higher than the other, his hammerhead close to the snow. His horse needed some more hay. Just a little bit of hay he had smuggled from the Rawson spread—the hay he had carried in his arms—had helped the horse. He would ride down to the Rawson outfit, despite the danger; he would steal some hay—and oats—for his horse. As for himself, he opened his last cold can of meat. He did not light a fire for there were no twigs around; snow was high. He chewed the cold meat with diligent thoroughness. The beef was tough, as is all canned beef, but it had nourishment and strength in its stringy fibres, and these were what counted.

On this day that was drawing to a close, he realized Rawson and Ganns had not had the dogs out for exercise—if that meant anything, and he doubted if it did. His meal finished, he rode toward the Rawson farm. His horse, weak though he was, was glad to be moving, for movement made his blood move, and it took warm blood to fight the incessant cold.

He left the horse in the same spot where he had picketed him the night before. The sun had gone with vast suddenness, the dusk had come with swiftness to depart just as readily, and now the moon rode the majestic sky and touched the snow with cold, magic fingers.

He was in the barn, stealing some oats in a bucket, when he heard the overshoes coming toward the door. He doubted if he had time to get out the back door.

Therefore he climbed hurriedly into the haymow, leaving the bucket of oats in the bin. By luck, he heard some conversation, then, and he got his first break in this deadly game, and he thus got it by pure accident.

A voice said, "A cold ride ahead of us, Ed," and the voice belonged to nobody but Al Ganns.

"But a good ride," another voice said, and it was the voice of Ed Rawson. "Tonight we take the cream off the pan, Al. Out there on Beaver Crick them beaver are as big as small cocker spaniels. Them hides will be prime and worth money. I'll ride this buckskin here. Which horse you takin'?"

"My sorrel."

"You don't sound happy, Al. We'll make a few thousand tonight, man. How else could you make a stake overnight, fellow?"

"That halfbreed."

"Dupree?"

"I don't mean thet purty halfbreed girl who works for Doc Hamilton. Me, I couldn't get mad at her. I'd like to have her for a partner. Better lookin' than you, Ed."

Al Ganns added something more about Mary Red Robin. This made Bill boil, but he, of course, did not tip his hand. He lay in the hay with his ear to the ground, listening for all he was worth.

"Maybe we had that halfbreed pegged wrong," Ed Rawson said.

"You mean—he might not have been a game-warden?"

"He seems to have left the country," Rawson said.

"I . . . wonder."

He heard the saddles being lifted off the rack, and he heard them hit the back of the horses. He wished he could see what was going on below him. He saw a place where a knot had fallen out of a floor board. The distance was about ten feet away. There was no hay on this section of the haymow; there was just loose dust. Bill inched toward the knot-hole, which was about as big as four-bits. He had to move without a sound. He hoped his forward movement—the drag of his body over the boards—would not send dust down through a crack. He was about a foot from the knot-hole when he had to freeze, fear going through him.

"What was thet noise I heard in the mow, Ed?"

Damn that Al Ganns . . . he's got ears like a housewife when she catches her husband sneaking in come a night . . . Bill Dupree moved not a muscle. In fact, he almost stopped breathing; blood pounded at his ears. There was a short silence. To Bill it seemed as though the whole wide world hung in abeyance—there was no wind, the earth was snowbound and silent, none of the men below him moved, the horses stood silent. Then this moment was gone, shattered by the rough voice of Ed Rawson.

"Prob'ly one of the cats up there. One of ours or some wanderin' tom belongin' to some of the farmers. Good thing they're in the mow—they keep down the mice."

"Reckon that was what it was," Ganns said.

By this time Bill had his right eye over the knot-hole. He had an eagle's-eye view of the barn below. Both of the men had already saddled their horses. Both were dressed for a night's outing. The lantern, hanging on a hook by the front door, showed them clearly, their shadows moving against the yellow light. Both wore long sheep-skin overcoats, overshoes and woollen pants, and muskrat caps with the ear-flaps tied down.

"I still figger that 'breed was a gover'ment man, Ed."

"Uncle Sam ain't gonna disgrace himself by hirin' halfbreeds, Al, when lots of white men are goin' around beggin' for jobs."

"He ain't!" Al Ganns snorted like a bull pawing the earth. "The gover'ment is loco, Ed. Them bigwigs would hire anybody they want to, I tell you, no matter what colour his hide is."

"Well, forget it," Rawson said.

Bill noticed that there were two picks and two shovels leaning against the wall. Evidently the pair had taken these with them into the barn. Bill scowled and watched, hardly daring to breathe. He got a leg cramp in his right leg. It knotted the muscle, making him grit his teeth; he wanted to rub it, to move his leg—but he dared not do this. Slowly the cramp untied itself. He gave his full attention to the scene below. Ganns was the next to speak.

"I'll get the dogs, Ed."

"I'll tie the tools onto our saddles."

Ganns went out the door. Bill watched Ed Rawson tie a pick and a shovel to each saddle. Each saddle, he also noticed, had a rifle in its scabbard, stock protruding upward ready for a man's grip.

The shovels were long-handled. Rawson tied them along the edge of the saddle-holsters which was about the only way they could be carried. Tied in this manner they were flat under the off-side stirrup. The picks were tied behind the cantles of the saddles. He was tying the last pick into place when Al Ganns, surrounded by the dogs, came into the barn, the dogs leaping around him.

"They're ready for a night's work," Ganns said.

Bill Dupree scowled at this information. It did not make sense to him. But when he thought of it, lots of things that had happened to him lately had not made sense. He remembered old Jim Overcast sneaking into this barn. That didn't make sense, either.

The dogs opened their mouths, but no sounds came from their jaws. Suddenly one stopped jumping and his mane stiffened and he growled noiselessly. The others, catching the fever, also stopped leaping; they stood there and looked around, suspicious and alert. Bill knew they had smelled him.

"What's the matter with them?" he heard Rawson ask.

"They smell somethin' they don't like."

Rawson said, "Maybe your feet," and said, "come on, pooches. Snap out of it. Brindle, come along, dog."

120

"They smell somethin' suspicious," Ganns said, and looked around the barn with a slow gaze.

"Let's get out of here." Rawson led his horse outside. "The night is so clear a man could read a newspaper. Us for some work, Ganns. Hit the saddle."

They were out of Bill's vision now. He heard the barn door slide shut. That was to protect the horses they had in the barn from the cold. He heard hoofs make sounds on the frozen packed snow, and then the sounds were heard no longer as the riders rode away.

Bill hurried to the hay window. He opened it a little, the hinges noisy in the cold as the door swung out. Below him was the Rawson spread, washed in the gentle moonlight, the buildings standing out in darkness, clumps against the snow. But he was not interested in the buildings. His interest was in two riders galloping away in the night, moonlight showing them with gaunt clarity. Even the dogs could be seen—the leaping, running dogs with their short legs, their mouths that opened but made no noises. And Bill Dupree had, at this moment, an odd thought: why had they silenced these dogs forever, and who had performed these operations? Had they silenced them so they could go about some task—some nefarious task—in silence?

That was the only answer. Then another question reared its head in desire for an answer. What was the nature of this task?

One thing was settled now in his mind, and the answer was as he had guessed. Ed Rawson and Al Ganns were poaching beaver. His suspicions had been correct. But how had they been getting the precious pelts out of the Milk River valley? By pack-horse, over the snow? By bobsled, by train? He would have to find out, before this case was closed.

He gave the building a raking glance. The house was dark, squat and ugly in the moonlight, but the bunkhouse had a lamp lighted there, and the yellow rays cut through the frost-rimmed windows, becoming lost against the moonlight. Did Rawson and Ganns ride alone to the beaver-grounds on Beaver Creek? Or had they sent men ahead of them—already on the ground?

Bill did not know. He wished he did know. He figured the odds against him might be high. Even if no Rawson men were along the creek, he still had two men to face—the odds, even at the lowest, would be two to one.

He wished he had some help. But he did not know to whom to appeal. The sheriff was at Malta, but Malta was a number of snow-thickened miles away. By the time he rode to Malta and got the sheriff and a deputy or two, the night of beaver poaching would be through—daylight would be walking across the snow, not moonlight. Dodson had a town marshal. His bailiwick consisted of the town proper; beyond its meagre limits he had no authority. He, therefore, was eliminated. Bill knew he would have to go it alone, no matter what the odds against him.

But he could do no good standing in this cold haymow and doing some thinking. He had to trail Ed Rawson and Al Ganns. He ran across the hay and came to the ladder; he went down it with speed. He ran out the back door. For a moment he leaned against the barn's wall, looking across the moonlight. He saw shadows, for the moonlight made many shadows. He thought, moonlight can be bright but never as bright as day. He saw nothing that spoke of danger so he ran across the clearing. No rifles talked to stop his progress, and he darted over the bank. He slid down and came to the creek bottom, and he ran to his horse. The animal was cold and he nuzzled his master, hitting him with his bony nose. Bill went into saddle, taking his rifle with him; he turned the horse toward Beaver Creek.

He did not ride far without stopping, though. About a quarter of a mile further, he heard hoofs coming in from the south, and he hurriedly reined his horse off the trail, darting into a bunch of willows. While the willows were not dense, the moonlight showed them as dark and Bill was hidden here. The hoofs came closer, a rider drifted into his vision, dim and distant; then, the rider was gone—the moonlight had reached out and pulled him out of sight. The sounds of his hoofs ran out, and the silence of winter held the range.

Bill had held his rifle half-raised, weight on one stirrup. Now he stood on both stirrups, peering after the rider, but he could not see him. Had that man been astraddle a mule? Had the rider been old Jim Overcast?

He was sure it had been the old man on the mule.

Bill swung his thoughts over to Overcast, but, as usual, he gained no definite point—his thoughts moved around an empty area. He realised that this problem was drawing to its close; the mouth of the bag was being pulled shut. Rawson and Ganns were going to clean the beaver out of Beaver Creek. That was all that counted. He remembered the big beaver dam, a dark wide line across the ice—the dam made of sticks and mud and logs, with a spillway for the ice-cold waters to tumble through. And he remembered the beaver dens above the dam, and because of the number of dens he knew there were many beaver back in those dens.

How would they catch the beaver?

There was only one answer to that: they had to set traps. But they had taken only shovels with them; yes, and picks, too. And they had tied sacks to their saddles. No traps. There was an answer to this, also. They had stationed a trapper on Beaver Creek. He had the traps for the night's work.

Bill realized they could not clean the creek of beaver in one night. Some of the dens, he figured, would hold maybe as many as a dozen beaver, and a trap can catch only one at a time. There were a number of points about this that did not make sense, and this was one of them— they rode with their dogs and had talked like this would be a night's work—one night, no more, no less. And that was not logical, he figured. Because of these assumptions, he realized he might watch them set traps, then he could ride into Malta for the sheriff and help, and he and the sheriff could catch the two in the act of taking beaver from their traps. A game-warden had to have evidence; he could not get a conviction on suspicion only.

So maybe things were not as dark as they seemed. He swung his horse, heading for the higher reaches for, from a higher point, he could watch the riders below him. And soon he was on a small hill, and the valley lay clear and white below him.

Two riders moved across the snow-covered wilderness.

They were about half a mile away. They pushed across the valley, one slightly in the lead, the other moving at the flank of the leading horse. That would be big Ed Rawson, there in the fore, with Ganns behind him, Bill knew. Rawson would take the lead—big and gruff and deadly. Rawson always took the lead spot. Bill swung his gaze, looking for another rider—a man on a mule.

But he saw no third rider. He remembered the rider drifting through in the moonlight, the white light shimmering and dancing on the snow, and he began to think that maybe his eyes had fooled him—that he had seen no rider. but he had heard the pound of shod hoods, and both his eyes and his ears could not have been wrong. He realized also he had been alone for some days in the wilderness, and he knew what the effect of loneliness and snow and cold could be, but he was sure he had seen and had heard the rider. He had not gone snow-crazy.

He had to be sure of that.

But still, though he looked hard, he saw no third rider—only the two, sweeping toward Beaver Creek. The two dark dots there on the snow-covered valley floor, the dots moving with fluid elasticity toward the dens of the beavers. These two, and no more.

The pinto stirred, pawing the snow; he wanted the trail, for the night was ice-cold. Bill was glad for one thing: there was no wind. He turned the horse; the pinto reared; he seemed to have found new life. Bill rode down off the hill, pointing the ears of the horse to the southwest. His plan was simple and to the point. He would ride along the hills, keeping the ridges between him and the men below, for if he followed them they might see him, what with the moonlight so devilishly strong.

He figured they would go first to the trapper's cabin. Anyway, they would head for the big beaver dam. He let the pinto stretch and the game animal, although gaunt and weak from fighting starvation and the cold, responded as best as he could, moving across the snow with great bounds.

Some places the drifts were deep. The pinto floundered through these, but Bill tried to rein him around such spots, for the horse had only so much energy and the supply was meagre therefore it had to be conserved and doled out. Bill knew that if he were forced to act on foot in this wilderness . . . well, a man would be out of luck—he had to have a horse. Even though the horse were gaunt and weak from starvation, he was better than being on foot.

Bill went along the edge of the foothills, riding the slopes where the snow was not so deep, where the wind had whipped the ground almost bare in some spots. By this time the two riders below him were out of sight; he saw no sign of a third rider, either. He rubbed his face with one mittened hand. He had frozen each cheekbone, and the skin was peeling. But his thoughts were not concerned with his physical appearance or comfort.

He figured it was about four miles to the cabin of the Rawson trapper. The pinto was sweating, hot despite the coldness, when he left the foothills and headed north, and ahead of him, a dark line in the moonlight, stretched the willows that bordered Beaver Creek—a ribbon of black, angling jerkedly across the expanse of whiteness. Occasionally a cottonwood reared its gaunt and ghostly branches, leafless and frozen to the core, grotesque guardians of the wilderness. Under their shade would be cattle when Spring had again walked across the northland, bringing leaves to decorate the branches now stripped and scraggly. Cattle that would bed down in the shade, sleek and fat from the native bluejoint grass; cattle that now stood against drift fences in the back country, or stood in cold groups and bawled for hay. They would seek the shade of the cottonwoods, but now they sought the sun of Spring. But these thoughts, fleeting and swift and fragmentary, had no position when placed against the savage duress of the present moment, Bill was quick to realize.

The cabin could be seen now, in between breaks in the willows. Bill figured he was about a quarter mile from it so he went out of saddle, stiff from the ride and the long session in the wilderness, and he took his rifle out of the saddle-holster, the steel sliding out of cold leather with the sound of ripping cloth. He did not check the rifle, though.

He knew that the magazine of the rifle was full of cartridges—steel-jacketed .30-30 cartridges, deadly and swift. A cartridge also rested in the barrel, for he had made sure of that; now, slipping off his mitten, he set the hammer on safety, the click dangerous and sharp in the stillness. He reached under his overcoat and pulled his Colt .45 pistol out of its holster. This, he knew, was also loaded; six cartridges in the cylinder, the hammer resting idly on one of them. He put the heavy six-shooter in his overcoat pocket—the right pocket—and he shoved it muzzle-down, the butt protruding upward and ready for his grip.

Rifle in hand, he moved toward the cabin. He thought of the dogs. If they were outside the cabin, they would run to him—they would smell him and come at him, a stranger. Then the thought came that they could not bark. And because they could not bark, they could issue no warning.

The cabin lay in a clearing ahead. Made of logs that were chinked against the wind and cold, it had oilskin windows that showed little light, but there was a lamp lighted inside—the glow came through the windows, looking like yellow, square jewels there in the moonlight.

Bill was about forty feet from the cabin. He could go no further unless he crossed the clearing. He had come in behind the cabin. He wanted to see the front of it, so he circled through the willlows, rifle poked ahead of him. True to his guess, two horses stood in front of the cabin, heads down as they panted from their run. No sign of the dogs, though—the dogs that opened their mouths but did not bark. They were evidently inside the cabin.

The horses, he knew, were the ones ridden by Ed Rawson and Al Ganns. One was a sorrel—a dark chestnut-coloured gelding—and the other was a yellow-cream buckskin, also a gelding.

Bill hunkered in the brush, watching the door. He wished he could have crossed the clearing, and could have moved in close to a window to listen. But he dared not do this, for, if somebody suddenly came out of the house—

So, he waited. He was patient and deadly. He was no halfbreed now. He was all Indian.

Big Ed Rawson had put his buckskin in the lead, with the sorrel carrying Al Ganns a pace behind the buckskin. He had not ridden too fast, for the dogs were short in the legs; they could not run like hounds—they did not leap, but they seemed to bounce. Therefore he held the buckskin in, sometimes hard on the latigo-leather reins, sometimes letting slack come into them. And the buckskin wanted to run. He was tired of the cooped-up stall in the barn. Rawson kept him up for hard, long rides. He always fed the horse plenty of hay, even if hay were scarce; twice a day the buckskin had received his measure of oats from the bin—golden oats, flowing from the measure, tumbling into the nosebag.

Al Ganns had said, "You set a hard pace, boss."

"The dogs—they're lagging?"

"We don't want them tired out before we put them to work, you know. I'd say drag rein a little."

Rawson had growled something, deep in his throat, but Ganns had not heard it. Sometimes the very presence of Al Ganns seemed to irritate him, to make him withdraw into himself, to make him fight off the man's presence. This was one of those times, for the man himself was full of frustrations: the big job was ahead—the job that would pay the high money. Rawson was this way, tough and angry and mean, but then logic moved across his character, telling him that he needed Ganns, that the man would be useful this night, just as he had been of use on other nights when the moon rode the cold cloudless Montana sky, when the beaver rested in their dens—the beaver with their rich-red pelts, with their beady rat-quick eyes, their long whiskers and their long yellow teeth. The teeth of an old man—only long and sharp—but yellow like an old man's fangs, not from tobacco but from the bark of willows, cottonwoods, and the red Indian brush.

He had glanced down at the dogs. They were travelling a well-packed road, the snow pounded flat by bobsled runners and hoofs of horses. The dogs were doing their best, but their best was not enough. Ganns' words held logic. Therefore Ed Rawson held down the buckskin.

"We can't let them get too tired," Ganns repeated.

"I heard you the first time."

Ganns looked at him, but said nothing. Ganns had been on these forays before. There was danger in them, but there also was something else—money. And money was what Al Ganns wanted. Money would buy the things his brain did not have power to earn for him. Whiskey, for one thing; women, for another. He had little, if any, regard for his wide-shouldered, tough partner. There was no respect between them, and without respect men cannot have a firm relationship. There was greed between them, and this was the binding tie—it was not solid, though. It was flexible and thin in spots, and when the income stopped the greed would be severed like a sharp knife cuts a string. Ganns was aware of this and so was Rawson. Neither paid the idea much attention, though. Both were somewhat fatalistic, though both would not know the meaning of the word were it broached to them. A man lived until he died, and he needed money because money bought things. When his time came to die, he died; there was that, only that, and nothing more. Ganns did no thinking. Ed Rawson, he figured, could do the thinking. Ganns hated work, and thinking was work—much harder work than skinning out dead woollies.

Rawson glanced at him, and then went back to his thoughts. He went over this in his mind, and one thing bothered him—if the beaver pelts were traced back to this section, he might have to leave it. He would have to pull stakes or go to the pen. He liked this area. He wanted to build up his cow-outfit and become big and powerful. Maybe he should never have started this illegal beaver-poaching? Did it threaten his future on this grass?

He did not know for sure.

He wished, then and there, that he did know, but he did not know.

Ganns moved his horse close. The wind was very cold, and the wind was manufactured by the speed of their mounts.

Ganns said, "Cold night, Ed."

"No hurry."

They drew down to a trot, and the trot became a long walk. The dogs trotted, too, tongues dragging, short legs working. The frozen earth threw back the ringing sound of horseshoes on snow-packed ground. The hills seemed to tower to the south, a long line of frozen icicles, and the points of them were sharp against the moonlight—they seemed to threaten them. What did they hold? Did the cougar move through them, treading on velvet-soft paws, looking for fresh meat—looking for a deer in the underbrush, a deer to mangle and kill and to feel a hot gush of blood, splashing out of the artery? Was the cougar tired of dead sheep, of winter-murdered cattle? And the bobcat, stalking the cottontail? The bobcat, sitting there silent on the bend, behind the rock; the wild cat, waiting for the cottontail rabbit to hop out? The world moved and somewhere the sun was bright, dappling the dark waters of a lake, lifting with the crests, falling with the troughs. They were soft, these waters; they were the clean lap of a woman, hands folded around her child. And a woman laughed, somewhere in Rio, and the light overhead—the gaudy light with its dangling facets of glass—showed her smooth red-yellow shoulders, the curve of her breasts, the fullness of her naked thighs. These were the thoughts of this man—the gaunt and deadly man who rode the buckskin here on these frozen Montana wastes. These were part of his thoughts—merely fragments of them—and they were like black minnows in white water. They ducked, they weaved, they beat against the edges of the bowl, and then they flashed away in their swift blackness.

"Damned odd dogs," Ganns said.

His words pulled Ed Rawson back to the present. The snowdrifts were there, piled around the sagebrush and hiding them; the woman with the soft white thighs was gone, moving swiftly into forgetfulness. Rawson glanced at Ganns and saw the man's amused smile as he looked down at the short-legged mutts.

"Hard dog to get," he said.

Ganns said, "What a hell of a way to get beaver." He was solid in his saddle, and he seemed to be shaking with some stranger inner mirth. "Nobody in God's green earth would ever guess."

"Not green earth," Rawson said, and looked again at the snowbanks. "Snow and cold, the earth."

"The earth," said Ganns, "is a queer ball."

Rawson said, savagely, "Forget it, man."

Ganns said nothing. They came to the willows and they crossed the creek, the ice covered with snow. They went along the willows, following a trail left by a bobsled, and the dogs trotted behind, in single file now, for the trail was narrow and would not permit two of them to gallop abreast. The run had left the canines and they were low to the ground and ready for action. Rawson did not look at them again until they came to the trapper's cabin. There was no light and Rawson and his partner went down and Rawson called, "Hello, the house."

Ganns watched the hills. He did not look at the door. He stood there, reins in one mittened hand, and his eyes were on the rimrock to the south, and so he stood there and watched the hills. There was no answer from inside the house.

Ganns said, "He's asleep, I reckon."

Rawson said, "We'll wake him up," and he kicked on the door. It was bolted from inside, a two inch wooden bar across it. The kick moved the door back against the hinges.

"He never expected us," Ganns reminded.

Rawson stabbed a glance at him. Ganns was still watching the distant, moon-shimmered rimrock. Rawson heard a man stir in the house—the creak of a bunk, the sound of blankets, the movement of a man coming out of sleep. Ganns still sent that long and careful glance probing the distance.

Rawson said, "No danger, Al."

"There might be," Ganns said, and he spoke in a very low voice. "There is always danger, for such as we are."

"God," Rawson said. "A philosopher." He spoke to the door. "Open this damn' door, or we kick it in."

"I'm comin', men."

Ganns said, "We take in the dogs, too."

"Why?"

"They're cold," Ganns replied. "They got work ahead of them. They'll get muddy and wet, and the dirt and grime will freeze on them. Warm them good, for they are good little beasts."

Rawson looked at the moon. He said, to the moon, "The man has feelings. He has sympathy and pity. Each ride, he shows me something new, he does. When does he get out his soap-box?"

The moon did not answer.

Neither did Al Ganns. His face went dark, but the shadow of his muskrat cap hid this, and at this moment the door opened.

"Come on in, dogs and all."

# TEN

Bill Dupree was in the brush about ten minutes. Actually, it seemed like an hour, for his feet were getting cold, the coldness moving through his overshoes and his heavy socks. The calves of his legs were cold, too. He shifted weight, moving from one foot to the other; this, though, did little good to push back the cold.

He kept watching the cabin. He wondered what the conversation was about. There were still many points not clear to him about this set-up. The main one was this: how could they trap beaver without traps?

He reached only one conclusion on this point, the only logical one he could reach. He would have to be patient and wait and see what happened. But he did wish the men would leave the cabin and get to work. There would be three of them, then—Ed Rawson, Al Ganns, and the trapper.

The horses stood in front of the cabin, patient and cold. Then Bill's attention was jerked back to the cabin door. The door opened and the three men and the dogs came outside. Bill hoped the dogs would not catch his scent. Rawson's voice came to the hidden game-warden.

"You sure two sticks of dynamite is enough?"

Rawson spoke to the trapper. His reply came clearly to

Bill, too. And the trapper said, "Sure, two sticks is enough, Ed."

"You dead sure?"

"I know powder," the trapper said. "Two sticks is plenty, Rawson. Well, guess we'll get movin'—the night will be long, but we got lots of work to do."

Ganns was watching the dogs. "What's wrong with Mutt?" he asked.

Bill saw them turn and look at one of the dogs. The dog was opening and closing his mouth; plainly, he was barking. He was looking at the point where Bill Dupree was hidden. Bill figured the dog had caught his scent. He hoped the mutt would not come over to him. The snow was deep between him and the dog, and to get to him the dog would have to leap through the loose snow. Possibly this alone was what kept him from running over to where Bill was hidden. For once Bill found himself being thankful for the deep snow.

"He must smell somethin'," the trapper said.

They all looked toward Bill's hiding place. The game-warden almost held his breath. Time seemed to slowly inch by. He was sure they had spotted him, and he cursed the brilliant moonlight. Well, he would jump up and fire and make a fight of it, but first they would have to move toward him, or holler or shoot at him. Then he realized his fears had been groundless for the voice of Ed Rawson said, "He might smell a deer. Can't tell about a dog . . . or a human. Well, let's get movin', you beaver skinners."

"The other dogs are lookin' the same direction and barkin'," Al Ganns said. "Must be somethin' in thet brush."

"Hell," said the trapper, "I remember, now. Saw a bobcat in the brush there this afternoon. Went for my rifle, but he beat it and I never seen him again. They must smell his tracks."

"Prob'ly," Ganns said.

This seemed to satisfy Ganns' curiosity. He called to

Mutt, who trotted over to him and put his forelegs on the man while Ganns petted him. Rawson said, "So you got some gunny sacks cached down by the beaver dam, eh, trapper?"

"Ready to tote the dead beaver into the cabin for skinnin'," the man said. "Well, here we go."

"I'll ride my horse and lead yours, Ed," Ganns said.

"All right."

Ganns mounted with difficulty, for he had on much clothing—the long sheepskin coat, coming almost to his ankles, also made it difficult for him to swing his leg over the saddle. He caught the reins on the buckskin and rode after the trapper and his boss, who strode ahead as they went toward the beaver dam, about a quarter mile away. They were walking from Bill. He was glad of that. The dogs followed their masters into the moonlight.

They were gaunt figures—two walking and one mounted—as they moved away across the snow.

Bill was still mystified. He had seen them take no beaver traps from the cabin. Nor had they taken an axe to cut through the ice to get at the entrance of the dens. He remembered the trapper saying he had cached some gunny-sacks down by the beaver dam. Might he also have cached some number three or number four traps there, also, and an axe or two?

But what did Rawson and Ganns intend to do with the picks and shovels they had tied to their saddles? Bill could see some utilization of the shovels. Snow would have to be removed from the ice. But these were not snow shovels—they were round-tipped number 2 shovels, the kind used to dig into earth, not snow. Bill Dupree decided to torment himself no more with unanswerable questions. He decided to let the future unravel the ball of yarn.

He moved back into the willows, for the Rawson men were out of range now. He worked himself back toward the creek, heading for the big beaver dam. His overshoes made too much noise in the snow, it seemed. Or were his senses just more sharp than ordinary, honed by the stone of danger? Once he stumbled over a stump, and he almost fell. The stump was the remains of a tree cut down by a beaver's sharp teeth and almost covered with snow. Bill landed on his right knee, managing to stay partly upright. He held his rifle high to keep it out of the snow. Snow in the breech might freeze, and foul up its action. He got to his feet, cautioning himself; from here on, he would take his time and be more careful. Had Rawson or his hands heard him?

He listened, heart pounding. He was sweating under his sheepskin coat. But he knew it was excitement and not exertion that caused him to be wet with perspiration. He heard no alien sounds. There was, for a long moment, only the great elastic silence of the frozen northlands, mystic and without voice. Then this was broken by the voice of humans, working at the beaver dam.

The three stood on the big beaver dam. The black line of the dam, stretching from bank to bank, was a ribbon of sticks, mud, and logs, spanning the frozen surface of Beaver Creek. Rawson stood to one side, leaning on a shovel. He was wide and bulky in the moonlight; a sinister figure of darkness. Ganns had caught the dogs and he was putting leashes on them; they were soon in a group, with him holding the ropes that ran to their necks. Bill wondered why they had leashed the dogs. But it was another question without answer at this time.

The trapper was working on the middle of the dam with a pick. The pick rose and fell, but it was rusty and therefore made no reflections in the moonlight. Bill heard the dull thud of the adze-blade on the mud and sticks. The dam, he knew, was solidly constructed, the logs and sticks interlaced skilfully. He wondered why the man was testing the construction with the pick.

He heard Ganns say, "All the dogs is tied up, boss."

"Good," Rawson said. "How is it going, trapper?"

The trapper leaned on the pick. "Tough goin'," he said. "Them beaver sure must go to school to learn something about arteetecture work, Rawson."

Rawson said, "Keep it up, man."

The trapper went back to work, the pick rising and falling. Bill was so interested he forgot the cold feet inserted into his overshoes. He forgot the coldness that was creeping along his thighs, pushing through the sheepskin coat and the heavy woollen pants and red underwear. He was about two hundred feet from the workers. They took turns working with the picks. This went on for about fifteen minutes, the dogs sitting on their haunches and watching. They talked as they worked, but many of the words were spoken in a low tone of voice; Bill could not catch them all.

What were they trying to do? Destroy the dam? And for what reason?

Finally the trapper straightened, and his words came to Bill. "We got enough dug out by now," he said.

Rawson looked at the hole they had made. Bill could not see it, because it was too far away and level with the ground; he figured they had not made much of a hole in the dam, though. Their picks had not pulled much debris upward to lie on the snow and ice.

Rawson asked, "Will that powder blast off, under the water thataway?"

"Sure will, boss."

Rawson spoke to Ganns. "Move the dogs back to the bank, Ganns. We can't afford to let any of them get kilt when this dam is powdered-out."

"Come along, dogs," Ganns said.

Ganns and the dogs went to the north bank of the creek and stopped there in the brush. The trapper dug into the sack and came out with the two sticks of dynamite. Rawson picked up the picks and went over and stood beside Ganns. Both of them watched the trapper work.

Bill watched the man, too.

Evidently they intended to blast out the middle of the dam. That would drain the water out of the lake back of the beaver dam. Bill did not see any sense in this. But there was a lot here he did not understand.

There was a silence of about four or five minutes. Then the trapper lit a match, the flare showing his gaunt, wind-cracked face, and this match touched the fuse. Then the man ran over to where Rawson and Ganns and the dogs were.

"Move back more," he said.

Bill watched the sputtering fuse in fascination. They had evidently dug a hole in the dam, inserted the dynamite; now, the blast should be heard any moment. The world—the snow-filled world—seemed to be in abeyance, waiting for its stillness to be shattered.

Then the dynamite exploded.

Crouching there in the underbrush, hidden and safe because of distance, game-warden Bill Dupree watched the dynamite break the beaver dam. It reminded him of a club breaking the back of a snake, coming down with such force that it broke the snake in two parts. For the dynamite smashed the dam, tearing it apart, breaking it in the middle.

The roar was not loud. In fact, it was not a roar; it was more of a crackling sound—a sound made by tearing logs apart. Very few logs left the dam and the few that did went but a few feet beyond their starting place. But the dam, unlike a stricken snake, did not writhe or move in pain—it remained staunch and solid and dark, except for the breech.

And through this breech—through this aperture— suddenly gushed the cold water, darting out from under the thick ice. The water was suddenly freed; it broke for the opening in its prison; it danced and laughed and gurgled, seemingly enjoying its new-found freedom. It spurted out, shooting in foamy spray, a blue-green sheet of liquid power. It tore at the sides of the area, ripping loose more sticks, more mud; it did what the dynamite did not quite accomplish—it made a clean and wide channel, and through this channel drained the waters of the lake made by the beavers.

The Rawson men stood and watched, the dogs seated in the snow. The area below the dam became flooded by roaring cold waters that danced over the snow, changing it to water, sweeping it on with its force. Bill Dupree still did not see the reason for breaking the dam. But the dam was broken, and the water was roaring out. He figured it would take some time for the water to completely leave the lake, and he was right on this point: it took about thirty minutes, for the dam had impounded lots of water.

But even before the water in the lake had become all freed, the ice had begun to crackle and break, for the water was not under it to hold it upward—it was now hanging across the area, a bridge with a platform but with no pillars to hold it upright. And this bridge, made of clear-blue ice, carrying a burden of snow, now began to sag, and then, when the weight of the sagging became too great, when the centre of gravity had become too low, the ice began to break and the bridge began to collapse.

This crackling was louder than had been the sound of the dynamite. The ice broke with sharp metallic sounds, like the greatly magnified sounds of a woman breaking twigs. The first sounds ran through the ice, making it shiver and quiver; then, the weight snapped it, and the ice broke in the middle. Bill watched in curiosity. The scene was not long of duration. The ice pitched, rolled, tossed; the cleavage became more apparent; the cracks widened. And, within a few moments, the clean smooth surface had disappeared; the ice lay in jumbled huge blocks, rising here, plunging into the mud at this point. The whole scene had shifted, taken on new points and meaning; the serenity of the ice had been shattered, and chaos was king.

And all the while the water had jetted out of the broken

dam, a stream shooting into moon-silver space, thundering down on the ice below. The water groaned and rolled, like a stricken beast suffering death-throes. The ice pulled away from the banks, sliding downward in the mud, and then Bill realized, with a suddenness, what motivation was behind this manoeuvre from the hand of Ed Rawson and his crew of two. And the entire meaning of this spread out before him, and he understood now every facet, every phase, of this undertaking.

This left him a little breathless. First, he had to admire Rawson's brain, for the plan was a good one; secondly, the audacity of it was surprising—it did not seem logical, yet all the time the evidence was in front of him, and the evidence was strong and substantial.

Now the scene was one of weird and tumbled desolation, made more eerie by the light of the moon which watched with no interest. Bill never forgot the scene left by the jagged broken blocks of clear ice and far bank of Beaver Creek. The ice had slid down off the banks, acting like small glaciers moving downward with the pull of gravity; they had pushed mud ahead of them. A few fish, mostly carp, were stranded; they flapped lazily and stupidly between the blocks of ice, and then they soon froze to death, dying in the freeze-tightening ooze left by the retreating waters. But Bill had no interest in the dying throes of a fish. His eyes were on the opposite bank, and he knew now why Rawson did not use beaver traps to catch beaver. And he knew now how Rawson and his crew trapped the beaver.

There had been about fifteen minutes of wild shooting water—water spearing through the broken dam—and the force of the water had widened the breech, making it allow more water to flow through. The ice below the dam was hidden by the water which had quickly dissolved the snow. The level of the lake had receded with great rapidity; the wider the hole in the dam had become, the faster the water drained out of the lake. The water had become tame, now; it did not have the potential force behind it—its energies had been turned to kinetic. And it was at this time that Bill Dupree heard the booming voice of Ed Rawson say, "Well, water is low enough to allow us to work, and the beaver holes are wide open."

"We might have to move some blocks of ice," said Al Ganns.

The trapper now spoke. "They'll be easy to move, what with that slippery mud to slide them around on."

"The mud," said Ganns, "is freezing."

"Don't worry about such small things," Rawson said, and he gave the brush a long scrutiny. "I wonder if we oughta post us a guard."

The trapper laughed, and the laugh held scorn. "And why should we have a guard out, Rawson?"

"That halfbreed," Rawson said. "He might have been a game-warden, at that. He's a foxy devil."

"He's left the country," Ganns said.

Rawson said, "We don't know . . . for sure."

"He ain't been nosin' around this region," the trapper assured. " 'Cause if he had been around here—well, I'd have seen him."

"You never saw nobody, huh?" Rawson asked.

"Nary a soul, boss."

Rawson said, "I guess we'd better get to work."

Out there in the brush, game-warden Bill Dupree suddenly stiffened, warning shooting through his veins like stabs of wild fire. He stood tense and solid, a dark upright line in the moonlight, and he listened and he heard the sound again—somebody or something was moving through the buckbrush behind him!

For he had heard a foot hit a twig, making a sharp small sound.

# ELEVEN

Here was an aged cottonwood tree, trunk gnarled and rough with time and wind, and Bill moved over close to it, putting himself in its dark shadow. Overheard, the spiny arms, leafless and frozen, stretched in a canopy made of shifting lines, and under this he stood . . . and he watched . . . and he waited.

Had a deer been scared out of the underbrush?

That was his first thought—a deer had bounded away, legs like spikes as he had cleared the brush. He had touched his hoof against a twig, and had bent it and broken it. But then Bill knew the sound had not been made by a fleeing mule-tail deer. For Rawson and his men had dogs. The deer would have lifted his head, smelled the dogs, and he would have retreated long ago—when Rawson and his men had first come on this wilderness scene.

Maybe the sound had been made by a slinking cougar? Had a great cat's paw come down, had the weight of a feline body settled on that paw, and had the twig been under that wide pad with its long and deadly claws?

No, Bill thought; no cougar. Cougars had no need to come along the creek. Cougars had dead woollies, back in the gullies; they hunted the higher wind-bare ridges. A cougar was out.

And the smell of the dogs would also have driven a mountain lion to shelter, long before this.

There was just about one animal left to consider, and he walked upright on two legs.

Impatience was strong in Bill Dupree. He decided to make his play; he had been out of this far too long. He moved out of the shadow of the cottonwood tree and he was a redman now, and the core of him was wild. Every bit of training his mother had given him came in handy. She had taught him how to silently part the brush ahead of him, how to progress through the thickest brush in fast silence, and he did this now—he was a shadow now distinct, now indistinct, moving toward the source of that mysterious sound. She had taught him to crouch and wait, to crouch and watch, and then, the trail clear of danger, to move ahead again—the way a lion stalks and crouches and advances. Bill used this lore, too. He moved about a hundred yards, and then he came to a trail. This was a narrow ribbon, moving through the brush, and it had been made by deer going to the dam to drink in the free-running water, by cottontails and bobcats.

Bill knelt beside it and he studied the trail. He could see the imprints of rabbit paws and here the wide pad of a bobcat. But no boot or moccasins had marred its surface; it held no trace of civilization, only that of the wild. And this puzzled him a little, and he thought maybe his calculations were all awry—that he had let his imagination gallop off with him.

He remained crouched, and he gave an ear to the wilderness. From along the creek came the occasional sound of a man's voice—dim and low and without meaning. This came from the Rawson gang, going about its nefarious employment. These sounds died, and then he heard something else, and it came from his right. It was a slithering sound, a short sharp sound, and he thought, "That was a bit of cloth rubbing on the thorns of a wild rose bush."

A man, moving through the underbrush, had rubbed against a spiny wild rose bush. He was sure of that. It could be no other sound, because he heard then the fall of a foot on a rock. This surprised him. Rawson had three men, and they were at the creek; he himself was the fourth, and now a fifth man moved out there in the moonlight?

Bill moved ahead. Vigilance was with him, pouring warning into his blood; he was stalking the biggest prey of all—a man. He had to find out who this man was, what his part in this consisted of, before he could move in on Rawson and his men, because he had to have his back free—he had to keep eyes from watching him from behind. He did not think that Rawson had a man—a fourth man—out in this brush. The talk he had overheard at the dam had not hinted toward this, for Rawson had mentioned stationing a man in the brush as a guard.

No, this had to be somebody else—somebody not on Rawson's payroll. Bill was sure of that—but who was this mysterious man?

He aimed to find out, as soon as he could.

He cut away from the creek, rifle in hand. He came to another trail, and this was a wider ribbon. He looked at it and saw no human tracks, and that told him the man had not gone this way. He moved back in the brush and waited, and soon the man came along the trail, heading toward him.

Because of the height of the buckrush, Bill could barely make out the man—he occasionally caught glimpses of his outline, and could not see his face. He heard the man stop. He could see part of him. The man stood there and listened, and then he turned, and he moved in the direction from whence he came.

Bill realized he had to get the man out of the way. This was a dangerous game, a game of death, and he had to be sure no rifles were on his back, no bullet would zoom out of the moonlight to break his spine. He swung around through the brush, moving with the redskin's silence, and he came in behind the man. Just as he hit, the man heard him; he started to turn.

But the man never completed the circle. Even as he hit, Bill Dupree recognized the man; yet, his gun-butt came in, the shoulder-plate fitting hard around the man's neck. The man lurched ahead, and Bill was afraid, for a moment, that he had broken the man's neck. He had used the rifle as a reverse-bayonet; instead of jabbing with the stock in his grip, he had held it by the barrel. By this time, the man was on the ground, rifle out ahead of him.

The rifle slid in the snow, then stopped. Bill went to his knees and listened. The unconscious man, head down, breathed with a rattling noise, and Bill realized his nose was in the snow. But Bill did not turn him over at this time. He listened, wondering if Rawson and his men had heard the commotion, listening for the sounds of over-shoes to come toward him. But he heard no voices raised in questions, no overshoes crunched snow. They had not heard the commotion. Only then did he roll the man over. A small man, wiry and tough, and his face stared at Bill, ugly as a dried prune—looking like a prune in one way with the skin leathery and dark, wrinkled as a prune too.

A homely face but, nevertheless, the only face that Jim Overcast would ever have!

Bill looked at the unconscious oldster, and thoughts flooded him and sought answer. Was Overcast working for Rawson? Was he stalking this brush to protect Rawson and his men from behind? That assumption was not long of life. He remembered Rawson debating about station-ing a man on guard, and he remembered the trapper laughing his boss down. Was Overcast in cahoots with the trapper, then?

Bill could see no tie-up between these two. He had another idea, and it came smashing in, moving into his brain. Jim Overcast had come to his aid when he had fought Ganns, when Rawson had slugged him from behind. Had he done this for one reason, and the reason being that he wanted to gain the confidence of one man, a man named Bill Dupree?

Had this oldster hoped to get into the good graces of one Bill Dupree in an effort to get evidence that Dupree was, indeed, a game-warden? That was possible. But Bill had not tipped his hand; he had told old Overcast nothing along this line. He remembered the old man and the mule drifting into the cold of the Montana night, and he remembered other scattered incidents—these added up and made the assumption logical.

Anger lit its way across the dark, high-cheekbones of Bill. But then this was gone, for it had no real basis. Rawson had wanted to post a guard and therefore Rawson had not known that old Jim Overcast was haunting the brush, rifle in hand. And that assumption shattered Bill's hastily-gathered logic.

What was the role of this oldster here in this drama of death? He walked the frozen land, and his rifle was in his grip, and he fitted into this somewhere—but where was his place?

Bill thought, he'll come to soon and then we'll pow-wow, by hell.

He felt the old man's neck. His muskrat cap had broken some of the blow. The neck was complete, not broken; had it been broken, the head would have moved easily, and would have lopped to one side. But the neck was complete; the man was just unconscious. Bill rubbed the prune-like face with snow.

The snow grated under his mittens. He could hear the Rawson men talking down along the creek, the sounds coming across the brush and dying against the snow-covered hills. Bill saw the old man's eyes flutter open, then close. The next time they opened, they stayed open. Old Jim Overcast sat upright, surprise scrawled across his wrinkled, whiskery face.

"What the hell happened to me?"

Bill said, "I slugged you, you old reprobate. Came in behind you with my rifle, and knocked you cold."

The watery eyes were on him. Bill felt admiration for this oldster—he had a keen brain. He had opened his eyes and instantly his brain had taken command, and he now showed no surprise—only pain was in his eyes as he rubbed his neck and twisted his head, loosening the muscles.

"You move like a Injun, Dupree."

He even kept his voice down low. He was himself all the time—wiry and aged and tough.

"I'm half Indian, remember."

Jim Overcast kept on rubbing his neck. He twisted his head slowly against his neck muscles, seeking to drive the pain out of his bones.

"Thought maybe Rawson had slugged me," he said. "Either him, dang his soul, or one of his toughs."

"Why would he slug you?"

The hand came down and the head stopped pivoting against the muscles on the scrawny neck. Bill saw the oldster glance at his rifle about ten feet away, barrel in the snow. Then the seamy eyes moved back to cover him in grim speculation.

"Rawson and Ganns and a trapper are down along the crick," Jim Overcast said slowly. "They blasted out the beaver dam and now the bottom entrances to them beaver dens is wide open."

"I saw that," Bill said.

"Never seen you in the bresh. And man and boy, I've travelled bresh for years, in my job."

"What is your job?"

Again, the old man seemed to be picking his words. Bill got the impression he had five cards—a good poker hand—and each card would be played with quiet deliberation. Half of the game of poker consisted of bluffing.

147

Of feeling out your opponent, to get him to make a bad play. Jim Overcast was using this technique now, Bill was sure, and his own guard came up.

"I could ask you the same, Dupree."

Bill said, "Enough of this countering and talking. I'm tying you and gagging you. I can't have you interfering, Overcast."

Shaded eyes, thoughtful eyes, probing eyes. "Interferin' . . . in what, Dupree?"

"My business, not yours."

"Rawson and Ganns and that trapper are out to wipe the beaver out of this crick. The only job you could have would be interferin' with them, the way I look at it . . ."

"That's your version. Mine might be different. Maybe I'm a guard out for them, coverin' their back?"

"No."

"Why not?"

"You never come to the dam with them. You sneaked in behind them, and you just admitted that."

"A guard doesn't travel sometimes with the man or men he is paid to watch over," Bill reminded.

Again the gray head shook in negation. Again the lips opened, the eyes showed a tough, hard, glittering light.

Overcast was getting ready to play another card. An important card, Bill figured, and curiosity was strong in the game-warden; he held this under stern reins, neck bowed.

"You're a game-warden, Dupree."

Bill laughed huskily to cover his consternation. "That's a good one," he said. "Come again with another joke."

"A federal game-warden. Working for Uncle Sam."

Bill laughed again. "All right, you say I'm a game-warden, and then you analyze it down to where I work for the government. Why not for the fish-and-game, the state, out of Helena?"

"You don't work for the fish-and-game."

"How do you know?"

"I know everybody on that staff, from the office-boy to the top bigwig. And you're not on that staff, Dupree. You had me stumped for a while. I figured you as a game-warden, but one thing was against you."

"And that?"

"You're a halfbreed. I never knew an Indian—a halfbreed—was working for the Uncle Sam men."

"Maybe I'm not."

Again, the eyes were thoughtful. Across the brush came the sounds of men—Rawson's men.

"I would have tipped my hand before," said Jim Overcast. "But I wasn't sure, Bill. When I stepped in that day you fought Ganns—those two, I figure, would have killed you—they wanted to kill you—"

Bill asked, "You got a job on this grass?"

"I have. I'm a state game-warden, out of the capital in Helena."

Bill Dupree said, "Well, I'll be hanged."

It was clear, then—the parts of the puzzle fitted, moved into their proper places. A mule and a rider, drifting through the snow-filled night . . . the stealth through the brush, the moment of danger . . . these all became part of the whole. The state had moved in this warden—this aged, tough old rooster—and he had posed as a farmer, for this was a big game—and the stakes were high. Bill Dupree had a partner now. But still, caution was with him. He showed the old man his credentials and the oldster grinned and dug in the breast-pocket of his dirty flannel shirt. He came out with a folded piece of paper. Bill unfolded it and read it and handed it back.

"Sorry I slugged you, Jim."

"Forget it, Bill. Good to have a partner. We got a job ahead—a dangerous job—and we'd best get about it."

"That's right," Bill Dupree agreed solemnly. He looked at the moon in the cloudless cold sky. "Danged moon is so bright I could read thet credential letter of

149

yours, and I guess a guy could find the sights on a rifle then, huh?"

"He sure can, Willie."

# TWELVE

They squatted and drew their campaign of action. Old Jim Overcast talked in a low tone of voice. Bill had been wrong on one point: the old man had not come into Milk River valley as a game-warden. He had been retired from the service and had come in and bought a homestead to live the last of his days in this basin. But his former boss had got wind of beaver-poaching and had asked him to settle the affair and to bring the guilty parties before the court. When it was all over—which should be soon—he intended to go back to his farm and leave the service again, and he chuckled.

"For good this time, Bill. That is," he added, "if I'm still alive."

"Ain't anything that can kill you." Bill hoped his voice sounded hopeful. He was glad—very, very glad—to have a partner. He had been bucking this problem alone for a long time. Riding the snowdrifts, camping in the snow. Now he had a man to side him and for this he was thankful. More thankful than he cared to admit. With a gun beside him, he had more chance of riding into Dodson and to Mary Red Robin. He thought of the girl with more than fleeting thought. Seemed ages—yes, ages—since last he had seen her dark-haired, olive-

151

skinned beauty. Despite the seriousness of the job ahead of him he got a fleeting picture of her in a kitchen—his kitchen—with an apron and a housedress, and she was baking pies for the kids, who were in school. A man, he decided, thinks of many things, when faced with danger.

"These boys might not like bein' took alive," Jim Overcast whispered hoarsely. "They're right tough hombres, Willie."

"Think they would fight to the death over a beaver pelt?"

"They get caught, and it means up to twenty years in the federal pen, it does. The law is really whackin' down on beaver poachers. If they don't, them beaver will done get like the dodo and that means they won't be around no longer—they'll be extinct."

Through the coldness came the sounds of the Rawson men and Ed Rawson. They were directly south of Bill and Jim Overcast. Bill outlined a plan. They would split up and come in on the three poachers, one from the east, the other from the west. "We'll catch them in the act, Jim."

"But what if they're acrost the crick, on the south bank? We can't go across them jumbled icebergs without them seein' us."

"We'll have to wait for them to work the north bank. From what I judged, they aimed to work the south bank first, looked to me."

"We'll get them workin' the north bank of the crick, then come in on them. Well, good luck, Bill."

"Good luck, Jim."

Other questions were bothering Bill Dupree. But they would be answered later, he knew. Old Jim Overcast moved out of sight in the buckrush. Bill realized he had been a good woodsman to be able to sneak in behind the old game-warden and knock him cold, as he had done. For Jim Overcast moved through the brush with the ease and speed of a cougar.

Bill turned toward the creek. He had moved about

three hundred feet or so—maybe a few feet further—
from the Rawson gang. He carried his rifle in his hands
and had his six-shooter in an overcoat pocket, muzzle
pointing down. He knew that before he jumped the
Rawson men he had to remove his mitten from his
trigger-finger. But that would not come off until the last
moment. He could not afford to go into this without
having a warm and limber hand. A hand almost frozen
stiff has rigid fingers; a man needs limber fingers to slip
around a rifle, and find the hammer and trigger swiftly.

He stepped around a clump of rosebushes, dark in the
moonlight. Cautiously he worked his way forward, heart
beating like a Sioux tom-tom. His heart beat so loudly he
was sure the beaver poachers would hear it. Then this
wild thought drew a smile to his lips, and this smile
moved some of the tension out of him.

Overhead, gaunt cottonwoods reared scraggly
branches, throwing shadowy images on the snow. A
snowshoe rabbit came out from under his feet, was visible
for a few jumps, and then became part of the wilderness
whiteness. He had scared Bill. Bill had jumped back.
Again, he smiled. He was tense—very, very tense. And to
act fast he would have to drive the tension out of his body.

He came to the creek bank. Before him was the
vastness of the jumbled, broken ice, looking for all the
world like a field covered with boulders made of mica.
And beyond the boulders on the south side of the creek
worked the Rawson men. Bill had guessed at the reason
for having the barkless dogs. Now he saw that his logic
and his guesses were correct.

When the ice had slipped downward, it had left open
the bottom entrance to the dens of the beavers. Now
these openings, which were about two feet in diameter,
were dark holes in the mud of the creek-bank. The top
openings or doorways to the dens, situated level with the
water-line, were also discernible. Thus one doorway was
above the other there in the muddy soil.

With the water gone from the front of their dens, the beavers would not run out, for a beaver is, above all other things, a swimming animal. Bill knew that a beaver had the main room of his den up in the bank, high above the level of the water, where it was dry. Now the beavers were huddled in these rooms.

They would be sitting there in the bank. Entire families of them would be in the dens, and sometimes a beaver-family, Bill had read, was composed of even a dozen, or fourteen or thereabouts, beavers. There would be grand-parents and parents and grandchildren. They would be able to hear the men on the bank outside and because of the voices they would not dare run out.

So, if they would run out, how would Rawson and his beaver-poachers get them out of their dens?

Bill Dupree had figured the short-legged dogs would come in about at this point, and this assumption had not been wrong—the actions of the Rawson gang now proved this theory was right.

Bill Dupree watched. Every movement made across the ice was discernible. The trapper led two of the dogs to the entrance of a beaver-den. He slipped and almost fell down, for the freezing cold had not yet frozen the mud left by the retreating water.

"Damned slippery job, men."

Rawson said, "It'll freeze soon. Then the going will be better."

"By that time," said Al Ganns, "I hope we have our pelts and are out of here. I'm suspicious."

"Of what?" scoffed Ed Rawson.

"We've done bin awful lucky," Ganns said.

"This is the last big haul," Rawson said. "Our luck will hold out, fellow. Get a coupla dogs and get to work."

Bill had listened to this conversation, but his eyes had been on the trapper. The man had slid and skidded his way to the entrances of a beaver den. Then he got on his knees and unleashed his two dogs.

"Smoky, you take the top hole," he told one dog, shoving him into the entrance. The dog, short and squat, darted into the hole. Now Bill knew why the curs had such short legs. Had they the usual dog-legs they would never have been able to get into such a small entrance. The trapper turned the other dog around, and he darted into the hole.

"There'll be some fun soon," the man said.

Rawson had two dogs, getting them ready to go into entrances. Ganns also had a pair of curs. But Bill watched the trapper. This was a new way to trap beaver. New to him, anyway—and his job was to keep up with the methods used by poachers. The Big Boss's ears would swing up when Bill told him about this way of getting beavers out of their dens.

That is, if he lived to tell the Big Boss. Bill Dupree was not joking himself; this was a dangerous mission. Other game-wardens had gone into the wilderness . . . and had never returned . . . or had never been heard of again. But he had to keep such thoughts from his mind. He was glad of one thing: this was pulling to a close. The sack was being shut. The drawstrings were sliding together.

These dogs, he realized, were trained for this work. They had to be tough, fighting dogs. For a beaver has long sharp teeth—teeth that can hew down a good-sized tree in just a few minutes. Some of these beaver were big—almost as big as the dogs, he figured.

The trapper said, "I kin hear them fightin' in there. Goin' 'round an' round, they is."

"Must be a hell of a commotion," Ganns said.

"Them beavers," said Ed Rawson, "don't like them dogs for company. Man, things are sure boilin' in this hole."

"Not so damned loud," Ganns warned.

Rawson laughed. "You jabber like an ol' maid what's tryin' to snare a man, Ganns."

"Okay, okay, okay."

Bill realized the voice-boxes on the dogs had been silenced to keep them from barking because their barks on a still night would betray their location and the nature of their work. On a dangerous job like this one, Rawson could not afford to have dogs that could bark—and without dogs he could not poach beaver in this manner. His attention was taken back to the trapper.

"Here comes out my top dog," the man said.

The cur came backing out of the den, dragging a dead beaver. Both he and the beaver were covered with mud. First the dog's rump came out of the aperture, then his body, and soon he had the beaver out, lying there dead in the mud. The trapper put the beaver in a sack.

"Go get more of them, dog."

The dog shook mud in a circle, then went back into the hole. Other dogs were backing out with beavers—some were dead, some were alive. Bill saw that the dogs knew their business. They would get the beavers by the head, crunch their skulls flat, and then drag them out. Most of the beavers were dead. Blood was probably on the dogs, for it was only logical that the beavers would get in some good licks, but Bill, of course, could not see this because of the distance.

Bill realized the dogs were really tough. Besides having fangs, the beavers had long claws; the dogs would have to dodge these while crunching flat the powerful heads of their foes. One beaver—a big old buck—was dragged out alive. The dog, once in the open, tried to shake him; the beaver was too big. The mutt braced his forelegs and tried to shake, but the beaver would not budge. He lost his grip and the trapper killed the beaver with a club.

And into the sack he went.

"My sack," said Al Ganns, "is almost full."

"More over on what is left of the dam," Rawson said. "Man, this is a real pelt, this one is. Draw down good dough in St. Louis."

Bill wondered, how do they get them to St. Louis? But

this question would be answered later. He and Jim Overcast had caught the poachers in the act, which was just what they had wanted. He wished the men were working this side of the creek. They were killing lots of beaver. Were they working this side—the north back— he and Jim Overcast would have forced their hand, thereby saving much of the beaver population. He looked at the jumbled, chaotic mass of broken, twisted ice. It would be impossible to cross this area without being seen. And that would turn the rifles of these three on him and Jim Overcast. No, he would have to wait until they reached the north bank, then make his play.

The Rawson men would soon have to cross the ice, he knew. They were running out of beaver dens on the south side. Bill waited, not minding the coldness now; he was warm under his sheepskin and clothing. One of Ganns' dogs came out dragging a live beaver. Instead of taking him by the head, he took him by the back. Rawson saw this and said, "Don't let him tear the hide."

Ganns batted the dog to one side with the flat of his shovel. The dog had to release his grip. The beaver apparently half-dead, started to waddle toward the den, and the shovel came down with another hard *smack*, hitting the beaver over the head and killing him.

"Damned dog knows better'n grab a beaver anywhere but in the head," Rawson said.

Ganns said, "We ought to send him to high school again, huh?"

The trapper said, "I'm glad this muck is freezin'. A man can stand upright now. Well, we got about three more holes to work, and then we got to cross the crick. I got to get a new sack. Mine is full of beaver. We'll have a job skinnin' in my cabin. Lots of money here in these sacks."

"I'll get some more sacks," Rawson said, "and you boys work these last two holes. There are more up the crick on this bank, but most of them is around this dam.

So we'll work the north bank and then go up the crick."

Bill saw Rawson go to the dam and get some more gunny-sacks. He wondered where old Jim Overcast was hidden. He had seen no trace of the oldster since they had parted in the brush, but he knew the old man was ready for whatever came his way. And Jim Overcast, he knew, could handle anything that came his way. Bill sure was glad the old man was on his side.

Rawson did not return to his two men. He crossed the creek on the remainder of the dam, because it was easier walking there than slipping and sliding over the blocks of ice. The south bank had been rather steep, but the north bank was more sloping in construction. The cold weather had frozen the mud and made walking easy. Rawson passed by Bill Dupree by about thirty feet. Bill was in the brush, squatted there, rifle over his lap, watching the beaver poacher. Rawson led his two dogs, but the breeze blew toward Bill and therefore the curs did not smell him, and for this Bill Dupree was thankful—he needed all the breaks he could get. Rawson stopped by a set of beaver holes.

"You men done over there?" he called.

"Our last holes," the trapper said.

"Come on over when you get done."

Ganns said, "Damn it, man, but you're noisy. Somebody once said the night has ears, you know."

"You got that wrong," Rawson said. "Not the *night* has ears, but the *walls* have ears, fella."

"You go to hell," Ganns said.

Rawson said, to his dogs, "Do your dirty work, boys," The dogs went into the holes and Rawson stood there. He had his rifle in his hands and he looked carefully at the surrounding rim of the brush. His eyes went to the point where Bill was crouched, and they seemed to linger there for a long second—or did Bill Dupree just imagine this? Then the eyes moved on. Rawson put his rifle, stock-down, against a block of ice, and picked up his shovel and waited for his dogs to come out of the holes. Bill looked at Ganns and the trapper. They were crossing the ice, having tough going; they had their dogs on their leashes, they carried each a sack filled with heavy, muddy beavers, and they carried their rifles and their shovels. Ganns slipped once, almost falling down.

"You clumsy ox," the trapper joked.

"You ain't funny." Ganns was not joking. "I'm cold an' muddy and filthy, and I wish to God we was out of here."

"Think of the dough we're makin'."

"I could stand a hard shot of red-eye," Ganns grumbled.

"Well," said the trapper, "that wilderness of ice has been crossed, like little Eva said."

"Who is Eva?" Ganns asked.

The trapper had no reply to this. The two moved over to where Rawson was killing a big buck beaver, shovel rising and falling. Bill knew the time was here. He slipped his right mitten off and let it hit the ground. He felt of his six-shooter, there in the pocket of his overcoat, and decided the hammer would not catch on the rim of the pocket, if he had to suddenly reach for the gun. He gave the three men a raking, probing scrutiny. Rawson was putting a beaver in a sack. The other two were unleashing their dogs. They were about forty feet away. He thought fleetingly of old Jim Overcast, and then this thought was gone. He looked at the cold, impersonal moon. Then he thought, well, this is it.

The steel of his rifle was ice to his bare hand. He carried the Winchester under his right arm with the barrel protruding. They did not see him until he cocked the rifle. Then the sound of the hammer coming back— brittle, dangerous, steel on steel—jerked them around.

And they stared at him.

For a moment it was a moon-frozen tableau. Rawson was of solid, dark ice, frozen against the darkness of the brush, holding the beaver by the tail. Ganns was on one knee, crouched over a dog, and the trapper was staring at him, mouth open in surprise.

Then this was broken by the voice of Jim Overcast as he came out of the brush, pistol in hand.

"You men are under arrest!"

They jerked then, puppets pulled by the same sinister string, and they stared at him. Then Rawson let the beaver thud downward into the sack and he let the sack go loose in his grip, and it folded limply and objectively and fell to one side. But nobody noticed this.

"We're game-wardens," Bill Dupree said. "I'm working for the Stars and Stripes and Overcast is working for the state. We caught you in the act. Now, if you want to get out of this alive, raise your hands."

Only the moon was neutral. The cold and impersonal moon in the high and cloudless sky. Only the moon had no part in this.

The shock had left Rawson, and his voice was ugly and tough. "Maybe we won't give up, you damned half-breed!"

Bill said, and his voice did not sound like his voice. "Then we shoot it out, here and now!"

Then the trapper screamed, "Not me, not me, not me. No gunfight for me, I'll cave in!" He was crying and sobbing, but he was still dangerous, Bill Dupree knew. He had just lost his control for a minute.

His sobbing was sharp and strong. A dog lifted his head and howled, and the two sounds broke across the wilderness—one canine, one human. Weird, piercing sounds, they were—they were files on the sinews of the men.

Rawson said, huskily, "Shut up, you damned fool!"

The trapper stopped. He stood with his eyes wide. He looked at Ganns. He looked at Rawson. The dog kept on howling. The trapper kicked him. The dog stopped howling.

Old Jim Overcast asked, "Are you raisin' your hands,

you damned beaver poachers? Or do we have to move in and slug you down to gain some respect?"

Bill realized he was clammy calm, now. He was sweating, though—he could feel sweat on his forehead. He only hoped they would not fight. He did not want to have to kill a man. He had never killed a man before in his life. He had often thought of the awfulness of killing a human.

Rawson said, "So you turned out to be a warden, eh, Dupree. Damn it, I would have killed you that day in the sheep camp, if this old button hadn't horned in! I was suspicious of you."

Ganns said, "I told you he never left the country. First off, he's fell for that 'breed nurse, down in Dodson. A man don't ride off an' leave a woman like her. Then I—"

"Close your mouth," snarled Rawson.

The trapper repeated, "I want no part of this, Dupree."

Bill said, "Then step to one side—with your hands in the air, trapper. Make it quick now—"

He never got to finish his sentence. He did not finish because two things happened in a flash. Rawson had his .45 in his overcoat pocket. He pulled the gun and before he could shoot at Bill, old Jim Overcast got in a shot. But Overcast missed and Rawson's gun exploded. Bill shot and Rawson shot; their echoes broke, blended, smashed against each other.

Later, Bill Dupree realized he had shot to kill—shot for the heart. And he realized that, when the show-down had come, when it was his life against that of a man who burned to kill him, he had no compunctions about taking a human life, for he killed Ed Rawson.

Rawson said not a word. Bill's bullet went through his chest, tearing at his heart. Rawson went down over the sack, and he and the half-filled sack toppled, and both lay without moving in the snow.

Bill found himself sagging. He realized, then, he had

been shot in the right leg, somewhere above the knee. He had a foolish thought, and this rang through his head: many times he had wondered what it would feel like to be shot. Now he knew. First, it had been as if a fist, swinging out of thin air, had hit him—a hard, cruel fist that drove him back. Then, there was the shock, and with it were mingled feelings, the strongest being the feel of blood. For blood was running down his leg. He sat down, looking foolish.

He found himself sitting about five feet away from another man, who also was sitting down. This man was bending forward, holding his head, and hollering something—the words were dim and far away. Then they came in and Bill realized old Jim Overcast had slugged Al Ganns to the snow.

Ganns was saying, "Don't hit me again. I'm out of this—"

Then the trapper was screaming again. Bill saw Overcast go up to him and rap him over the head from behind with his rifle's barrel. The trapper looked very stupid, mouth open but no screams emitting. Then he went down on his face, mouth buried in the snow.

Jim Overcast came over and knelt beside Bill. "Where did he shoot you, son?"

"In the leg."

"I'm a hell of a poor shot," the old game-warden said. "I missed him a mile. You kilt him plumb dead."

"I'm sorry I had to do that," Bill Dupree's voice was somewhat steadier now.

They came into Dodson with the dead Ed Rawson tied across his saddle, with the trapper and Al Ganns riding ahead. They had left the dead beavers at the trapper's shack, and the dogs trotted around their horses—the muddy and bloody and battered, short-legged dogs, that could bark but could not be heard.

"How do you feel, Bill?"

162

"You tied my leg up good," Bill Dupree told Jim Overcast. "I was lucky that no bones were broken. From here on in, Mary Red Robin will take care of me . . . I hope."

Jim Overcast chuckled. "She'll be right happy to," he said.

"I'm mighty happy I'm riding to see her," Bill Dupree said, and smiled. "Here's the doc's office. We'll get the town marshal to get word to the sheriff at Malta, and these boys can go behind bars. Say, there comes the marshal now, coming out of the hotel."

They sat their horses and waited for the marshal to reach them. Bill let his mind run back. The trapper had revealed the rest of the plan used in getting beaver pelts out of the country. Bill had been sure that the sheep hides had played some role in this game. This conviction the trapper had affirmed. When the sheep hides had been shipped out they had been shipped out flat, because a sheep and beaver are skinned in the same manner and both pelts are flat. The flat beaver pelts had been placed between two sheep hides, woolly sides down. Now Bill knew why Rawson had been so anxious to buy dead woollies. He needed the pelts to smuggle out the beaver skins.

Bill's attention was jerked back to old Jim Overcast. The old game-warden had cupped his mittens around his whiskery mouth. His yell would have driven a Sioux buck to shame.

"Hey, Mary! Red Robin!"

"Shut up, you ol' fool! You'll wake up the whole town!"

"That's what I aim to do. Oh, Mary Red Robin! I brought your man back, Mary!"

The marshal panted, "She's a nursin' Mrs Wilson in the hotel. What the hell has happened? Rawson there—dead?"

Old Jim Overcast chuckled. "Here she comes." He screamed. "He's over this way, Mary!"

With difficulty, Bill dismounted. Mary came running. Bill met her. She met Bill.

Old Jim Overcast grinned and spoke to the marshal. "Bill's gonna file on a homestead right next to mine. Mary an' him'll be danged happy—a fine young couple. I hope they have lots of kids. Them kids might even call me gran'pa!"

"Okay, Gran'pa," the marshal said. "Start explainin', please."

Old Jim paid him no attention. "Gran'pa Overcast. Man alive, they'll make it soun' good, them kids will. Hey, marshal. Look at them two young-uns!

"What about 'em?"

"Ain't them two ever comin' up for air?"

# BUCKSKIN CHALLENGE

# ONE

Spring came early that year to the Territory of Wyoming. A Chinook wind, coming from the northwest, had suddenly come down from the snow-clad Rocky Mountains, cutting the snow and turning it to water that roared down into the creeks and rivers. The Chinook came during the night.

By morning the warm wind had melted the snow and lain bare the dark earth. Then had come the flowers out of nowhere—the crocuses and sweetpeas and bluebells.

And the land rejoiced for the Chinook had liberated it.

Ed Jones had difficulty getting his traps out of the sets along the creek. When he'd gone to his lonely cabin bed that night before the creek had been frozen solid and snow-covered from bank to bank.

But next morning snow-water ran over the ice. By wading out into the ice-cold water he had managed to free his traps, taking the last of this year's beaver from them.

The trapping season was over. Warm weather was at hand. Beaver and mink would immediately now start slipping their fur and getting thin summer coats.

Now, his pack of plews on his back, he came through the brush and he came upon the old-timer, who was digging a grave along the creek. The old man had been working hard, shovel hacking through the damp clean soil, and Ed was almost on him before he saw him. And the old man leaned on his shovel and looked at the stranger through beady and bright eyes almost covered by huge brows.

"Howdy, stranger," Ed said, and he slipped out of his pack. The pack was heavy. Despite the width of the elkskin straps, they still cut into his shoulders. Ed was a gaunt man, around six feet tall, and he was close to thirty. He had never married. The wilderness had been and was mother and wife to him. He had his giant malemute, Chief, with him. They were a wilderness pair. Now Chief, who had squatted flat beside Ed's moccasins, was growling softly. A deep rumbling sound, low in his massive throat. And the dog's eyes were sharp and missed nothing.

"Howdy, trapper."

"Diggin' a grave?" Ed asked.

"A grave, sir."

Ed glanced at Chief and said, "Shut up, dog," and Chief put his big head on his paws, his growling stilled. Although the spring air was warm and good the malemute was trembling slightly. He was looking at the dirty canvas tarp that was about fifteen feet away. There was something under that tarp. Ed wondered, Is it a dead man? and he too caught the sudden chill that seemed to have come into the air. He shifted as he squatted, watching the old man work.

The old man was around seventy, Ed figured. He had a slender old frame, now covered by greasy buckskins. Ed could tell by the beadwork that the buckskin jacket and trousers had been made in a Sioux camp. The old man was almost bald and a muskrat cap sat perched on the back of his dome. He had a long nose and his mouth was red from the kinikinick he was chewing.

He seemed to have forgotten Ed's presence. He dug in monotonous rhythm, shovel rising to deposit the earth, shovel going down into the damp soil. He had dug until he stood in the trench about to his waist.

A bluejay, raucous and scolding, had been following Ed and Chief through the brush, but now, for some reason, he was silent. The only sounds were the sounds of the shovel, the grunting breathing of the old man, and the tongue of Chief licking his forepaws. Ed had a tight feeling across his back. He again looked at the tarp. The form it covered could be that of a man, he realized.

"Buryin' your partner, ol' man?"

The oldster stopped digging and leaned on the worn handle of his old shovel. "You ask a hell of a lot of questions," he said uncivilly. "But then you trappers who has been alone all winter is full of questions." He spat out a gob of red kinikinick juice. "For your satisfaction, I ain't got no partner. I've had about eight squaws in my life, but I outlived them all. Smallpox don't touch me for some reason. Look under the tarp an' satisfy your curiosity."

Ed grinned. He moved over the lifted the tarp. Now he knew why Chief had been growling so softly. He had thought the dog had growled at the smell of death—human death. But no human was under the tarp. A big malemute dog lay under the old canvas. He was a beautiful dog. As big as Chief, almost, who weighed close to a hundred pounds; but he was silvery-blue. And he was dead.

He had been shot through the head. Ed let the tarp fall. He felt sort of sick and unsettled inside. The dog had not apparently been sick. He looked like he had been in good flesh. Then why had he been shot?

Ed swung his serious eyes to the old man, who watched him. "Your dog?" he asked.

"No."

"He don't look to me like he was sick. Why was he shot?"

"Damn you, trapper, you got too many questions on your tongue!"

Ed felt his face flush. He was somewhat angry—he loved dogs. Chief and he had spent the winter together. Out tending trap-lines, out hunting elk and deer, and when night had come and the blizzards had raged around the log cabin, Chief had lain before the fireplace, warm and with the red light glistening on his thick grey fur. He seemed to know and understand every word his master said.

"Don't get huffy, old timer."

Suddenly a hot and feverish look flashed across the old man's sunken eyes. It gave them a maniacal look. Suddenly, and without warning, he started to chant, his cracked red lips opening and closing. From out of those lips came a chant, low and deep, gathering purpose and strength. He would answer no more questions. He apparently had forgotten the existence of one Ed Jones.

The song was weird. It was not a war song; it was a chant to the Manitou. Ed felt the impact of it. He wanted to leave this scene of death. He got to his feet, lifting his pack. Ed Jones was tall and hard work had made him too thin. The high ridges, with their howling snow-laden winds, had turned his face to seamed rawhide. The bitter coldness, when sometimes the thermometer stood at sixty below, had hammered a stubbornness in him, turning him to whalebone and elkskin. He slid into his pack, picked up his Winchester rifle, and glanced at the chanting old man. He got the impression that this oldster was somewhat touched. He had sprung too many traps in wilderness camps while living by his lonesome. The wilderness sometimes did that to a man, when he lived alone. Ed had a thought: Maybe in time the wilderness and its loneliness would get him, too. Well, what happened . . . would happen.

"So long, old man."

If the oldster heard, he gave no sign. He kept on chanting. He worked with his muskrat cap pushed back to show his scraggly grey hair. Ed said to Chief, "Come along, boy," and the dog fell into pace behind him.

And so they left the demented man who was digging the grave for the dead silvery-blue malemute.

Ed Jones had his thoughts.

He was pretty sure he was walking into trouble. Three miles or so below this point the Soda came roaring into the Green River. The Soda came out of the mountains, and now it was in flood stage; it would be sweeping along trees and icebergs; the water would be dirty and foamy. The waters of the Soda would blend with the wider waters of the flooded Green. And here, at the confluence, of the two rivers, was Fort Green.

Ed trotted along, moving like a buck Cheyenne, his gait smooth and effortless, and Chief trotted behind him, his small pack bobbing with each pace. They followed an old trail made by Indian moccasins and by elk and deer going to the river for water. The wind of the last two days had dried the earth very much. But snow still clung stubbornly to the base of trees and behind the boulders. But grass was springing to life in the mountain parks rimmed by huge pines and firs. Soon the lupine—the blue and deadly lupine—would rear their heads over the grass. But Ed had no eyes now for the beauties of this Wyoming highland.

Ed's thoughts went back to a conversation a week ago. Ed had trapped that winter on the headwaters of the

Soda, where the group of creeks had come together to form the river. His camp was fifty miles away. He had come in during the fall and had built his cabin. Now he was abandoning the log shack. Somebody else could use it. Such was the way and method of the wilderness trapper. He had been turning a deer steak on his griddle when Corporal Hank Williams had come into the clearing with his pack. Corporal Hank Williams of the Territory of Wyoming Police. Ed had cut off another steak and fried it for his old friend. He had been surprised to see the Corporal out here this far from his headquarters down in Laramie, miles to the southeast. But he had said nothing outside of casual conversation. But Corporal Hank Williams had come with trouble. And, after eating he explained the nature of this trouble.

"Ed I want you to help me."

"Sure, glad to be the best-man at any weddin', Hank. Which squaw are you aimin' to hitch with? Take a Cheyenne, 'cause they work harder and don't want to fight as much as a Crow."

But the humour had been lost on Corporal Hank Williams. "I'm married already, Ed. Done hooked-up with a Fort Cheyenne girl, daughter of the factor there, last fall after you and Mack Hanson headed out for your winter trappin' grounds. She already expects a baby, so we ain't lost no time. But it's Mack Handon I'm worried about, Ed."

"Why worry about Mack?"

"There is a new tradin' post down where the Soda comes into the Green. Called Fort Green. It was built last fall. Big outfit, too."

"I never knew about that post. Much closer than Fort Bridger. I might do my tradin' there. Time to git outa this country, what with Spring here and fur startin' to pull." Ed had chewed a hunk of steak. This venison was rather tough, and he had cooked it right—he was a good cook.

He should have shot the doe instead of the buck, he figured idly. He had decided to wait until Corporal Hank Williams felt due to explain his trouble.

This Corporal Williams had soon done.

The Green River Trading Post was owned by one Big John Remington. He had come down into Wyoming Territory out of Canada.

"I have heard the Mounties told him to git outa Canuck country. Why they ran him out, I don't know. But anyway, he's down on the Junction, and he is open for trading. So far, to the best of my knowledge, he has had one customer. And that customer went to the post . . . and ain't been heard or seen since."

Ed had looked up, fork filled with venison. "And who is that customer, Hank?"

"Your old partner, Mack Hanson."

Ed Jones had frowned. "Hank, what are you tryin' to do—tell me a scare story, fella?"

But Corporal Hank's earnestness soon convinced Ed that something was wrong at Fort Green. Mack Hanson had come in with his winter's catch of beaver, marten, mink and muskrat plews. He had come into Fort Green . . . and had been seen no more. This puzzled Ed no end. He and Mack Hanson had trapped together for over ten years. But this last winter they had not been trail partners. That was because of a Shoshone squaw. Mack had wanted to take her out trapping with them. Ed Jones had stomped his moccasin at this idea. He had figured the squaw would have caused nothing but trouble between them. The three of them would have spent the winter together. And when two men go trapping, there might be some strife because of their characters; but to these two men add a woman, and Ed Jones had known trouble would be sure to rear its ugly head. So Mack, in anger, had taken the young squaw and had made his winter camp about thirty miles away, at the head of the Beaver.

Ed had not kicked about it. He figured that Mack would soon tire of the Shoshone, as pretty and young as she was. He figured also that he and Mack Hanson had been partners a long time. A winter apart would show Hank his error and would only cement their friendship even stronger. So they had split up partnership and Ed and Chief had headed out alone to the headwaters of the Soda. This was the first word he had heard about Mack Hanson since he had parted with the man down in Jim Bridger's fort, miles to the south.

"What about Raven Wing?" Ed had asked.

"Raven Wing?"

"Yeah, the squaw. The Shoshone that went out with Mack."

"Oh, she quit him about January. Headed back for her people. Mack told me she was a bitch to live with, and lazy besides. He was sorry you and him broke up over her."

"And now he has disappeared?"

"Him and his pelts—they're gone."

"You think he met with foul play from the hands of Remington?"

"That's what I figger, Ed."

The corporal had continued talking and eating. He had seen Mack Hanson twice that winter. Mack had really caught some good fur.

"That Beaver Crick is good trappin' area," Ed Jones had said. "Continue, Hank?"

"He had lots of mink. Yes, and black long-haired muskrat, not to mention ermine and a few marten. Prime furs, Ed. I figure he had around four thousand bucks in furs. I was in his camp the day he broke it, Ed. He said he'd go down to Fort Green and wait for you. Spring busted out earlier on his side of the Rockies. That was about a week or ten days ago."

"You stopped in at Fort Green, I take it?"

"Yes. Two days back. And Mack Hanson wasn't there."

"Maybe he changed his mind about joinin' up with me again? Maybe he done went down the Green to Bridger?"

"No, he wasn't at Bridger, either. I met Harry Smith back along the rim of the Tetons. He had just come outa Bridger. And Mack had never come into that camp. Mack never got down-water no further than Big John's Green River Post."

"Then you think Mack has met with foul play?"

"Four thousand bucks is a lot of money, Ed."

Ed had stared at his coffee cup. Maybe the suspicions of this territorial policeman were unfounded. Maybe they were genuine. But if Big John Remington had done away with Mack Hanson, he had another man to contend with—and his name was Ed Jones.

"Why don't you go down and investigate, Ed?"

"Ain't that your job, Hank?"

"Sure, it is my job. But Big John knows me, and he plays it calm with me around. He don't know you. You can work from inside. Me, I don't figure that big Canuck built that post to trade and buy fur. I think he built it for another reason."

"What would that be?"

"I don't know. But Big John Remington knows I'm a cop. I can't make a bit of headway around the Fort. But if you—a stranger—came in—See my point, Ed?"

"Yes, I do."

"Work with me, Ed?"

"Sure will, Corporal Hank!"

The corporal had to head north around the geysers, for there was rumour of a killing and robbing up there. He had left within the hour, a stocky man moving with his pack to bring justice and law to an area bigger than many European countries. And Ed Jones had broken camp. He had left most of his cooking utensils, taking only a frying pan. He had put a pack on big Chief. This carried muskrat furs and some ermine. He himself carried the chief and highest priced furs in his pack. One of these pelts was that of a silver fox. It was a prime plew. A silver fox was a rarity, seldom seen in this area, ranging usually north along the Arctic Circle. But the storm had evidently driven him south. He had been very trap shy. But finally he had been lured into a Number 4 steel trap. His pelt was glossy, glistening in the sunlight; it was worth well over a thousand dollars.

His catch had been good, but the silver fox catch had been the high point. Now Ed Jones went through the brush, remembering the dead malemute. He had been afraid, at first, that the tarp had covered a dead man. He had been afraid that that dead man might have been his partner, Mack Hanson.

He heard the rumble of the Soda, tossing against its walls of igneous rock. He moved forward, moccasins slipping sometimes in mud. The rubble grew louder. He could see only a few feet ahead because of the thickness of the brush and the timber. He smelled the aroma of wild roses. The earth was damp, the earth was fresh; the world was awakening to the magic of summer.

The roar of the two rivers became louder. It beat in steady rhythm against his ears. Suddenly he came out of the timber. He was on the edge of a giant meadow that ran in V shape to the meeting point of the two rivers. It had few trees on it. The trees that dotted its expanse were cottonwoods, wide and spreading. The pines and firs had stopped at this point, seemingly unwilling to invade this mountain meadow. From here he could see the raw green poles, driven upright into the earth, that constituted the stockade of Fort Green.

Ed Jones stopped and looked at the fort. He remained hidden in the brush. He could see the tops of buildings. They had sod on their roofs and weeds and grass was starting to sprout there, giving them a green-topped appearance. They were barely visible over the top of the stockade. The fort was about half a mile away. Big John Remington had picked a good spot whereon to raise Fort Green. Because of the two rivers, driving in together in a gigantic V, the Sioux and Cheyenne could not hit from the west, east, or the south—to do so, they would have to cross the Green and the Soda, and they would be ducks sitting on a pond. They could only hit the fort from the north, the direction whence Ed had come.

For about half an hour, Ed watched Fort Green.

The huge gate, hung on bullhide hinges, was open. A few men moved in and out, and Ed wished he had fieldglasses, but he had none. The post looked almost deserted, and it had an ugly air about it. On the southwest corner was a guard house, built higher than the stockade fence; another guard house was on the east side of the gate. Ed wondered if a guard, stationed at that altitude, had seen him. Was he being watched through field-glasses? Or maybe even a powerful telescope? Some of these forts had telescopes in these turrets. Telescopes that could pick out clearly the smallest movement of wilding or man, even though miles away.

Ed crouched there in the tall brush, watching the fort through a break in the rosebushes, and Chief lay beside him, resting from the weight of his pack. Ed kept remembering the old man and his wild and crazy eyes. He remembered the weird and ugly chant; he thought of the dead malemute. Where did the old grave-digger and the dead malemute fit into this drama? He was sure they fitted in somewhere, but he did not know where. And was his partner Mack Hanson really dead?

Had he been murdered for his furs?

Watching the fort, Ed's mind went back to other points in his talk with Corporal Hank Williams. The policeman had told Ed about The Bear. The Bear was Big John Remington's right-hand man. He was, according to Corporal Hank Williams, a human bear—a human grizzly. He was a huge and shambling giant, walking with the lumbering gait of a bear, slow on the mental trigger but fast on the trigger of a rifle or pistol. Ed had never met him, either.

"Chief," he said, "we hide some of our plews, includin' our silver fox pelt."

Chief was tired. His tongue lolled out. His tail made a fan-like motion against the grass. Whatever Ed had said was okay with him, was his expression.

"Come along, mutt."

With Chief following him, still concealed in the high brush, he came to the Soda. He slid down a bank and came to the edge of the river. Here a big boulder stuck out into the muddy water. An iceberg crashed into it, stopped, and then the current turned it slowly, moving it again to free water. Here was a small area where the water was calm, an area of backwash. Ed had the silver-fox pelt wrapped in an oilskin. To this pack he added some of the costlier furs, mostly fine ermine. Then he bound the parcel solidly with some elkhide thongs. He waded out in the water, on the lee sid of the boulder. Here the water was calm, although ice cold. With his hands, he dug a hole under the boulder. Into this he put the parcel. He dug around and got some rocks to put over it. Water was already washing silt and mud over the cache. Within a few minutes, the parcel would be hidden.

Hidden under a layer of silt, of rock, and hidden by the swirling cold water. Ed waded back to the shore. He looked at the landmarks around him to establish forever the location of the cache in his memory. Now he packed furs of lesser calibre. A few beaver pelts, some mink and a marten or two. He checked his pistol. It was a .38, secure under the wide moose-hide belt around his middle. He knew his .30—30 rifle was in good shape. He always kept it oiled and loaded, a bullet under the hammer and the magazine filled.

"Okay, Chief, okay. Let trouble come, eh?"

Chief, for some reason, suddenly whined. A puppy-like sound, something he had not done since his puppyhood days. Ed glanced at him in surprise. The big malemute seemed troubled.

"What's the matter, boy?"

The big dog put his wide wet nose against Ed's hand. His nose was cold and Ed did not like its coldness, for some reason. Usually the big dog was very calm and stable and even of temper. But today he was nervous. Was it because he had smelled death—the dead malemute—back there in the clearing?

They came to a small creek. Moccasins and paws made splashing spray. Ahead of them was a strip of brush that consisted of willows and brush. Ed found a trail, made by coyotes and rabbits and deer, and he followed this, the dog behind him. Suddenly the malemute grabbed Ed's buckskins. He grabbed his master by the slack of the buckskin on his right leg. He stopped his master.

"Boy, what is wrong?"

The hackles stood on the giant thick neck of the malemute. He was growling savagely deep in his throat. His ears were pointing down the dim trail, and his nose was working. Plainly he had heard or smelled something Ed could not hear or smell.

Then he heard a voice say, "Where the hell did she go, Bear?"

The voice came from their right. Ed judged it was about two hundred feet away. Chief had stopped growling. Ed listened and wondered. He heard another voice, also a deep voice—but much deeper than that of the first speaker.

"She's somewhere in the brush."

"Hell, I know that. We can't lose her!"

"We won't."

What was this?

Suddenly a woman came running into the clearing. She came silently, and she came out of nowhere—one moment there was no woman, the next she was running into Ed. She did not see him and Chief. That was because she was glancing backwards. Ed jumped to one side, trying to get out of her way. She hit him then, and he heard her gasp. She turned, and the blow of their meeting made her stagger. She wore buckskins—a buckskin skirt, and a deer-hide blouse. She had moccasins on her small feet. Ed figured she was a young squaw.

Ed said, "Easy, woman," and grabbed her, for she was falling. He caught her by both arms. She jerked back and stared at him. She was winded. Evidently she had run for some distance. She was a pretty woman and she had a cut on her right cheek. A nasty cut, about an inch long, and it was bleeding. Blood was on her jaw and throat. Her eyes had a terrible frightened look. Ed was surprised to see she was not a squaw. She was a young white woman.

He held her in a firm grip. "Woman, what's the matter?"

"Let go—of me—"

He held her by effort. She kicked at him. She tried to bite his hands. Surely the men, threshing and calling in the brush, had heard them. Ed didn't know what he was getting into. But he could not let this woman run alone into the wilderness. She had no pack, no gun, no grub. She would die in this tanglement of brush, under the cold shadows of high peaks.

And she was a white woman. A white woman was a rarity here in the wilderness. Trappers married squaws or lived with squaws. Ed had not seen a white woman for two years, and that had been in Independence over in Missouri. He was as surprised as she. Her pretty lips formed angry words.

"Let go of me, you Remington dog!"

"I'm not a Remington man," Ed said.

She stopped trying to bite him. The words worked like magic. She stopped kicking his legs. Her eyes, blue and wild, lost their wildness. Was it hope that speared through them?

"You mean—you're not part of Remington's crew?"

"I wear no man's collar, woman."

Her lips quivered. For a moment, no words came. Then she said, "Oh, Thank God, Thank you, God," and then her knees gave away. She started to fall. Ed pulled her close to hold her. She was limp and womanly in his arms. He liked the feel of her firm young body. She had fainted. Ed laid her on the grass and stood over her and wondered. Chief smelled the blood.

"Move back, Chief."

The malemute moved back in obedience, then sat down. Ed knelt beside the girl. He heard the men threshing through the brush. Somebody hollered, "Did I hear a man's voice ahead?" and it was a savage and deep growl. The girl rolled over and looked at him. Her eyes showed a wildness, a fear, and then, on recognizing him, lost these things.

Ed said solemnly, "Don't be afraid of me, girl."

She clung to his arms. She tried to sit up but he held her down. "I have to run. I have to escape. I got to get away."

"No, I'm with you. I'll watch for you."

Her blue eyes roamed over his strong face. "Thank God you came," she whispered. Her voice was husky. "Oh, to see an honest man, a good man, again . . ."

"How did you cut your cheek?"

She sobbed suddenly. They were deep and racking sobs, tearing at a man's vitals. Her words came in jerky suddenness.

"The Bear—His blacksnake whip—The lash, it cut my cheek."

Ed stood up and she sat up. He was in turmoil and this must have shown on his face, for she said, "The Bear did it. Who are you?"

"Ed Jones. I trapped on upper Soda. I'm heading for—"

Ed never finished the sentence. For a man was coming toward them. He ran with a ponderous, thick gait. Ed knew he would be big and solid. And Ed said, "This way, man," and the man hollered, "Somebody over here, Big John. Over in the brush."

Then the speaker crashed through the diamond willows and brush. He saw them and he halted. He was a human moose. Huge hands, complete with thick knuckles, hung at his sides, almost reaching his knees. He carried a coiled blacksnake whip. Made of moose-hide, braided and pleated by a Cheyenne squaw. A deadly stinging destructive weapon, when handled right. Ed saw a huge and ugly face, bloated by drink and dissipation, and on either side of the wide flattened nose were two eyes—grey slabs of granite folded in by heavy jowls and thick dark eyebrows. He knew he was looking at The Bear.

"Here she is, Big John. And they's a stranger with her."

Then The Bear just stood there, bole-thick legs spread wide. His eyes studied Ed with a slow and animal-dumb intelligence. He opened his mouth and a tongue the size of an elk steak moved out to touch the thick lips. The eyes left Ed Jones then and went down to the girl. They sent fear across her tiny bloody face.

"Don't let him get me!"

She screamed the words. They hung in sharpness across the underbrush. They did not effect The Bear. He still held that animal look on his wide and coarse face.

The words did not touch him.

"This way, Big John."

A man was coming toward them. He was still hidden by the brush. Now he came into the clearing and for the first time Ed Jones saw Big John Remington. The name Big John fitted him, for he was also a big man. But he was not as huge as The Bear. He wore greasy buckskins. His face was wide, marked by pits—he had had the smallpox years ago. He had dull-coloured eyes and sandy hair and his lips were thick. His teeth were brown with tobacco.

Those dull-coloured eyes went down the girl, then shot up to look at Ed Jones. "Who are you, stranger?"

Ed had made up his mind not to enter Fort Green under his own name. "I'm Hans Martin, a trapper. I trapped back on Warm Crick last winter. I am heading for Fort Green. I aim to mebbe do some tradin' there with the new factor, Big John Remington."

"I'm Remington."

"Glad to know you," Ed said.

"How come you find my squaw?"

"Not squaw," Ed corrected. "White woman."

"They're all the same—red or white."

"She ran into me," Ed explained.

The Bear was growling like a malemute. Without warning his blacksnake whip licked out. The lash wrapped itself savagely around the woman's right ankle. She screamed. The whip came singing back; the man's face was that of a savage. Ed was afraid of the blacksnake, but his fear overcame his logic. The girl screamed in pain. Ed hit the big man in the mouth.

Ed hit with all his strength. The blacksnake fell from The Bear's grip. He went back a step or two. The blow had come unexpectedly. Ed thought, I have to close in, for I have him stunned. I got to work fast. The girl was still screaming. Chief was snarling.

Ed felt blood on his knuckles. He had split the thick

185

lips of The Bear. He had not been looking for trouble. But the savageness of the whip, lashing out to wrap its thongs around the woman's ankle, had been too much. He dug his moccasins into the damp earth for leverage, and he hit again. He smashed a fist into The Bear's belly.

He heard breath leave the huge man. The Bear spread his legs and slugged. Ed made two blows miss him. He hit the man and his blow landed on The Bear's thick chest. It was like hammering solid grey granite.

By now the stunned look had left The Bear's eyes. Ed Jones was conscious of many things. One was that Chief was snarling, and the sound was rumbling and deep in the malemute's throat. The white woman had got to her feet. Big John Remington had been drawing the pistol from its holster. The white woman had clamped both hands around Remington's forearm. She was hollering in Sioux. She was wrestling with him, trying to keep his pistol out of this trouble.

The Bear was rushing him.

Ed Jones figured he had bit off more than he could chew. He had hit The Bear with every thing he owned. He had stopped him and The Bear was coming back strong. He only hoped the girl could keep Remington's pistol out of this. He knew he could not whip The Bear with his fists.

He heard a snarling, terrible sound. He saw Chief launch his weight through the air. The dog sprang like a huge uncoiling spring. He was tackling Big John Remington. Ed Jones thought, Good boy, and then The Bear hit him. The blow was a mauling blow. It came from the butt-end of a battering ram and it hit Ed in the ribs. It almost knocked him out. Shadows danced, blood roared in his head. He had to use his pistol, he realized. He had it in his right hand. He decided to use it first as a club. Then, if it failed to drop The Bear, he would use it as a weapon. For The Bear was out to kill him. To maul him, grapple with him, break his bones.

He hammered down with his pistol-barrel. He missed the shaggy head. He was going backwards now. He knew that soon he would go down. Suddenly he saw the back of The Bear's neck. The man had lunged past him. With all his might, Ed brought down the heavy gun. And it hit The Bear at the base of the skull. The sound was a sodden thud.

The Bear slid ahead, landed on his side, and lay moaning on the damp earth. He was out of the fight. Ed Jones whirled, gun still in his hand. But Big John Remington was also out of this fray.

For the girl had grabbed Ed Jones' rifle. She had the big man backed against a cottonwood tree. He had his hands in the air and his face wore a look of anger, and mingled with this anger was discretion. The barrel of the Winchester was about two feet or so from his big belly. She had brains enough not to move the rifle barrel too close for he then could have batted it to one side. Chief was crouched beside her, belly flat on the ground. He was watching Remington with careful scrutiny. Remington's buckskin trousers had a long gash on the right leg. Blood showed on the dirty yellow deerhide.

"Call off your dog, trapper!"

Ed said sternly, "No more, Chief," and the malemute got to his feet and walked away about ten feet. Then he sat there and watched. Occasionally he growled deep in his shaggy throat.

The Bear sat up. He held his throbbing head in his giant hands. He kept his eyes on the ground.

Ed said, "You oughta teach your man some manners, Remington." He spoke in a husky voice for he as yet had not found his breath. "That bullwhip is for bulls and mules, and not to use on females!"

Remington looked at The Bear. A crafty look came

into his sunken eyes. "He's a wild one when he gets the prod." Now he spoke to The Bear. "Get to your feet and cause no more trouble."

But The Bear did not get to his feet. He lifted his head from his hands and looked at Ed Jones.

"I'll kill you, Martin! I'll break your neck!"

Ed had a sudden thought. When the woman had run into his arms, he had told her his name was Ed Jones. And he had told Big John he was Hans Martin. He hoped she would keep this knowledge to herself. He looked at her and said, "Did I tell you my name was Hans Martin, woman? In the tussle, I guess I never got to properly introduce myself."

"Hans Martin," she said. "I'm glad you came along."

She understood.

The Bear lumbered upright, gained his feet, and stood with wide-spread legs. He reached down and got his bullwhip.

Ed ordered, "Use that whip, and I'll gutshoot you!"

Remington said angrily, "Forget that blacksnake, Bear!"

The Bear looked at Ed. Then his eyes swivelled over to Big John Remington. He coiled the whip automatically.

"I won't use it," he mumbled.

Ed said, "Girl, put down the rifle."

She moved back a few paces. Then she sat at the base of a tree. She put her head in her hands and started to weep. She wept almost silently, her shoulders moving. She was tired; she was spent; she was sick at heart. Ed Jones' heart went out to her. He kept his face stern.

"Now what the hell is this all about?"

Big John Remington said, "This girl was sold to me by her father. He sold her to me two days ago. Then he left my post. He was a trapper. She doesn't like me and she tried to run away."

Ed said, "They don't sell white women. They only sell

188

reds and blacks."

"He sold her to me," Big John repeated, and anger flushed his whiskery face. "You walk in a wide circle, trapper."

"Blacksnakes were not made to be used on humans."

The girl flared, "They lie! Both of them lie! My father—he never sold me—" She looked up. Her small face was pale with fury. Blood was on her cheek and the cut was a vivid slash. "These men—they murdered my father! I know they did! They killed him because Remington wanted me—for his wife—and his slave. But I'd die first! I'd kill myself first!"

"She's a damned good liar," Big John Remington said. "I bought her and her father left for Utah."

The whole situation was rapidly becoming clear to Ed Jones. Evidently a trapper and his daughter had stopped at Fort Green to trade plews. And the trapper had disappeared, just as had Mack Hanson.

Ed thought, I got off to a whale of a bad start. But what has gone by had happened, and I'd best try to repair the beaver dam.

He had hoped to work into the confidence of Big John and The Bear and then find out what had happened to Mack Hanson. But because of this woman, he had tangled right off with Big John and The Bear. He did some quick thinking. He had two alternatives. The first was to get the girl and take her away from Fort Green. To head with her into the brush and thereby procure her freedom. But this would not solve the disappearance of Mack Hanson. He had to find out if Mack had died in Fort Green. So to do this, he had to get into the good grace, if possible, of this pair. And if the girl returned to Fort Green, he could see she got a fair shake. He wished he knew for a surety whether Mack were dead or alive. Hank Williams might have been wrong. Hank might not have had trouble at Fort Green; he might have gone on down the Green to Fort Bridger. But he thought, I have to find out . . . for sure.

He noticed that Big John was looking at his pack of plews, and that the eyes of the factor also were taking in the small pack on Chief.

"You wanta trade your furs?"

"That's the reason I was headin' for your post."

Big John said, "Let's fergit what just happened. We all got off on the wrong moccasins. Come along to the post, Martin, an' we'll dicker later on. That all right with you?"

"On one condition."

"What is thet?"

"Don't manhandle or beat this woman again?"

The big man grinned. He let his wide shoulders fall. "We all got het up under the collar. I'll agree with you, Martin."

Ed said, "Then let's go to the fort."

The girl looked at him for some time. Her eyes appraised him. She must have liked what she saw.

"I have no other choice," she said.

But now her voice held hope.


One glance told Ed Jones that Fort Green was built in about the same order as Fort Pcck, up north on the Missouri River. Yes, and on the same plan was Fort Union, over in the Dakota land, where the Missouri and the Yellowstone met. And on the same plan was other scattered wilderness fur-trading posts.

When you cleared the two huge gates, you stood in the compound. Here the soil had been packed and rutted by the hoofs of horses, mules, dogs and humans. The buildings inside the stockade were set a few feet from the wall. At the far end was the trading post itself—a long log building housing the trading-supplies and the furs and the barrels of whiskey and beer. The building had a long porch with a floor made of native rock and concrete.

A halfbreed buck hoed weeds in what seemed to be a small garden, set on yonder side of the stockade. A squaw sat on the porch in a rocking chair. She seemed to be unaware of their existence.

Big John Remington had become somewhat talkative on the trip back to Fort Green, but The Bear ambled along and said nothing. Big John seemed to have a streak of subtlety in him, and he became rather friendly. But not too friendly, Ed Jones was quick to note. The man had brains.

"Hell, Martin, a woman always gets a man into trouble," the giant factor had said. "Get two men together and they can become good friends. But get one woman with them, and they become enemies. Come down to my fort and we'll look at your fur and maybe so we can dicker. I offer top prices—good as any price you can get down at Bridger. You can take it in gold or in tobacco an' a new rifle, or in grub and supplies or whatever I got that you want."

Ed Jones had nodded. "We'll talk it over, Big John. Yeah, we all make mistakes. Bear, if you'll overlook our tussle, so will I."

"All right with me."

But The Bear did not sound too willing.

The girl said, "I'll walk with Martin."

Martin, eh? Well, she had caught on. Ed found himself wishing he had not given her his right name. She might forget sometime and make a miscue, which was an easy thing to do. He'd have to talk to her when he had a chance, he saw.

Things had sure started off wrong.

"I'll see what price you hand me," Ed had said, "an' if it ain't to my likin', I'll trek to Bridger."

"We'll find a common ground," Big John Remington had assured.

Ed had stepped to one side. "I'll travel behind you."

The implication was clear. He did not trust Big John or The Bear. He saw this register on the factor's face. The man's jowls hardened. His lips pulled in a little, then relaxed. He took the trail and The Bear had swung in behind him, and behind The Bear was the white girl. Ed and Chief then trailed them. And now they were in Fort Green. Ed had an eerie feeling. What was the mystery—if any—of this wilderness outpost? Time would tell.

The fort stood at the head of navigable water on the Green River. Now and then a river packet, low and wide so it would not draw much depth, would brave the swift current to make the dock which was right outside the gate that opened onto the river. Ed Jones knew this packet came about once or twice a year up from Fort Bridger. It toted in supplies. Also, Big John would pack supplies overland from Laramie by mule trains. Maybe now because of Fort Green the packet boat came up more often. Ed did not know nor did he care. It was just an idle thought fitting into this wilderness of gigantic peaks and eternal snow.

Ed had noticed that a guard had been in the cupola built beside the gate. An upward glance at the cupola had told him that. He wondered how many men were at this fort. The place had an air of desertion. The gate was an enormous affair—split into two sections—each section hung on thick bullhide hinges. This fort was solid and strong. This fort could repel man and beast. But could it shove back Death?

The gate swung shut behind them, pushed closed by the halfbreed gardener. Then the fort surrounded them, heavy and strong and deadly. Although he tried to fight it off, still a tension grew in Ed Jones. This feeling of danger tightened the muscles along his thighs and gave his tongue a bitter and wry taste.

They went across the packed compound, moccasins

whispering against the earth, and they went past the silent windows and doors, and they entered the store.

The room was wide and long. Across the plank floor was a long counter with shelves behind it on the wall. Here two or three rifles were raised in a rack and short-guns hung from wooden pegs. A barrel or two stood in the middle of the room, and the stove was a huge one—pot-bellied and brown—with wood piled behind it. Ed caught the odour of prunes and dried beans and mingled with this were other smells—spices and dried fish, and the ugly dry smell of gunpowder.

The Bear said, "I take her to her room, Big John?"

Big John nodded.

The girl looked at Ed. Her wound had crusted over and was not now bleeding.

Ed said, "You'll be all right. I'll see to that, girl. Don't lay a hand on her, Bear."

"He won't," Big John assured easily.

He said it too easily, Ed noticed.

The Bear and the girl went through a side door. Ed glimpsed a hall beyond the door, and then it was closed to shut off his vision. Soon The Bear came back. He growled, "Was I back soon enough to suit you, Martin?"

"You're a good boy," Ed said.

The Bear reached under the counter and came out with a bottle. He was chuckling. A deep rumbling sound, like water cascading—deep in his barrel-thick chest. He uncorked his bottle and drank deeply. Big John reached across the counter and took a quart of whiskey from the shelf. He slid it down the bar to Ed Jones.

"First quart is always on Big John Remington."

Ed looked at the bottle. He saw it was not sealed. Perhaps it had left the distillery without a seal or perhaps it came from Big John's private still. He put the bottle down. He reached over and got The Bear's bottle. He poured a small drink into the water tumbler made of clay.

"This looks better," he said.

Big John said nothing. The Bear scowled but remained silent. Ed heard a door slam and then he heard the sound of pots and pans. Evidently the squaw had left her rocking chair and was getting ready to do some cooking. The whiskey was powerful. It kicked like a mad mule. It reminded Ed that his belly was empty. From the north door came the smell of cooking food. Smelled like a good old mulligan stew. He could hear a woman moving in there.

Big John reached out for the bottle, too. "Won't open that one," he said. "Save it for later on."

He put the unopened bottle back on the shelf.

The bottle went around again, but Ed turned down the second drink. "Been away from likker for months," he said. "That's like swallerin' a hot brandin' iron. I'm gaunt to my ribs, men."

"Trade?" Big John asked.

Ed shook his head. "Tomorrow."

"My squaw is in her kitchen." Big John moved around the corner of the counter. "She must have some chuck cooked up. Bring the dog along."

Ed carried his furs into the room, walking behind Big John, with Chief following with his pack. The squaw had lit a fish-oil lamp. It cast guttering light across the dark kitchen, reflecting on the heavy cooking utensils. She was evidently a Sioux, or so Ed guessed because of her high cheekbones. Her face was dark and wide and expression-less; her body was wide and thick and without form under the old cotton dress evidently made of flour sacking. She regarded Ed with slow scrutiny and then looked down at Chief. She did not nod or in any way give any knowledge to the presence of a stranger and his dog.

"Where the girl?"

"In her room," Big John said.

"I wish she had got away."

"Well, she didn't."

The mulligan boiled in a copper kettle on an old cook stove. She stirred it with a wooden spoon, evidently hewed out by bowie knife. The stew smelled good. "One squaw enough for any man," she said. "Only one squaw to each man. Man no need two squaws. Wish she go."

"Close your big mouth!"

"I no close my mouth!"

Big John slapped her open-handed across the cheek. Ed knew that the blow had stunned her and hurt her. But she took it without flinching. She kept on stirring the mulligan. She did not even reach up and touch her face. She watched the wooden spoon and the mulligan.

"One squaw enough," she repeated stubbornly. "Many Feathers enough squaw for you."

Big John did not slap her again.

She raised her head and her eyes met Ed Jones's. For one brief moment it seemed to Ed that something ran across those dark eyes. Was it hate—or was it fear—or was it contempt? Or was it love for this shambling giant? Ed did not know nor did he care. Then her attention was on the mulligan again.

Big John was saying, "Woman is all the same, be they black or red or white or yellow. Bellyachin' all their lives. Take a chair, Martin." He spoke again to the squaw. "Many Feathers, get some chuck for his malemute, too."

Many Feathers was ladling out the mulligan onto thick plates made of pine. "You no like dogs."

"Feed his animal, too."

"You want to act like you big of heart. Hate the dogs, you do. You killed the other dog—the dog that looks like his dog." She shuffled over to the table and set down the plates. "You like to kill his dog, too."

"Don't try it," Ed Jones warned. "You'll have to kill me first."

"The dog tried to kill me," Big John explained.

195

Ed Jones' mind went back to the meeting with the old man who was burying the dead malemute. Who had owned the big dog? And wasn't it about time the oldster was returning to Fort Green?

But he knew better than to ask too many questions.

The Bear ambled in. The squaw dished him some mulligan. He grunted and tied into it, spoon rising and falling. He crammed whole slices of bread down his throat. Ed noticed that the bread was made from rice. The Bear washed down the rice bread with great gulps of coffee. He was noisy and all animal. Big John Remington busied himself with his grub.

The squaw came back from the stove with a big buffalo bone. "This for your dog," she told Ed. "He eat it outside."

Ed shook, his head. "He eats it not outside. He eats it in here or no place."

"I jus' mop the floor."

Big John looked up. "The dog eats it inside, like his master says. You can clean the floor later on. You got a lot of time."

Chief took the bone. He chewed on it, holding it between his forepaws. Occasionally Ed tossed him hunks of the rice bread. Down the Green River a mile or so there were sloughs where the river spread out. Here in the stagnant water grew wild rice. Ed figured Many Feathers had gathered this rice and had ground it. It was good bread. And the mulligan was first rate, also.

Ed Jones ate slowly.

He had his thoughts.

There were very few people stirring about this post. That seemed odd. Other trappers should have been in by now. Usually a few hangers-on and trappers were around each trading post.

Because of high peaks shutting off the sun, darkness came down with amazing suddenness. It folded itself around the darkened buildings. Only in the trading post did the fish-oil lamps dance and flicker, sending dull rays out to die against the dark log walls.

Ed heard moccasins coming down the hall. He wondered if the person were the young white woman. But when the door open it admitted the old man who had been burying the malemute. He saw Chief lying there chewing his bone and he stopped just inside the door. Ed saw a wildness come into his eyes, and he opened his mouth and chewed on spit in surprise.

"The dog—He's come back from the grave—I jus' finished sayin' a prayer over his grave—"

Big John Remington showed a smile. But it was not pleasant; it was angry and mean. And his words, although low in tone, also carried anger.

"Sit down, you damned ol' fool! This ain't the same malemute you buried, you idiot! This is another dog!"

The vacant and horror-filled eyes turned on Ed. They burned down on him in fanatic intensity.

Ed asked, "Do you remember me?"

The eyes were hot gimlets. "Sure, I remembers you. I met you two years or so back up in Fort Peck. Up on the Yellowstone, I met you."

Ed shook his head. "Fort Peck is on the Big Muddy and not the Yellowstone. And you never saw me there. The first time you met me was back yonder when I come across you diggin' that grave."

"I don't—remember that."

Big John said, "He's slipped his picket pin, Martin. He's set too many lonely traps. In other words, he's crazy."

Ed asked, "What is your name?"

"My name?"

"Yes, your name."

The Bear muttered, "Crazy man. Go to hell, all of you." He kept on wolfing his mulligan.

"Me, I'm Ol' Man."

"Jes' Ol' Man," Big John said.

The old grave-digger sat down, fitting his bottom to a rawhide-seated homemade chair. "Ol' Man. That's what they call me." He cocked his dirty whiskery head in thought. "Once I had another name." He shook his head. "But I forget it . . ."

The Bear glared at him. "You never had no other name," he corrected. "All your life you been the Ol' Man."

"You're right. I never had no other name."

Ol' Man cackled. It was evidently a big joke. He had a sharp nervous laugh, the high-pitched laughter of the insane. Chief growled and looked up at Ed for another bone, which he did not get. Chief was nervous. Maybe he smelled the odour of the dead malemute on this demented oldster?

Many Feathers shoved mulligan in front of the oldster. "You eat this." Her voice was tender. It sounded like a mother talking to a wayward little boy. "Do you good. Make you get big and strong."

"Me, I wanna be strong."

The oldster made loud noises as he ate. He seemed to be unaware of any of the others; his attention was on his mulligan. Ed got to his feet and Chief arose with him. Ed picked up his pack and that of his malemute.

"You got quarters for me, Big John?"

The factor shoved back his chair. "We sure have got quarters, Martin. But we could do some dickerin' tonight, if you cared to. Evenin' is still a young cub. Me, I'd cotton to look at your furs."

Ed grinned. "I ain't got much. I have a few mink, some marten, and a few fisher. My trappin' grounds were almighty poor. Poorest I've hit this side of the Platte. Most of my pack is muskrat. Some are light; some are dark—but not much count. Seems to me you built your post in a bad spot."

"How come you say that?"

"Well, they ain't many trappers in this area. Most of them are on the other side of the Divide. They go down into Fort Bridger or to Fort Keogh or Fort Peck. Some head northeast even as far as Fort Union."

"They'll come over this way when they all hear about my post. This is their closest tradin' post. An' my pay will be as high as any other factor, if not higher. I'll see to that."

"Had many trappers so far this year?"

"Only one, but the season is young. That was the white girl's father. He traded his plews and he traded his daughter."

Ed spoke evenly. "There was a trapper over the ridge from me. I met him once last winter, about in February. I forget his name—was never no hand for rememberin' names. Faces, yes; not names. Figgered he might head this direction, had he heard of your post. An' word gets around fast in the wilderness, although I don't know how it does. Figgered he might have come to Fort Green."

"Ain't seen him so far. Too bad you don't remember his name, so I could welcome him for you . . . . if he does come to Fort Green. But I'm expectin' them to trek in any day now, what with the Chinooks over with and Spring bein' here. Well, come along—we'll bargain tomorrow."

"Tomorrow, Big John."

Big John led the way down the porch, moccasins making dull sounds on the gravel. Ed and Chief followed. The big man opened the door to a cabin set apart slightly from the rest of the trading-post headquarters. Ed gave it a studied survey. It was about five feet from the thick stockade-wall. Big John opened the door and it swung in silently on its bullhide hinges. He entered ahead of Ed and lit a sulphur match that flared up and showed the bunk and the table and the two opposite windows, sealed with oilskin. He found the fish-oil lamp and lit the wick. The smell of sulphur and burning fish-oil was strong in the closed-up cabin.

"Here you are, Martin."

Suddenly Chief snarled. Big John jumped back slightly, caught his balance, and looked down at the dog, anger in him. Ed thought for a moment the giant would kick at Chief. But Big John held his temper.

"I hate them damned malemutes," he growled.

"He won't hurt you," Ed assured.

Big John killed the match. "See you come daylight." He watched Chief cross the room and lie down in front of the bunk. Chief licked his paws but his eyes were on the factor. "Have a good night of sleep, Martin."

"Same to you, Big John."

The big man closed the door and Ed heard him shuffle along the gravel, then he heard another door open and close. He and Chief and the night were alone. Ed sat on the bunk and thought, Well, this is Fort Green, but where the devil is Mack Hanson? Things had piled up fast. His knuckles were skinned and sore from hitting The Bear. Had he made an eternal enemy out of the shambling giant?

He figured he had.

From now on, Bear, I watch you, and you're not gettin' behind me at any time, Bear.

He crossed the room and extinguished the lamp. This plunged the room into inky darkness. He sat on the bed. Chief put his wet broad nose against his hand. He stroked the malemute's wide forehead. Chief pushed against him.

Maybe Corporal Hank Williams was in error?

Maybe Mack Hanson had never come to Fort Green?

Ed played with this thought. But then he knew Hank Williams was not wrong—Williams played his cards close to his chest. He made sure of his statements before he uttered them. Mack had come to Fort Green.

Was Mack dead? Murdered—robbed—buried? They had killed the girl's father. She had screamed out that information. The Bear and Big John knew she had told him this fact. They had heard her scream it. Big John and The Bear would be watching him, for what he knew was dangerous to them. Ed had a sudden cold thought. He had heard too much. He knew too much.

And, because of this, he knew that he, too, was marked for death.

And this thought was as icy as glacier water.

Ed sat there for some hours in the dark. He listened to the wind and its slow push against the rough logs. The cabin became cold. Chief curled up on the bunk, nose covered by his tail. He was with his master and he was content. But there was no contentment in Ed Jones.

He had got into Fort Green easily enough. But he knew that in order to get out alive, he would have to fight for his life.

He wished then he had not brought Chief into this. Big John had killed one malemute; he hated malemutes; he would try to kill Chief. Who had owned the dead malemute the insane oldster had buried? This was another part of the riddle. Ed took his mind from this thought—the dog was dead, out of this.

Had the dead malemute belonged to the white girl who had tried to break away from The Bear and Big John Remington?

Ed waited for what seemed to be hours. The post was quiet and there was only the murmur of the night wind. When he slid out of the door he had Chief at his heels. He left both packs of plews in the cabin. He knew that the pack on his back would only hinder his movements, were there to be trouble. And this fort, he thought wryly, should have been named Fort Trouble, not Fort Green.

201

He toted his Winchester.

He stood there for a long tense moment, scanning the dark. He could barely see the dim outline of the buildings and the stockade. His eyes fell on the turrets. Were guards up there—guards who watched him? He toyed with this thought, and it was not a good thought. Then the realization came that the overhang of the porch hid him from possible eyes in the turrets. The overhang, and the darkness were his friends. Well, he needed every friend he could get!

A dim light flickered in the trading-post proper, evidently a night light. The rest of the post was in darkness. He wondered how many people were on the post. Well, it made small never-mind. Only one would be on his side. That would be the white woman, with the scar on her cheek. With the wound made by the snapping lash of The Bear's ugly blacksnake whip.

He saw nothing of danger, so he and Chief moved ahead after he had muttered, "Heel, Chief," and the malemute had obediently slid into pace behind him.

His plan was to attempt to look over the buildings comprising Fort Green. He had a wild idea—perhaps Mack Hanson was still alive, a captive in one of the buildings? This, he realized, was a wild hope, based on desire. He knew the odds were vastly against it. For Big John and The Bear would not keep a prisoner. They would rob him and kill him and bury him.

His thoughts went over to Corporal Hank Williams. Williams had said that after he had gone to the geyser country, he would then hurry back to Fort Green. He would get his partner, Bill Smith, who was up in the geyser country, and they would come back to this fort here where the Soda tossed its flood-muddy waters into the Green. They would camp in the brush outside the fort and await his coming to them with whatever news he would be able to find out concerning Mack Hanson.

He wondered if they were now out in the brush.

That hardly seemed logical. But it had taken him a couple of days to break camp, and by that time Williams and Bill Smith might have solved the rumour of the murder, which might have proved false, and they might even now be in the brush, watching and waiting.

This was a strong and good thought. But another question kept running around the rim of his mind, and it was not good nor was it strong. And the question was this: Why had Big John Remington built this wilderness out-post?

Surely he had not constructed it in order to trade with trappers. For in order to make a trading-post popular, to make it pay a profit, a factor had to curry the favour of the trappers, and not go out and kill them. Another angle came into this assumption. This area held few trappers when considered in the light of the trapping area across the High Divide. And to buy plews, a man had to have his post located in an area where there were many trappers, not just a few buckskin men.

Then why had Big John Remington built Fort Green?

His mind did mental gymnastics. Across the mountains, in the Territory of Idaho, gold had been discovered the year before. Yellow gold, precious gold—gold that man and women had fought for, had died for, had killed for. Yellow gold, panned from rushing mountain streams, sluice-boxed out of roaring mountain rivers. Hank Williams had told him about this, too. And Corporal Williams had said the lawlessness and murder and robbery ran riot in the Idaho gold country.

Williams had said that miners had been murdered, then robbed. They had been shot in the back bent over their pans and their sluice boxes. Was this stolen gold then being smuggled across the mountains to Fort Green? Was it then going by bull boat or packet down the Green and out of the country into circulation in far-away

Saint Louis or Independence or some other distant river-port? Williams had mentioned this as being one reason Big John Remington had built Fort Green.

This theory was possible . . . and probable, Ed Jones reasoned.

There was another angle, too.

Unrest and rumblings of warfare were moving along the Wilderness Trails. Railroads were pushing steel ribbons to the West, always West. Buckskin men were settling down. They were building cabins on land claimed by the Indians. Their ploughs were ripping up soil claimed by the Sioux, the Cheyennes, the Crows, the Bloods, and the other scattered redskin tribes. The war between red man and white man was soon to boil into bloody border warfare.

Out on the Plains, the buffalo were being slaughtered not by the thousands, not by the tens of thousands, but by the millions. Their flesh was not being used. It was left to rot on the prairies, to decay in the high buffalo-grass and bluestem and bluejoint grasses. Only the hides were being salvaged. They were going out all over the world to become robes and coats. And the Plains Indians—the Sioux and Crows and Cheyennes, to mention only a few tribes—depended upon one animal for their food, their sinews, their teepees, their lives. And this animal was the shaggy short-horned animal known to them as King Buffalo. They looked to him for their subsistence.

With him gone, they would have no food. With King Buffalo dead, they would be forced onto reservations, to become wards of white men, of the Great White Father. And they were fighting for their livelihood, their way of life.

And to fight white man, they needed the white man's weapons. Bows and arrows and war spears were no good against deadly rifles and pistols.

Uncle Sam had to keep the redskins from getting their

hands on rifles and cartridges and Colt pistols. So far he had been fairly successful. But unscrupulous traders were smuggling rifles to the Sioux, up in Montana Territory. They were riding war ponies and brandishing new government rifles. Where were they coming from? Had Big John Remington made this trading post as a place to smuggle rifles north? There was this possibility for bull boats and packets could take the rifles up the Green to this fort. Corporal Hank Williams and he had discussed this possibility.

Was Big John posing as a trader to sell and trade rifles to the redskins? Was this post, then, only a blind for bigger game, for more money? Indians would trade beaver pelts packed flat the height of a new Sharps rifle. The beaver pelts were worth many, many times the cost of the firearm.

But Ed Jones wasted not much time with such thoughts. His job was to find his old partner, or to discover his grave . . . or to find out what had happened to Mack Hanson. And to accomplish this, he was endangering his own life.

Accordingly he went ahead, a black shadow in the black night. He worked his way along the wall, the logs rough against his hands. He headed for the trading post proper, and now and then he paused; he stood dark and hidden against the log building, Chief at his moccasins' heels. And he watched, and Chief watched; he listened, and Chief listened, too.

Suddenly, about forty feet ahead of them, a man moved into the night. Ed went to his haunches, his hand on Chief's broad head.

"Quiet, boy, quiet."

The dog remained silent. The man moved with a jerky motion, as though physical action was hard to accomplish. Ed then recognized him as the Old Man. Surely this demented man was not his guard? Then Old Man was gone, a part of the night: the night had opened its black jaws and had swallowed him. He had headed across the compound toward a cabin. Maybe he was just going to go to bed?

Ed and his dog crouched there for some moments. But they saw no more of Old Man. Ed thought he heard a door open and close, but he was not sure. These bullhide hinges made no squeaking sounds.

He thought of Many Feathers. He remembered the terrible look in her eyes when Big John had slapped her. She did not like the white girl. The white girl was an enemy of hers, for plainly she wanted to hold Big John. Ed wondered if her jealousy, properly handled, could not be used.

He went to a window in the kitchen. He looked in. There was a light in the kitchen. The window pane had been made out of buffalo hide. A knife had worked diligently and carefully on the hide, scraping off the hair. The hide had been carved to a parchment-like thinness. He could see through it. He listened but he heard no conversation. He saw the squaw across the room. Evidently she was washing dishes in the wooden tub. She hummed something—a weird redskin tune. Evidently she was alone, singing to herself. Ed thought, I'll take the chance.

He went to the door. Slowly he tried the latch, lifting it slightly. The door was unlocked; it opened slightly.

He murmured, "Chief, you watch from outside," and the malemute nuzzled against him, nose pushing against his buckskin-clad leg. Ed did not know whether or not the dog understood, but he had to take a chance.

He slid into the kitchen. The squaw heard him, and she turned quickly despite her bulk. But nothing changed in her face. No surprise, no fear—nothing but the wide and dark and bland face.

Ed closed the door behind him.

"What you want, White Man?"

"I want to talk to you."

"We talk about what?"

"You hate the white girl, huh?"

"I hate her. Big John, he want her. She take my place. I have to go back to my tribe. They no take me, because white man has slept with me. She will drive me out. I no have home."

"You came from Canada with Big John?"

"Yes, he bring me here. Long time I been his squaw. Three papooses, all they die. He father them."

"You love him?"

"Why you ask?"

"You like Big John?"

"He my husband. He father my dead papooses. Why you ask all this, white man? You want white girl?"

"I might take white girl with me."

"You do that, I give you anything you want. You been without woman for long time. I give you what you want."

Ed grinned. "Maybe we're kinda mixed up as to what I want, Many Feathers. I don't want to hit the sougans with you, woman."

"You—sick?"

"Never felt better in my life. If I take white girl with me, you tell me something? Something I want to know?"

Shrewd eyes watched him. She wiped her gnarled hands on an old and dirty dishtowel. Ed studied her and had his doubts. But he could do nothing but lay his cards on the table. He had nothing to lose except his hide. And he knew that to keep his hide without bullet holes, he had to get out of Fort Green. But how would he get out? He was like the white girl . . . a prisoner . . .

"You take white girl with you?"

"Yes."

"What you want to know?"

Ed decided to shoot the whole jackpot. "There was a

trapper, and he came in here with his furs." He made a flat motion three times to designate in Sioux the possible period of time. "This trapper he was my partner. He came to Fort Green, and then he was gone. I never seen him again."

"What you want to know?"

"Where is he?"

"I did not see him."

"You speak the truth?"

"I do, White Man."

Ed wondered if she were not fabricating. He decided to try another lure. "I have a silver fox fur. No, it is not in my pack. I am not that stupid, Mother."

"You have no silver fox fur. Foxes do not come this far south. They up north, where Manitou lives."

"I cached it. I would not be fool enough to come in here with a silver fox fur. But I have a deal to make."

"Deal?"

"Yes."

"What kind of deal?"

"If you tell me about my partner, the silver fox he is yours."

He saw something move across her eyes. This gave their fullness a savage light. This flashed across her eyes for a moment. Then it died.

"There are no silver foxes this far south. You do not tell Many Feathers the truth, White Man."

"But one came south, and I trapped him. The fur is worth much. I will lead you to it, if you do not believe me."

"Where is fur hid?"

"Along the river."

She smiled. "You have no silver fox. You lie to me. You are like all the mens—white or red. They all lie to the womens. I do not believe you. I know nothing."

Ed realized he had run into a stone barrier. He could

not climb over it. Nor could he go under or around it. Maybe he had tipped his hand too far? She might tell Big John. He wondered about that. He decided on a plan.

"You tell Big John I talked to you, Many Feathers, and I won't take the white girl with me. Big John doesn't want you no longer. He wants to kick you out and live with the white girl. With the white girl gone, you are not in danger."

Her eyes were dark shadows.

"He will sleep with the white girl. Not with you. He will keep you as a slave—to scrub and wash and cook."

"He will do that," she said.

"Why don't you run away?"

"The whip."

He nodded.

Her voice was low and thick. "You saw the girl's cheek?"

"I did."

"The girl, she ran out the gate. The whip did that—it cut her cheek. Big John, he can use the whip, too, but not like The Bear."

"They whip you?"

"My back, it has the cuts. Maybe I show it to you?"

She started to slip off her cotton blouse. Ed saw a huge meaty shoulder crisscrossed by recent scars. His blood ran cold. He saw the lash marks across her sagging full breasts. Then she restored the blouse to its original position.

"Big John he beat me when I tell the truth. He beat me when I tell the lie. So I say nothing, and I not get beat. I not tell them you talked to me. I'm afraid of the whip."

Ed thought, even as rotten as it is, the whip is an ally in this deal. He had another thought: If they caught him in her kitchen, she would suffer for it under the lashing blacksnake whip. He would have to get out of here for her sake. He did not want her to suffer because of him.

He tried another question. "Where is the white girl?"

"I do not know."

He knew she was lying to him. She lied because she feared for her own safety. She lied because she was afraid of the whip.

"That dog that Ol' Man buried—the malemute—Who owned him?"

"White girl's dog."

Ed pulled back against the door. She stood with her big hands in dirty dishwater. She was solid, she was wide, she was ugly. But yet there was a strong sense of character in her. Ed was aware of this. She had had her troubles. She still loved Big John. Women, he decided, were odd things. The best women seemed to fall in love with the most worthless men. But he had not much time for this thought. Time was piling up; Time was demanding he move on.

"You want to leave, Many Feathers?

She cocked her heavy head. She seemed to be listening to inner voices. "No, I love Big John. He beats me 'cause I am his woman." She waddled to the water bucket and lifted the thick wooden dipper and drank noisily. "Now white man go and leave Many Feathers, or she get the whip."

"Goodbye," Ed breathed.

He slid out through the door. Chief rose and pushed his nose against him. So far he had accomplished exactly nothing. He had not learned a thing about Mack Hanson. Fear of the lash had sealed Many Feathers' thick lips. He wondered where the white girl was. The Bear had taken her to a cabin. But which cabin?

He was cold with fear inside. He was sure that Mack Hanson was dead. Murdered and buried in some lonely spot. While that fear had been with him for some time, it now became stronger and more powerful. He wished that Mack had gone trapping with him—why had they had to part over a squaw? But such were the ways of men and of Time. There was nothing he could do about the past. What had happened had happened. But he had to make sure that Mack had really been killed.

He stood there for a moment, a dark shadow against the dark log wall, and he gave his attention to the night. Fort Green apparently slept under the dark blanket of the Wyoming night. But the sleep was deceptive and it was uneasy; the fort was not inert and senseless—it seemed to throb and vibrate with danger. He wondered if the moon would soon rise. He had not paid much attention to the moon lately. If it did rise, would it be a friend—or an enemy?

He thought about this momentarily. If it did rise, he could see his way about more clearly; but, by the same line of thinking, eyes could catch him and watch him. He was sure his cabin was being watched. By this time The Bear and Big John Remington—He stiffened suddenly.

Had he heard something?

He listened, head canted. He noticed that Chief had not growled. That told him that his nerves had been playing him false. His nerves were as taut as fiddle-strings. His leg muscles were trembling. He heard the wind moving around the corner of a log building—the lazy and indifferent mountain wind. Chillness was in the air, coming down from the high peaks with their glacial ice and snow.

Where was the white girl? He saw a cabin that had a light in it, the light dim through the buffalo-hide pane. He decided to take a chance. He had no other recourse. Of course, he could turn back toward his cabin, and wait for tomorrow. Maybe that was the sensible thing to do? To play his cards closer to his chest—not to rush ahead as he was doing? But he was in danger. Every moment he spent at Fort Green was freighted with ugly and red danger.

Chief at his heels, he moved toward this window. He tried to peer through it, but it was not scraped thinly enough to allow vision. He tried his best to see clearly into the interior of this cabin, but it was no use. The pane was too thick. He went to the door.

He knocked on the door. Nobody answered. He tried the latch; it was bolted from inside. He knocked again.

A voice said, "Go away, Big John, you liar and killer!"

His heart jumped. It was the voice of the white woman! He put his head close to the door.

"This is the trapper, white girl."

"The trapper who helped me?"

"Yes. I want to talk to you."

"They'll kill you—if they find you here—"

"Open the door. I have to see you. I'll take the chance."

Above the soughing of the wind, he heard her movements. She was coming to unbolt the door. Recklessness flooded him and momentarily drove away the feeling of danger.

Maybe this recklessness caused his lack of alertness.

For suddenly Chief growled. A terrible, ugly growl. Ed turned, hand going to his gun. But he never got to pull the pistol. For the whip came out of the night, coiling its thundering length around his arms. The whip smashed in and pinned his arms to his side.

The whip pulled him ahead, throwing him off-balance. He caught the blurred outline of The Bear. Then he was going down. Something smashed across the back of his head. Right before the inky blackness came in, he heard the guttural voice of Big John Remington.

He had one terrible thought before the blackness claimed him. They might kill Chief!

Then there was nothing.

For years he tumbled across the empty wilderness of

black space. He fell end over end, turning in the eternal darkness. He whirled through the stars and they had no light; they too were wrapped in eternal blackness. They were not then stars, for stars are quick and bright. Then finally across the wilderness came the sound of a voice and it held a strange familiarity. Finally the voice broke into parts and these sections became independent words.

> Oh, the wild fox, the wild fox,
>     A wise old fellow is he:
> Some say he's a wild devil,
> Some say he's a wise man,
>     But he's as wild as can be!

Ed thought, I recognize that song, and memory tried to come back, piercing the veil of pain and blackness. He became aware of sight. All seemed black around him. Memory returned quickly—the whip, the club behind his head, and Chief growling. Fear for Chief shot through him. Had Big John killed the malemute? This was short of life, though. A tongue came out of nowhere and wrapped itself around his face. It seemed the size of a cut of deer flank. But it belonged to a dog, and the dog was Chief.

He tried to reach out to bury a hand in the thick fur of the malemute, but he could not move his hands, and at first he could not understand why—then he realized they were tied behind him. And he tried to move his feet and they too were stationary, and the realization seeped in that he was bound hand and foot.

He felt a rough wall behind his back. He turned his head and rubbed against it, and he found it was made of rock and mortar.

He was in a dungeon.

Despite his short beard, the stone and mortar had been rough on his face. But this sensation was lost as the voice again took up its mournful dirge.

> The c'yoties run in killer packs,
>> But the wise fox runs alone:
> C'yoties hunt in the dark of night,
>> But the wild fox hunts in the moon—
>> For he is wise as can be!

Ed heard a voice snarl, "For God's sake, man, stop that wildcat yowlin'," and the voice, he realized, belonged to himself.

A voice said, "Ed Jones, don't tell me you're already comin' out of it! You've only been in here about ten minutes." The voice was very familiar. "I know because I've run through only twelve verses of my song."

Ed thought, somebody knows my real handle, and here I told them I was Hans Martin. Suddenly he recognized the voice. Despite the pain roaring through his skull, he felt a lift of elation. This smashed through the pain-red barrier and brought him happiness that tore aside the veil.

For the voice belonged to Mack Hanson!

This is a wild dream, he thought. Mack, you're dead— The Bear and Big John—they murdered you! Have I gone across the Big Ridge, and are we in the Promised Land? No, I have my body.

"Mack—Mack Hanson?"

"The same, Ed Jones. Your ol' pal, in the flesh. What is left of the flesh, that is. Mack Hanson, tied to the wall. You're tied down too, eh, Ed?"

"My hands is tied behind me. My feet are tied. But my hands ain't tied to the wall. I'm jus' settin' against the wall. Mack, I thought you was dead, man?"

"I sure ain't, Ed."

"What happened to me, Mack? I remember the whip wrappin' itself aroun' me. I was tryin' to get into the white girl's cabin. Then they clubbed me. We're in a stone walled cellar, eh?"

Ed could hardly hear his old partner's low words. He felt somewhat good now, finding Mack Hanson alive. Even if they were tied up like two shoats in this cellar. Mack was alive, and that counted.

"Big John and The Bear heaved you in here, all tied up. Big John tried to kill Chief. But Chief done tackled him teeth and nail, and Big John was almighty glad to get shut of him in this cellar. He threw Chief in, too, and Chief chewed the hell out of Big John's arm, looked to me. But here we are, man, and what we goin' do about it? And how come you're in this outpost of hell?"

Ed Jones' throat seemed filled with cotton. He could hardly talk he was so dry. He told about the visit of Corporal Hank Williams.

"So . . . I come lookin' for you, Mack. Figgered all the time they had killed you for your plews. Wonder how come they never killed me?"

"When they threw you in here, I heard Big John say somethin' about you trappin' a silver fox, an' cachin' the pelt. Sure enough, Ed, did you trap a silver?"

"I got one. I cached the hide. I told the squaw about it, tryin' to bribe her. But I reckon I done tipped my cards, for she must've told Big John and The Bear right pronto. But by golly, it saved my life, at that. Now they'll keep me alive until I tell them where I cached that pelt."

"You done right tellin' Many Feathers about thet fox plew, or else they would have kilt you like they done kilt that Malone trapper."

"Malone?"

"Yeah, he was the gal's pappy. I met him as I come down to Fort Green. Met him an' his daughter on the south fork of the wilderness. He and her had trapped back along the Tetons, and we all decided to try out Fort Green. They kilt him. The gal's name is Nacie. Nacie

Malone." Mack Hanson tried to spit, or so it sounded in the dark. "I'm dry as a ol' beaver den. How is Nacie?"

Ed told him what he knew about the girl. "She tried to break free, and she ran into me—The Bear cut her cheek with his blacksnake. I couldn't let her go into the wilderness alone—one woman with no gun or supplies—but maybe I done wrong in holdin' her, at that."

"Nacie is quite a gal."

Nacie. Nacie Malone. Pretty name. The name fitted her. Ed liked that name. Nacie.

"But how come they didn't kill you, too, Mack?"

Mack Hanson's dry chuckle moved across the darkness. By this time Ed Jones' eyes were becoming accustomed somewhat to the inky blackness. He could make out Chief, lying beside him, and he could dimly see the outline of Mack Hanson, seated across the dungeon, about ten or twelve feet away. The thought that Mack was alive—really and truly alive—was still with him, the wonder of it causing him happiness despite his bonds and his throbbing skull that had a big wild goose egg on the back of it where Big John's billy-club had slashed down to knock him unconscious.

"That silver you caught, Ed? Was it a vixen or was it a dog fox?

"What the heck you blabbin' about?"

Again that dry chuckle. "I done put a question to you, Ed. Was the fox a she or a he?"

This sounded silly to Ed Jones. Maybe his friend had slipped his picket pin, and his brain was addled? This was a terrible thought. But then this left, for Mack Hanson's words were coherent, his sentences complete—not the words of a demented man.

"Well, if it makes you any happier, I'll tell you I caught a she fox. But why such a loco question?"

"That ain't out of the ordinary. You see I caught a dog fox. I caught her mate."

"You got a silver, too?"

"I sure have. An' I did like you did—I cached it while I scouted Fort Green. But I made one error."

"An' what was that?"

"Big John an' The Bear got me leaded down with whiskey. I got so drunk I blabbed about ownin' the fur, but I never tol' them where it was cached. They lowered the boom on me, like they did you."

"How many days back was that?"

"I dunno. They ain't no days in this dungeon. We got only nights."

Ed had a moment of thought. This was, in a way, rather ironical. Because of a vixen and a dog silver fox, they were here in this dungeon. And the possession of these two expensive plews had saved their lives.

"Big John an' The Bear has tried to make me tell where I hid my silver, but so far that blacksnake whip ain't had no luck."

"They've hammered you?"

"I'm cut kinda had around the rump and back an' chest. Now I know how them pore ol' black slaves felt like down south years agone. But they can't hammer it out of me, Ed."

"Reckon they'll work on me, too?"

"I sure do. We'll share our misery together, man."

"They'll never get the location of that pelt out of me, Mack."

"Nor me, either."

Ed Jones said, "I'm goin' roll over to where you are, Mack."

With difficulty, he rolled across the floor. It too was made of native Wyoming sandstone. His head felt better now—more like it belonged to him instead of sitting out there throbbing in the dark. Chief went with him, growling as he moved. He slid forward on his belly. Suddenly Ed rolled against Mack. The feel of his old partner, the thought that he had company in this prison, did him much good. He got his back against Mack Hanson's moccasins. This way he could feel the man's leg-ties. He was tied with buckskin, the knot solid and secure.

"Think you can untie it, Ed?"

"I'll try, but I doubt it."

"Ed, if we can get loose—"

Ed's mind had cleared to almost normal by this time. He still had a splitting headache, though. But his kind had been keen enough to detect the high note in Mack Hanson's words. The realization came that his partner was close to breaking. He was on the edge of losing his mind.

"I can't make it, Mack. Them thongs—they was soaked in water—they've pulled in tight. How does your feet feel?"

"They ain't no blood in them no more. I can't even feel them on the ends of my legs. Wonder if with the circulation cut off, I might lose them?"

"I'm goin' roll over and try your hands."

His partner's wrists were tied to an iron loop embedded into the wall about a half-foot from the floor. This buckskin had also been soaked in water. The knot was iron hard.

"Wonder why they never tied me to a iron loop, Mack?"

"Only one in the dungeon, I reckon. This 'pears to me like it might have been built for a meat house or a root cellar."

"Where's the door, Mack?"

"To my right about five paces."

Ed rolled over and found the door. He got his back to it and felt it. It seemed to be made of young cottonwood logs bolted together after being hewed and fitted. It was as solid as a door could be. If there was a latch or bolt, it was on the outside: for he managed to get to his feet, using the door as an aid to keep his balance. And he could find no lock or latch. He sank down with a groan. He now had his back to the door. Evidently it opened out. The door stops told him that. He pushed against it but it had no give. It was as solid as the Tetons.

Suddenly, Chief growled.

Ed heard another door open. That meant the dungeon had two doors. Quickly he rolled across the cellar to his original position. Chief followed and sank on his belly beside his master. Ed got his back to the wall and let his head drop into his chest, acting as though he were still unconscious.

He heard the door go closed. Then he heard moccasins shuffling toward them. Evidently a tunnel ran from the outside door to the inner door. He looked up covertly. He saw the outline of light around the door. The moccasins stopped. He heard a bolt slide back and then the door opened, letting in the light. The light was caused by a huge candle of buffalo-fat with a lamp wick in it. It sputtered and guttered, and you could hear the grease melting. The grease stunk. Soon the stink filled the dungeon. But Ed was not interested in the grease. The candle was carried by Big John Remington. Behind the factor of Fort Green came the wide and terrible form of The Bear. Candlelight showed on the coiled blacksnake whip.

Chief growled, deep in his belly. Ed said softly, "Down, Chief, be good," and the dog remained flat on the rocks, belly hard against the stones. His eyes were on the two huge men.

Ed got a glimpse of a passage-way beyond the door. Evidently a tunnel led to this dungeon. The candle-light had glistened on the rocks. This dungeon, then, was sealed by two doors.

Big John spread his thick legs wide and looked down on Ed Jones. "So you finally come outa it, eh, Jones?"

219

"How did you find out my real name?"

Big John chuckled, a rumbling sound. "When we dragged you in here Hanson got so excited he babbled out your real name. You figgered you was purty smart, huh, sneakin' into Fort Green under a different name. What you drivin' at, Jones?"

"I don't get your meanin'."

"To hell you don't, man! You came in here for some purpose. Otherwise you'd not have changed your handle like you did. Anybody send you in here to scout my post?"

"Why would anybody want me to look over your rotten tradin' post?"

"How come you come to Fort Green, then?"

Ed did a little bit of lying. "I went over to Mack's cabin. He had already pulled stakes. He had left a note for me sayin' he was goin' try Fort Green. So, I followed him. That satisfy you, you big devil?"

Big John scowled. He rubbed his whiskers. The sound was loud in the silence. "Might . . . and might not," he finally said. He seemed deep in thought. The Bear watched him, sunken eyes reflecting the yellow light. The Bear fingered his coiled bullwhip. It looked like a long and dark snake coiled in his thick hands. Now he wet his lips with his huge tongue. He seemed fascinated by his boss's stern face. He had the appearance of a dog waiting for his master to give him the word. Candle-light showed the deep ridges of Big John Remington's rugged face. "I'll dicker with you, Jones."

"In what way?"

"You got a silver fox pelt cached somewhere. You tol' thet to Many Feathers. I want you to give me thet fur."

"Oh, yeah? And what about me?"

"Give me the fur, and you can go free."

Ed scoffed, "I ain't got no fur. I was only lyin' to thet female Indian. Just lying to her to try to get information out of her."

The Bear's deep voice cut in with, "We don't think so, Jones. Me an' Big John saw a pair of silvers off in the distance last winter when we was runnin' our trap line. A he and she fox. They was too far away for rifles. I still reckon you an' Hanson here caught them."

Mack Hanson broke in savagely. "You're damned right we done trapped them! Their pelts is worth around a thousand each in Fort Union or St Louis. An' I can tell you one thing fer sure—and for damned sure—you'll never get your lousy hands on my silver pelt!"

Ed said, "Mack, watch your tongue. It might get you into trouble, fella. Play your cards close, Mack."

The Bear's gnarled hands were slowly uncoiling his bullwhip. His eyes were on Mack Hanson who stared up at him in belligerent silence. The candle sent flashing light across the ugly planes of The Bear's huge face and became lost in the narrowed slits of his bloodshot eyes. He pulled his lips back and showed his dirty tobacco-dark teeth.

"Maybe I give you the lesson with my whip? How about that, Big John? I make him talk."

"You could kill me afore I'd talk," Mack Hanson gritted.

"I work on him, Big John? Tell The Bear to go to work on the trapper. Big John say yes."

"Not now, Bear."

"Why . . . not?"

"Oh, shut up, you fool!"

The Bear settled back and started to recoil his whip. Ed saw something move across Mack Hanson's bearded face, and the trapper swallowed and wet his lips. He got the impression that Hanson was close to the breaking point. He decided to do some talking to Big John Remington.

"Hold your hosses for a minute, Remington. I want to

powwow with you. You say that if I lead you to my silver, you'll let me go free?"

"That I will."

"I don't believe you."

"You have my word."

"It ain't logical," Ed Jones said. "You know damned well I'd git the territorial police and lead them back here an' have them smoke you two out of Fort Green. I think you'd get the plew and then kill me."

Big John Remington grinned. "You got a head on them shoulders, Jones. I got a good deal here at Fort Green. Fact is, I could use a man like you—one what can think, and can fight. I might arrange to take you into this deal, if first I know you want to make money an' if you'll let bygones die as bygones."

"Gold?"

"You'll find out . . . if you want to work with he."

"He's a liar," Mack Hanson said huskily. "He jes' wants your silver. He'll get it and then shoot your spine in two, Ed."

Ed wished then and there that Mack Hanson would keep his mouth shut. They were in a dungeon tied like pigs going to market in a peasant's wagon. Could they manage to get outside, they might have a chance; here they had none at all. But he did not speak to the trapper again.

"We'll let you set here in the dark for a few more days," Big John said. "Maybe when you git hungry enough, you'll dicker with us. Bear, keep that whip coiled for now, savvy!"

"I want to use it!"

"Not today."

At this moment, Chief growled. Big John turned hurriedly and looked at the dog, and for a moment his eyes were wild.

"I oughta kill thet cur!"

"You kill him,' Ed Jones said levelly, "and I'll kill you, Remington. I'll climb outa my grave to do it if I have to!"

"I give him the whip?" The Bear's voice was hopeful.

"Forgit that damned blacksnake!" Big John Remington roared the words. Apparently he had reached the limits of his patience. "You two think it over."

"We sure will." Mack Hanson was cynical.

"Get out, Bear," ordered Big John. With The Bear in the lead, they went toward the door.

"How about the girl?" Ed Jones asked. "Where is she?"

Big John shoved The Bear out the door. Now Ed could see the tunnel clearly. There evidently was another door at the far end.

"You jes' forgit the girl," the factor warned. "If you want to stay healthy, forget that female."

"I'm hungry," Mack Hanson said.

Neither Big John nor The Bear had any answer to that. The heavy door closed behind them. Ed listened carefully and he thought he heard a chain rattle and a bolt move into place. Then moccasins moved down the tunnel. He heard another door open and close. Then, there was only the sound of Mack Hanson's harsh breathing.

"Hang onto yourself, Mack. We can't get no place by goin' off without a full charge of black powder."

"I guess . . . I'm goin' down . . . Ed . . ."

Ed managed to roll next to his partner. He remembered how the candle-light had shown Mack Hanson's face. His lips had been quivering and despite his dark beard, his face had looked thin, the cheeks sunken. This damp and dark dungeon—coupled with the terror of the bullwhip—had sapped him and he was close to caving.

"Some day . . . I'll Kill The Bear, Ed."

"Not if I beat you to him," Ed said. "But we got to get out of here. If we promise to take them to our silvers, we can at least get out of the dungeon. They won't kill us until they get them plews in their hands. If they killed us, they'd never find out the location of the caches."

"Can you . . . untie my hands?"

Ed shook his head. "My own hands don't belong to me no longer. The buckskin is cuttin' into my arteries, I believe."

"Chief?"

"What about him?"

"'Member how he used to like to play with a rope? Grab it and tug and pull. Would he do that . . . on your wrists?"

Hope speared through Ed Jones. "I can try that. He might chew the buckskin in two. Come here, Chief."

The malemute crept across the blackness. Ed heard him come but he could not see him for his eyes had not yet synchronized themselves again to the gloom. Soon he felt the huge dog beside him. He got around and he roughed him with his numb hands. He could not feel the dog because his hands were so dead.

"Chief! Play, Chief, play!"

The big dog did not understand. He whimpered and whined like a lost puppy. His long tongue snaked out to lick Ed's wrists. But he would not chew the thongs. Finally he pulled his head away. He whined.

"He won't do it, Mack."

"We ain't got no luck."

Again, Ed tried. But Chief got to his feet and glided away. He was not in a playful mood. He was hungry and gaunt and he was thirsty. A dog only played on a full belly after he had lapped up a pan of moose milk or clear mountain water.

"He won't do it," Ed repeated.

This time Mack Hanson did not answer. Ed leaned against the wall beside him. He heard the man snoring softly. Soon the snores were louder. Mack Hanson had been claimed by exhaustion.

He slept a deep sleep.

Ed himself was almost asleep when the second visitor came. The sound of the outside door opening—a thin and distant sound at its best—brought him fully awake. He listened and he heard the shuffle of moccasins on the rock floor of the tunnel. Again the doorway was limned by light. This light seemed stronger. He heard the bolt slip out of its socket and then came the dull clang of the chain. The door came slowly inward, admitting the light. He had judged, from the sounds of the moccasins, that only one person was coming into the dungeon. And in this assumption he was correct. The visitor was a female.

She was the heavy squaw, Many Feathers.

She carried a lantern with a dirty chimney. It cast a stronger glow than had the candle held by Big John Remington. It clearly showed the cavern. Ed guessed it as being about thirty feet long. There was no other opening except the door. His gaze came back to the massive hunk of flesh. Many Feathers carried a pail in her other hand. It was made of moosehide with red willow staves. Ed smelled the good odour of mulligan. His head had cleared and he realized he was terribly hungry.

"You damned liar," he said. "You said you wouldn't tell Big John."

She said nothing. She made no reply. Her face was a massive hunk of expressionless beef a dull-red colour in the light of the lantern.

She placed the lantern on the floor, putting it down carefully so it would not tip.

"I bring you grub."

She also put the pail on the floor. She brought out two tin plates that were almost hidden by the wide elkskin belt that held in her enormous belly. She squatted and the lantern light made her look even more grotesque and even larger. Her shadow was cast against the rock wall.

Ed Jones said, "Damn you, woman, you lied to me."

But she still did not say anything. She had a wooden spoon in the mulligan. She ladled mulligan onto a plate. She got it full and then filled the other. Mack Hanson continued sleeping. His head was down and his breath was hoarse and rattling. He was a pathetic figure.

Ed found himself studying her impassive face. He wondered what thoughts, if any, ran under its dark and emotionless surface. He figured two strong emotions were hidden there.

One was anger. Anger toward her man, Big John Remington, for getting in a young squaw, a young white squaw. Then there would be also jealousy. Nacie Malone would be involved in this jealousy, just as the anger centred around her pretty being. She had, against her will, moved into this squaw's territory.

Ed sat there in silence with his back to the rock wall and considered these two possibilities and wondered if there were some way to utilize them. But he could not think straight. He had been beat up and he was bound hand and foot. Nothing came from his mental gymnastics.

He wished he could walk. He wished he could have moved his hands. For the first time in his life he realized the predicament of a wilding caught in one of his traps. He felt revulsion toward his trade. He was a wildcat caught with both paws in a Number 4 trap. He was a grizzly who had tumbled into a deep and deadly deadfall. He was a wild animal trapped and ready for the *coup de grâce*.

To keep from thinking he watched the squaw work. He knew that she would have to feed them by hand or else untie their hands, and he knew she would not do this. Then why had she brought two plates? This was ironical and it drove the terror from him. It took his mind momentarily away from his condition and predicament.

But she filled both plates with the steaming mulligan. Chief whimpered and inched closer and then stopped and she seemed unaware of the malemute's avid attention. Chief made sweeping movements with his broomlike tail. His eyes were glued on her, and hunger was in them.

It was a grisly scene. The lantern kept flickering, making her dark shadow dance in grotesque hugeness on the opposite wall. Ed smelled good deer meat in the mulligan. It had a strong and clean odour. He caught the quick scent of wild sage she had used for seasoning. She was a good cook, he realized.

"You will feed me and my dog, too? And my partner?"

She did not answer.

"Where is the girl? Where is Nacie Malone?"

She raised her head and he saw her dark eyes and full face, but her thick lips did not move, and then her eyes went back to her work. Just the ladle dipping. Stirring, finding the venison chunks, filling the spoon, then rising to deposit them on the plate. He heard the rustle of her doeskin blouse and the rattle of wood on the tin plates. There were these sounds and there was her big form, without shape and without hope.

He tried again. "Where is the white woman?"

The eyes rose again and found him and watched him. They seemed to hold him in a silent grip. She was very thoughtful and very deliberate, or so it seemed to him. And then she said, "You love the white girl, trapper?"

Ed Jones scowled. Her question puzzled him. What did she mean by the word *love*? He had just met Miss Nacie Malone. He wondered if she, with her limited vocabulary, had selected the word she had wanted.

"I love her?"

"Yes, do you love her?"

Ed grinned. "I *could* love her, I reckon. That is, if she is willin' to be loved!" He laughed a little at his answer.

"Why do you ask such a thing, Many Feathers?"

"Do you love her?"

My God, she was persistent. What was behind all this? Ed lost his boyishness and his joking attitude. She was serious—deadly serious. He decided to become serious also.

"Yes, I guess I do. And that is odd, isn't it?"

"Why?"

"Why, I just met her once."

"Once is enough."

She said nothing more for some moments. She was still stirring and selecting hunks of boiled venison from the mulligan. She put them on the plate. Chief whimpered and drooled, but he came no closer to her. The malemute had his eyes riveted on a plate.

She raised her head again and she watched him. She had the eyes of a hawk. A circling, watching hawk. They glistened in the lantern light. They were sharp as the eyes of a hawk, too.

"Big John, he has not slept with her. I have watched him too close. Neither has The Bear, the bastard. I have watched them both. If Big John he tried, I will kill him with a knife. I will murder him if he goes into her cabin. I will kill him, and he knows it."

"What about The Bear?"

"He cannot go, for Big John will kill him."

Her voice quivered with hate and jealousy.

Mack Hanson kept on sleeping. Chief kept on watching the plates. Ed wondered what all this was leading up to. Could he use it to gain his freedom? He decided to ask more questions.

"You hate Big John?"

"No, I no hate him. I should hate him. But The Bear, I like to kill him. Cut his throat!"

Ed tried something. "Why not turn us loose?"

"Why I do that?"

"We will take the white squaw with us. And then you will have Big John all to yourself."

She had no answer to this.

She had both plates filled. She gave one to Chief who went to work with great haste. He gulped hunks of venison so fast he never even tasted them, Ed figured. She held the other plate under Ed Jones' face.

"I feed you."

"No, Mack first. Mack, damn you, come to wake!"

Mack Hanson awakened with a start. He stared around himself and then saw the mulligan on the plate and then he saw Many Feathers.

"I'm hungry," he said.

She fed him from the spoon. He was a little child and she fed him and for some reason there seemed much beauty in the scene to Ed Jones. She was the mother of men, the eternal female; she was feeding a man. Mack Hanson looked at Ed and gravy dripped from his beard.

"You eat like a dog in this deal, Ed. But she is a good cook. Wonder how many men good cooks have killed by feedin' them too much good food and they foundered themselves?"

"An' then some kill them by bad cookin'," Ed said.

She had some rice bread, too, and she fed a slice or two of this to Mack. He ate in great gulps. Finally he said, "No more, Mother," and she wiped his beard and chin with a doeskin handkerchief she took from the wide belt. She looked at Mack Hanson, whose head had again sunk to his chest, and was it pity in her eyes? Ed wished he knew. He kept harping on Big John and the white girl. Big John would kick her out. He had a young woman now—a white woman. Squaws were cheap and easy to get. But not white women.

"You say no more, Jones."

"But it is the truth."

"No talk about it now. You make me mad."

Good, Ed thought. Good.

She ladled up more mulligan and moved over to feed Ed. Chief growled at the Sioux smell of her and Ed said, "Be quiet, boy," and the dog let his growls die in his deep throat. But he kept his eyes on her. She squatted and fed Ed. She was huge and dark. The mulligan was good. There was plenty of venison in it, and this was well-cooked and had much nourishment. It had some vegetables in it, too: Ed remembered the halfbreed hoeing in the garden. The halfbreed had his freedom. When you took freedom of movement away from a man, you took away his life. Ed was getting to think in a confused manner. But with the grub in him, his headache was leaving. He was glad for that.

Chief whimpered, for he was still hungry.

"You can clean the pot, dog," Many Feathers said, "after this man gets more food. You want more, Jones?"

"Another plate."

But he did not eat all of this, and it went back into the pot. Chief licked it clean. She said, "Later on I bring water for you and the dog," and she stood up and gathered her utensils.

Mack Hanson snored.

"When will you bring water?" Ed Jones asked.

"Soon."

"I'm thirsty."

"I bring water."

She waddled away then and the door came open and closed, and again her moccasins moved down the tunnel to the outer door. Time moved on and Ed was almost asleep when she returned. She had a pail of water and a dipper. She gave them drinks and Chief lapped out of the pail. Ed kept working on her. So did Mack Hanson, but Mack was rather far-gone. Ed did most of the work. Impatience was raw in him. He had to get free. He knew he could not free his hands and his feet. The thongs were deep in his flesh and his hands were numb. He figured there were only three possible ways to get out of this dungeon. One was through Corporal Hank Williams and his assistant. But Williams would not know they were prisoners in this dungeon. Were Williams to come into Fort Green, he would be welcomed by The Bear and Big John Remington, and he could scout and look but never find them. Then there was the girl Nacie. But she was also a prisoner; she could not bring about their escape. The best and only outlet was this thick Sioux squaw. So he kept working on her, putting his words to her.

"You turn us loose, Many Feathers. We give you our silvers. You can take them and go. You be rich Sioux."

"I no leave Big John."

"Big John will kill you some day," Mack Hanson said. "Kill you so he can have the white squaw all alone."

"Maybe I kill her before they kill me?"

Neither Mack nor Ed relished this theory, but neither spoke. Each time she came, Ed Jones worked on her. He found that she had a great sense of pity and mercy. She even made friends with Chief, and Ed had figured this was an impossibility for a woman, either red or black or white. But she did make friends with the surly malemute. She fed him and petted him and stroked his ears and he licked her dark wrist. Ed figured she felt sorry for him and for Mack Hanson. Neither man could tend to his body habits properly and they became stinking hunks of humanity. Time dragged on and on, or so it seemed. There was no day but only night. Every once and a while The Bear and Big John Remington would come into the dungeon. Always The Bear carried the whip. Only one time was he allowed to use it. Then he lashed with savage intensity, and the bestial cruelty was on his wide and grisly face. Ed took the cutting blows without a word. But it took all his energy to keep from screaming. Mack Hanson screamed and then passed out; for this Ed had been glad. Then Big John had come in and stopped the rising and falling blacksnake with its cutting lash with beebee shot on the ends. He did it not because of mercy. The big man had no mercy; or, if he had any, he never showed it. Chief snarled and with difficulty Ed kept the malemute beside him. He did not want the dog to get killed. During the lashing, Big John Remington watched the malemute with steady and alert eyes. He was afraid of dogs. He was afraid of Chief.

Ed figured he had got lashed about twenty times. The lead-tips cut his buckskins to strips and his back was warm with blood. He swore to himself that he would some day kill The Bear. He would kill Big John, too, if he ever got a chance.

"Where are those furs, Jones?"

"You go to hell."

"Will you take us to your fox cache?"

"Not now." Ed cursed as only a wilderness man can curse. "You'll never see my silver fox pelt. I'll die in this damned hole first!"

And he meant it.

So Big John had made The Bear coil his bullwhip, which The Bear did with a scowl of dislike.

"They'll tell us after a few more days of this," the factor said. "Come along, man."

And he and his human dog left the dungeon.

And it was Many Feathers, the Sioux squaw who had herself felt the lash, who doctored Mack Hanson and Ed Jones. She smuggled in a lotion she had made of turpentine and bear grease. It burned like mad at first, making Ed's eyes have tears, but then the grease, when smoothed out, had a cool and good feeling.

"You feel better, now?"

"Better, Mother."

Both of them called her Mother. Both did not know why they did this. She went to Mack Hanson and rolled him on his belly. She spread the grease gingerly, working with her gnarled and big hands in a delicate manner. Ed watched her face. She kept it impassive. The lantern light made it look darker and the lantern light showed the wrinkles. Ed wondered at her age. She was not over thirty-five, he guessed. These red women worked hard and faced the wind and snow and the sun; their lives added years to their bodies. They worked and they did not complain. They asked only a handful of beans and some venision and rice bread. And they, like all humans, wanted love. She wanted her man. She wanted to belong to him. Ed kept harping on this chord. He kept reminding her of Nacie Malone.

"Do not talk to me like that, Jones."

"But it is true. You free us, and the silvers are yours."

"I do not want your furs. I do not want money. I want only peace, and I want my man."

"But what if he doesn't want you?"

"He will, when white woman is gone."

He had no answer to this.

"You turn us loose, and we take Nacie with us. We go out of Fort Green and never come back."

"You promise?"

Ed hated to lie, but he had to lie. "Yes, we take her . . . and you see us never again."

She shook her head. "You tell the big lie. Hate is strong in you. You can never forget the lash. Nor The Bear. Nor Big John."

"You have my word, Mother."

She looked at him. He wondered if pity was a part of the colour in her dark obsidian eyes.

"I go now."

She left and darkness claimed the pit.

"I don't know," Mack Hanson said.

Ed said, "Our only way out, Mark."

"My hands . . . my flesh. It must be rotting."

Ed said, "Maybe we should tell? Maybe we could get out then. I'll tell them, Mack."

"No."

"We can get out of here then. We can lead them to our furs."

"Then they will kill us. We might have an outside chance if we stay here. We'll have none if they have us lead them to our silvers. They'll get the furs and then shoot us down like sagehens."

Ed knew the man was right.

She came again and Ed said, "You are a good squaw, Many Feathers. I like you. Don't let them kill you. Watch behind your back all the time."

"I watch good. Don't worry about Many Feathers."

"Help the girl get away. You can do that. You can get her over the wall, and into the brush."

Many Feathers was sitting flat on the rock floor and she was petting Chief, who had his broad nose in her lap.

"She go over wall, then what happen to her?"

"She will get away," Ed said.

"You talk like fool. You are the fool. White man fool. She will go into timber. Even with rifle, she will die. She cannot take care of herself. No woman can do that in wilderness."

Ed had to admit to himself that she was right.

"Her father, he is dead. Her dog, he is dead. The Sioux or Cheyennes—they find her. Kill her or make her slave. Or else she get killed by grizzly or lion, in the brush."

"She'd have a chance," Mack Hanson pointed out.

"I cannot have her blood on my hands."

And that was that. Final. Complete. All finished. Her face showed this. She kept on petting Chief.

You could hear her hands rubbing the thick fur of the malemute. He licked her hands and his tail made movements on the rocks. She looked at Mack who lay slack and almost dead. The stench was bad in the room. She looked back at Ed. His eyes were lit with fever, his body was almost dead.

"I feel sorry," she said.

She climbed laboriously to her feet. She picked up her mulligan pail and her lantern and left them. The chain clanged; the bolt slid home. Her moccasins moved away and then the outer door went shut hard.

The darkness seemed even thicker.

The world was a million miles away.

Somewhere the Soda River danced over rocks and smashed its way over Liberty Falls, foamy and wild and free. And it came into the Green and made the Green wider, and it danced down toward the Colorado. Somewhere the giant trees grew and in them hopped a magpie—that gaudy and saucy black and white scavenger of the bird family—and you could hear his raucous and demanding voice. Men walked the streets and women smiled, and somewhere a baby cried in the night. But all that was a million miles away.

Who cared for two dying men, bound hand and foot?

Chief slept with his head close to Ed's thigh. He was content because his belly was full and he was close to his master. Ed was glad he had the dog. The dog was company.

Ed tried to think.

It was a hard job.

He figured that at least three days had gone by since he had been thrown into this dungeon. He based this conjecture on the number of times Many Feathers had fed them and the number of times he had had to fill nature's demands. He knew he could not last another three days. He figured that Mack would be lucky to last two more. But Mack, he knew, was a stubborn cuss.

Finally, he slept.

He did not wake of his own accord. He came out of a troubled slumber and he was aware of the voice of Mack Hanson. It held a high note of excitement, feverish and hopeful.

"Do I hear something', Pard?"

Ed come wide awake. He listened and beside him, Chief stirred and growled.

"Hush, Chief."

The dog kept on rumbling. Ed pushed him with his hip and finally silenced him. Then he listened.

"Behind us . . . in the wall."

His heart leaped. Had Hank Williams found out about their imprisonment, and was he digging toward them? Ed knew instantly this was not probable. He heard the sounds—they came from behind the rock wall. Was it a muskrat grawing in a newly-dug hole, along the bank of the Green?

"Sounds like a rat, Mack."

"I think . . . it's a pick, Ed."

Ed said, "God, man, don't feed us false hope!"

The sound, dim and remote in the earth, died as suddenly as it began. There was a long pause. Ed was aware of the wild and uncontrolled beating of his heart. Chief sat up and looked at the wall. He too had heard the sounds. He walked to the wall and smelled of it and whimpered.

"Don't bark, damn you," Ed snarled. "Come back here and lay down, Chief!"

The dog returned slowly to his old position. He wanted exercise and he wanted to run the cottontail rabbits out in the high brush. But he lay down and put his head on his front paws.

Ed and Mack listened for an hour or so. They offered suggestions. A muskrat? A beaver? Just a common house rat? Or had Nacie broken loose and was she digging toward them? Or was it the squaw?

"She would be afraid," Mack said.

Ed remembered the sympathy in her eyes. He had nothing to say on this angle. Then they heard a definite sound. It was the sharp end of a pick hitting the rock wall. That took the muskrats and beavers out of the picture and put a human into it. And hope was wild in both of them.

Mack now had a clearer voice. He wondered just where the dungeon was located in relation to the other buildings in Fort Green. He had a hunch the dungeon was close to the river. Ed had also had this assumption. The air was very damp and the rocks behind them very cold.

"But if it was the squaw, Ed, she'd smuggle on out the tunnel at night. She wouldn't be diggin' in to us."

"But I don't think it can be Williams."

"Might be Nacie. She might've got away."

"Many Feathers said a few hours ago that she was still locked in her cabin. I don't get this."

"Somebody is tappin' on a rock with a pick."

Ed breathed, "God be with us, and keep Big John and The Bear out of here. Pray, Mack, pray."

"I'm danged near prayed-out, but I'll try agsin. That pick is knockin' loose the mortar. A hunk fell outa the wall on me. There goes the rock—it's free. Watch out, Chief."

Chief jumped as the boulder fell to the floor of the dungeon. It rolled on the stone floor and then rocked to a stop. Neither could clearly recognize the human head that suddenly appeared in the wall. But both knew the voice when they heard it. For it was the voice of Many Feathers!

"I dig to you."

Ed thought, the miracle has been accomplished. But I still think it was because she had pity for us, and not because she wants our silvers. She must have really had a struggle with herself. Fear against pity, and pity had won.

Well, it went to show one thing—all humans, black or red or white or yellow, had a streak of pity and fair play in them. She was risking her life to free them.

"I have to get another boulder loose. I am so big, I cannot get through. I could not let you die."

Ed could only say, "Thank you, Mother."

The pick went to work again. It made loud sounds as it chipped out the strong mortar. Ed smelled water. The smell was coming through the shaft she had dug. He heard the lap of water. Their guess had been right. They were in a dungeon close to the east wall of Fort Green. Close to the river. She had gone out of the post and found a point in the river's bank and had dug in. The distance could not be very far. Otherwise they could not have heard the water.

"How far did you dig, Mother?"

"Oh, ten feets."

Ed said, "Is it night or day?"

"Night."

"About what time?"

"After midnight."

"Then The Bear and Big John—they are asleep?"

"They sleep."

"Good," Mack Hanson said.

She dug some more and none of them spoke. Then she said, "Rock he fall now, so watch out," and the second rock tumbled to the floor. It rolled over on Ed's legs, but he squirmed and got the boulder off them. The rock had scratched his legs. But what was another sore spot?

"I come in now."

They saw her huge bulk squirm through the hole. She came in headfirst and her buckskin dress slid up and showed her wide behind. Then she was on her feet, pulling down her dress.

"I got a knife."

"Cut Mack loose first," Ed said.

Chief came up to her. He wagged his tail and fawned on her. Had Ed a tail, he would have wagged it too. The world had suddenly become a good place. And an hour before, it had been a hell-hole.

The rawhide was iron tough. Although her knife was sharp it had a hard time severing the strands. Also she had to be careful not to cut the man's flesh. She finally got the trapper's wrists free. Ed listened and prayed that The Bear and Big John Remington were deep in the arms of Morpheus. She seemed to work with a great and exasperating slowness; he knew, though, she was working as fast as she could. She finally turned to him.

"Now I cut you loose, Jones."

"Hurry, Mother."

He felt her long-bladed skinning-knife sever the rawhide. She nicked his wrist, but he said nothing; the wound was on the outside, and not close to the artery. It bled. His hands were free. He tried to move his arms. He got them around with difficulty. He wanted to put his tongue to the cut place. He finally got his elbows to bend.

Mack Hanson was trying to stand up. He crept up the wall, but his hands were numb; his knees were water. He toppled down and tried again; again he fell. Now Ed's legs were free.

I wonder if I can stand.

He braced himself against the rock wall, grasping onto the rough boulders. This way he pulled himself upright. His knees held, then gave way; he toppled down over Chief.

"I help you, Jones."

His head swam. Eddies of pain washed through his legs, his arms, his belly. He was aware of Many Feather's wide shoulder boosting him upright. Between her and the wall, he managed to find his feet. Mack Hanson had fallen again. His voice was thin as he said, "I can't walk."

"We'll drag you out," Ed said.

"God, Ed, we're free!"

The awe of it was in his voice. It gave his voice a hollow sound. Now Mack asked, "Why do you do this, Mother?"

"You promise to take white woman away."

Ed said, "Is that the reason?"

She said nothing for a moment. "Yes, that is it. Now into the tunnel. Get moving."

Ed said, "Big John will whip you."

"He will not know I dug the tunnel. I will pull lots of dirt into the dungeon, or what you call it. He will think you two got loose and dug out, with the dirt in this room."

"You bring us our side-arms or long guns?" Ed asked.

"No."

"Why not?"

"I do that, Big John he miss them. He know then somebody else help you get out of cave."

"Logic," Mack Hanson said. "You got to help me, Ed."

"I can walk purty good now," Ed said.

Chief was standing with his forelegs and head in the hole. Ed pushed the dog into the small channel. The squaw had dug hard and fast, moving the dirt back and throwing it into the river. But this was a loose sand more than a compact soil. River sand, washed in for centuries. Ed and Many Feathers got Mack Hanson's head into the pit. Chief seemed to understand this. He got his fangs in Hanson's buckskins, back of his neck, and he pulled. They got the man into the hole. Chief backed up, legs digging; he pulled. Ed Jones pushed the limp man. Toward the end, Mack got on his hands and knees; he crawled of his own accord. The tunnel was not long but it seemed endless. Soon Chief was backing out into the night. They were all three—the dog and the two trappers—then on the bank of the Green. Overhead the stars were brilliant bits of polished diamond.

"They look good," Mack Hanson croaked. "Where is

the squaw, Ed?"

"She stayed back in the tunnel. She loosened another rock and was draggin' dirt down to make it look like we left the dirt at that end. No dirt here. She's carried it back in a bucket er sumpthin' an' tossed it in the river, I reckon."

Behind them a few feet was the long stockade that surrounded Fort Green. Ed sent a nervous glance at the cupola beside the gate. But it was wrapped in night, and he could not see it. The smell of the river was wet and strong. They could hear the river, too—the lap of water on the bank. It sounded but a few feet away. Under them the ground was wet. River foliage—cat-tails, moss—had its smells. The world was good.

"Sure wish we had our weapons," Mack Hanson said.

"I got her long knife."

"Help me to that log over there? I wanna soak my feet in water. My hands—they almost feel like they belong to me now. A man comes back fast, eh, Ed?"

"Don't talk so loud."

"Didn't know I was talkin' loud. I was close to the edge back yonder. Thank God for Many Feathers."

"We still got to get the girl out of the fort. We promised her that. How does the water feel on your feet?"

"Cold as billy hell. Bringin' blood down to them, though. Lord alive, how they hurt."

Ed said. "That's a good sign. Blood is flowin' through your flesh. I feel all right now, except for the cuts on my wrists and ankles. Chief, dang you, lay down, or I'll crown you."

They sat there for about twenty minutes. They did little talking. Chief took a long drink in the Green, his tongue noisy and splashing. Both of them soaked their feet, not taking off their moccasins.

"Seems to me like I hear her belly-slidin' through the tunnel," Mack Hanson whispered.

Soon the thick squaw was with them. She brushed dirt from the front of her buckskins.

By this time Ed and Mack had stripped to their hides and washed their buckskins in the Green. They were wet and chilly, for the night was cold. But neither paid much attention to the chillness of the mountain air. Their clothing hung on them, but it at least was now clean. Ed said jokingly that he felt almost like he was still alive.

"Now I get the girl," Many Feathers said.

"How do you aim to get her from behin' the stockade?" asked. "Smuggle her out the gate or boost her over the logs?"

"Not one of those. I get her and take her into dungeon, and then she go out tunnel to the river."

"Good idea," Ed said.

"But how you gonna get back into the fort?" Mack Hanson asked. "Climb over the wall?"

She laughed quietly. "No, I go back down tunnel. Before I start to dig, I unlock the two doors to the pit. Now I go up tunnel and out doors and come out in fort."

"Can you get Nacie outa that cabin?" Ed asked. "Ain't Big John got a guard posted over her cabin?"

"Not at night. Only guard in south look-out. But she locked in. Windows are with bars across them."

"How do you intend to get her out?" Ed asked.

"I saw bars, maybe. Have the saw in my kitchen. Saws iron. I saw bones with it."

Ed glanced at the sky. Dawn was not too far away. "Maybe you'd better git movin'," he said.

"Send her back with some firin' irons an' side pistols, if you can," said Mack Hanson.

"I might not be able to get her out of cabin."

Ed said, "We'll wait, and if she doesn't come inside a hour or so, we head out into the brush and leave her with you."

He did not, of course, mean this. He said it only as a spur to drive her to greater effots. He knew she wanted one thing in the world: that was to get rid of her competition, one Nacie Malone. She had freed them so they could take Nacie with them.

"Go now," she said.

She got on her hands and knees and crawled into the tunnel. Chief growled at her sudden disappearance. Mack Hanson lay with his back against some buckbrush that the flood had washed in. The smell of dead fish, trapped and dead in high water pools, was strong for a moment for the wind had shifted. Then the wind changed directions again and the rotten odour left them.

"I'm almost all in," Mack said slowly.

Ed said, "You take it easy, Mack. I'm goin' scout down the river a little. Jes' scout aroun'."

"What fer?"

"Jes' give the lay of the land a look."

"I'll wait here, but don't get into no trouble."

"I'll be back in a little while. Not more then ten minutes. I'm gonna work downstream toward the gate, and look around a little. Might not be a guard in that stockade, at that."

"Don't draw his fire, if he is there."

"I won't."

This was mating time and a mockingbird made his noises, despite the fact it was night. He was singing to his mate who was nesting in the diamond willows. The river chuckled and murmured.

Ed made Chief stay with Mack Hanson. He did not want the dog along because he might be seen from the turret and thereby give away their plan. The dog lay down beside Mack Hanson, who was lying in the cat-tails. Ed moved downstream. He wondered where Corporal Hank Williams was. Was the policeman scouting Fort Green? He thought of his furs. They were still in the fort. All except the silver-fox pelt, cached there along the edge of the river. The silver-fox pelt that had indirectly saved his life.

Anger was in the lanky trapper. But it was not a flaring anger; rather, it was old and cold and, because of its age, burned with a steady flame, not with a jetting flare. He decided he would get his furs back. He decided he would make The Bear and Big John Remington pay for each lash of the blacksnake and for each hour they had had him tied in the dungeon. He was certain of that. He made a vow that he would leave Fort Green only after he had taken his revenge on its owner and The Bear. He realized that to bring this about he and Mack Hanson had to have weapons. Weapons and ball and powder or cartridges. They had only a knife between them.

So, thinking these thoughts, Ed Jones moved along the river, keeping hidden under the cover of the night and the spread of the giant cottonwood trees. The cottonwoods were dropping their down, and in some places the whiteness of the cotton gave the ground a whiteness, almost the colour of snow. He came out of the timber and came to a dock built out into the Green. He was surprised to see such a big dock. It seemed made of heavy logs laid on other logs which had been driven into the river. It extended about twenty feet into the water. And he was also surprised to see a river boat moored to the end of the dock, anchored to a cottonwood pillar.

It was about fifty feet long, this river boat; as big as the ones they ran on the Big Muddy between St Louis and Fort Benton, up in Montana Territory. It loafed in the water, moving slightly to the current; it was dark and sombre and low to the river.

The size of the boat rather surprised him. He had not thought a boat this big could navigate the Green. Evidently it drew little water for in some places the Green was rather shallow. Perhaps it could come this far north only during the flood season. It was big enough to carry lots of supplies into this wilderness outpost. Of course, its full cargo had probably not all been consigned for Big John Remington's fort. It had undoubtedly dropped cargo at other trading posts up the Colorado and the Green.

There were no lights in the compartments. Evidently the crew was asleep. Ed looked at the gate of the fort. It was thick and rigid and a man couldn't go through it or under it or over it, he reasoned. He could not see a guard in the cupola. But darkness was still thick. He had accomplished nothing by his scouting trek; he had only limbered stiff muscles. So he went back to where his partner lay with Chief in the cat-tails.

He told Mack about the river boat.

"Big one, eh?"

"Sure is. Big as them what tie-in at Benton."

"Come up the Colorado and then into the Green. Prob'ly come out of Fort Yuma with supplies that have been freighted overland from San Diego, I reckon. End of its trip, here at Green."

"Wish thet squaw would come in with Nacie," Ed said.

"Be daylight come a hour or so."

"We'll wait about thirty minutes or so, and then if they ain't here I'll go into the tunnel."

"What if the doors are bolted from the outside?"

"I doubt if they are. Many Feathers might have bolted them; she might not have. I got to take that chance."

"I'll go with you."

Ed shook his head. "You sure won't," he said stoutly.

He had to talk his partner out of it. Mack Hanson was very weak; weaker than he himself really realized. He had a difficult time impressing this fact on Mack. There was danger ahead in Fort Green. It would take a man who was nimble, one who could walk and move fast, to get Nacie Malone and rifles and cartridges. It was not the job of a

245

cripple.

"Reckon . . . you're right, Ed."

"I know I'm right, Mack. Much as I'd cotton to have you side me, your job is stayin' here. Chief will stay with you. A man can't slink around from cabin to cabin, with a dog trailin' him."

Mack Hanson's scrawny hand tightened in the thick fur around the malemute's neck. "You're dead right, Pard. My hands are gettin' to move right good. Day or so, an' I'll be myself again. But if you don't come back, I'm takin' Fort Green apart log by log—even if I have to do it with my bare hands!"

"I'll be back, Mack."

"You'd best get back."

Ed spoke in a serious vein. "But if I don't make it, don't fool around alone. You and Chief head out pronto. Wait a hour for me and then if I don't show up, you know they recaptured me or killed me. Head out with Chief and report to Corporal Hank. He should be around somewhere. Maybe he is in the fort right now. He should have another lawman with him. But if I don't come back, make for the brush. That's the deal, Mack."

"Wish to hell I could go with you, Ed."

"You're better off here."

"You'd best head into the tunnel. Dawn will soon be here. What if you can't get into the fort through the tunnel?"

"Jes' won't get in it. We'll have to let the girl go until Williams comes in, if he ain't in this country by now. Take to the brush, keep away from The Bear and Big John, and report to Williams."

"I'll do that, Ed. But be danged sure you come back."

"So long, Mack."

Then Ed Jones was on his hands and knees going into the tunnel. He thought, Hell, I'm a human angleworm, and this made him smile. He had some of his old strength

246

back; not all of it, though. But Many Feathers had fed him and Mack rather well, and to the squaw they owed much. They had had a bit of luck in one way. Had not Nacie been a prisoner at Fort Green, he and Mack would never have been able to talk Many Feathers into turning them loose. Such was the hand of Fate and its wobbly writing.

He came to the dungeon and its fetid stink. It was warmer here in the earth; the air along the Green had been damp and cold. His buckskins were drying. The big test was ahead. Had Many Feathers locked the dungeon door behind her?

He crossed the dungeon and found the door. He put his weight against it; it held. It had not a bit of give. It was a heavy door. She had locked it, behind her. Now he could not get to Nacie. Angrily, he rammed a skinny shoulder against the panel. This time it grudgingly gave. Then he realised he was trying to push outward on it and the door opened inward. He was in a somewhat confused state of mind, he realized. He should have known that the door did not swing out. He had tried to open it the wrong direction. Now he pulled and it came open and the shaft was ahead, dark and ominous.

He had never been in this shaft. Oh, yes, he had been there—but that had been when they had toted him into the dungeon, knocked cold as a beaver hammered over the head by a club.

He felt his way along the rock wall. He had heard another door open when he and Mack had been in the dungeon. He came to this. He got a surprise. To open this door he had to push upward, for the door was in the floor of a cabin. This was a heavy door and hard to open, but finally he stood in the cabin.

The cabin was about twenty by twenty. It had two high and dirty windows, covered by cobwebs. Evidently it was used for storage for his fingers found a chain of traps hanging from the wall. It had some boxes and other things in it. But he had no matches, so he did not know if it also held a rifle or two. And he did not take time to find out, much as he needed a weapon for protection.

He listened for a moment, poised in the darkness. From somewhere came the sound of men's voices, and then there was a sudden loud laugh. It had a certain drunken quality to it, he thought. He found the door and moved outside and stood for a moment with his back against the log wall. He gave the compound a long and serious scrutiny. From the trading post proper came the blaze of whale-oil lights. The post was wide awake. He heard the voices again and he decided they came from the dining room. He figured that the crew of the river boat was celebrating with Big John Remington and The Bear.

He went toward Many Feathers' kitchen. He came into the back yard and to the back door. A glance through the corner of the window told him she was at the stove and she was alone. Slowly he opened the door. She was cooking something, and the smell of elk steaks was good in the air. She was very busy. But she saw the door opening and she hurried over, casting an anxious glance at the door leading to the dining room.

"I no get away. When we in tunnel, river boat come. Crew in there with them, all getting drunk."

"Where is the girl?"

"She in building. Down the hall, she is. Back of where Big John and men drink. She locked in. Crowbar at end of building. I put it there, when I want to get her out—but the crew come, and I have to cook."

"I'll get her out of here," Ed said.

The squaw swore in Sioux. "Take the damned heifer out of here. If you don't I kill her."

"I need a rifle."

"No have none. No small gun, either. Get to hell out of here. They come from dinin' room—see me talk to you—

248

you get killed and The Bear use his whip. I lock the doors behind you, so it looks like you escaped. I have to do that, or they beat me."

"Be danged sure we're in the tunnel afore you lock them, woman. I don't want to get locked into this hell-hole."

"I watch you through window."

Ed had no more words with her. Every moment he spent in this doorway was a moment of danger. He went along the wall and found the crowbar. It leaned against the log wall. It was made of steel and was about three feet long and it had a sharp end, the end being shaped like the head of a small axe. He juggled it and it was heavy in his grip. He went on further down the building, the sounds retreating behind him. He was in an aisle-like area between the high stockade and the building. He had the feeling of being trapped. It was not a comfortable feeling. He came to the door and he knocked on it. There was no light in the room. He thought he had gotten the wrong door, for there were three others, for he got no response to four knocks. He worried. Time was running out. Then he heard somebody stirring and he heard Nacie's voice.

"Who—who is there?"

"Me, the trapper. Ed Jones."

"I can't open the door . . . It is chained, from outside."

"I know that. I have a crowbar. I'm goin' twist the chain off. You get ready to go—You got a weapon?"

"Why, no. That is a foolish question."

"I knew it, but I wanted to know for sure. We got to get some side-arms, woman. Dress, if you ain't already dressed."

"I'm dressing . . . now."

Ed's groping fingers found the chain. It was a small chain and it ran through a hole in the heavy door and was bolted outside to a eye-beam in the wall. Ed got the crowbar between the chain and the door. He laid back on the bar. The chain held and the door creaked. He was wet with sweat and he was trembling. His week knees and ankles threatened to drop him. His forearms throbbed and his wrists had little strength. He could not open the door in this manner. He did not possess enough strength. He would have to get the chain around the crowbar, and twist down on it, hoping to tear it out of the door or the eye-hook.

"I'm dressed. How did you get out?"

"Can't talk, now."

From the dining room came the roar of sudden laughter. Big John and The Bear and the packet-men were whooping it up. This was good for their noise covered what sounds he made as he juggled the chain and the crowbar. Finally he got the purchase he wanted. He pulled down on the free end of the bar. For a moment, it was nip and tuck; then, the chain ripped loose from the wall. He almost fell down. But he maintained his balance with difficulty. The crowbar clattered to the rock floor. It made a loud noise. The door went inward, suddenly released. He leaned against the wall, gasping for breath. Had they heard the clatter of steel on stone?

Suddenly Nacie was beside him. "You dropped—the crowbar."

"Do you think—they heard it?"

From the dining room came another roar of masculine laughter. That was their answer. His hand went up and touched her cheek.

"The cut—left by the whip—?"

"Almost healed."

"Good."

"We got to get out of here, Jones." Her hand was in his—soft and feminine. "But how can we? Climb the wall?"

"I have a way. But where can we get a rifle?"

"I don't know."

Her hand remained in his. They moved forward. Ed did not know where he could get a rifle or short-gun. They were at the edge of the building when the door of the trading post opened and a man stumbled into the night. He was a huge man and he carried a coiled bull-whip. He was about fifty feet away. He was heading across the compound toward the house that had the tunnel under it. Ed had pulled Nacie back into the darkness of the log building. His heart was in his throat. Evidently The Bear was going to pay a visit to the dungeon. Whiskey and hard drink had inflamed him and he was going on his own hook to use his bullwhip? But he did not go into the tunnel. He went instead into the small cabin next to the gate, and disappeared.

Ed realized he did not have time to get a rifle or pistol. He had to get himself and this girl out of Fort Green. Corporal Hank Williams and his man would have rifles. The main thing to do was get Nacie away from the grip of The Bear and Big John Remington.

"Come on, girl. Run like hell, and follow me."

"Lead the way, Ed."

He ran as fast as he could across the clearing toward the cabin. Behind him the girl was a scampering doe fleeing for safety. Any moment he expected to feel a bullet hit him in the back, to hear her cry out above the roar of a rifle. The distance seemed endless. It seemed miles and miles and miles across that darkened strip of moccasin-pounded dust. His legs were wak. She caught him and ran abreast of him. He hoped The Bear would not leave the cabin. Then they were in the cabin that hid the tunnel. And the door was closed behind him. He was breathing like a wind-broken moose. She was not breathing that hard.

"Where do—we—go now?"

"Tunnel."

"Where?"

"Give me your hand."

Soon they were in the shaft leading to the dungeon. They came to the door opening onto the pit. Ed closed this behind them. He found the tunnel that Many Feathers had dug. He stumbled over the heap of earth. His groping hands, flailing in the dark, found the opening of the tunnel.

"Here, Nacie."

"What—"

He got his skinny hands around her thin waist. He boosted her into the tunnel. "Just crawl and crawl, and you come out by the river."

"Yes."

He was climbing into the tunnel when he heard the bolt snap on the door. Many Feathers had followed them and she was locking the door. He was glad for that. Now The Bear and Big John would think that he and Mack had escaped of their own accord. They would wonder how the girl had made her escape. Maybe they would blame it on Many Feathers. Yes, they would. No matter which way he viewed the situation, the squaw would lose. Which was tough, but there was nothing he could do about it.

Now he was following Nacie down the tunnel. Again, it seemed endless, but there was no definite need for haste. Then the girl was standing up right, and Mack Hanson was there, and so was Chief. Chief jumped on Ed and almost knocked him down.

"Chief, for God's sake, dog—go easy on an old man."

Nacie was weeping. She sat on the river bank and held her head in her hands. She was exhausted and she was weak and she was free. The combination of these things had suddenly hit her and she wept in silence. Neither man said anything to her; there was nothing to say.

"You were gone for ages," Mack Hanson's thin voice said. "I was scared stiff. I almost climbed back into that tunnel."

"I worked as fast as I could. They're havin' a drunken brawl. The ship crew is with them. The squaw—they made her work—they watched her—She couldn't come back."

"You never got no rifles?"

"Never had time. The Bear was on the prowl. Bullwhip and all. He headed for the out-house, and I thought he was aimin' to pay us a visit. Scared me stiff, Mack."

"Sure wish we had some weapons."

"If wishes were horses, all beggars would ride. Well, we got our freedom. We got a knife. We ain't got no supplies, but we're free."

"What do we do next, Ed?"

"Get t'hell away from Fort Green. Head for the thick brush and make a camp, an' get our strength back. Then we contact Hank Williams, and we blow Fort Green all to hell!"

Nacie suddenly sprang to her feet. "And I'll be with you to the end!" she cried through her tears.

"Good girl," Ed Jones said.

They headed for the mountain back of Fort Green. Mack Hanson set the lead pace and behind him trotted Nacie and then came Ed Jones and Chief. And it was the girl who first spoke, and then her words came between pants.

"My father, Mack? Are you sure he is dead?"

"I think so, Nacie girl."

"They took him from me," the girl said. "But I do not know for sure—if they killed him. They killed my dog—my malemute—" Her voice held an edge put there by hysteria. "But maybe they never killed—my father—"

"I only know what I heard," Mack Hanson said over his shoulder.

Dawn was coming swiftly to Wyoming. Dawn was bright on the mountains now, reflecting from the glistening glaciers and the eternal snow. Dawn was on the lodgepole pine and the fir and cedar. The day would soon be clear. Ed pulled great gulps of cold air into his lungs. The dungeon had stunk and the air had been rotten.

"What did you hear?" Nacie asked.

"The Bear and Big John, talking when they made me dance the whip dance. They said they weighted his body with rocks and wrapped it in a buffaler hide and threw it into the river."

"They said that?"

"I heard them, Woman."

"I could cut their throats," she said. "I could kill both of them and never feel sorry about it. They are murderers and killers."

"They'll pay," Ed Jones said.

They were on the bank of the Soda. They would wade through the water along the edges of the river. This way they were throwing off any possible trackers. Big John and The Bear were, above all, wilderness men; therefore they were good at trailing. Logic told them this. The girl shuddered at the cold water. Ed wondered if it was caused by the coldness of the glacial stream or the fact its waters held the body of her father.

"Rest time," Ed said.

Mack Hanson said, "We cain't afford to take five, Ed. We got to get miles atween us an' them hellions. They'll find us gone soon, an' all hell will bust loose at the fort."

"We rest," Ed said.

Nacie sat on a boulder. Mack Hanson sank to the ground and lay on his back. He gazed at the greying sky.

"Never figgered I'd see dawn again. Never figgered I'd see the sun set again. Ed Jones, I'm deep in your favour."

"A friend and a friend," Ed said.

Mack Hanson rolled over in the tall and green beargrass. He clung to the grass, knotting it in his hands. He smelled of the damp clean earth. Then he started to sob.

254

He lay on his back, face buried in the grass, and he sobbed. Nacie looked at Ed. She had sympathy in her eyes. She had paced the floor and she had not slept and she had waited for either The Bear or Big John to lumber in and destroy her. But this had not happened because of the jealousy of another woman. A waddling, huge Sioux squaw. To Many Feathers she owed much. More than she ever had owed anybody, man or woman. And Ed owed Many Feathers, too. And so did Mack Hanson. Jealousy was in this case a good force, not an evil thing. He wondered how the squaw would fare. Big John could not accuse her of helping him and Mack Hanson escape. That escape would look as though it were engineered not by the squaw but by themselves. But she would probably have to pay for the freedom of Nacie. For they would swear she had broken the chain and spirited the girl out of Fort Green.

Mack Hanson rolled on his side and said, "Bawlin' like a Cheyenne papoose, I was, and me a grown man."

Nacie said, "It did you good."

Ed said nothing. The river made its endless talk as it sucked against the bank and its waves lapped and rolled. He could see the turret at Fort green. He could hardly see it above the high diamond willows and the timber. He remembered the big river boat tied to the dock. The crew and Big John and The Bear had been celebrating. Celebrating what? Had the packet come up the Green to deliver necessary supplies to Big John? Rifles and ball and powder and cartridges to trade to the trappers for their plews? Yes, and bacon and other grub. Or had it carried some other cargo up the Green to the nefarious fort? Big John had offered to cut him into his game. And what was that game?

Ed played with this thought and got nowhere. The dawn was fastly changing to daylight. The snow did not glisten now—it shone with steady cold whiteness on the high peaks. The air was slowly losing its high-altitude chill. And it was time they pushed on again. Hell might be breaking loose back at Fort Green. Surely by this time Big John had missed Nacie.

"Gotta move on, people."

Mack Hanson got to his feet slowly. "I'll lead the way," he said. He started out at a dog-trot. He had gone about a mile when without warning he fell, landing on his face. He was winded and sick and weak. The back of his buckskin jacket was cut to ribbons. Under it you could see the proud and festering flesh. The terrible blacksnake whip of The Bear had done its job well. The lash, shot-laden, had cut and cut.

"I'm all . . . in . . ."

"Help me, Nacie?" Ed asked.

Of the three, she had the most strength. She had been fed better and had not been tied hand and foot. She got on one side and with Ed on the other they got Mack Hanson back on his wobbly knees.

"Leave me behind, people."

Ed said, "We're in this one for all and all for one. Come on, Mack."

"Put your weight on me," Nacie said.

"Leave me behind."

But they did not leave the whip-lashed trapper behind. To do so would have been his death at the bullwhip of The Bear, for they were not far from Fort Green. The seriousness of their predicament caused sudden alarm in Ed Jones. The fact they were unarmed was an alarming fact in itself. He helped his partner. Sympathy for the wounded and spent man was strong in him. He silently damned the squaw that had made them split the fall before. But then he realized this thought was in itself foolish. What had happened had happened. And it had been his fault and the fault of Mack Hanson as much as that of the pretty little squaw. So he pushed this forever from his feverish mind.

He and Nacie half-carried Mack Hanson for about a mile and then suddenly a new strength seemed to flow into the wasted and hacked body, for Mack pushed them to one side.

"I feel stronger, now."

"Mostly your nerves," Ed said.

He himself was winded. The girl was the stronger. Chief walked and watched, making side scurries as they travelled. He was looking for a young cottontail rabbit for dinner. He came back with one between his teeth. The rabbit was limp and dead and wet from his jaws. Ed hated to do it but he took the rabbit away from the big malemute who growled and snarled at him.

"Food," he said. He grinned. "Food."

"He might catch another one or two," Nacie said. "They're thick this time of the year."

"But he might be wise and not take it back to us," Ed Jones said. "He might have learned his lesson."

This assumption proved correct. Chief had decided not to waste time and energy for two-legged creatures when his own belly was flat and his flanks drawn. He made a few more side trips. He came back from the fourth with bloody jowls. He had caught another rabbit but he had not brought it back to be robbed of it. He had torn it apart and eaten it where he had caught it.

The day was clear now. Ed figured they had gone about five miles from Fort Green. They were at the base of the mountain. They were climbing steadily. They came to a park that had kinikinick and beargrass. Wild lilies and sweetpeas were little stars in the grass, peeping up at them. The beauty of the mountain was lost on Ed Jones. For inside of him was a great sense of urgency and of speed. But he had to throttle this.

A jackrabbit bounded out from under the shadow of a boulder. Chief did not chase him. He knew he could never run-down the long legged Rocky Mountain jack-rabbit. Being a smart dog, he knew his limitations. When he had been a year or so old, he would have chased the jack; but he was wiser and older now. So he merely stopped and looked at him. A white-tailed buck leaped out of the brush, stuck up his flag, and on stiff legs bounded out of sight. Had Ed had a Winchester, one shot would have sent that deer crumpling to the forest floor. But he would not have dared fire the rifle for it might have been heard back in Fort Green. They pushed slowly on for another hour or so. The terrain lifted and changed as they climbed the toe of the mountain. The land spread out below them. There were thousands of miles of native timber and the creeks leaped down from the snow and the glaciers. Despite his physical condition, Ed Jones saw the beauty in this tumbling endless land. For centuries it had known only the moccasins of the redskin. Now it was being violated by the axes and the guns of the white man. Small wonder that the Sioux rode the Black Hills with rifles across their horses' withers. Small wonder that the Blackfoot had unsheathed his long war-spear and rode with it loose in his grip, ready for the whites.

Ed wondered if this wilderness area held Corporal Hank Williams and his fellow lawman. He could see no trace of smoke across the green expanse. He could see the Soda, roaring to its meeting with the Green, and the fort lay below them—complete with stockade and buildings. It looked like a checkerboard with some of the checkers in place. Because of the distance he could not see men move across the compound. Nor could he hear the din and noise caused by the discovery that the two trappers had escaped the dungeon and that the white woman had somehow made her get-away, also.

"When we get a little higher on the slope, we dine off this cottontail," Ed cheered them up.

"I can't go much further, Ed," Mack said.

"Let's make camp for a while," Nacie said, "and rest up a little. Get some good food in Mack, and he'll be ready soon."

"Over yonder," Ed said, "in them big boulders."

Their buckskins had dried. Because of their physical movements, the buckskins had dried in a pliable state. Had they been washed and hung up to dry they would have come down stiff and unyielding. They reached the boulders and Nacie held the band together, for courage was in her small body. She smiled and worked with Mack, her arm around him, with his weight sagging sometimes against her small body. But they gained the protection of the boulders. Here the Cheyenne had made his camp many times across the millions of years. The inner side of a boulder was dark with soot where they had built their fires. Mack Hanson went down in a limp heap, and after a while dragged his broken body to a boulder to sit with it against his back. And his smile was small and tired.

"Wish I had a slug of hard good ol' forty-rod, Ed."

"It would kill us both," Ed joked.

Nacie said, "I have a few matches. I saved them for an emergency. Ed, you scoop out some water, and I'll get some twigs. Don't know if I can get any dry ones, though."

"Go in the brush and pick some dead limbs off the willows. The air should have dried them by now, seein' they're not close to the damp ground."

"Good idea, Ed."

She was not gone long. But during that time Ed Jones had dug with his hands a small channel, and into this the snow water was seeping. When the little pool had become filled, Mack Hanson lay on his belly and drank. Ed thought, Will he ever stop drinking? but finally his partner sat upright and wiped his beard.

"Feel better now."

"Better'n forty rod," Ed joked.

He skinned the cottontail and gutted him and threw Chief the head. Chief got it between his forelegs and started to gnaw. His teeth made sharp sounds as they knifed through the bony skull. Nacie knew how to build a camp fire. She used only one match. Soon she had a small fire burning in the lee of the boulder. It made little if any smoke. She had pulled dried dead branches off the willows. Soon she and Ed were broiling the rabbit. She turned her meat slowly and let the heat turn it brown. Chief smelled the aroma and whined. But he got not a bit of the meat. He got the bones and they were small and of little account. He cracked them and gulped them.

Ed had not realized he was so hungry. His belly heaved and flattened against his backbone. His back was sore where the lash and ripped him. He had taken off his coat and sat with his back bare to the sun for the sun would heal his wounds. He had slowly and laboriously taken the buckskin jacket off his partner. The terrible rawness of Mack Hanson's broad back struck him and made in him even a great hatred. But this hatred would have to be controlled until Corporal Hank Williams was found. For the policeman would have arms. And it took firearms and guts and raw red fire to defeat Fort Green, he knew. You couldn't whip The Bear and Big John Remington with only a single long-bladed knife.

Nacie did not eat the piece of flesh she had cooked. She took it over to Mack Hanson.

"For you, Mack."

"But you're hungry. You need it, woman."

She shook her head. Her smile was ironical. "I got fed well. I was the prize heifer waiting for the big bull, so they fed me good. You boys never got fried prairie chicken one day and grouse the next."

"You eat it, Nacie."

"Don't be a damned polite fool!" She spoke angrily

but Mack did not see the covert wink she sent Ed Jones. "You eat this or I'll put you on your back and jam it bones and all down your gullet!"

"She means it," Mack said, and took the meat and smiled. He ate slowly. "Got to get all the good and all the strength out of it, people."

She took the forepart of the rabbit and adjusted it on the red willow stick and started the job all over again. She sat crosslegged and she looked like a pretty Blackfoot squaw. One of those light-skinned Blackfeet, Ed thought. She was all woman. Despite her ability to fight and to rough-it in the wilderness, she still clung to a woman's role. This pleased Ed. Ed also ate slowly. He wondered how they would get more grub. They would have to build grass snares and catch more rabbits. Or else a grouse or sagehen or a prairie chicken. But that would come later.

The main thing to do now was rest.

"I saw some blackberries back yonder," Nacie said, tossing the bones to Chief. "I'll pick some while you boys rest."

"Sure be nice if one of us had a hat," Ed said, "for then you could put the berries in it."

"I'll make a basket out of my jacket."

"Don't stray too far or get lost."

She looked at him and smiled. He liked the way her eyes made wrinkles on each corner.

"Buckskin Man, Nacie was raised in the brush. Nacie was raised runnin' a trap line, and Nacie can't get lost."

Ed joked, "But Nacie maybe could be led astray?"

"With the right man, she could."

Ed said, "I've been put in my place. A round peg has been put in a square hole. Take it easy, woman."

"You goin' with me, Chief?"

But Chief would not go. He would not leave Ed. So she went into the brush alone.

Mack said, "She's all woman, Ed."

"And then some."

"She'd keep a man's cabin clean and his bed warm."

"And she'd come fresh every nine months, too."

Mack had his head on his chest. "Be nice to have kids runnin' around a man's cabin. Argue with them and their mother. I'm goin' lay on my back and let this sun hit me. Wonder if they can find us?"

Ed shook his head. He was terribly sleepy. "We ran through water a lot. They might have dogs at Green, but I heard none make any barkin'. An' even if they has dogs, the water will throw them off. They got nine million acres of timber and water and boulders to look behind."

But Mack Hanson had no answer. He slept with his back to the warming sun. Ed remained awake a while longer. Then suddenly he was asleep, too. Both slept the slumber of two men completely and finally exhausted. Mack Hanson woke up once and he was screaming. Nacie was in camp and she put her hands over his mouth and watched him struggle from sheer terror to complete consciousness. When sanity returned to his bloodshot eyes she let her hands leave his bearded mouth. And her smile was that of a mother.

"You were screamin'," she explained quietly.

Mack glanced at Ed, who was still asleep. "The Bear," he said, and his body was broken and limp as was his voice. "The Bear . . . and his bullwhip."

She touched the scab on her cheek. "I felt it, too."

"The dirty devils."

He was soon asleep again. She sat there and had her thoughts. She had lost her father and her dog. The world had moved swiftly the last few days. She looked at the scarred and swollen back of Ed Jones. Her eyes were thoughtful. She looked at the whip lashes on the naked back of Mack Hanson. She was alone in the world. Her mother had died years before of smallpox over on the

Yellowstone in Montana Territory. She did not feel too much regret at being alone. She had been reared in the trapping country. But she did feel one definite thing: And that was a desire for revenge—to revenge the death of her father and the death of her malemute. And the odd thing was that she was more desirous of avenging the death of her dog than the passing and murder of her father. She analyzed this emotion. It was based on one thing; Her father had never been too kind or good to her. Before the death of her mother, it had been different. But when the smallpox had come sweeping across the plains, moving from Indian camp to camp, it had taken her mother. And from that day on her father had been a changed man. He had pulled back even deeper into himself. He had in his way only tolerated her. Now he was gone and she felt no keen regret. He had a number of times threatened to kill himself. Now he was part of the river—the eternal ever-flowing river. She put her head down, but she did not weep. She was sitting there with her back against the boulder and her head down when Ed Jones awakened. He sat up and looked at her. He did not speak for he thought she was asleep. Then she heard the rustle of his buckskins against the beargrass and she looked up and her eyes were dry and without thoughts. He moved over and sat beside her and took her hands in his.

"It will all work out all right, Nacie."

She had a bruise on her arm. The fingers of The Bear had made it. Big John had reached out and had pulled the big man back and had backhanded him across the mouth. The Bear had stood there and growled and then Big John had pulled his pistol. The Bear had backed down under the threat of the gun. She did not mention this bruise to Ed Jones. She thought, I'd like to kill The Bear. She did not mention this, either.

"They always work out right, Ed."

It was The Bear who discovered that the prisoners had escaped. The time came to feed them and Many Feathers was doubled in her kitchen, holding her belly. She had been moaning and carrying on. Her belly was on fire. She had gone to bed and Big John had been smiling. Big John was rather drunk. So were the crew members of the boat tied to the dock. The Bear was rather drunk. So were the crew members of the boat tied to the dock. The Bear also wobbled a little on his thick knees.

"She's sick, Big John."

"Good."

"Somebody has got to feed them two trappers."

"You do it."

"I'm no cook."

"Dip some mulligan out of the pot, and take to them. We can't let them die. They'll start talkin' soon about them silver pelts."

So The Bear had dished some mulligan into the pail and had started across the compound in the dawn. The day would be rather warm, he thought absently. He unlocked the first door and went down the tunnel and unlocked the second. He carried a lantern. The door swung open and he said, "Chow time," and then he stood with his mouth flopping open. The fact seemed to register slowly in his dull and drunken mind. He moved over and gawked into the tunnel that led to the river. He looked at the pile of dirt that Many Feathers had pulled back into the dungeon.

"My God," he said, and his words were hollow.

Then he was lumbering across the yard. Big John and the skipper and the crew were at the long dining table. The Bear had wild eyes as he came through the door. He leaned over Big John and breathed. "They're gone."

Big John had been raising the bottle. He lowered it and stared at The Bear. "Who's gone, you fool?"

They were staring at them in surprise. Big John

scowled and said, "Well, don't jes' stand there with your mouth open!"

"They're gone, Big John!"

"Them two trappers—gone—?"

"They dug out!"

The crew did not know, of course, what the conversation was about. One roared, "So trappers dig now . . . 'stead of settin' traps!" and the others fell into drunken shouts. By this time Big John and The Bear were out of the mess hall, hurrying toward the cabin under which was the dungeon.

"They've dug out an' come free outside the fort," The Bear said.

"Was the doors locked when you went down?"

"The two padlocks was locked, Big John."

Suddenly the giant factor halted. "That girl!" He ran toward her cabin with The Bear on his heels. They did not enter the cabin. The condition of the chain and the open door told them the girl had made her escape. Big John was suddenly becoming sober. The Bear stared at the chain and the door.

"She's gone," he said.

Big John said, "Somebody has busted that chain from the outside. She never done it. They got loose and then come back an' got her free."

"How come they get back over the wall?"

Big John had no answer to this. His mind was working through the haze caused by the whiskey. He added the points in his mind. The doors leading to the dungeon had been padlocked. He turned and looked at the kitchen. Many Feathers was there, sick at the belly.

"Lemme look at the pit."

They went into the dungeon. Big John looked at the mound of fresh earth. He squinted down the tunnel. He was too massive to crawl down it. He looked on the ground.

"They was tied with buckskin," he said. "They ain't no sign of them buckskin strings around here. And to digga hole like that, they had to have their arms free. An' legs loose, too. An' thet looks like shovel work."

"Maybe somebody dug into them from out along the river?"

"Why then would the pile of dirt be at this end?"

The Bear let his wide shoulders fall and his tongue snaked out to wet his thick lips.

"I ain't much on the thinkin' end," he admitted.

Big John said, "Let's go outside the wall an' see where this hole comes out."

They did this. A guard was in the cupola. He looked down at them and waved. Neither man returned the greeting. Soon they were on the bank of the river looking into the tunnel. Big John said, "No dirt out here. That means they dug out from inside." He looked at the ground. Many Feathers had carefully brushed the ground with the end of a cedar twig to erase the marks of her big moccasins. There were only the tracks left by Ed Jones and Mack Hanson and the malemute. The river paid them no attention. The river chuckled and boiled and went down toward the Gulf of Mexico. The river had no troubles.

"They went this way," The Bear said.

"Three sets of tracks now," Big John said. "The girl is with them. Now with them doors locked, how did they get over the wall without one of the guards seein' them?"

"You got me stumped."

Big John Remington's mind was gathering data. The main thing was that the prisoners and Nacie Malone were gone. Around this was the core of his thoughts. He said, "We'll check with the guards," and they did this. The guards were mystified and surprised. Nobody had come through the gates except the authorized persons and nobody had been seen scaling the wall. Big John cursed them out in a loud voice. That made him feel better. Then he went in and looked at Many Feathers. She had managed to drag herself to her bunk.

"The girl is gone," he said. "So is them two trappers out of the dungeon. What do you know about it?"

She stopped grimacing and looked up at him. "I know nothings," she said. "I am glad the girl is gone. She do you no good."

"What do you know about it?" Big John Remington repeated.

"Nothings, I tell you."

The Bear started to uncoil his blacksnake lash. "Maybe this will jar her memory." He drew back his hand, the lash uncoiling and getting ready to strike. "This looks like it was done from inside to me."

The squaw rolled over on her back and held her hands over her head. She had a wide back and thick thighs. The whip went out, the shot-laden tip cutting her buckskins. She did not wince or holler or move. She was impassive and dead to the world. Big John grabbed his partner's arm.

"No good," he said. "Don't cripple her. We need her for work."

"Maybe her memory will come back? Another one or two, Big John, and her memory might know something'."

"No damn it!"

"But, Boss!"

"Get outa here."

Many Feathers was moaning now. Low moans, like those of a stricken dumb animal. Blood was trickling down and dripping onto her bed. Big John snarled and smashed The Bear across the mouth with the back of his hand. It made a loud noise. The Bear did not move back, though. He wet his numb lips and tried to say something, but at first the words would not come.

Then they came and he said, "Some day I use the whip

on you."

"Try it and get killed!"

The Bear turned and went outside, grumbling to himself and with one hand to his mouth. Big John glanced at the blood and followed his partner. The sun was becoming brighter as it went higher.

"How about them men in the mess hall?" The Bear asked.

"Leave them where they are. Tell them nothin'. We might need their rifles later on."

The Bear had uncomprehending eyes. "I don't foller you."

"This might lead to trouble. Them three might come back with the Law. There might be gunfire."

"Mebbe we should clear out?"

"An' leave all them rifles and cartridges behind? Man alive, there's a fortune there. Them Sioux will trade thousan's of beaver for them rifles an' that powder. We got a small fortune at our hands, an' you talk about leavin' it."

"They might not come back. They might be so glad to be free they'll light out of the country for good."

"There's that chance."

"Then where would they git the Law? They would have to go overland all the way to Laramie an' by the time they got back the pack-train would be here an' the rifles would be gone up north."

"That's got some good meat in it," Big John said.

"Let's see what tracks we can find?"

They went out toward the main gate. An Indian came out of a cabin, stretching as though he had just climbed out of his sougans. He was a short man who had come into Fort Green the night before. He had had a few furs in a pack and he had traded them for whiskey. The furs had been of poor quality and he had not had many, about ten muskrat and three beaver. He had eaten supper and then gone to his cabin with his two bottles of firewater. Big John had not liked his looks. He looked like a tramp Blackfoot buck. He had made a little profit on the deal, though. He had been of half a mind to run the buck out after the trading but he had not done this, and now he stopped and said, "Get your pack and get to hell out of Fort Green, you damned bum!"

The Blackfoot studied him, evidently surprised. "You talk to Mike Has-a-man, factor?"

"Yes, if that is your name, I'm talkin' to you. I don't want no bums around Fort Green."

The brown eyes shifted. They had lost their surprise and a hardness had seeped into them. For a moment Big John figured the man would show rebellion. But this he did not do.

"I go."

"Right away, too."

"I go get my pack and go. To black hell with you."

Big John grinned. "You'll be there with me," he said, and he and The Bear went out the main gate.

The buck got his pack out of the cabin and went out the gate. Big John had guessed wrong at his tribe. He was not a Blackfoot. He was a Crow. He had not a hair on his head and therefore the white men called him Curly. He was not a bum Indian, either, who had jumped the limits of his reservation. He was a man who worked for the Territory as a scout and a law officer. He had come into Fort Green in the capacity of a Lawman. He had hoped to scout around a little in a sort of shiftless way, for he was supposed to be a bum. But now he could not do this. He was looking for two white men who had come to Fort Green and had disappeared. Big John and The Bear had seemed rather excited. What had caused this, he wondered.

But he knew he could not stay at Fort Green. He went out the main gate. The rifleman in the cupola looked down at him and said nothing. The river boat was at the dock, water lapping around it. A guard stood at the gangplank. He had a rifle leaning beside him. He also watched him and said nothing. The red man said, "Hello," but the guard did not answer. The red man stopped. "I get job on boat, maybe?"

"We got a full crew. An' besides we don't hire no redskins, an' especially not ones that has jumped their bounds."

"What boat take to Fort Green?"

"Onions," the man scoffed. "Nine million tons of green onions. Come closer an' I'll jam one down your filthy throat!"

The Crow played ignorant. "Big John he plant the onion farm?"

The guard grinned. "Keep movin' or the river will be floatin' a dead Injun." He made a motion toward his rifle.

"I go."

The redskin swam the river. He got on the other side and wobbled out of the muddy water. He went into the brush and was lost from sight. He climbed a high hill and sat and let himself dry and he watched the area below him. The wilderness stretched out with Fort Green across the river in the timber. But his eyes were not on the fort. His eyes were for Big John Remington and The Bear, who were moving slowly up-river on the opposite bank.

Evidently they were tracking something or somebody. They moved in and out of the brush, visible now and then hidden in the buckbrush and wild rosebushes. They stopped on the edge of the river once or twice. Curly the scout found himself grinning. Whoever they were tracking had waded into the water. And water leaves no tracks. He watched the men for a while and then looked on the opposite slope. He had a pair of army field-glasses in his old moose-hide pack. They were old but they were good and he put them up and adjusted them to fine precision. For over three hours he was a motionless piece of flesh watching that mountain. By this time Big John and The Bear had returned to Fort Green. Curly did not watch them. The river boat lay in silence, bobbing on the current of the Green. It had not yet been unloaded. He wished he knew for sure what cargo it held. Had he been allowed to stay at Fort Green, he might have been able to find out the nature of the boat's cargo. But Big John Remington had put the run on him.

He kept on watching the mountain. It was the dog, Chief, that he saw first. The malemute was out hunting cottontail rabbits. Curly thought, That's a wolf . . . a timber wolf, and then the glasses showed it was a tame wolf, not a wild one. The dog moved through the brush. He went flat and crawled forward and then when the grouse left her nest the malemute was on her. He was in a scatteration of feathers. Then he was trotting away with the dead grouse in his mouth. He moved up the slope of the mountain, coming and going out of clumps of timber. He was heading high on the slope and he went into a bunch of boulders, scattered through the pines. Curly did not see him leave the area of boulders. Curly thought, He's gone into a camp, and he watched, and he felt the touch of a strange elation. Maybe his journey to Fort Green would not be a waste of time and effort?

He realized he should never have a dog. A dog was no good on a job such as his. Had it not been for the malemute he would not have been able to find this camp. He watched the rocks. At long last he saw a man move out of them. He kept his glasses on the man but he did not recognize him because he had never seen him before. The man had a snare along a trail. He checked it and Curly saw him take a cottontail rabbit out of the snare. Then the man returned to the rocks.

Curly had seen enough. He swung his glasses back to

Fort Green and watched the fort for about half an hour but he saw nobody around the ship. He glanced at the sun. Almost noon, he figured. He got into his pack, slipping the wide elkskin straps over his thin shoulders, and he skirted the toe of the mountain. He went at a dog-trot across the timber area. When he tired he fell to a walk that could cover many miles in an hour. Two hours later he came to a camp along a creek. Four men were there, dozing in the shadows of a clump of igneous boulders. He slipped from his pack and settled down next to one man.

"Hank, I was to Fort Green."

"You must've had good luck to find out what we wanted in such a short time," Corporal Hank Williams said. "Any sign of Hanson and Ed Jones or the girl?"

"They must have escaped."

"You never saw them at the fort, I take it?"

The Crow told them about being chased out of Fort Green. He told about the camp on the hill and he described the man who had come out of the boulders. He described him in minute detail. He spoke good English for he had gone to the white man's school at Carlisle.

"That was Ed Jones," Williams said.

He told about the river boat. "I don't know what cargo it held. They haven't unloaded it. The crew got drunk and was in the cabins when I got chased out by Big John."

The other three men were listening. They did not seem to be very excited about his words. One was another member of the Territorial Police. He was a young man built like a rock house. He was not tall but he was solid granite. The other two were trappers. They mined in the summer and they trapped in the winter. They had known Hank Williams for some years now. They liked him and they liked the work he was doing in bringing law and order into the wilderness. They had been sworn-in as special deputies. Each knew he might get killed on this job. But each had the philosophy of the timber-lands: Every man had to some day die. They were not brave; they were just level-headed. And Hank Williams had asked them to help him, so they were here.

"That dog was Ed's dog," Hank Williams said. "His name is Chief. The girl had a malemute too. She had a father, too. But you say you saw just two men, and one is Jones and the description of the other fits Mack Hanson."

"Only two men," Curly said.

Hank Williams got to his feet. "Time we was moving," he said. He spoke to one of the trappers. "Don't fall with thet dynamite, Matt."

Matt smiled through his beard. "If I fall, we all go to kingdom come," he said.

"Time to move," the patrolman said.

Ed Jones had a feeling of being watched. Chief was growling as he lay beside him. Mack Hanson slept in the shade. Nacie was out on guard. Ed got to his feet. He moved out of the circle of rocks. He heard something move in the brush and he stiffened against the bole of a fir tree. The sound was not made by a bear, he figured; bears made more noise than that. Chief was growling.

Ed said, "Get him, boy."

Chief dashed into the brush and became lost from view but not from sound. Ed heard a voice say, "Call off your mutt, Ed Jones."

"Hank Williams?"

"That's who it is, Ed."

Mack Hanson had staggered to his feet. "Do I hear voices?" he croaked. He was gaunt and broken and then his mind returned. "Come out of the brush, men!"

Nacie called, "Who is there, Ed?"

"Come in," Ed called to the girl.

She came running through the brush, the long-bladed

273

knife in her hand. "These men—they got through me—I never heard them!"

Ed said, jokingly, "Some guard you are, girl."

She stopped and said, "Corporal Hank Williams." She looked toward their rifles. "Rifles and pistols."

Ed Jones noticed that her voice had risen and had a savage note. He then realized fully for the first time the terrible desire for revenge that was in her lovely body. He felt a little bit of nausea. A woman should not hate the way and with the intensity she hated.

"Pistols," said Mack Hanson. "And rifles."

"Yes, and black powder, too," one man said.

There was much talking. They joked the girl about being such a poor guard. She took it in good nature. Ed noticed that the cut on her cheek was almost completely healed. The sun had sunk rather low and a coolness was coming from the glaciers and the high snow. They explained everything to each other and then they made their plans.

"I want to find out what is in that river boat," Hank Williams said. "So to do that, we scout Fort Green."

Nacie asked, "How did you know my father and me had gone to Fort Green, Corporal Williams?"

The corporal had checked at the Malone camp and had found the cabin empty and the furs gone. He had figured that the father and daughter had gone to Fort Green.

"What happened to your father?"

She told him that her father had been murdered. "They even killed my malemute," she finished.

"A murder charge, then," the corporal said. "But unless you saw him killed, it would be hard to prove in court."

"Big John will never go into court," Ed Jones said. "He's got too much on his black soul. This will be a fight, Hank."

Mack Hanson had settled down with his back against a boulder. He was eating a hunk of jerky that one of the lawmen had had in his pack. He chewed the thick hunk of meat slowly, letting every ounce of strength flow into his body. His eyes had lost their maniacal glow, Ed saw. Now the hate seemed to be supplanted by the light of hope, or so Ed guessed.

The others were scattered around among the boulders, listening to Ed and the corporal talk. They made guesses as to the number of men at Fort Green. There were the two guards and Big John and The Bear and the crew of the river packet. And maybe one or two more, like the man who had been hoeing in the garden. Yes, and the Ol' Man. Ed thought of the demented oldster. He would be of little use to Big John in a fight. Yes, and this surmise might be wrong. Ed took his mind off the old man. His thoughts went over to Many Feathers. He wondered if she had got into trouble over his escape. He did not know. He had a soft spot in his heart for the big greasy old Squaw. But then logic told him she had not helped him because she liked him. She had released them so they could get Nacie and take her away from Fort Green.

Ed asked, "How come you find our camp so easy?"

Williams told about seeing Chief catch the grouse on her nest. Ed said, "Well, we got off lucky, at that. I was afraid the malemute would sneak out of camp. He might just as easy been seen by Big John or The Bear as you men. Nacie, your job is cut out for you."

"I take care of Chief?"

"Tie a leash on him. Use some buckskin out of my jacket. Cut it into strips and tie it. Jacket is no 'count now since the whip cut it all to pieces. We can't afford to let thet dog run loose."

She took the jacket and went to work with the long-bladed knife. By this time the day was almost gone. Curly the scout was dozing with his back against a tree. He had sampled some of the rot-gut and he had slept little the night before because of the carousing and the shouting. They decided to break camp and move to a new site. There was an outside chance that Big John or one of his men had also glimpsed the malemute and might be planning a night foray on their camp. They moved to the north about two miles, away from Fort Green. They also went higher on the mountain. They had been watching the river boat but no cargo had been dispatched that day. Ed figured the crew had got so drunk they were sleeping off their jag. Or they might still be drinking. The Bear and Big John had come out of the fort twice and were scouting along the river. They were still looking for tracks. Ed had seen Many Feathers through the field-glasses. She had moved across the compound and had gone into a building and then had come out and had returned to her kitchen. He figured Big John and The Bear were in a rage. And in this assumption he proved correct.

"We should've killed them," The Bear said angrily.

"We wanted them silver fox plews. They are worth over a thousand each, I'll bet. Two thousand dollars . . . lots of money."

"But we never got them furs. An' now they're out in the timber somewhere goin' for the law."

"Take a week or so for them to go to Laramie. By that time the Sioux will be in for their rifles. An' we won't be here maybe, huh?"

"Burn the fort an' run off?"

"We can get somebody to run the fort. We can take a *vacation*, savvy? Then when it blows over we can come back."

"We can fin' them three an' kill them. Then the law won't come. Damn it, man, we should've murdered them when we found out they wouldn't tell us where them fox furs was!"

"Water over the beaver dam, you fool. No use talkin' now about what we should do. Let's head out an' scout some more, huh?"

So they had scouted along the river. They had walked past the point where Ed Jones had buried his silver fox fur in the river beside the bank. But the river told no tales. You can't put footprints into water and make them stay, any more than you can write your name in water. Fort Laramie was miles away to the southeast. There might have been a chance they could have driven themselves hard and circled and come in ahead of the trio, stationing themselves between them and Fort Laramie and killing them from the brush. But this plan, though probable, was not logical. Big John Remington had given it some thought and then had abandoned it. For one thing, the two men and women, despite their weakened condition, would move fast and would hike and run to get as many miles between them and Fort Green as possible. And he did not know how many hours start they had, also; this was important. Besides, he was needed at Fort Green. There was no use in sending The Bear out alone. He was half-crazy and he was no hand at tracking. He was only good for one thing: his whip. So Big John Remington had discarded this plan.

He was not sure in his mind whether or not the trio had had help from inside Fort Green.

He knew there would be no use in beating Many Feathers. The squaw would die before uttering a word. Therefore in this case The Bear and his bullwhip would be useless. The thought came to him that The Bear and his whip had been useless all the time, for it had not made the trappers talk. With this thought in his mind he whirled suddenly, moving fast for such a big man. His right fist rose. The Bear had not expected the sudden hard blow. The fist hit him on the jaw. He dropped and was out cold.

Big John rubbed his knuckles and grinned. He felt happier now. With one blow, he had knocked-out The Bear. Just one swinging hard blow, and the man had fallen over his coiled blacksnake whip. Big John's grin grew wider. He leaned against a lodgepole pine and looked at the unconscious man. The Bear had fallen on his belly in the tall beargrass. A little blood was on his lips. He lay there for about three or four minutes. Then his mouth started to move but no sounds came from it. He rolled over and his jaw kept on twitching. He opened his eyes and they were wild and he sat up quickly. He waggled his jaw and his memory returned. He roared to his feet, the whip uncoiling. Big John Remington stepped in and grabbed the stock of the bullwhip. He pulled it savagely from the big fist. Then The Bear was unarmed. Big John made the whip talk. He sent the lash curling around The Bear's wide legs. The lash locked and he jerked on the whip and upset the man again, only this time The Bear did not land on his belly. He landed sitting on his wide bottom. His anger was gone now, driven away by fear.

"I'll be good, Big John."

Big John had roared with laughter. He had stood there in the mountain park with the beargrass almost to his knees and he had bent his big body almost double at the belt as he had laughed. He had always guessed that The Bear had had some cowardice in his makeup but now that cowardice showed through the man's words and his bloodless face. It was in his trembling hands and his cowering huge body. And Big John Remington roared with laughter. He did not know why he laughed. He could not put a finger on the absolute reason that motivated his laughter. He only knew that this was a comical sight, one he might never again see, and he wanted to make the best of the moment.

The Bear lost his fear and became angry. He got the

lash untangled and the bullwhip fell free and The Bear got lumberingly to his moccasins. He stamped like a bull moose. He bellowed like a bull moose, too. But he made no move toward Big John Remington, who waited with his legs spread wide and his fists up. Big John wanted to fight him, to hit him, to tear him with his fists, to pound him down and break him. The Bear knew this. The Bear had often woundered if he could whip Big John. Now the factor was inviting him to fisticuffs. But The Bear would not take the open challenge. Within a few minutes violence left his gross body and he stood and grinned like a schoolboy who had been caught putting a girl's pigtail into his ink-well. A childish and stupid-looking grin.

"You win," he said.

Big John had stopped laughing. He looked at his partner with narrowed eyes. "You turnin' down a fight?"

"We got nothin' to fight about."

This was the truth. Big John thought, 'Stead of fightin' each other, we should be workin' together. His mind flicked back to other things The Bear had said across the five years or so they had been trail-friends. The Bear was not so dumb. Not as stupid as he appeared.

They had met in the Oregon country and had joined forces for some unknown reason, maybe because both men were huge men and therefore they had been somewhat out of place among smaller men—maybe because they were two of a kind in body size, if not in mind and appetite. They had mined gold and had got drunk and had wrecked saloons and had lain with the garish and painted harpies over saloons and in red light districts. Their records were not clean. The Bear had killed a miner in Kellogg, wrapping his lash around his throat and almost decapitating him. That had been three years ago. They had fled the mining town ahead of a posse. Big John had killed a cowpuncher in the Black Hills with a single chopping blow of his huge right hand. That also had almost led him to the hangman's hungry noose. Then they had stumbled onto trading whiskey to the redskins for pelts. This put the War Department on them. From whiskey they had graduated to rifles. Thus had come into being Fort Green. Each had wanted to put up a cloak of respectability. The fort had been hatched in the brain of Big John Remington. We turn into traders, see. We work apparently inside the Law, see. So the connections had been made and here they were at Fort Green and the river boat had five cases of new Winchester rifles bound for Sitting Bull and the Sioux. Custer was stationed at Fort Lincoln, miles to the northeast in the Dakotas. Miners had moved with burro and pick and shovels and pans into the Sioux hunting grounds of the Black Hills. The Sioux were ready to fight. The Sioux had gold stolen from miners they had scalped. The Sioux had beaver and other furs. And soon Sitting Bull's men would come down and trade and trek north with rifles. And Fort Green would make money.

But they had made one mistake, and that had been this one they were now trying to correct. And logic came in and took control of Big John Remington.

"I'm danged sorry, Bear."

"All in fun, Big John."

They had shaken hands with solemn faces that hid the distrust of the other. Big John had braced his legs wide fearing that The Bear would suddenly jerk and send him flying to the grass as they gripped hands. But this The Bear did not do. He had no anger toward this big factor. Anger was a momentary thing to The Bear. It came, roared like a meteor flaring across the skies, and then, like the meteor, died as suddenly as it came. He was not angry at Big John. That had gone. He had no feeling of revenge. To him the world was grey and pine trees wavered and the centre of it was a bullwhip. A long and curling and terrible bullwhip with its lashes loaded with shot. Only the whip was real.

"We look for their tracks," he said, and so the incident was ended.

But what tracks they found led into the river and the river hid them. They circled in the brush. Ed Jones and Corporal Hank Williams watched from the heights of the unnamed peak. The field-glasses held the two big men with absolute accuracy. Ed had Chief back at camp with Nacie and the dog was leashed and therefore he could not betray their position as he had done to Curly the scout. Ed and the patrolman had seen the two big men scuffle there in the mountain park surrounded by pines and spruce and fir.

"They're mad at each other," he had said.

"Wonder if The Bear will call him?"

"Be like two bull moose lockin' horns," Ed had said.

They had watched and Williams had said, "They ain't gonna fight," and disappointment was in his voice.

For The Bear and Big John, their search finished, were going toward Fort Green, walking side by side.

The captain of the river boat and his crew were in the mess hall. Some were eating and some were drinking. The captain looked up and said, "When do we unload?"

"When the Sioux come and trade."

The captain was a short man and he wore a deep scowl. He wanted to discharge his cargo and turn back down the Green. He knew the danger of keeping the rifles on board his ship.

"When will that be?" he asked.

"Tomorrow, maybe. Next day, maybe."

"Look, Remington. I have to discharge that cargo. I got to get back to Fort Yuma. I've got a cargo to take down the Mexican coast to Mazatlan."

Big John rubbed his beard and grinned. "You afraid somebody might jump the outfit, an' fin' rifles on your boat?"

"I am."

"Well, be afraid for a while, man. Do you good."

Big John turned to go but the captain said, "Come night, we discharge our cargo. Either that, or we take them rifles back to Fort Yuma."

Big John turned. They locked eyes. The captain meant every word he said. He figured that Big John had the money to pay him gold for the rifles. And he would take only gold. He knew the big man wanted those rifles and that powder and the cartridges.

His bluff worked.

"Leave them on the boat tonight," Big John said. "Then if the Sioux don't arrive by tomorrow evening you can unload and I'll pay you in gold and you can go down the river."

"Tomorrow night, eh?"

"That's what I said."

Their eyes held. Men watched them. The mess hall was silent. Only the wind made a sound, and it talked against the logs.

"All right," the captain said, and sat down.

The water was icy cold. Occasionally an iceberg floated past the river boat, rubbing against its thick ribs. Ed Jones wore only his buckskin pants. He had discarded his jacket back along the river bank. For a man cannot swim well with a heavy jacket.

His only weapon was the long bladed knife and he held it between his teeth as he swam. The night was dark but soon the moon would be up. He swam with long strokes the way a beaver swims. With his head high and with his closed fingers pulling the water. A few feet away swam another man, also naked. Ed glanced at this man and saw his head in the dark and realized that Hank Williams was also a good swimmer.

They had built their plan ahead of time and now they

executed it to perfection, almost as brilliantly as if it had been rehearsed, which it had not been. He would go around the aft of the boat and come in from the south side and Hank would come over the north rim of the vessel. The boat came into sight and it was dark and low against the swiftly-running current. It did not move sideways with the current, for it was roped solid to the solid dock; it merely rose upward and then settled down again, riding the crest.

Ed Jones swung around the end of the ship and swam along its side. He was in the lee of the current here and the water was still. He leaped upward when he reached the shallow area toward the front of the boat where he could stand on his feet. He caught the edge and pulled himself on board. He lay against the darkness, listening and watching and wondering.

He lay on the deck. The boat was longer and wider than he had anticipated. Its looks had been deceptive. He was shivering. The night was chilly. It was close to midnight. He had not been the one who had sired this plan; it had come from the brain of Corporal Hank Williams. He wondered if their expedition would give them any information as to what cargo the boat carried. Both had been sure that cargo had not been unloaded. Curly the scout had kept an eye on the boat while at Fort Green. After he had been ordered out of the fort the others had kept a stern eye on it through field-glasses.

The wind was cold for it came down from the snow and the glaciers. The cold wind and the ice-cold water had its effect on him. He was armed only with a knife. A pistol or rifle is of no account after it has become water-soaked. Therefore both he and the patrolman carried knives.

Cautiously he raised himself on his hands and looked around. He saw no sign of a guard. When he had climbed onto the deck he had glimpsed a man standing on the landing. There evidently was a guard stationed. He had seen the dim outlines of the man, who was squatted in the shadow of a piling. This told him the ship carried some mysterious cargo or otherwise no guard would be posted.

He wondered how Corporal Hank Williams was faring. But he had to get moving, or else the cold would get him down. His thigh muscles quivered and jumped under his wet buckskins. He went across the deck on his hands and knees, hoping he made no noise. His wet skin pants made a purring sound as he crossed the deck. He could not see the guard because of the rise in the deck. Logic then told him that the guard could not see him.

He and Corporal Williams had discussed the plan to some detail, and now his thoughts went back to their conversation there in the hidden camp in the tall timber.

"Sure give my back teeth to know what that ship carried, Ed."

Curly said, "They unloaded some supplies. Canned stuff and other supplies. Some traps and some barrels of sugar and salt. I seen them unload that much. But I still think the big cargo is still on board."

Mack Hanson had asked, "What would that be?"

Nacie Malone had listened. She sat with her back to a granite boulder and Chief had had his head on her lap. Chief seemed to have taken a great liking to her. This in itself was odd, for up to now the big malemute had been a one-man dog. Ed had looked at her and their eyes had met. Ed had felt a little embarrassed. He had had a squaw or two in his life but that had been only for a short while. He had never been around white women much since he had left the farm. And that had occurred some years back.

Ed thought, I like her, and he entertained more serious thoughts, too. He wondered if she were really as beautiful as she seemed or did she look prettier than she actually was because she was the only white woman in the camp? Were there more women, and therefore comparison, would she look so beautiful? He had a sneaking hunch she would stand out in any crowd any place, be it the wilderness or in a crowded city. He liked the way she looked at him and, being a young man and healthy and strong, he had his hopes, and his desires.

"Rifles and powder and ball and cartridges," the territorial policeman replied. "The Sioux are gettin' ready to raise cain. There is talk of movin' the 7th under General Custer out of Fort Lincoln to the Yellowstone country, for the scouts say the Sioux are gatherin' there."

"The big shots in the army would never figure that rifles would come from the south," a trapper said.

The red-headed trapper said, "We might all be wrong. We might be spittin' ag'in the wind."

"Seems odd they wouldn't unload the rifles, if they had them on board." These words came from Mack Hanson.

Ed Jones had the answer to that. "Mack, I think that line of reasonin' ain't hard to deduct. You an' me an' Nacie here escaped out of Fort Green. That put The Bear an' Big John ahind the tow-sack for good. He don't know that Hank here an' his men are in the vicinity. He'll figure we headed out for Laramie to notify the territorial police. That's a long distance overland. Take some days to come and for the police to arrive. He ain't in no hurry to unload that packet. The Sioux should come in any day for them rifles, if he has rifles. So why not leave them on the boat?"

"Yeah . . . Reckon that's good logic."

"There's another angle there, too," Corporal Hank Williams had said. "With them rifles on the boat, they're easy to move. Trouble rise either from the territorial police or from the Indians, and all they have to do is cut the line and steam down the Green, safe as can be."

Ed Jones had said, "Why then try to find out the cargo's nature, Hank?"

"We got to get evidence, Ed. We're all actin' on guesswork. But the Law—the Law, well, it is different. To prove somethin' in court, you got to have evidence. Not hearsay evidence, either. Or guess somethin' in court, you got to have pure evidence. Me, I'm swimmin' out to thet packet, come hell or ice water or icebergs. I'm goin' to do my best to find out what thet cargo is."

"I'm swimmin' stroke by stroke alongside you," Ed had said.

So the plan had been conceived and now they were carrying it out. Across the river were two of the trappers. Mack Hanson and the girl had stayed in the mountain camp. Curly the scout had swum the Green, too. But he had not gone to the packet. He had crossed the river above it and he was watching Fort Green.

Ed was still a little lerry of this plan. It was not the danger involved that worried him as much as one other point they had discussed. What if they ran into a guard and either had to knock him cold or kill him? This would tell The Bear and Big John Remington that an enemy lurked in the brush.

"If that happens, we steal the packet boat," Corporal Hank Williams had explained. "Cut the moorin' line an' let her drift down the Green. We got the evidence we need, if rifles are really on the boat. Was it an honest boat, there'd be no guard stationed."

"But there is a guard," Curly had said. "I saw a guard posted all the time I was at Fort Green. The captain an' his crew took their bed rolls ashore and are bunkin' at Fort Green. I hardly blame them, either—those cabins are small an' hot, even though the nights do get chilly."

"Well," said Ed, "we'll see what we see."

So they had left camp and had gone to the river. Ed missed the companionship of Chief but at a time like this a dog was a detriment and not an asset. Because of Chief, Corporal Williams had found the location of his camp. Maybe by the same line of reasoning, Big John Remington had also located their wilderness camp? But this was not logical. Had Big John or The Bear or any other of the Fort Green men spotted the malemute, by this time the camp would have been raided.

They had stripped to their pants and had plunged into the cold river. At first the shock had been like that of falling endlessly through space for the cold water numbed a man right off the bat. But after a dozen or so strokes circulation had started again. The stream had been treacherous with icebergs and roots and entire trees that the flood had loosened. The Chinook wind had cut the snow fast and had turned the Green and the Soda into roaring streams of mad water dashing down toward the Gulf of Lower California, about a thousand or so miles to the southwest. And now Ed was on the packet, sneaking into the lower areas. And he only hoped he would not have to slug the guard, or silence him forever with the sharp hunting-knife that had a razor tip and edges honed as sharp as a cutlass.

He came to a stairway and went down it, knife in his hand. His eyes searched the darkness. He stopped at its base and squatted, knife between his teeth. He heard nothing out of the ordinary. The hull squeaked occasionally as it lifted and fell and rubbed against a fir piling. The river lapped and made its eternal noise. There was the fetid smell of the river, also—the ugly stink of muddy highwaters. But these registered on him only with casual and passing interest. His eyes probed the darkness and became somewhat accustomed to the blackness. He moved forward and came to a door. It opened inwardly at his touch. The hinges squeaked in an oil-less protest. He stiffened, fearing the guard would hear the high-pitched squeaking sound. He stood against the door jamb and listened. But there was no sound of footsteps approaching. His wariness had made the sound even sharper and even higher in pitch than it actually had been.

His heart pounded. It seemed to want to break out of

his ribs. He realized he was weak and jittery. The memory of the dungeon—black and stinking—came back, and he rubbed his right wrist. The scar was deep and was healing. Anger came into him then and loosened his muscles and filled his body and being with a terrible emotion. At that moment he could have cut either of the throats belonging to The Bear or Big John.

He could have cut them with pleasure, just to watch the blood jet forth.

But he summoned logic from the deepness of his person, and this came to his rescue by calming his thoughts. He realised he was still yet close to the breaking point—that mythical point where being dissolves and goes into flaming action. He would have to concentrate his thoughts on the present and shove the past out of his mind, if this was possible.

He realised he had opened the door to a cabin. He got the odour of dirty socks and clothing, and he crossed it and felt the bunk. There was nothing here. No use lighting a sulphur match to look over this set of quarters.

Commonsense told him the cargo would be in the hold of the ship.

He knew nothing about ships. This was the first time he had ever felt a deck under his moccasins. He figured that the cargo would be stored in the bowels of the ship, but how to get to it—that was another thing. He figured a stairway would lead down to the hold. His objective was to find this stairway.

Suddenly, he heard a strange noise.

He stiffened against the wall of the cabin behind the door. He heard a man coming. He was whistling a gay tune. His boots came along the walkway and stopped in front of the cabin door. Then the door opened. It did not open to its full width, though; this told Ed the man was not entering. He had his knife in his hand. The guard never knew how close he was to death.

For a moment, the world seemed to stand still. Then the door closed, the latch snapped shut, and the boots moved on, their owner still whistling. Ed heard him go around the corner and then he heard his boots on the opposite side of the cabin, and this told him the guard was returning to his post on the deck. And Ed Jones found his breath again.

He left the cabin, hanging close to the wall, and went to the aft of the ship. Here he found a stairway leading downward. He went down it silently and then a whisper said, "Ed?"

Ed had stopped, heart cold. Then he realised the low voice had come from the bottom of the stairway. He recognised the voice now.

The voice belonged to Hank Williams.

"Hank?"

"Down here at the door, Ed."

Ed was beside him then, feeling his presence in the dark. Hank's words were a muffled whisper in his ear.

"The cargo . . . It must be behind this door, Ed."

"Did you see the guard go by?"

"I was hidin' ahind a pile of rope on the deck. That man never knew how close he came to runnin' into a sharp knife."

Ed felt the door. He saw that it was made of heavy lumber—evidently three by eights—bolted together. It had no hasp. It had a chain that ran through a metal rimmed hole in the door. Then the chain ran through the wall and it was bolted by a huge steel lock.

"That chain is two inches wide," he muttered.

He felt for the hinges, but he could find none. That was because they were on the inner side of the door. He pushed against the door. It was like trying to move a huge boulder.

"We can't do nothing with that door," he said quietly. "If we had an iron-saw, we could saw through the chain, but that would take a lot of time—and the saw would make noise." He grinned in the dark. "But we ain't got no saw, man."

Hank Williams voice held disgust. "We're really up against a blank wall, and I'm not jokin'. We'd best get out of here, Ed."

"Lissen!"

Again, there were boots on the deck. They came off the landing and pounded on the hardwood deck. They heard the voices of men. From the pound of the boots Ed judged about three men were coming toward the cabins. He heard their voices and decided they were drunk. They walked unsteadily, too.

A voice said, "Everythin' okay, guard?"

"Nothing' out of the ordinary," the guard said. "I still figger we're loco to have a guard out. Who is there in this damned wilderness to raid a boat?"

"You're not runnin' this ship!"

The boots went into a cabin. The door was not slammed shut, Ed noticed. He could still hear the voices, although they were muffled now. He was aware that Hank Williams was gripping his right arm. The man had talons as strong as those of a Rocky Mountain bald eagle.

He put his mouth close to Williams' ear. "We got to get out of here, Hank."

"They've lit a lamp," the corporal said.

They were at the top of the stairs. The hurricane-lamp sent light out on both sides of the cabin and this light made the deck very clear. Some of it came through the open door and the other side was illuminated through the two windows. The men had evidently settled down and were drinking for the words came, "The bottle is under the bunk, there."

The guard was about twenty feet away, settled down against a piling. He was a dark and compact figure. They could not pass the cabin to get to the aft of the vessel.

290

They had only one choice and that was to dart across the desk and go over the rail. And to do so they might be seen by the guard.

"We got to crawl," Ed said.

"Lead the way."

Ed went down on his hands and knees and then onto his belly. He wriggled forward like a human worm. His heart was beating like that of a doe with a hunter and hound in chase. Because they were so low on the deck, they were in darkness. Still, the guard might see them. Or hear them.

He felt, rather than saw, that Hank Williams, also on his belly, was beside him. He kept his eye on the guard. The man was sitting with his side toward them, and he was smoking—you could see the coal of his cigar or cigarette, whichever it was, glowing and falling back as he inhaled. There was also the possibility that the men might suddenly exit from the cabin. But this danger was not as great as that personified by the guard, for the cabin door was on the opposite side. The greatest danger was the guard.

Ed found himself scarcely breathing. His wet buckskins seemed to make a very loud noise as they dragged on the deck. Actually, the sound was not loud; in fact, it was little more than a very low murmur. Yet it seemed loud to him.

The tendency to rise suddenly—to run and dive over the rail—was strong in him. But somehow he managed to control it. So far nobody but Hank Williams and he knew they had visited this ship. And it was best this knowledge was not disclosed to the guard, if possible.

He got a sliver in his hand. He paid it no attention. Now they were across the deck. One thing was in their favour now. Because they had moved positions, the guard was hidden by the piling against which he was sitting. Ed Jones lifted his leg and crawled over the railing. He hung to it and let his feet touch the water. It seemed even colder. Beside him hung Corporal Hank Williams. Hank also let go of the rail and they slipped into the chilly water. The effect was one of shock, but there was only one thing to do and that was to start to swim and bring back circulation through physical movement. They glided through the water, keeping in the lee of the vessel for the water was calm here. They came to the end of the ship and swam out into the turbulent water.

"Hey," came a stern voice, "did you fellows hear something? Out in the water, there?"

The three men came out of the cabin. They went to the rail and peered down at the dark water. The light from the cabin showed them rather clearly. But Ed and his partner were already about fifty feet away, the darkness of the night hiding them as they swam.

The voice of the guard said, "I never heard nothin'." You could hear their voices across the water with great clarity.

"Sounded like somethin' overboard," a man said.

The guard said, "Might have been a family of beavers. I seen some swimmin' aroun' right about sundown. Prob'ly got flooded out of their dens with this high water. Mebbe one got scared and went down an' flapped his tail ag'in the water."

Somebody else spoke but distance stifled their words. A huge iceberg, dirty grey and cold, came sweeping along, and Ed and his partner had to swim around it, and then it was on its way south again, a mass moving into the darkness. Ed swam as best he could. He was not a good swimmer. The corporal was a better hand in the water, and when they reached the bank he was already standing there, shaking himself much as a spaniel shakes to get rid of water.

Ed was shivering. His words came out shakingly. "A wild goose chase, but maybe it netted somethin'."

"Who knows," said Hank Willaims, teeth chattering.

Now a figure glided out of the brush and a voice said, "Curly, men," and the redskin was beside him. "What did you find out?"

Ed grinned despite his coldness. "That the water is ice cold," he said jokingly.


Next morning at daybreak a Sioux scout came into Fort Green, and the gate swung and let him into the stockade. He was a short and wiry man of undeterminate age and he wore only moccasins and a breech-cloth. He met first the Sioux squaw, Many Feathers.

"I look for factor," he said in Sioux.

"Big John?"

"I look for him."

"He asleep. He drink too much."

"Where is he?"

Many Feathers had been coming from the well. She carried two wooden pails filled with clear water. She nodded and said, "I take you to him," and the scout walked beside her. She was as big as two of him.

The scout asked her if she were not a Sioux. Upon receiving a positive reply he asked no more questions. She had deserted her tribe for a white man. She had not selected a man of her own race. This the scout did not like. So he said nothing more to her, and she understood why.

Big John lay naked on his bunk and The Bear, wearing only his buckskin pants, slept on the floor, bullwhip coiled beside him. The scout gave him and the whip a long glance and then Many Feathers was shaking her lord and master. It took her some time to bring Big John out of his drunken sleep. When finally he opened his huge eyes they were bloodshot and ugly.

"Go away, you damned Injun."

"Scout, he come."

Big John then sat up. His chest was a matted mass of black hair turning slightly grey. He was not a pretty object sitting there naked. He looked at the scout who had a dead-pan face.

"Sioux?"

"Run the Deer."

"You came ahead of your bunch—your tribe?"

The scout talked in broken English. His men were three days behind him. They had pack-horses and they were coming after the rifles and ammunition. They had beaver and marten and mink.

"Beaver pelts packed flat," the factor growled. "As high as a rifle, for each rifle. Three plews for each pound of shot and powder. Five for a box of cartridges. If you don't want to trade that much, turn around an' head back for Montany."

The terms were steep. Very, very steep. But Big John knew he had the redskins over a barrel. They had to have those rifles and that powder and ammunition. So the scout could merely nod and say, "We trade. I go back to my men."

And he turned and left.

Big John rolled over on his back. Then he became aware that Many Feathers had not left. He turned his head on his thick neck.

"What do you want, Squaw?"

"Nothin'."

"Then get to hell out and make it speedy."

To emphasize his remarks, he reached down and looked for something to throw at her. But she scurried out the door, moving quickly despite her size. He grinned and lay on his back again. He looked at the ridge-pole in the roof. The Bear kept on sleeping. Big John's head had a Flathead powwow in it. He knew one thing that would kill the stampeding moccasins, so he reached under his pillow and came out with a flat flask of whiskey, and he killed it with savage gulps. He threw the bottle on the dirt floor and it hit a rock and broke. This made The Bear groan and rolled over but he did not open his eyes.

Big John grinned and went back to sleep.

The guide went out the gate and the heavy gates swung shut behind him, Ol' Man pushing on them. Ol' Man grinned at him and asked, "You got the dog?" and the guide glanced at him and read his insanity and said, "I got the dog."

"Bring him aroun'. We cut his throat."

The scout said nothing, and then he was outside Fort Green. He had a bad taste in his mouth. He looked at the river boat and went into the brush. He moved upstream, and then it was that the field-glasses of one of the trappers, high on the mountain, picked him out, held him, and brought his image close with clarity.

"A Injun. Looks like a Sioux, judgin' from the bead-work an' porcupine quills on him."

Ed Jones was lying on his side, getting some sleep. The sun was gaining heat and Ed needed heat, for the chill of the river was still in his bones.

"Watch him," he said.

The trapper took the field-glasses and moved out of sight through the buckbrush. Ed said. "The sun is gettin' some heat."

"My aching bones," Hank Williams said.

Mack Hanson smiled. He was getting himself together now, but the memory of the hell-chamber would be with him the rest of his life, just as that memory would also haunt Ed Jones. Ed looked at Nacie. She had cooked breakfast and was sitting against a boulder, with Chief beside her. She did not meet his eyes. She was petting Chief on his wide intelligent head.

"I even lost my dog," Ed mourned.

She smiled then, said, "He's still your dog, Ed. When

you were gone he was restless and he wanted to go with you."

Ed said, "Jes' a joke, Nacie."

"I wish we had some coffee," she said. "We're all out of java. Some more hot coffee would drive the river chill out of you."

Ed smiled. "She's gettin' o'nery, Mack. Guess we'll tote her feet-first down to Fort Green and sell her to Big John."

"No, not Big John. He's got one squaw. We'll peddle her to The Bear."

Nacie said, "That's no joke."

"Reckon not," Ed said.

There was nothing to do but spend the day loafing and building plans. The sun heeled high and at noon the trapper returned.

"He went up the Green. Reckon he's a scout for the pack train comin' to Fort Green. Do we move tonight, Ed?"

"Ask Hank."

Hank Williams drew lines in the damp earth with a twig. "Tonight we use powder and ca'tridges," he said. "When the moon comes up about midnight, we rip the hell out of Fort Green."

Nobody had anything in reply. Each knew his part in this and each knew the plan of procedure they had carefully drawn. That afternoon The Bear scouted the brush for tracks they might have left. The Bear was drunk and he was sweating and he was sick from a hangover. He carried a quart of Old Maple Leaf. He drank from this and it chased his headache away. He was like a grizzly moving through the brush. Ed Jones trailed him. Ed wanted to kill him. But Fate seemed to intervene, and he could not come within head shooting range of The Bear. He did not want to shoot the man down from behind; he wanted to face him and his bullwhip and kill him. But he never got this chance. Finally The Bear returned to Fort Green and Ed Jones went back to the wilderness camp. Nacie said, "What did you see?" and he said, "The Bear."

"Oh?"

"He scouted, drank from his bottle, and then went back to the fort. I tried to get close to him to kill him, but I had no luck."

"Might be for the best," Mack Hanson said, and his sunken eyes were on the ground. "When he failed to return to Green, Big John might have got suspicious. An' part of our plan is to hol' down his suspicions and hit his fort with him thinkin' we are miles away."

Ed nodded. "That held me back, too."

So they spent the rest of the day resting for the terrible chore ahead. Buckskin men, waiting to answer a buckskin challenge. And fear was in all of them, for tomorrow some of them, by all rights, should be and might be dead. This thought was not pleasant. Nacie came over and sat beside Ed. Their hands met and became one. She had selected him, and this was in her silence and in the grip of her small hand, and the world was big and there was goodness in it; yet with this thought was the thought that he might die this night under the round and yellow Wyoming moon.

But neither mentioned this.

Down at Fort Green, Big John was continuing his drunk. The captain and the crew were with him, and there was only the guard at the river boat. The captain was mad. He wanted his boat unloaded and he wanted to go down the river with the furs he would take from Fort Green. He did not understand the reason for this delay. Even though his crew was drunk they could still unload rifles and cartridges and powder. But Big John kept repeating that there was no need to hurry. No need to unload the rifles and then take them from the warehouse when the Sioux came in with their pack-train. And the Sioux would bring many, many furs. The river boat would have to wait to carry out these furs. He could not afford to let them lie until the boat returned that Fall. He would have to pack the plews in salt in a cellar; even so packed, some might slip hair. This appeased the captain to some degree. For he would get his cut of the money these furs would bring down at Fort Yuma. So they drank and raised a wild yelling.

Many Feathers stoically tended to their wants, fiilling glasses and serving food. She wondered what was going to happen. Or maybe nothing would happen? Maybe the two trappers had taken the white squaw and had gone overland? This was the most logical thing. Two men were not fools enough to storm Fort Green. And they had no weapons, only the knife. No, they had gone over the mountains, glad to be out of the dungeon, fleeing from the whip of The Bear. She batted down the hands of a young sailor who wanted to drag her into a side room. She said nothing to him, but she saw a dark cloud pass over Big Jonn's face. This might end in a free-for-all. If this happened she would lock herself in the kitchen armed with her longest and sharpest skinning knife.

She cut hunks of buffalo meat from the roast and hacked off great slices of rice bread, and her face was impassive and she had no thoughts. She went into the mess hall only when the bellowing voices demanded more whiskey and more grub. When the Sioux scout had come into Fort Green he had given her a look of dislike and mistrust. She had abandoned men and squaws of her own colour and race. She wondered if she really loved this hulking brute of a man called Big John. But there was no answer to this; she wanted to be with him, and that was that. So . . . she let it go at that, and went about her menial chores in silence.

The afternoon was hot. Then the sun sank behind the

jagged sawteeth of the peaks, and the high chill came creeping across the land of timber and wild streams. Some of the men had passed out. This made Big John angry. He walked among them and slapped them and awakened them with curses and drunken roars. One man wanted to fight, and The Bear whooped and his whip went out. He wrapped it around the man's legs and pulled and the man went forward. Big John at this moment hit him an enormous blow on the side of his head and the man was unconscious before he hit the floor, The Bear lumbered over and unwrapped the coils of his whip and grinned as he examined the shot-loaded lash with great care.

"The squaw sure laced them shots in," he said. "Did a good job."

The captain had a face as red as a prime marten pelt. He started out of his chair and Big John waited and he had his fists hard and big at his sides. He wore a twisted and satanical grin. The captain settled back.

"You shouldn't have did that," he mumbled.

"He wanted to fight," Big John said. The factor glared at The Bear. "Next time keep your whip out of it, hear me?"

Ol' Man was sitting on the floor with his back to the log wall. He cackled in his toothless way and it sounded as shrill as a packet-boat's whistle.

"Hear you, Big John! You're bellerin' like a bull moose stuck in a bog! They can hear you even to Fort Yuma!"

Big John caught himself. "I'm gettin' drunk," he said.

He went outside. The night air was chilly. He lumbered across the compound, stumbling over a stump in the dark; he kicked it and cursed it. First he checked the guard at the cupola over the main gate. The man was sober—he was a short stocky man with red-hair—and he never drank. He did not smoke, either. Big John could not understand a man who did not drink or smoke or had any bad habits. His life must of necessity be terribly uninteresting.

He braced his legs and hollered up, hands cupped to his whiskery mouth. "How is the night, Mike?"

"Nothin' stirrin', Big John."

"Keep away from your bottle," the factor joked, and he went to the other cupola, across the dusty yard. He hollered to this man, too, who was the halfbreed caretaker, and he got the same reply, only this time in the Cheyenne tongue. Thus satisfied, the Big Man lumbered back to the mess hall, where he got a glass and poured it half full of whiskey.

The man he had slugged was sitting up, wondering just what had happened to him. Big John grinned and said, "Come an' wet your gullet, Casey."

"What happened—to me?"

"A beam fell off the roof, an' hit you on the head."

And they roared at this. Heads back, they laughed in boisterous drunkenness that echoed past the fort, going over the heavy logs that made up the stockade. And then it became lost against the eternal sound of the Green River and the murmuring of the wind in the pines.

One man heard the roaring laughter.

He was along the stockade in the buckbrush, scouting Fort Green. He moved through the high brush as silently as a buck deer going down to a water hole which was being watched by a cougar.

He was Curly the scout.


They were ready to move against Fort Green. They were in the mountain park, with the smell of the damp beargrass in their nostrils, and they waited for two men. One was Ed Jones. The other was Curly the scout.

Mark Hanson said, "They might have run into trouble."

Nacie glanced at the full moon. She said nothing.

Chief stood beside her, a dark wolf in the moonlit washed area. Somewhere the lupine were blooming. Their odour was nauseating, smelling rusty and aged. Nacie Malone shivered and her hand went down and found the malemute's thick neck-hair. She remembered her own malemute and she was silent and thoughtful.

Corporal Hank Williams said, "They can take care of themselves, those two." But his words were rather low.

An hour went by, and the moon moved across a sky without clouds. Moonlight reflected on the glaciers and the snow high on the peaks. They seemed to be ringed-in by a white band of flame as the moon touched the white snow. The scene was one of beauty, with moonlight dappling the wilderness of timber, but there was no contentment there. Rather there was the raw push of men who wanted to move against the foe . . . and have it over with.

One of the trappers, lying on the ground, raised his head. "I hear something comin' this way," he said, and he put his ear to the ground again and nobody stirred. Finally he looked up. "Moccasins," he said.

"How many?" asked Hank Williams.

"Two men, I think."

"That will be them," Mack Hanson said.

Ed Jones trotted into the clearing with Curly on his heels. Ed squatted and said, "Gettin' old, I reckon. Puffin' like a wind-busted bull elk. Either that, or my strength ain't come back yet."

Curly went over and got a drink from the spring. Ed caught his breath. They had scouted outside of Fort Green. Two guards were in the cupolas. Both of them had been smoking and he had seen the coal of their cigarettes. And Curly had heard them shouting and yelling. Ed had been on the far side of the wall at that time, and had not heard them.

"They must be drunk," Curly said, wiping his mouth

with a buckskin-clad sleeve. "Raisin' hell an' puttin' blocks under it."

"Good," a trapper said.

Corporal Hank Williams said, "Time we get movin'. First, let's go over this again, and each man know where he should be and what he should do."

There was an area by the spring where there was only damp earth, and in this earth the corporal outlined Fort Green, and he pointed with his twig as he talked in a low tone of voice.

"There are six of us, not countin' Nacie, who ain't gonna get into this fight. She wants to fight with us, but no women are fightin' our battles, as we agreed. So she stays back."

"With Chief," Ed said. "I don't want the dog killed. No use an innocent animal dying for man's mistakes."

Nacie said nothing. She had argued and she had lost and now she was content to wait, as women have waited for their men from the beginning of time. She had a leash on Chief. She gripped this leash and said nothing.

"The main thing is to keep them away from that boat," the patrolman said. "We want that boat to sail down the Green when this is over. So we hit at the cupolas first, of course. Ed, you know how to handle black powder, seein' you mined a year in copper down in Arizona Territory. You take the main gate. Blow it to kingdom come, and knock out that guard. You take Mack with you, and Curly too. I'll take the others, and hit the other guard. We got to get that wall down and knock those guards out of their posts."

"We'll do that," Madck Hanson said.

"Then we break through into the compound. From then on, it's each man for himself, and the devil grab the hindmost."

"We should have a watchword," Ed said. "A word we can holler to identify each other so we won't shoot the other in the dark."

"What'll it be?" a trapper asked.

Nacie said one word, "Malemute."

"Good," Ed said. "Malemute it is."

Corporal Hank Williams nodded. "That'll be the word. Shoot and shoot to kill. This bunch is worthless and they're killers. Those rifles can't go north to the Sioux. If they do, Custer and Crook will lose soldiers. We'll holler when we get ready to toss our dynamite. After we part, I'll start counting and when I reach two hundred, we should be beyond the fort and under the guard. Then I'll yell *Malemute* and throw the dynamite!"

"That will give us three time to get to the front gate," Ed said. "So we'll wait until you holler." He looked at Nacie. "Where will you be a-hidin', girl?"

"In the willows, right above the river boat."

"Good place," Williams said.

"Check your arms," Corporal Hank Williams ordered.

Each man was armed either with a rifle or a pistol. Ed had a pistol one of the trappers had given him. Mack Hanson carried a rifle given to him by the other patrolman, the short and blocky young officer. Curly had his rifle and his pistol was in his belt. They had cartridges and they had dynamite and they had sulphur matches and the dynamite was complete and ready to explode, fuses in place and caps ready.

"Here we go," Ed said, and took the lead at a dog-trot. The others fell in behind him with Nacie and Chief taking up the last position. It was about three or four miles to Fort Green. He kept up a steady dog-trot. They went through the willows and found the trail that led down the river. A grey owl made a mournful noise from his perch in a high tree. Once three white-tail deer leaped out suddenly ahead, their white tails high as they bounced into the moonlight. A cougar moved into the brush on silent paws but they did not see him. Man was on the move and man was dangerous, and the wildings fled in silence. Chief smelled the air and growled but he followed the girl. The river lapped against its banks, sullen and angry with muddy water, and icebergs were grey and they moved swiftly along, pushed by the stern current. Ed kept up the pace and he became tired and then he got his second wind. He was still weak but his strength had come back to a great degree. But the cuts on his wrists and his ankles kept reminding him of the terror-filled dungeon, and the slashes across his back brought his mind always to The Bear and his snarling bullwhip.

They all had the same thought at some moment as they made the trek, and they all wondered if they would see the sun rise. But this thought came to each and did not stay long, for there was a job ahead. On their rifles and short-guns would rest the fate of many other men—men who rode with Custer and Crook and Howard. They were accomplishing two things: they were seeking revenge and they were going to keep rifles and cartridges out of the hands of the Sioux—rifles that could and would kill cavalry and infantry-men.

Then the bulk that was Fort Green was ahead of them, dark and threatening under the moon. The stockade reared its height, and the cupolas stood out against the light sky. And here they split up.

"Good luck and lots of it," Corporal Hank Williams murmured.

Ed said, "And the same to you men," and he took the path to the right. Behind him came Mack Hanson with his sunken eyes and scarred wrists and scarred soul, and behind Mack came the redskin called Curly, and the girl left them at this point, taking Chief to hide in the willows. Ed Jones glanced back just as she left the trail and the red willows claimed her and his malemute. They were walking now, bent over to keep concealed, working their way toward the main gate. They went along the river's bank. They came toward the landing where was tied the river packet. The boat lay flat on the dark waters. There were no lights in it. Evidently the crew was spending the night in Fort Green. Ed Jones wondered how many men were in the fort. Each man was an enemy. They were running against tough odds, he figured. But there was no percentage in letting this thought stay in his mind, so he did his best to get rid of it. Still it persisted in bothering him, moving across his brain with infinite slowness.

Back in the clearing, both he and Hank Williams had practised throwing three sticks the length of a stick of powder. They had tied the powder together with a buckskin thong. They had taken three sticks just about the same weight and size of a stick of dynamite and they had practised throwing these to determine how far they could pitch the black powder. So he knew just about how close he had to get to the gate. now the gate was ahead of him by about two hundred feet. He could not see the guard in the cupola nor could he see the glow of a cigarette or cigar there. But he figured there was a guard.

He held out his hand, palm spread, and it touched Mack Hanson, who in turn stopped Curly. This was the signal that Ed was to move out alone to do the dirty work. He felt the quick push of Mack's fingers against his, and this gave him some measure of assurance. He did not feel so lonely. They stayed there on their haunches and he moved ahead. He worked with care but with speed. He had been born to the timber, the timber was his home, and his job was trapping and stalking the wildings. This had given him great skill and a greater patience. The boat rose and fell in the water, lazy and dark. He moved through the willows, always conscious of the purr of the river. Somewhere in the buckbrush the wild roses bloomed and they sent out their sweet and secret aroma.

Usually he liked the smell of the wild rose; tonight, though, he disliked it.

His heart was a pounding thing, jarring the ribs of his chest. He judged his distance and saw it was right and he settled down. He got a match in one hand and he was hunkered behind a boulder. And so he waited. He seemed to wait for years; actually, it was only short minutes. He looked at the round and yellow moon. The moon, though, had no sympathy, no regard for him. The moon was cold and without thoughts. He glanced at the river boat and then back at the gate. He would put the powder at the junction of the two heavy gates, the point where they met. He would blast it from its hinges and take the cupola and guard down with the gate. The guard would be due for a surprise but Ed judged the surprise would not last long. The dynamite would roar upward and kill him.

He had no compunctions about taking the life of the guard. He hoped he would kill him and he hoped this with a savage intensity. The guard was low and needed death, for the guard was in this with Big John Remington and the hulking devil called The Bear.

The seconds dragged out and became minutes, and the minutes were long. He waited for two things: either the call of *Malemute* or the flaring roar of the exploding dynamite. Either would send him forward, arm back for the throw. Either would send the match into life, send the fuse sputtering.

From inside the fort came the sudden sound of laughing and roaring men. The drunk was still going on.

Then, from across the fort, the world turned red and roaring. There was no cry of *malemute*. If there had been, it had become lost in the smashing roar of the exploding dynamite.

The match came to life with one stroke. The fuse caught and he went forward, hearing the roar of the explosion. He heard the high-pitched cry of the guard in the cupola. He threw the dynamite the way a man puts the shot. It arced, it hissed, it had a red tongue. It landed directly in front of the gate. He had his pistol out and he sent a shot toward the cupola. A bullet came back, the rifle spitting flame, and the bullet hit the boulder. Then, the dynamite exploded.

Ed Jones remembered it until the day he died.

He had been running backwards when the dynamite exploded. The world changed instantly to a red and roaring hell. The gate went sailing upward, ripped from its leather hinges. The two sections of it seemed to float as though they had wings. Debris went soaring after them. The cupola went back, suddenly disappearing. The dynamite blew out part of the stockade, too, one each side of the gate. And where the gate had been was a wide hole in the stockade of Fort Green.

"Come on in, men!" Ed screamed.

Then he was moving ahead, his pistol in his hand. Behind him came Mack Hanson with his sunken and broken eyes. Mack Hanson, with his great undying hate, with his scarred wrists and ankles, with the unhealed cuts of the lash on his broad back. And behind Mack came Curly the scout.

The stockade was burning. But the spring rains had been wet and many, and therefore it did not burn fast. They moved through the hanging dust and the stink of the black powder. One of the gates came down, scissoring as it fell, and it hit a building, cutting through the sod roof. It was suspended upright, caught and held by the timbers. A glance told Ed it was the house over the dungeon. The other hit the river, splashing down with silvery spray.

They burst into the compound, coming out of the dust. The guard had been thrown from the cupola which lay on the ground a mass of shattered timbers. He was dark against the destruction, and Ed knew he was out of the picture and for good. No human could stand the roaring pressure of the black powder that had hit the guard. He gave a quick glance at the opposite cupola. It, too, had been blasted to earth, but that section of the fort was not burning.

"Spread out," he ordered hoarsely, and the roughness of his voice surprised even himself. "Each man to himself and remember the *malemute*, and kill all you can!"

"With pleasure," Mack Hanson screamed.

Curly the scout said nothing. He swung away and moved toward the south, and he was squat and heavy and deadly. The scene was one of chaos. The twin blasts had shaken the log buildings to their foundations. It had blasted Many Feathers away from her stove and had thrown her bleeding and startled into the wall. The stove had tipped over from the concussion. Fire was on the floor and was starting to lick up the dried walls of her kitchen. She got to her feet and then fell down, and she got up again and staggered out the door. Ol' Man had been sleeping with his back to a wall out in the compound. A hunk of the stockade hit the logs over him, came down and almost crushed him. The heavy log lay across him. He tried to crawl out, but blood was in his brain and his head, and then he tried to crawl no longer, for he became the third casualty in the destruction of Fort Green. The two guards who had been in the lookout-towers had beaten him across the Big Ridge.

Big John Remington and the captain and three of the crew members had been playing poker in the mess hall. Big John was in an ugly mood that had been caused by his continuous losing and by the whiskey he had drunk. He was also impatient because the Sioux pack-train had not come at the regular and appointed time. He was thinking of two men who owned silver fox furs and who had broken out of his dungeon against odds that he had figured were impossible. He figured those two men had had help, but he did not know who had helped them. He was suspicious even of The Bear. He knew that The Bear had a greedy streak in his make-up. He was fostering the thought that perhaps the two had traded their secret to The Bear for their freedom. He had even sent The Bear out on a scouting trip and he had in turn followed his right-hand man to see if he went to dig up two silver-fox pelts. But The Bear had blundered half-drunk and half-blind through the brush and had dug up no pelts nor had he taken silver-fox furs out of their hiding-place. Big John Remington was somewhat at a loss. He felt baffled and puzzled, and he hated this feeling. He wanted to be the boss and he wanted to rule this fort, and he had not done a good job. This rankled him and fed his inner anger. And his continual losses in this endless poker game did not add to his happiness.

Had he been clear-minded and sober he would have realised he was bucking a cold deck. He was one man playing against three or four others and they were working him. He guessed this but his wavery mind could not grab any conclusive evidence or point. It was all honest enough to the naked eye. One would bid him up high and then would get the signal and turn him over to the man with the best hand. It was very simple. One man cannot beat four men when they work together. A matter of uniting forces, nothing more.

When the blast came the big factor had been shuffling the greasy deck of cards, and he had been livid with anger. The blast knocked the building rocking on its stone foundation. It came with stunning surprise. At first they thought an earthquake had shaken the house and then when the other roar came—the second concussion caused by Ed Jones's dynamite—Big John Remington knew it was no earthquake.

"Black powder!" he hollered.

The explosion knocked The Bear out of his bunk. He rolled out on the floor and then he sat up and looked dazedly for his bullwhip. The room was wild with shouts and conjecture. Big John Remington had scooped his rifle from its resting place beside the door. The explosion had knocked the rifle to the floor. He did not check the barrel or the magazine to see if they had cartridges for he kept the rifle loaded all the time and he kept the magazine filled.

"What happened?" The Bear hollered.

He got no answer. The men were pouring out of the door, which had been knocked open. Big John Remington had been the first one out. One glance told him what had happened. The main gate was an aperture gaping in the moonlight. The south wall was burning. Smoke was coming from the kitchen. Flames were eating along the beams of the building and scarlet tongues were licking out the windows.

"Them damned trappers! They've come back an' blasted the hell out of the wall! They've got help from somewhere—"

The Bear came roaring out of the building. He had his coiled bullwhip in one hand and his pistol in the other. He was now wide awake. He realised he could make a good target there in front of the open door with the light behind him so he ran to one side, crouched and heavy in the night.

He went to one knee and knelt like that, looking into the moonlight. A log came hurling down, the last of the gate, and it hit the kitchen on its sod roof, shaking it and tearing into the sod as the log slid off the roof and hit the ground.

The captain had a pistol in his hand, and he and his men were ready and armed. They always went armed. Theirs was a dangerous game—this game of gun-running—and therefore to be armed was to be prepared. He was a thick-set man, ugly of face and loose-lipped, and he had made his living by dealing outside the pale of the law. Now he had but one thought in his mind and he put this into words.

"Get the boat, men! We got to hold the boat!"

Big John hollered, "Spread out, men!" and his voice was a croaking bellow. "Spread out and take them as they come!"

"Work toward the boat!" the captain ordered.

The Bear lifted his pistol and fired twice at a man coming toward them, bent low. The man went down on his belly. The Bear wondered if he had shot the man, or if he had fallen of his own accord.

Many Feathers came out of her kitchen. She was screaming like a wounded she-wolf, shot through the vitals. It was the high-pitched scream of the Sioux tribe, and it cut across the gunfire with knife-like sharpness. It cut into a man's nerves, making him even more nervous. She stopped screaming when she fell over a log. She lay on the ground, whimpering like a lost wolf-cub. But she had sense enough to lie low behind the thick log.

"Get along the buildings," Big John ordered, "and fight them! They're in the open, and we got the upper hand!"

He was correct in this statement, and his words came to Ed Jones. Ed was advancing toward them, bent over and low against the moonlight. Corporal Hank Williams and his three men were moving in from the south. They darted for the safety of a log building used as a store house. Ed saw them running forward, scurrying like sagehens running in front of a marauding coyote. But he had no eyes for them. This was a battle where each man had to fight alone and fight for his life.

He did not know whether bullets were coming close, but he did know that he had not yet been hit. From the darkness of the log building ahead came the stabbing flame of rifles and intermingled with these sharp jets were the thundering reports of short guns. He was aware that Mack Hanson was still on his feet. He could see him from the corner of his eye. Curly the scout had disappeared against the stockade wall, hidden there in the shadows.

"Get out of the clearin'!" he yelled at Mack Hanson.

Hanson hollered, "Kill them, Ed!"

"Get into the protection of the buildings!" Ed hollered back.

The burning buildings added further brightness to the night. The red of the flames became intermingled and gaudy in the yellow of the moonlight. Mack Hanson darted for a small building at the end of the burning kitchen. Ed knew he could not make it. He felt sand and gravel spurt up and hit his buckskin pants. He remembered a huge black boulder that was in the compound. Evidently it had been too heavy and huge to move, so Big John Remington had left it in the compound. He glimpsed this to to his right about forty feet and he ran for it, bent over and in a hurry. He came to it and he dived into its dark shadow, putting its igneous bulk between himself and the rifles and pistols there along the wall. He heard the vicious whine of a bullet as it hit the rock and then slid off harmlessly into space. A rifle ball, he thought, and then he had his pistol lying on the flat surface of the rock.

Big John and his men were lying on the ground along the base of the building, and they were part of the shadows there. The only thing that betrayed their positions was the flame of their weapons. Ed realized that things were not going too well. Their attack had been built on the element of surprise, and this was now a thing of the past. From now on it would be a pitched battle. And the odds were in favour of the factor and his men.

Also, he had to be conservative with his ammunition. He had to make each shot count. Even with the light of the burning kitchen, he could not see his enemy. They were hidden by the shadow of the log building.

He gave the matter some thought. One thing was necessary: that was to burn down the building which now housed Big John Remington and his men, for he was sure the men had retreated into the building, for now the fire came out of rifle-holes in the logs and from the doorway and the windows. Big John had built Fort Green well. Each building had rifle-holes. Ed had noticed this when he had been in the fort before the dungeon had claimed him. Now the enemy was behind thick log walls and was firing through those holes and through the openings. They had a distinct advantage.

Ed thought, we got to get that building on fire.

He thought of throwing a firebrand. But a firebrand if it landed on the roof would not set fire to the building for the roof was made of thick sod over sheathing, and ground does not burn. He wished he had had some more dynamite. A stick of black powder thrown forward with fuse flaming could have blown the enemy into bits, and he had no compunctions about this method of fighting. But they had spent their dynamite in blasting down the gate and the two guard lookouts. So wishing for dynamite was as useless as wishing for the moon.

The firing had died down to spasmodic bursts. Ed and his gun had run into a blank wall studded with angry guns. From the cabin housing Corporal Hank Williams and his fellow patrolman and the two trappers came an occasional shot, but they were at a distinct disadvantage, for they could not see the men in the log cabin. They were in a cabin at the south end of the mess hall which protected Big John Remington and The Bear and the crewmen of the river boat.

Curly was somewhere along the north wall, crouched

there and also impossible to put in a shot, for a man cannot send a bullet through a wall of log which is at least a foot thick, and he cannot see through logs, either. Mack Hanson was somewhere close to the burning kitchen, Ed guessed.

Ed and the boulder were alone in the clearing.

There was also another point to consider, his racing brain told him. Dawn would soon be here and when daylight came the odds would more than ever begin the favour of Big John and The Bear and the river-boat crew. Something had to be done, and done in a hurry.

A sudden burst of firing came from Hank Williams and his hands, and this was the cover Ed Jones needed. He left the shelter of the boulder like a jackrabbit leaping out from under a sagebrush when suddenly scared by a wolf or coyote. He did not fire. He had no time to raise his pistol and fire. He had about a hundred feet to go until he reached the burning kitchen. And he had to get to that kitchen. Head down, heart in his throat, he sprinted, moccasins digging dust.

"There runs one of them!"

The shout had come from the cabin housing the enemy. Ed saw the flame of a rifle stuck out through a hole in the logs, but he did not know where the bullet went. He had about twenty feet to go when the bullet hit his arm. He had been pumping his arms back and forth to get more speed. And the bullet hit his arm when it was back of him, and it tore through the bone and muscles. The blow sent him skidding ahead, and he rolled into the area behind the flaming and smoking kitchen. The flames hid him from the rifles and pistols of Big John Remington's men.

He came ploughing in and he rolled over, and his left arm dangled. The bullet had broken the arm between the elbow and the shoulder. His buckskins were wet with blood and he was shocked and he was nauseous. The bullet had gone through his arm and had burned a trail across the muscles on his back and he had blood also on the back of his jacket. With his good hand, he felt his back, and he realised the bullet had just grooved him, tearing a scooping trail across the thick muscles of his back. He had been lucky. So had the man who had shot him. The man had been a good shot . . . or a lucky shot. For he had been a fleeing and uncertain target.

The first effects of the bullet left him, and he felt the heat of the burning kitchen. It was burning on the east side, which was the side facing the main gate. He got to his feet and staggered around the north end of the log building. This end was starting to burn but the west side of the building was not as yet on flames. Here he saw a log—a thick cottonwood log about thirty feet long and about three feet thick—and he went behind this. And here he found the squaw called Many Feathers.

"White man, you came back?"

He could see her face. The broad face of the Sioux was smeared with blood. She lay on her back. She was heavy and she was sick, for the shock had jarred her terribly.

"We came back to wipe out Fort Green."

"You used the dynamite?"

"We blew the hell out of the south wall and the main gate."

"When you do that—you hurt me inside."

Ed said, "Mother, we had to get in. We got to kill this nest of snakes. Other trappers would come—be killed and robbed—like the girl's father was killed—like we was throwed in the dungeon—"

"They are in the cook hall. Where they eat, they are."

"We got to burn them out."

"There is kerosene—coal oil—in my kitchen."

"Whereabouts in it?"

"By the door, there—the back door. A can of it. Fires in my stove—I started them with it—"

Ed said, "I've had some luck."

A man moved around the protected end of the kitchen. Ed swung his pistol on him and then recognition came in.

"Mack, this way."

Mack Hanson was soon on his belly beside them. "We got tangled up," he panted. "We fouled our own nest."

"We got to burn them out."

"Curly—he got one."

Ed asked, "Hurt bad?"

"He's dead. Along the wall."

Ed cursed the guns of Big John. Many Feathers lay and sobbed. Her throat and lungs rattled.

"We got to burn them out," Ed repeated. "She says there's a can of coal oil in the kitchen. By the door."

"Then what?"

Ed looked over the log at the mess-hall. It was about a hundred yards or so away.

"I'll get that can."

He got to his feet, and his arm dangled. Mack Hanson said, "You got shot?" but Ed had no reply. He ran toward the door which was about thirty feet away. Flames were appearing on the south end of the kitchen. Flames lighted the scene with ghostly glow.

He drew no fire on his dash for the door. The door hung on one hinge, and he had to push it back to get inside. But the can of coal oil was there. The heat was intense and it smashed against him, but he grabbed the can by the bail and then moved out of the doorway, squatting beside the log wall. He could feel the heat through the thick pine logs.

He was panting, and sweat held his buckskins to him. His arm and back had stopped bleeding. He was dimly aware of this fact, and the pain had lessened. He could feel the ends of the bones grate in his broken arm.

The can had a top that had a wooden cork in it. He pulled this loose. A spud had been jammed over the spout and he took this loose, too. The can was about half full. He took it in his good hand. He said, "Here goes nothing," and he dashed toward the mess-hall, can poised and ready to throw. He drew a bullet but he was moving fast and the light from the burning building, coupled with the glow of the moon, was still not clear. Shadows danced and made for hard shooting. He threw the can the way a football player throws a shuffle-pass. Underhanded, he threw it; it crashed against the side of the building, then fell at its base.

He ran backwards, and reached the side of the building. He hesitated there for a moment, and he considered his luck—he had done his job. The thing now was to ignite the kerosene. He ran to the log and rolled across it and a bullet hit the log, making a thudding sound heard even above the crackle of the flaming kitchen.

"The squaw—she's dead, Ed."

Ed panted, "Too bad. I liked her," He looked at her immense body. "We got to get flame to that coal oil. I'm all in. Get a firebrand—from inside the kitchen—and throw it on the kerosene."

"My job, Ed."

Mack Hanson ran for the kitchen door. He was a gaunt skeleton of a man, running on his guts. He got to the door and came out with a flaming rag tied to what looked like a broom handle. He threw it the way a man throws a javelin. The bullet hit him as he threw, and he went down on his face. But the flaming brand landed beside the kerosene can, about a foot from it.

Ed hollered, "Mack," but got no reply. Coal oil had jetted out of the can. The brand touched it and it broke into wild flame. Coal oil had been dashed on the logs. The building sprang into flame in an area about five feet across. The wind licked the flames upward across the logs.

Ed hollered, "We got their house on fire, Hank. They

got to make a run for it soon. I'm watchin' the back."

There was no reply, so he screamed the words again. This time a reply came back, indistinct and distant because of the gunfire and the burning building.

"Kill them, Ed."

Ed lay there and he put his pistol across the log and he waited. Many Feathers did not move. She lay with her face in the dust. Ed felt sympathy for the heavy Sioux squaw. She had been an innocent person, and she had died because she loved Big John. Or did she love him?

The world was a crazy, mixed-up thing. The moon rode at a weird and fantastic tilt in the sky. Back along the willows, a malemute and a girl waited. A pair of silver-fox furs were cached in the wilderness. Because of them there had been the dungeon, the lash of a whip. Ed waited and he called again to Mack Hanson. And this time, he got a weak reply.

"I got shot . . . in the chest."

"I'll come after you, Mack."

"No." Mack Hanson cursed with savage intensity. "I'm safe here—behind this stump."

"I'll come to you."

"No, you'll get killed. They'll come out soon."

The mess hall was burning rapidly. Ed heard the cries of men. They had to get out, for soon the heat would be too intense. The building had two doors—one in the front, one in the back. Corporal Hank Williams and his men would watch the front door. He would watch the back.

There seemed to be a moment of long duration, and then the back door broke open. Two men, crouched over their pistols, came dashing out, and Ed thought, One is The Bear, and he did not know the other. The Bear did not have his bullwhip now. He had a Colt .44 pistol.

Ed hollered, "Here they come, Mack."

He heard the voice of Mack Hanson scream, "The

Bear—He's my meat, Ed. Him an' that bullwhip—"

Ed was on his feet. Mack Hanson had also staggered upright. Ed shot at the man who ran ahead of The Bear. He knocked the man down, and the man shot and missed and lay silent. Ed swung his smoking pistol over to cover The Bear.

But he did not let the hammer drop.

For Mack Hanson had already fired. Gaunt in the red of the flames, a living skeleton, he stood there and his piece was hot and ugly. One bullet caught The Bear in the face, breaking through his wide nose and coming out the back of his ugly head.

Ed watched in terrible fascination.

The Bear slumped ahead, dead on his moccasins. But even in death, he dimly remembered his whip—his right arm started back as though he were lashing out with the bullwhip. Then death took complete possession, and he was down on his face.

"You got him, Mack."

Mack Hanson turned and looked at Ed. "I paid him back—for those lash-marks . . ." Then he, too, was down.

Ed ran to him, sick at heart. He felt his partner's bloody chest, putting his palm over his heart. But there was no beating there. From the front of the building came the roar of rifles and pistols. Ed got to his feet and moved ahead, and then he heard the bull-like voice of Corporal Hank Williams.

"Big John—Ed, he's goin' aroun' the corner toward you."

Ed and Big John met in the clearing. Big John was without a rifle or short-gun. He was shot through the belly. He was very, very sick. He said, "No gun on me," and he stood on wide-spread legs. He looked down at Many Feathers. He was stunned and shocked and wounded. He was whipped.

His big eyes, bulging in straining sockets, looked down at Many Feathers. His thick lips moved.

"She's—dead?"

Ed watched him. "Dead," he repeated.

Again, the bloody lips moved. "I'm tired. Big John— he's gonna lay beside her—" He took a step forward. Then he fell on his side and lay with his head against the ground.

His hand reached out, finding the buckskin skirt of the squaw. Ed stood there and watched the huge hand twist the soft buckskin.

Three days later the Sioux came to Fort Green. They came out of the timber with their pack horses—pintos and bays and sorrels and duns and greys and blacks. The Sioux came for rifles and powder and ball and cartridges. But they did not get these things, for Fort Green was no more.

Fort Green was only black ashes.

The Sioux were puzzled. They saw fresh graves and they poked around through the ashes looking for loot until their moccasins were black. The river boat, too, was gone.

They were led by a chief called Pushing Ahead. Pushing Ahead did not know that at about that moment in Fort Bridger, about sixty miles below Fort Green, they were hanging two men to a makeshift scaffold.

Those two men were the river-boat captain and Big John Remington. The captain whined and wept as the noose was fitted but Big John Remington, wounded and sick, died without a word of protest. His eyes were on the high horizon. Was he thinking of his squaw, Many Feathers?

Pushing Ahead did not know that two hours after the hanging there would be a wedding at Fort Bridger. A man named Ed Jones was to be married to a wilderness girl named Nacie Malone.

And what would Ed Jones give his wife as a wedding present?

A set of silver-fox furs, of course.

# GUN QUICK

# ONE

A quarter-mile ahead of Matt Harrison rose a rounded Montana hill covered with buckbrush. From behind the hill came the sudden snarl of a rifle. Matt hurriedly reined in his trail-tired horse.

He automatically counted the shots. Four . . . He sat a tense saddle, blue eyes searching the hill's rocky surface for possible danger.

He saw no suspicious movements. Only the wind, there across the brush, the endless prairie wind.

This side of the hill showed no skirling powder-smoke. He had seen many similar hills on his ride fifty miles south from the Canadian border into wild Montana Territory.

He had immediately recognized the shots as rifle reports. A rifle makes a savage, singing sound, a six-shooter a roaring boom.

He studied the hill.

Gray sagebrush grew along its base. Huge sandstone boulders were flung here and there.

Hard breathing made his bronc's ribs rise and fall under his Hamley saddle. The cayuse was leg-tired. The afternoon sun was blisteringly hot.

The horse needed water. He'd drunk last when crossing the Frenchman creek just below the United States — Canada border.

Now the horse pulled at his bit. Matt Harrison figured the sweat-coated bronc smelled water ahead.

He saw no sign of green growth on this side of hill. Where there was water, there were trees and green brush.

Harrison looked down at the trail he was following south. Hoofs had ground deep into the arid soil. All tracks pointed ahead. Evidently those hoofs — cattle, deer, horses, elk — were headed for water?

Harrison heard no more shots. This land was strange to him. Never before had he ridden across this north central section of Montana. Tension slowly left his tough young body.

He looked about, a tall young man loafing in the saddle. Despite the heat, despite the drought, he liked what he saw, for the barren wilderness, burned brown with its short grass, seemed to hold a studied loneliness, an appeal of its own.

For drought held this lonesome land. Grass was short and brown, even this early in the year. Evidently there'd been little snow last winter to form spring water. Also spring rains apparently had been very scarce.

Harrison again thought of the four rifle shots. Maybe he read danger into something where danger did not exist?

Maybe some cowpuncher had downed a deer or antelope or elk for cabin meat? Harrison had seen skinny cattle in this sagebrush wilderness.

He was jerked back to reality by the tug of his bronc on his bridle reins.

Harrison knew horses. And he was sure the bronc smelled water ahead, so he gave him rein south on the rutted trail.

He circled the base of the hill and before him unfolded a long draw some three miles in distance, he figured — and about a quarter-mile wide.

Straight ahead across this valley stretched a low rim of hills, also covered by buckbrush and sagebrush and here and there a scraggly greasewood. Halfway up this slope Harrison saw a small patch of greenery.

He read the distant green as cottonwood trees and bullberry bushes. These told him a spring of water came from that side hill.

Still, caution rode his shoulders. Those four rifle shots had come from this area. Search the hill as his eyes did, they could detect no sign of life — of man, cow or wilding — on the hill's rocky side.

Harrison then saw the reflection of sunlight on galvanized steel. That would be from a water-tank below the spring to catch the run-off water, for water was worth its weight in gold here.

He gave the horse his head. The thirsty animal loped toward the spring. He crossed the valley and took the upward track — and as Harrison rode into the area around the tank, he realized instantly he'd given his horse too much rein, and his foolishness had led him into trouble.

For two dead cows lay between him and the tank. He pulled in and studied them, heart hammering against his ribs.

Both cows had been shot in the head. Blood still oozed from the bullet-holes. Harrison remembered the rifle shots and a cold spot suddenly froze in his belly, for the rifle-man could still be hidden, back in the cottonwoods.

Common sense told him it was too late to turn and ride away. Men that would kill harmless cattle were not beyond putting a bullet in a man's back.

So he rode ahead, moving around the two dead cows. To his surprise he saw that the cows were Holsteins; this in itself was odd. Cattlemen raised whitefaced Herefords, not black and white Holsteins. Farmers usually raised Holsteins because they were such good milk cows. And since riding into Beavertail Basin some fifteen miles north he had not seen any sign of a farmer. This did not make sense.

Now he was at the water tank and he noticed something else. Somebody had placed two bullets into the tank low down close ot its base. Twin streams of gray water spouted out.

But the tank was still half full and the bay plunged his nose into the water, sucking noisily around his bit. Harrison carefully folded both hands on his saddle horn. He looked slowly about but saw nothing suspicious in the cottonwood grove.

"I want no trouble," he said loudly.

His words died in space. For a long moment the only sound was that of his drinking horse. Perhaps the rifleman had already jerked stakes and had ridden over the hill and the grove was empty.

But this assumption proved false when a harsh masculine voice said, "Just stay where you are, cowboy! Keep your hands on that saddle horn! Don't make a move for your weapons!"

Harrison studied the point where the voice had sounded but the brush and trees were too thick and he saw nobody.

"I'm no fool," he said.

Two men rode out of the cottonwoods, horses braced against gravity. The lead rider rode a big sorrel. He rode with his massive boots deep in stirrups. Sunlight shimmered on the silver of his expensive hand-tooled saddle. He carried a rifle. Matt judged him to be somewhere around fifty.

The second rider was a slender, lithe man of thirty odd. He rode a chunky black gelding. He also carried a Winchester. Matt read the Circle Y brand on the right shoulders of the saddle horses.

The older man moved in on Matt's right, the younger on his left. Neither spoke. The older man leaned in his saddle, hawkish eyes taking in Matt's tired bay, finally locking with Matt's gray eyes. Those eyes appraised a six foot cowpuncher wearing runover boots, plain steel spurs, well washed levis and a faded chambray shirt. Matt smelled whiskey on both men.

Matt said nothing, carefully watching the older man. Plainly this man was boss of this duo. The younger man was a follower, not a leader. The big man, Matt realized, was a local cattle king — he had met this arrogant type before.

Most of Montana cowkings were transplanted Texans who had trailed Lone Star cattle north into Montana Territory following the war. Tough riders, they had spilled wild cattle over these tumbling Montana rangelands, claiming their land by settlement, not by registered deeds. They were tough men. They had had to be tough. This land had then been owned by Sioux and Crow and Cheyenne.

They and their hard riders had done more to put the redskin on reservation than had the U.S. Cavalry. They had built empires by the brute force of their fists and their guns.

"Who the hell are you?" the cattle king demanded.

Harrison's belly was solid now. "I could ask you the same," he countered.

The dull eyes narrowed. "What's your name?"

"Harrison. Matt Harrison."

"I'm Wad Martin. This is my range-boss, Jocko Smith."

Harrison looked at Jocko Smith. Smith leaned forward in saddle, eyes on Harrison. Harrison saw a long jaw, a long nose, and two close-set yellow eyes.

"Glad to know you, Martin. You too, Smith."

Martin grunted. Smith said nothing, eyes boring in on Harrison, evaluating him.

"I own Circle Y," Wad Martin said.

Harrison said, "I see the brands on your horses."

Martin leaned back, said, "There's a man down in Beavertail City. Name of Clint Harrison. He any kin of yours?"

Harrison debated momentarily. Clint Harrison was his only brother — in fact, the only remaining member of his immediate family. Finally Harrison said, "He's my brother."

Wad Martin smiled tightly, glanced at Jocko Smith. "Another god-darned nester! Get him, Jocko!"

Harrison whipped around in leather, boots braced — and grabbed Jocko Smith's rising rifle, getting both hands on the barrel. He fought for the rifle, teeth gritted, bronc standing solid — and all the time he knew he was an open target to Wad Martin.

From the corner of one eye he saw Martin spurring his stallion close. He dropped his hold from Smith's rifle, turning in saddle to meet this new threat.

He was too late.

Wad Martin's Winchester slashed down. Desperately, Matt Harrison flung up a hand — but not in time.

The rifle's barrel crashed across his head.

First there was shooting pain — and then only blackness.


Harrison hollered, "You trying to drown me?"

His head ached violently. His eyes focused, outlining a woman. She had golden hair, a sun-tanned lovely face — and then the water hit Harrison again, choking and blinding him.

"No more — please!"

"That's enough, Sis." The man owned a deep voice. Harrison thought first that Wad Martin had spoken.

He stared at the man.

He had never seen a man like this before. The man was about five-five, and he was almost as broad as tall — his shoulders were huge, heavily-muscled.

Harrison looked around. Two horses stood behind the girl. They wore only bridles — and farm-bridles, at that. The kind with blinders. There was no sign of Wad Martin and Jocko Smith.

Evidently that pair had hightailed.

Harrison's gaze returned to the man, whose ugliness fascinated him. He remembered a picture book his mother had bought him years ago when he had been a boy on the Texas Panhandle. That book had had pictures of men looking like this man. Gnomes, they had been called.

The man had a head as large as a water pail. Two huge eyes, damp and big as big marbles, rolled in red sockets. They were dull pale blue. He wore no hat. His mass of hair had the colour of ripe wheat. His nose was a big pear. His lips were thick leather.

Now the thick lips parted and said, "I'm Sig Westby. This is my sister, Jane."

"I'm Matt Harrison."

Ropelike yellow brows rose. "Harrison, huh? Any relation to Clint Harrison?"

"Clint's my brother. I mentioned that fact to Wad Martin and Jocko Smith and they went wild and slugged me."

Thick lips hardened. "Martin and Smith, huh? So they was the ones who killed our milkcows!"

Harrison realized he was sitting propped against one of the dead Holsteins. He got slowly to his feet, head spinning. He walked to the water tank and leaned with both hands braced on its rim, waiting for his head to clear, and finally it became normal and he looked at Jane Westby.

Her blue eyes were on him. She was a little beauty, not more than five two, Harrison guessed. Neatly built, she wore an old blue shirt and tight levis. Her small boots were worn and her tiny fingers held her old hat. She had used that hat to throw water into his face.

"Are you all right?" Jane asked.

Harrison grinned. "I'll live. All Harrisons were born with concrete skulls."

332

"You've got a bad cut on your head that'll require some stitches. You should go to Beavertail City and let Doc Seymour sew you up. He's only a vet but he's good with a needle."

"Where you from?" Sig Westby asked.

Matt had been up in Canada punching cattle and after a rough winter doling out hay to Canadian cattle had decided to return to the United States.

"Got in a poker game in Malta," Malta was the county-seat north on Milk River. "One of the boys there knew Clint, said he was in Beavertail City, and I haven't seen Clint in seven years, so thought I'd drop in and say hello."

"Clint's in bed. He's wounded," Sig informed. "Had a gunfight with Jocko Smith and Smith shot Clint through the right leg about a week ago."

"Five days," Jane corrected.

Sig Westby smiled. "Takes a woman to remember to the last detail."

Jane's lips slightly hardened.

"Well," Sig said, "we'd best get you into Doc Seymour. Town's about four miles south."

Matt nodded.

Sig studied the two dead milk-cows. "We won't juice those cows any more. Only milkers we have, too. Jane and I were out looking for them. I'd guess that Wad Martin and Jocko Smith shot them."

"I never saw the cows get shot," Matt Harrison said, "but they were dead when I rode up. That your water-tank, too?"

Sig nodded. "Just installed it last week, too. Cost us a purty sum. Those holes can be plugged. Cut a willow that size, tar it and wrap the tar with old cloth, and pound the willow hunks into the holes. But our two milk-cows —''.

Matt saw bitterness flash across the huge eyes. He got the impression that, once this gnome were aroused, it would take hard bullets to stop him.

"Give me first chance," Matt said quietly.

Eyes swung on him, probing him.

"I've got a score to settle with Jocko Smith. Yes, and with Wad Martin, too."

"That throws you on the side of us farmers," Sig said.

Matt slowly shook his head. He had to shake it slowly. Had he shaken it hard his brains would have rattled.

"I ride a middle trail," he said.

Jane Westby said, "Let's get him to town. We can talk on the way in." She went over to Matt's horse, standing hip-humped a short distance away, led him over and asked, "You need any help, Matt?"

Matt found a stirrup. "I can handle it, thanks." He mounted. He felt better in saddle.

The Westbys climbed on their old nags, the girl going up skilfully, pulling herself on her bareback plough-horse. They rode downslope toward the trail, Matt and Sig in the lead, Jane behind a pace. Matt heard hoofs coming from the north, the direction from whence he had ridden in.

"Circle Y's coming back!" Jane said tersely. "Martin and Smith have seen Sig and me ride toward the tank!"

Matt listened. "Only one horse," he said.

The young woman rode a magnificent sorrel. Sunlight reflected from her silver mounted saddle, making Matt remember Wad Martin's expensive rig.

Jane said angrily, "That bitch of a Margaret Martin! Wad's daughter, Matt!"

Matt glanced at Jane. Her lips were set in anger. He swung his eyes back to Margaret Martin, who drew in her horse. He saw a young woman as dark as a gypsy. Her hair was ebony black. She rode bareheaded, her Stetson hanging by its chin strap. She wore a blue silk shirt and creamy buckskin covered her thighs. Her Justin boots held a high polish and her Kelly spurs were heavy with silver.

She seemed to have eyes only for Matt, whom she studied a long moment, and Matt smiled but she didn't. Jane cut in with, "What do you want, Martin?"

Margaret took her eyes from Matt, but she did not look at Jane. She looked beyond Matt at the dead milk cows. "I suppose these cows were killed by my loving father and his no good foreman?"

Jane said, "They were!"

Now Margaret looked at Jane. "I just saw my father and Smith heading across the hills toward town. I'm out looking for a saddle horse of mine that broke out of the night pasture last night. So I thought I'd ride over the springs and look around."

"You've looked around," Jane coldly pointed out, "so why not keep on riding?"

"So sweet of you," Margaret Martin murmured. She looked at the water tank. "They shot holes in your new tank, too, I see. Childish thing to do." Her dark eyes returned to Matt. "I've never seen you around before. I take it you're new here?"

"I might be," Matt said.

"Your name?"

Matt laughed sourly. "Like father, like daughter. Arrogant, asking many questions — very impolite. Ask your father whay my name is. He knows."

He turned his horse toward the south. He rode away and within a few minutes the Westbys clattered up behind. Matt looked back. Margaret Martin sat saddle, watching them leave.

"She's a bitch," Jane said.

"But a pretty one," Matt said.


Beavertail City consisted of one main street lined with weather beaten, unpainted buildings. Matt read signs: *Martin Hardware, Martin Saddles, Martin Mercantile and General Store, Martin Blacksmith Shop.* Only the hotel, a two storey affair, did not have Wad Martin's name over its door. Its sign said *Beavertail House.*

The baldheaded clerk told Matt that Clint was upstairs in Room Eleven. Matt took the rickety steps two at a time. His brother's door was locked and he knocked.

"Who's there?" Clint's gruff voice asked.

"Your brother, Matt."

"Go to hell! My brother's in Texas!"

Matt grinned. "Old Pancho sent me, Clint."

Old Pancho had been the Mexican *mozo* on the Harrison Running M, out of Lubbock, Texas.

Matt heard, "My God, it is Matt!"

The door was unlocked, key rattling. It opened. But Clint did not open it.

A short, squat Indian opened it, stepping back, hand on his holstered gun, his shrewd black eyes narrowed slits in his leathery face.

Clint lay naked on the bed. A white bandage was on his right thigh. The room was hot as hell is supposed to be. Beads of sweat coated Clint's muscular frame.

Clint got on one elbow, staring at Matt. "Good lord," he said, "how'd you come to get into this jerkwater burg?"

"I could ask you the same."

Clint gestured toward the Indian. "Go buy yourself a drink. My brother will act as my body-guard, Slow Elk."

The redskin grunted, looked hard again at Matt, then waddled out, dirty buckskins leaving a stinking odor. He closed the door behind him. Matt noticed Clint watching the door.

Matt said nothing.

Finally Clint said, "Open the door, Matt? See if the son is eavesdropping?"

Matt opened the door. No Slow Elk outside. Matt looked into the hall. The Indian had just turned the corner to descend the stairs. Matt shut the door, frowning.

"Who's the redskin?" Matt asked.

"A renegade Crow I hired a few months ago to do chores on my farm. I'm a sodbuster now, Clint."

"I rode into town with Sig and Jane Westby. They told me you're also the leader of the farmers."

The fact that Cling was now a farmer had surprised Matt. Farming was hard work and Clint had always evaded physical labour. Matt realized that Clint would now be thirty-three, for Clint was eight

337

years his senior. Clint had been twenty two when he had drawn a twenty-five year sentence in the Texas state penitentiary at Huntsville. Matt had heard that Clint had got out of the pen a year ago. Evidently Clint had immediately headed north out of Texas for Montana.

"What happened to your head?" Clint asked. "Somebody's shaved off a big hunk of your hair."

Matt told about his trouble with Wad Martin and Jocko Smith. "Doc Seymour just finished sewing me up. He had to shave my head."

Clint's eyes narrowed. "So big Wad Martin slugged you cold, huh? You shouldn't have told him your name was Harrison."

Matt grinned. "How was I to know?"

Matt realized he and his brother had not shaken hands, nor had Clint offered his hand. Although the room was stinking hot, it still seemed to hold a stiff coldness. Matt wished he had not stopped in. He and Clint had never been very close.

Clint had been the wild one of the two brothers. Because he had loathed ranch work he had left the Harrison Panhandle spread when he had been seventeen. He had become a professional gambler — and a good one.

Clint was also a terror with a six shooter. Arrogant and cocksure, he had got into trouble during gambling and had killed three men before being sentenced to the Texas pen, for killing the fourth.

"The Texas boys let me out on one condition," Clint said. "I had to get out of Texas and stay out." His lips clenched as he fought pain. "I came right up here to Montana. But what gets me is how did you find out I was on the Beavertail?"

Clint told him about the card game in Malta.

"How long do you intend to stick around, Matt?"

Matt grinned and gingerly touched his scalp. "Maybe for some time. Me, I never did cotton to being pistol whipped!"

Clint's eyes narrowed. "You talk like a damned fool, Matt! Use your head if you have one. This Wad Martin and Jocko Smith are two dangerous men. Look at what happened to me. I can handle a gun — I'm still fast — but Jocko Smith shot me down, and in a fair gunfight too."

Matt said nothing. Again that thought came that Jocko Smith must indeed be lightning with a Colt. Clint had fairly lived with a six shooter in his hand or on his hip.

Clint had spent days practising down in Texas, even when he had been a mere boy. He had stood wide legged and then drawn, pistol leaping from leather. He had become so efficient six shots had sounded as a single sound. And after Clint had emptied his .45, a tin can would be battered and full of holes.

"Don't stick around town just because you think you can help me. I can cut my own water."

Anger touched Matt briefly. It seemed to him that his brother actually wanted him to ride out of Beavertail City.

"How nice," Matt said cynically. He decided to change the subject. "Where is your homestead located?"

"All twelve of us farmers — including Sig Westby — have taken up homesteads on Beavertail Crick."

"They tell me Beavertail is Wad Martin's biggest water supply. In fact, his only water for his Circle I stock during a drought."

"That's the deal, Matt."

"You're in trouble, Clint."

"You tellin' me?" Again, a grimace of pain. "I'm going to kill Jocko Smith! Just as soon as I get on my feet — You met this Martin filly yet?"

"Margaret Martin?"

"Yes."

Matt told about the meeting. "Her and this Westby chicken don't seem to see eye to eye."

"Never saw two females in my life that hated the other like them two."

Somebody knocked on the door. Clint reached under his bed and came up with a Winchester .30-30. He put it on the door. "Okay, Matt," he said.

Matt opened the door. Doc Seymour stood ouside, black bag in hand.

The veterinarian studied the rifle. "Ready for any emergencies, huh, Harrison?" Clint grinned and put the rifle again under his bed. "Martin and Smith would hardly shoot a man already wounded and in bed," the veterinary continued.

Clint laughed hoarsely. Matt watched the doctor unwrap the bandage from around Clint's thigh. Clint had been shot between the hip and knee, the bullet digging a clean shallow channel. Clint had been lucky. Matt had once seen a man die from being shot in the thigh. The bullet had dug deep and had grazed the hip bone, tearing in two the artery there. Blood had jetted out. Within minutes the wounded man had been dead.

Clint's wound was clean and without proud flesh. Clint would be on his feet in a few days.

Doc Seymour stepped back, eyeing the wound. "Looks good," he said. "Healing fast, Clint."

Clint said, "Sure doesn't feel good."

Matt went to the door. Clint said, "If you see any of my old girl friends down in Texas give them my everlasting love, huh?"

"I'll do that," Matt promised.

He went into the hall, softly closing the door behind him, a sour feeling churning his belly. Brothers should be close, not cold as had been he and Clint. He went down the creaking old stairway into the lobby. Slow Elk sat in an armchair there.

Matt said, "He's all yours, Slow Elk."

Slow Elk made no reply. His dark eyes were beady under heavy lids. Matt decided he would take Clint's advice. He would ride out of Beavertail City. Nothing existed between him and Clint but the memory of a boyhood together, and this boyhood had not been very congenial, even though he and Clint were brothers. Clint had always been overbearing and demanding, always the cock of the walk. He would forget big Wad Martin and Jocko Smith.

When he stepped out onto the hotel's porch the sun was sinking, but heat still clung to the parched earth. His throat cried for a cold beer. Across the dusty street was Wad Martin's saloon, its hitchrack holding quite a few tied saddle horses. Matt started toward the saloon, then halted.

He had recognized two of the saddlers tied to the tooth gnawed hitchrack. One was a big sorrel with a silver mounted saddle. The other was a chunky black gelding. The sorrel belonged to Wad Martin, the black to Jocko Smith.

Anger gripped Matt. He wanted to stalk across the street, enter the saloon, jerk Wad Martin around — and plant a handful of knuckles in the cattle king's arrogant big face. He hesitated, face drawn into bleak lines.

But if he did that, Jocko Smith might kill him. Or buffalo him cold again. It would be two against one again. The odds were too heavy. And besides, what would he gain? No, he would take Clint's advice, dust out of Beavertail City.

He turned in the direction of his bay, tied to a hitchrack down the street. He would get something to eat and then head south and make a night camp along some water hole with his bay grazing out on a picket rope.

Suddenly he froze in his boots. From across the street had come a harsh voice. He recognized the voice immediately. Jocko Smith!

"You pack a gun, Harrison! Use it!"

Matt crouched, spun, hand splayed over his gun. Smith stood across the narrow street, also crouched, both hands on his holstered guns, his face drawn in rigid lines.

He stood by the corner of Martin's Saloon. Matt got the impression that he had been waiting in the slot between the saloon and the store.

Matt said, "Why the guns, Smith?"

Smith laughed hollowly. "One Harrison alive in Beavertail is one too many! You might aim to ride out — and you might not be aiming that direction. So I'm going to make sure, Harrison."

"You're drunk," Matt said.

"Maybe I am. Maybe I ain't. But like I said, you got a gun — now use it!" And Jocko Smith started his draw.

Frantic thoughts smashed across Matt Harrison's brain with lightning like suddeness. Smith had him bested, for already the gunman's Colts were lifting from leather. Matt could do but one thing, and that to hit the dust.

He crashed to the ground, hearing a bullet sing overhead. He rolled off the plank sidewalk, aware of dust rising at his right. He rolled three times and came to a dusty stop on his belly. His gun came up, belched.

He shot hurriedly, not faking aim. By sheer luck alone, his bullet smashed into Smith's left shoulder. Smith lurched off the side walk, came to a jarring halt on one knee. Desperately, he started to raise his right hand gun, shock sagging his face muscles. Matt laid his pistol across his forearm, blood cold as he centered the sights on Smith's heart, but he never got to shoot.

From somewhere a lanky middle-aged man came on the dead run. Despite the threat of Matt's pistol he barged between Matt and Smith. He slapped Smith to the ground. Smith dropped his guns. Matt glimpsed a star on the tall man's gray shirt. His gun now in his hand, the lawman whirled, faced Matt. Matt got to his feet. "I want no trouble, lawman," he said.

"Holster your gun!" the lawman ordered.

Matt pushed his pistol into leather. He noticed his shirt tail had popped out. He noticed something else, too — his shirt tail had a bullet hole in it.

Sig Westby came running out of the Mercantile, his sister Jane following him. "That was fast work, Matt," he said.

Matt merely nodded, shaking inside. Beavertail City had come to life. Matt figured the entire town — all fifty of its occupants — were watching from the plank sidewalks. Now Wad Martin came from his saloon, a half dozen men trailing him. He stood wide legged and looked down at Jocko Smith, now grovelling in the dust. Then he lifted heavy eyes to Matt Harrison.

"You must be a heller with a gun, Harrison, to outshoot Smith." Matt detected surprise in the cattle king's voice. Matt said nothing, watching Martin closely. Martin got the blubbering Smith to his feet, shoved him toward the saloon, said, "Somebody get Doc Seymour, huh?"

"Here comes Doc now," a man said.

Two men ushered Smith into the saloon, Wad Martin looked at Matt who said quietly, "You ordered Smith to try to kill me, huh?"

Martin's laugh showed tobacco stained teeth. "Maybe I did and maybe I didn't. You can go either way with your thinking, Harrison."

The lawman cut in with, "No more of this talk, men!"

Wad Martin laughed again, then turned and swaggered into the saloon. Doc Seymour hurried up, panting hard. "You stop anything, Harrison?" Matt laughed shakily. "Only a hole in my shirt tail." Doc Seymour grinned. "There's a seamstress down the street," he said and entered the saloon.

The lawman said, "I'm town marshal, Jim Snodgrass."

"Am I under arrest?" Matt asked. "I claim self defence. Smith called, went for his gun, and shot first."

"I'll bear witness to that," Sig Westby rumbled. "I was in the Mercantile. I saw it all through the window. Like Harrison says, Smith drew first. My sister saw it too."

"I certainly did," Jane Westby affirmed. "And I'll testify if needs be that Jocko Smith shot first."

Matt said, "Thanks."

He glanced at Jane. Her pretty face was drained of blood. He looked now toward the open door of the blacksmith shop situated beside the Mercantile.

Two people stood there watching. One was the blacksmith — a heavy man wearing no shirt. The other was a beautiful, dark haired girl, Margaret Martin. For a long moment Matt's eyes held those of Wad Martin's daughter, and then Margaret looked away.

"Come to my office," Marshal Snodgrass said, "because I want a few words with you, Harrison."

"I'm powerful hungry," Matt said. "I was heading for the cafe when Smith jumped me."

"I'll get a tray from the cafe for you," Snodgrass said, "and you can eat it while we talk."

"Service," Matt said.

"Come along," the marshal said.

When Matt and the lawman passed the hotel Clint Harrison had his head out of an upstairs window. "Now my advice looks good, huh?" Clint cynically said.

Matt glanced up at Clint's bare torso. "You go to hell," he said shortly.

Snodgrass's office was a sod shack at the street's end. Weeds grew on its roof. The insides looked as though cattle had stampeded through the building. A billy goat slept in a corner.

Snodgrass kicked the goat to his feet. The goat lowered his horns, apparently wanting to rush the marshal, then turned and trotted out the back door, bleating angrily.

"Damned thing came in here about two months ago," Snodgrass grunted. "Nobody knows where he come from or who owns him. He doesn't know it, but when winter comes he's going to be my winter chewing."

There were a desk, loaded with papers, and two chairs in the office, one a swivel chair behind the desk, the other a straight backed chair weighted down with a Sears Roebuck catalogue, Snodgrass pushed the catalogue to the dirt floor. "Sit down," he said.

Matt sat.

The billy goat had stunk up the office, leaving a heavy odour behind him — a stink that made Matt think of Slow Elk, Clint's Crow Indian. Snodgrass moved his bulk into the swivel chair and put his run-over boots on his desk. Matt waited in raw impatience, wondering what lay ahead.

"Sig Westby and his sister was in my office a few minutes ago," the marshal finally said. "Told me about them holes in their new water tank and their shot milk cows. Told me too that Wad Martin had slugged you cold out at the tank.''

Matt merely nodded, waiting.

"You actually see somebody shoot them cows? Put them bullet holes in that tank?''

Matt shook his head. "I heard the shots but never saw who fired them.''

Snodgrass expelled a deep breath. "Then actually there's no evidence against Circle Y," he said.

"That seems to make you happy," Matt said.

Snodgrass's pale eyes pulled down. "I don't follow you, Harrison.''

Matt laughed shortly. "Don't play dumb, Snodgrass. I know cattle kings. Wad Martin got you this easy job. That makes you a Circle Y man.''

"Keep talking.''

"I had my sights dead on Smith's heart. A second more and I'd have killed him. But you barged in and saved Smith's life. You did it for Wad Martin.''

Snodgrass's lips worked. "You talk hard, Harrison.''

Matt got to his feet. "I don't see any grub coming over. You can't hold me. Smith pulled first.''

"You leaving town?''

Matt studied the lawman. "I might and I might not. Fact is I doubt if I could leave town, now.''

"What'd you mean by that, Harrison.''

"Use your head, Snodgrass. Quit playing ignorant. My bullet just laid up Wad Martin's ace gunhand. When I slammed lead into Smith, I waved a red flag in front of Circle Y.''

"You mean Wad Martin won't let you ride out?''

"Oh, hell, yes — he'll let me leave town. Then in a

few days somebody will find my carcass out in the brush. You'll hold a coroner's inquest, sure. Everything will be nice and legal. And the inquest's verdict would either be suicide or death by accident. Loading a gun is always a good one."

Snodgrass got to his feet, face livid. Matt watched him closely. Matt said, "What if I wanted you to swear out a warrant against Jocko Smith? He drew on me, you know."

Snodgrass wet his lips.

"I could demand a warrant charging Jocko Smith with an attempt to murder. Would you serve the warrant?"

Snodgrass's tongue snaked out again. He opened his mouth as though intending to speak, then clipped his jaws with a metallic click.

Matt laughed harshly. "I got you between the devil and the deep, huh?"

"You're a bastard," Snodgrass choked.

Matt stepped forward, fists clenched. Snodgrass moved back, fists coming up. Matt feinted, ducked — caught his fist in mid air. Snodgrass had leaped back.

Matt grinned sardonically. He turned and walked out into the clean Montana air. He still hadn't had his supper. He started down the street toward the cafe. He was cutting into a thick steak when Doc Seymour entered.

The medico took the seat at Matt's right. He put his bag on the bar and sighed and mopped his face with a big blue bandanna. "Jocko Smith'll be coming at you again soon, Harrison."

Matt only nodded.

"Your bullet never even broke his collarbone.

Just made a nice clean flesh wound. Now he's in Martin's saloon taking up his drinking where he left off."

Matt nodded again.

"You probably know it as well as I do," the veterinary continued. "You're in trouble, Harrison."

"Nothing new," Matt said.

"This may sound strange, but Jocko Smith has a lot of pride. Stupid pride, because Smith is a stupid man. But for years he's been the fastest gunman in this locality. He's killed a few men to prove it. Your brother boasted of his own gunspeed, but Smith took him fair and square."

"What you're trying to say is that Jocko Smith will come gunning for me again, huh, Doc?"

"That he'll be sure to do, Harrison."

Thirty minutes later Matt Harrison rode down a lane that was fenced with glistening barbwire on either side — the first time he had been in a fenced lane since leaving Texas. The barbwire hung taut and shiny on new cedar posts.

Matt hated barbwire as only a cowman could. Barbwire had come across West Texas and cut the graze into farming areas to put cowmen out of business. For without unlimited free range, the cattleman could not make a living — his margin of profit being so thin.

He saw Circle Y's point-of-view.

Were these farmers allowed to stay, others would come in — and Circle Y's doom was sealed.

But . . . there was still an answer — a way out — for the cowman. He'd seen it in Canada.

Canadian cattlemen had early seen the handwriting. They had known it was impossible to turn back the sod-men. Therefore they had had their cowpunchers file on homesteads and then deed them back to the cattleman.

This gave the cowman good water-holes. It also handed him grasslands, in many cases, where hay could be out for winter feeding.

For cattlemen had discovered two winters ago that cattle would winter-kill by the thousands unless cattle were fed hay during winter. The rough winter of 1886-87 had almost wiped out the cattleman. When Spring had finally come many Montana and Wyoming outfits had lost seventy percent of their stock to blizzards.

Over in the North Dakota Little Missouri badlands the winter had completely wiped out the spread run by young Theodore Roosevelt who had wisely abandoned the cattle-business and gone into politics.

Braced on stirrups, Matt twisted his wiry body in saddle and looked west at the purple peaks of the Little Rocky Mountains, some 20 miles away. He could barely see the mountains through the dusk.

Up in the mountains there was bound to be much beargrass and bluejoint among the pines. Because of their roughness, the Little Rockies would never know the impact of a plough.

Matt wondered if Martin ran his Circle Y cattle also in the mountains. He probably did. And when finally all of Beavertail Basin became fences and fields and homes, Martin would have only the range afforded in the mountains.

Matt glimpsed a rider coming in fast from behind him, dust lifting behind lazily. He waited with his hand on his gun. When the rider neared he recognized Margaret Martin. Again the beauty of Wad Martin's daughter hit him.

Margaret drew rein and said, "Hello."

Matt said hello.

"Riding out to see your brother's farm?" she asked.

Matt momentarily studied the dark face, the dark eyes, the glistening black hair. He breathed deeply. "Yes," he said. "Thought I'd look it over."

"You're going to stay, I take it?"

Matt smiled. "At least ten people have asked me that same question this afternoon." Tactfully he changed the subject. "Where are you going?"

"I'm still looking for my strayed saddle horse."

Matt wondered if she told the truth. In his thinking the horse would not have drifted into fenced lanes. He would have headed west toward the high foothills where there was bound to be more grass, not moving out onto the bottomlands where the grass was burned short and brown.

Two hundred yards away was a sod shack set along the creek. Behind the meagre building was a barn made of brush. "Farmer live there?" Matt asked.

"A sodbuster named Morgan. He's got a wife and four kids."

Matt scowled. "He'll starve to death on that land without irrigation. From what Sig Westby told me, all these farmers came in during the winter time — the worst part of the year."

"We had a mild winter. We had very little snow and not a blizzard. Without snow there was no snow-water this spring. That's one reason this range has such little grass."

"Westby told me my brother was the first one in, and a fellow named Hannigan came in a few days behind Clint."

"Yes, your brother was first. He sent ads back east to newspapers, I understand, and got the others in."

Matt kept a bland face. Something was wrong here. Clint was no farmer; in fact, he had hated farmers down in Texas. Clint was a schemer. If he had moved in these farmers, one thing was certain — Clint had made some money from each and every one.

"All right," Matt said, "my brother moved in these pumpkin rollers. Did he make any money from the chore?"

Margaret laughed shortly. "He located each farmer on a homestead. I understand his fee was three hundred dollars a location."

Matt understood, now. Clint still was after the easy dollar. He had cleared at least three thousand dollars by acting as a land locator.

"And I've heard your brother has more farmers coming in soon," Margaret said.

Still, it seemed like a hard way for Clint to earn a buck, Matt reasoned. He'd seen Clint clear over five thousand on the turn of a card in stud poker.

He wondered if anybody here — outside of himself — knew that Clint was an ex-convict.

Nobody would ever drag this from him.

"Your father fighting these farmers?"

"One of their spreads burned down about a week ago. Dad claims he did not burn it, though. But my father, when the occasion rises, can be an adequate liar."

Matt glanced at her.

"I have the misfortune to be the only child," Margaret said. "That is, living child. I had one brother — four years younger — who died of smallpox when he was six. My mother had a hard time when Jim was born, and the smallpox hit her, too. They were buried a week apart."

"I'm sorry," Matt murmured.

Margaret smiled cynically. "I could say I have a brother now, I guess. He's three. My father hooked up with a Crow squaw about five years ago. No benefit of clergy, as the books say."

Matt said nothing. Bitterness rimmed her words. Evidently Margaret had ruled the roost until her half-brother had come along. Matt got the impression her nose was now completely out of joint.

"I wish t'hell I could get out of here."

"That's simple," Matt said. "Just leave."

"And forfeit my right to Circle Y? Oh, no, Matt Harrison. Hell, I'm talking too much!"

Matt silently agreed. There were certain things in a family that, in his opinion, should be kept inside the family. Like Clint's prison term, for one.

"Just why are you riding with me?" Matt asked suddenly.

"Looking for my stray horse, of course."

Matt shook his head. "You rode with me to size me up. You tried to dig into me — get me to talk — but you ran off at the mouth instead. That it?"

She pulled in, eyes cold. Matt stopped his horse. Matt's eyes, amused, wordly, met her hot, angry eyes.

"I could hate you," she said.

"A number of people have. Right now, I'm not too pleasing to your father and Jocko Smith. If I live longer, more people will eventually hate me, I would say."

"Maybe you won't live much longer!"

Margaret whirled her horse on a dime and loped back-trail, stiff in saddle.

Matt watched.

He rubbed his jaw. He needed a shave. His whiskers made a rasping sound. He remembered her small, dark face, her dark and angry eyes. She was indeed a lovely woman.


Five minutes later he opened a wire-gate without leaving saddle, closing it behind him still mounted, and rode into the yard of a nice log house, set back against a small rise.

Chickens scattered before his horse. A collie dog stood beside the cabin barking. Gnome-like Sig Westby came from the pump carrying a bucket of water. Jane Westby had come to the cabin door.

Matt lifted his flat-brimmed hat.

Jane wore a blue house-dress that loved her tiny waist. "Why, Matt! What are you doing here?"

Matt smiled. "Visit."

Sig said, "Come in, Matt."

Matt shook his head. "Thought I'd look over my brother's place. I guess it's still down the road. I saw the sign on your gate. That's how I happened to know you two lived here."

"Clint's homestead is the last one in the lane,"

Sig said. "On the south."

Matt looked about. The cabin was set in a cotton-wood grove. To get to it from the lane he had crossed a wooden bridge over Beavertail Creek, which was not running but consisted only of pot-holes of stagnant water. He slapped at a mosquito.

"Aren't you leaving?" Jane asked.

Matt's brows lifted. "You sound if though you'd be happy to see me leave?" A joke, nothing more.

Plainly Jane's sense of humour — if she had one — had deserted her today for she said quickly, "Oh, I'm sorry, Matt. Do come in. I'm just making supper."

"Thanks again, but I'd best mosey on. You have a nice place here. Lots of work, Sig."

"We were the third family in," Sig said. "Your brother was first, then came Nels Hannigan, who lives just this side of your brother."

"Which farmer'd Circle Y burn out?"

"Hannigan. Torched his house and buildings and ripped up part of his fences. Happened at night. Guess Circle Y riders tied lass-ropes to posts and pulled the wire down."

"Nels came in a week behind your brother," Jane said.

Matt decided he would visit Nels Hannigan. He turned in saddle and looked east at a clearing evidently made by a plough. The wheat had sprouted, grown about six inches, and then the drought had killed it. "Wheat crop doesn't look so good," Matt said.

Sig smiled. "Dry-land farming is no good here. This land needs irrigation. Us farmers own water-rights on Beavertail Crick. We aim to build a dam further up, then divert water into a ditch along the hills." Sig's thick arm motioned. "We've been gathering boulders for the dam. You rode by the big pile we've gathered."

Matt had seen the enormous pile of boulders.

"We'll have a reservoir back between those two hills." Again, the blocky arm gestured. "Then when the crick gets too low we can tap our stored up water."

"Big job," Matt said.

"But it can be done. Money's scarce between us, of course — took our capital to build our buildings. But we're contacting the U.S. Bureau of Reclamation. Uncle Sam might help us, starting this fall."

"Uncle's helping lots of farmers to build irrigation systems. Dang it, I feel like filing, myself."

"Good idea," Sig said.

Matt looked at Jane but her small lovely face showed nothing. He had spoken the truth. He was tired of being a drifter, a saddle bum. He was weary of punching the other man's cows for a lousy forty bucks a month and a few crummy blankets. This thought of settling down was not new to him. It had been with him for some time now. With irrigation water a farmer could make a good living here on Beavertail Creek.

He could raise wheat and oats and barley and other head crops. With plenty of water this land would grow any crop adaptable to this climate. A man could run a few head of cattle back in the mountains and feed them on his farm during the winter.

"Circle Y ever bothered your farm?" he asked.

Sig shook his enormous head. "Never touched us here on the homestead. Only move Martin and Smith have made against us was killing those two milkcows and shooting those holes in our water tank." He grinned crookedly. "But I guess that's enough."

Jane said, "If you homestead here Martin and Smith will really be out to kill you, Matt."

Matt shrugged. "Seems like they're out to do that little chore now, even without me homesteading. Thanks for the invite for supper but I just ate in town." He turned his horse. "So long, folks."

He glanced back when he reached the gate. Sig had moved his bulk into the cabin but Jane stood watching him leave at the cabin's door. Matt lifted a hand. She waved back.

Matt did not know that Jane watched him with solemn eyes. Jane wanted to talk to Clint Harrison. A new danger had moved in on Beavertail grass. Suddenly she wondered if anybody suspected her tie-in with Clint. She hoped not and a coldness entered her.

She entered the cabin. She glanced at Sig, washing his face at the washstand. She started putting plates on the home-made table. She did not know that her brother watched her in the mirror.

Sig Westby's huge eyes were sad.


Next forenoon Slow Elk said, "Your brother Matt stayed at your farm last night."

Clint lay on his hot bed, staring at the Crow. "Matt. At the farm. Why?"

Slow Elk shrugged. "When I came to the farm Matt had all the chores did. But he slept in the hay in the barn. Why didn't he sleep in the house with me?"

Clint held his smile. Although Slow Elk was at the room's far end Clint could still smell him. "What did Matt have to say?"

"He said he might take up a homestead."

Clint's eyes widened. He studied Slow Elk's wide brown face. The Crow was not joking.

"Matt . . . a homestead. Why?"

"He said he was tired of working for the other mans. And with barbwire coming in, there would be no more ranches to work for, he said."

Clint laughed cynically. "You tell him how much hard work there is in homesteading?"

"I did. But he said hard work was good for a man."

"Oh, God," Clint said. "The idiot. There's nothing you can do here. Ride back to the farm, string some barbwire — get Matt to help you. He tangle with barbwire a long day and he'll change his mind about being a farmer."

"You don't need me for a guard?"

"I've got my Winchester."

Slow Elk shrugged, got to his feet. Clint reached over the bed, got his purse from his pants, tossed the Crow four-bits. Slow Elk caught it in mid-air.

"A bottle," Clint said.

"Thanks."

Clint spent an angry, impatient day sitting beside the window watching Beavertail City's main street. Riders came and went, most of them Circle Y men — he saw neither Wad Martin or Jocko Smith. At four

358

Jane Westby rode into town. She dismounted across the street in front of the Merc, entered with Clint's eyes glued on her lovely figure. She came out within a few minutes, went to her horse, glanced up at Clint's room, touched a hand lightly to her hat brim.

Clint waggled the window's curtain slightly.

Jane mounted and left town.

Doc Seymour came in at five, changed the dressing on Clint's thigh, studied the wound, said, "You can walk now, Clint."

"I'd best take another day in bed, don't you think?"

Doc Seymour shrugged. "Okay." He left.

At eleven that night Clint dressed, picked up his rifle, glanced cautiously up and down the dimly-lit hall, saw nobody, then went down the hall, taking the stairs leading from the second story to the alley. He had his horse in a barn across the alley. He saddled the big black and rode out of town and moved into the tall gray sagebrush, sure that nobody had seen him.

But a man had.

Slow Elk had hunkered in an abandoned shed beside the stable that had held Clint's black. Through the open door he'd seen Clint come silently down the hotel's backstairs.

When leaving Beavertail City, Clint had ridden directly past the shed. Slow Elk considered trailing Clint but abandoned that idea, for the night was dark. Later on — in an hour or so — would be a late moon, though.

Slow Elk weighed matters carefully, then got his horse from out of the shed, and rode toward the Westby farm, taking a trail that did not run direct but circled through the hills.

Slow Elk came in on foot behind the Westby farm, moving silently through sagebrush. He tapped delicately on a window. Sig Westby opened it.

"Clint left town about an hour ago. He rode north. Your sister?"

"Her bunk is empty. She sneaked out about an hour ago."

Slow Elk said, "Bad. Shall we trail?"

"What's the use?" Sig Westby said. "We know where she's going and who she's going to meet."

"I go back to town," Slow Elk said.

When Clint rode into the shadows of the high granite boulders on a hill three miles north of Beavertail, Jane Westby already waited, horse hidden back in the huge rocks. She hurried to meet Clint, who dismounted slowly, and her arms were around him immediately, her hungry warm mouth seeking his.

They kissed long, ardently. Clint's fingers dug into her back, and she shivered in sweet pain.

"It's been so long, Clint."

"A century, at least."

She kept her arm around him. "There's a flat space on that boulder. Be careful, now — your wound!"

Clint limped badly now. When coming down the hotel's backstairs, he'd not limped at all. He sat down on the boulder. Jane sat beside him, thigh touching his, eyes feasting on his face.

"I counted my money today," Jane said. "I have four thousand dollars. But that adds up. Almost eleven hundred head of stolen Circle Y steers at fifteen bucks a head split four ways. Margaret will have four thousand too. I don't like Margaret being in on this."

"We had to take her in. She's invaluable — spotting Circle Y cattle."

"I rode with her today. We met at Weeping Rock. We drove steers down toward Widetop Flat."

"Good."

"Never bunched them, of course. We just hazed them the direction of Widetop so they'll be handy when we want them."

"Anybody suspicious, you think?"

Jane shrugged. "Don't think so."

"What'd Margaret have to say?"

"Not much. Same old thing. Her father claims Circle Y is losing cattle."

"What'd you tell her?"

"Same old thing. She should tell Wad Martin that Circle Y's spring roundup must have missed steers."

"Hope Wad believes her."

"He did."

"Did you see Nels Hannigan today?"

"He stopped in at the shack this evening and said he was getting the farmers to meet tomorrow night at Alamada's. The farmers are going to talk about ways to hit back at Circle Y."

Clint frowned. "Maybe I should attend?"

Jane shook her head. "I think it's best you don't, Clint. Make out as though you are still sick in bed. With you in bed Nels will have more fuel to feed the farmers."

Clint grinned. "You've got a good brain in that

pretty head, Jane."

Hannigan and Clint had been cellmates in Huntsville penitentiary, Hannigan being released a month behind Clint, also on orders to get out of Texas and stay out. Clint had been the one who had hatched this plan of getting farmers into Beavertail and get them fighting Circle Y while he and Hannigan rustled Circle Y cattle.

By sheer luck, Clint had stumbled onto Jane and Margaret Martin. Despite Wad Martin's resistance he had taken Margaret to a couple of country dances. There her greed and unrest had broken loose and she had offered to help rustle her father's cattle. Jealousy motivated Margaret for when her father had taken Small Mocassins as a wife that had been bad, but when a halfbreed half brother arrived Margaret had then known for sure she was on the outside and Margaret wanted out . . . but not before she had a good stake. Hate and greed spurred on Margaret Martin, but greed alone motivated Jane Westby.

Without money, Jane's future was black. She would marry some poor dirt-farmer, raise a bunch of poorly-clad children, live her days in bleak poverty.

Therefore money was an obsession with her. Clint wondered how many times a day she counted the money got from Circle Y raids. He wished he had not cut her in. But she and he had been at a dance, both half-drunk, and he'd talked too much.

Jane hated Margaret. To poor Jane, Margaret spelled wealth. Silver-mounted saddle. Well-bred saddle-horses. Expensive clothes.

Jane tolerated Margaret only because Margaret was necessary.

"You're thoughtful tonight," Jane murmured.

"That damn' brother of mine. Slow Elk says Matt's talking about filing on a homestead."

"Matt told me that, too."

"Try to talk him out of it, Jane. Talk him into moving on. I've got enough troubles without adding Matt to them."

"Matt's a strong man. He seems like the type that once he gets his teeth into something, he won't let go. He's like you, darling. Strong and tough."

"Work on the idiot."

Clint got to his feet.

Jane came instantly into his arms, warm mouth against his, her tongue on his teeth.

Because of his bum leg. Clint had to stand spraddle-legged to meet her hard push. Heat then surged through Clint and he and Jane made love roughly there on the hard Montana soil.

"You make a move toward that Margaret bitch," Jane panted, "and I'll kill her, so help me!"

Savagery edged her words.

Then she was riding away, darkness hiding her. Clint mounted, grinning. *Sister, if you only knew*, he thought.

First, he was not getting fifteen bucks a head for stolen Circle Y cattle, as Jane thought.

He was getting twenty-five. His cut, from sales so far, was not four thousand — it was around ten thousand, with Hannigan having the same.

Clint turned his horse toward Circle Y. Margaret awaited in the grove of aspen trees on the hill behind Circle Y. By now there was a sliver of moon, showing the dark bulk of Circle Y below on the meadow.

Margaret came running to his arms, her lips grinding his. Again, Clint Harrison, to maintain balance, had to spread his legs wide.

"Darling, darling," Margaret said huskily. "I never thought I'd ever, ever be in your arms again."

Clint kept a straight face. "I love you," he said throatily.

Matt was stringing barbwire next day when Sig Westby rode up, riding a heavy-footed work-horse. "Where's the Crow?" Sig asked.

Matt sleeved his forehead. The forenoon sun was very hot. "Rode into town about two hours ago to check on my brother. I offered to ride with him but he said he wanted to go alone."

"He's an odd buck," Sig said. "Seems to think an awful lot of Clint."

"Sure looks that way."

"Clint's been good to him. Slow Elk came into this area about the same time Jane and I did. Clint took him in and fed him and gave him pocket money."

"Hannigan told me you've got two new milk cows."

Sig grinned. "I went out and drove in two of Wad Martin's Hereford heifers. They're sure wild, though." Sig pulled up a pant leg to reveal a big black and blue spot on his enormous leg. "They can kick like Missouri mules. I have to hogtie them to milk them."

"That's rustling cattle," Matt said.

Sig shrugged immense shoulders. "Martin and Smith killed my two cows, remember?"

"Martin might swear out a warrant with Snodgrass for your arrest. You could get convicted of cattle stealing. And that would mean a term in the territorial penitentiary."

"I'll take the chance."

"Or Martin might hit at you and take those cows back."

"I doubt that. Martin's only got around ten thousand head of cattle, I understand. I doubt if he'll fight for two head of them, him having that many." Sig moved his bulk to a more comfortable position on his skinny horse. "They say you're really serious about taking up a homestead here, Matt."

"Yes, I'm really thinking about it."

"No money working for the other man," Sig said. "When a man is a farmer, at least he's his own boss. If you need anything feel free to call on me."

"Thanks, Sig."

Sig turned his horse and rode back toward his homestead. Matt pushed back his hat and wiped his sweaty forehead. He thought of Sig for a moment.

Sig was ponderous, ugly, moved slowly — but he was brave. Had not he practically stolen two of Wad Martin's cows? Or maybe it was not bravery? Just sheer, bullheaded ignorance?

Matt had a waterbag in the wagon. He uncorked it, tipped it up, and drank deeply. The sun was blistering hot. He returned to work digging post holes.

Clint's homestead consisted of one hundred and sixty acres, the amount allotted by the government — a square with each side one half a mile long.

Clint had just fenced forty acres around his house and barn.

First Matt had put in a corner post, anchoring it solid by burying a dead man, a huge boulder. He then had strung a single strand of barbwire as taut as he could. This was his guide in making a straight fence. Fence posts were to go in a rod apart along the wire.

Actually this was a two man job. One man should sight the location of the post holes while another tamped them in. Working alone it was difficult to get the posts accurately aligned, but Slow Elk had been adamant about riding into Beavertail City and checking on Clint.

Matt hoped he was getting the posts in a straight line. He wanted to build a good fence. He twisted the post hole auger into the flinty soil, muscles wet with sweat.

A number of points puzzled him. To date Clint had not even dug a well and Sig Westby had said that well water was only twenty feet down.

All the other farmers except Clint and Nels Hannigan had their homesteads fenced, and these sodbusters had come into Beavertail Basin after Clint and Hannigan had come in. Also all the other farmers had sewed some crops, but Clint and Hannigan had not put a seed into the ground.

Matt shrugged away such thoughts. He was a fool for helping Clint, he realized — still, Clint was his brother. Unless Clint and Hannigan made more improvements on their homestead the Federal Land Agent might cancel their homestead entries.

Matt heard hoofs approaching. He looked up.

A bay horse was approaching, a bony man in saddle. Matt recognized Nels Hannigan, whom he had met for the first time yesterday.

Hannigan had Matt slightly puzzled, for Hannigan looked anything but like a farmer — in Matt's eyes, he had the appearance of a cowpuncher. But he might have been a cowboy, at that. Many cowboys were now giving up their saddles and taking up the handles of a walking plough.

"Howdy, Matt."

"Hello, Hannigan."

Hannigan leaned from saddle and squinted down the taut length of barbwire. "Looks straight as a die to me, Matt. Maybe when you get done fencing Clint's homestead you can run wire around mine, huh?"

Matt shook his head. "When I get Clint's farm fenced I'll be soon running fence around my own homestead."

Hannigan's brows rose.

"I've got to settle down somewhere some day," Matt said.

Hannigan shifted weight in saddle. "Only one thing wrong, Matt. We've found out this soil ain't as good as it looks. It's got some black alkali in it. Also they ain't much rain. And there's Circle Y, you know." He spat angrily. "Just look what Circle Y did to my homestead!"

Matt could not believe this soil held alkali. To him it looked like rich brown loam. As for not enough rainfall, irrigation would raise crops. And as for Hannigan's burned down shack, that was a horse of another colour.

367

Yesterday while Hannigan had been in town Matt and Sig Westby had looked over Hannigan's burned down house.

"He never had much to start with," Sig had said. "Only a one room shack made of crooked logs he'd cut along the creek bottom, Matt. And his barn had been made only of brush he grubbed out along the creek and wired around poles and somehow got a brush roof over."

"How much do you figure he lost?" Matt had asked.

"Not even a hundred bucks at the most," Sig had snorted. Now Matt said, "Alkali or no alkali, I'm still going to take a whack at it, Martin or no Martin."

Hannigan smiled crookedly. "Well, it's your rump, Matt. Me, I'd better be riding on. One of my work horses strayed off last night. Must be back in the hills somewhere." Hannigan rode down the creek.

Matt returned to work. Within ten minutes Jane Westby came into sight. She rode a gaudy black and gray pinto and girl and horse made a vivid picture.

Matt grinned. "My day for company it seems, Miss Jane."

"What do you want?"

"Well, Sig visited me; then came Hannigan. And now you, the prettiest of the lot, by far."

Jane blushed prettily. "What do you think of my new horse?"

"That pinto sure looks good."

"I bought him yesterday in town. Sig got mad. Claimed I should have saved my money for the winter but I made it myself off my hens and eggs."

Matt walked around the pinto. He had good legs, a stout barrel, and strong shoulders.

"He's only a three year old, Matt. A cowpuncher left him in the town livery barn a few months ago and never came back for him. The barn man sold him to me for the horse's feed bill." Her blue eyes studied Matt. "Is it true that you really intend to take up a homestead?"

"Sure is. I've even picked out the spot down the creek a ways. All I have to do is get to the Federal Land Office in Malta and point out the land on the map and pay my filing fee."

"Why are you going to homestead?"

Matt smiled impishly. "Maybe to be close to you, huh?"

Instantly her face hardened. Matt was surprised at the sudden change. Anger touched him slightly. Surely she must have known that he had been merely joking?

"I don't need a man, Matt."

Matt said, "Hell, I didn't mean to scare you out of a year's growth. I was only joking."

"I figured so, but wasn't sure. You're a fool to homestead, Matt. It's nothing but hard work."

"You and your brother are homesteading," Matt pointed out.

"I'm not, but my brother is."

"You evidently don't like homesteading?"

Jane coloured. "I'm sorry, Matt. I spoke too much and —"

She never finished her sentence. The rifle-bullet saw to that. The lead hit the steel rim of the high wheel beside Matt, then ricocheted screechingly into distance.

Matt screamed, "Get off your bronc!" and crouched low, Colt leaping into his grip. Dust geysered up ten feet ahead of him. The rifleman shot from the crown of the southern hill about two hundred yards away, hidden in the buckbrush.

Matt glanced at Jane.

She had wheeled her horse and now, bent over the pinto's neck, was racing for the safety of the cottonwoods along Beavertail Creek. Even as Matt glanced, the pinto plunged into the timber, hiding her.

Another bullet ricocheted off the wide tire-rim, screaming like a wounded banshee. Matt winced and rolled under the wagon. His wagon-team, ground-tied to two big sagebrush roots, fought their tie-ropes, eyes wide with fear, nostrils snorting.

Hidden now under the wagon, Matt could not be seen by the ambusher — and Matt lay quiet and thoughtful, Colt in hand. His saddle-horse, tied to the wagon's nigh side, fought his reins, forelegs slashing, but the sturdy cowhide reins held.

No more shots came. The horses quieted down. Lying there, Matt studied the hill. He was not safe under the wagon. The ambusher could work his way down yonder coulee, hidden by brush.

Squirming out from under the wagon, Matt untied his saddler, swung into leather and rode down-creek Cheyenne fashion, hanging to the nigh side of his bronc's neck, only a boot visible as he rode, spur hooked over the saddle's cantle.

The horse ran with thundering hoofs, ears back. Matt expected the cayuse to falter any moment, a bullet ripping into him, but man and horse made it safely into the timber, where Matt drew rein in the protection of trees and buckbrush.

He sat saddle, thinking. Had Circle Y sent a man out to ambush him? If so, the man had been a poor shot. He, Matt, had been a clear, open target — yet the man had missed.

This conjecture raised another thought. Maybe the ambusher had not shot to kill? Maybe he had shot just to scare? For surely at such close range even a poor rifleman could have killed him.

Matt heard horse hoofs coming. He swung his gun in their direction, then lowered it as Jane Westby rode in. "Circle Y tried to kill you!" she said angrily. "You were lucky, Matt!" Anger twisted her red lips. Her eyes were savage.

Matt shook his head. "I don't think that ambusher shot to kill me. He could have done that, easily. I figure he shot just to scare me."

Jane studied him. "You talk like an idiot, Matt Harrison! Why would anybody just want to scare you? That man shot to kill but he shot wide!"

Matt decided to drop this subject. "Maybe so," he said. He moved his horse ahead. Jane grabbed him by a forearm. "What are you going to do?"

"Ride into those hills and look around."

Jane's hand dropped. "You'll never find the ambusher. He'll be far gone by now. Back of that ridge of hills is a bunch of badlands. Rough coulees, deep gullies!"

Matt said no more. He rode down creek, intending to approach the hills at the point where they edged close to the timber. Within ten minutes, he was beyond the hill from whence had come the bullets.

Jane was right. Here were the Montana badlands, a miniature country of hell, marked by red buttes slabbed with yellow and green soil. Dark lava ledges protruded from gaunt hills.

Matt shook his head. Only a fool would ride into this rough area knowing an ambusher lurked there. He swung his horse up a hill, seeking the spot where the ambusher had crouched. He found the approximate spot, dismounted, walked to the edge of the hill, looked at his wagon and team below.

Here was a huge granite boulder, just high enough to lay a rifle across. Matt studied the loose soil at its base. Here was more wind; the ground held no boot prints. The ground stared back at him, mute and telling nothing.

Matt then searched the surrounding area for spent cartridge casings, but found none. He sighed, looked south into the badlands, saw nothing but hills and vivid colour. He had ridden a cold trail.

He swung again into saddle and rode along the crest of the hill heading west. Once a mule deer ploughed out of the brush, horns back, but Matt saw no hoof spore or sign of a rider. He trailed down off the hills and rode toward the creek, hearing a horseman ahead in the brush. He expected Jane Westby to ride out. He was disappointed, for the rider was gaunt Nels Hannigan, driving two big bay horses ahead of him.

"You found your horses, huh?" Matt said.

"Back along the brush, Matt. How come you ride this brush? Thought you'd be digging post holes."

Matt hesitated. Should he tell Hannigan about

372

the shooting? He decided he would. He had nothing to lose. Upon hearing of the ambushing, Hannigan's small eyes pulled even smaller.

"Either Jocko Smith or some other Circle Y killer," the lanky homsteader said. "Doubt if the rifle was handled by big Wad Martin. Martin would hire somebody to do his killing."

"You see any Circle Y hands riding around?" Matt asked.

Hannigan shook his head. "Not a one," he said.

Dusk of that same day Nels Hannigan rode in Beavertail City. He tied his horse to the hotel hitching rail, pulled up his sagging gunbelt, swaggered into the lobby and upstairs to Clint Harrison's room, where he knocked on the closed door.

"Nels Hannigan here," he said.

Slow Elk opened the door. Hannigan glared at the Crow and his flaring nostrils twitched. "Good god, Injun, but you stink! How in the hell does Clint stand you?"

Slow Elk's thick lips hardened but he said nothing. Clint lay on the bed, naked. "Move down into the lobby," he told the Indian. Slow Elk left with Hannigan standing in the doorway, eyes on the Crow's broad back as he went down the hall. Hannigan stopped watching only when Slow Elk had turned the corner and was out of sight going downstairs.

Hannigan entered and closed the door. "The clerk down in the lobby stopped me," he said. "He's worried about your rent bill being due, Clint."

"Tell him to kiss my rump. How did you come out?"

Hannigan pulled in a chair and sat backwards on it, leaning both arms across the chair's back. "Well, I went up in the hills, like we agreed. I shot a couple of times at the wagon. Hit the steel on the wheel the first time and it really raised a racket."

"You kill my brother?"

Hannigan shook his head. "You'd like to have had me kill Matt, huh? You're a vicious bastard, Clint! Matt, your own brother, from ambush! I might be a ex-convict and a no good, Clint, but I still can't kill from the brush!"

Clint laughed sourly. "Now listen to who's talking! Gone religious all of a sudden, huh? You're slapping this bull in the face with a red flag, Hannigan!"

Hannigan got to his feet. He seemed deceptively slow, a man merely rising to his boots, but his lips were solid and without give. Angry lights glittered in his piggish eyes. His hands gave him away, opening, closing, becoming fists, breaking out of fists.

He stepped toward Clint's bed, then stopped. For Clint had taken the .45 from under his pillow. Now the black bore of the big pistol stared up unblinkingly at Nels Hannigan.

Clint laughed sourly. "You've still got that hair trigger temper, Nels. That's bad. Well, this .45 has a hair trigger, too. Don't lose your head because I was needling you, man. You think Matt will hightail now?"

"How would I know. He might. He might not." Hannigan walked to the window. "Why so all-fired anxious to get shut of your brother, Clint?"

"You don't know him, Hannigan. First, he's tough — he gets his teeth in something, he ties on

374

like a bulldog. He might get in our way."

Hannigan turned. "How?"

"We're playing a tough, hard fast game here, Nels. Matt says he's going to file on a homestead — one right below mine. That'll make him one of the farmers. With Matt to lead them, those grangers could be a tough bunch."

Hannigan thoughtfully rubbed his whiskery jaw.

"I see your point, Clint. Wad Martin is howlin' wide and far that Circle Y is losin' steers. He says the farmers are rustlin' them. You and me — and the farmers — know they ain't. Them farmers'll naturally talk to Matt, say they ain't running off Circle Y stock. Matt knows you were in the pen. Does he know about me?"

Clint laughed hoarsely. He stuck his .45 under his pillow. "You think I'm completely loco, Nels? Why should I tell him about you being in Huntsville with me? I tell Matt nothing."

"Then Matt thinks I'm just a dirt-poor farmer, huh?"

"He should . . . unless either of the women tell him otherwise. And even a female wouldn't be that damned stupid, would she?"

Hannigan scowled. "There're too many women in this thing, Clint. Too many fingers spoil the pie, remember?"

Clint laughed sardonically. "You tell me nothing new. Margaret and Jane say they're drifting cattle down toward Widetop Mesa.

"When do we push them west, Clint?"

Clint Harrison considered. "How about three nights from now? Margaret will sneak in and see me tonight. I'll get her to ride the forty miles to Galena and notify George Emerson we have a herd for him. She can tell her father she's riding into Malta to buy some geegaws."

Hannigan nodded.

"What'd you think about Sig Westby, Nels?" Clint asked.

"What about Sig?"

"I don't cotton to him. He doesn't fit in here. I've questioned Jane, too — but could get nothing much about Sig from her. Sig and Jane came from around Helena." Helena was the territorial capital one-hundred-fifty miles southwest. "If he wanted to homestead, why didn't he file close to Helena? Better soil, more rain."

Hannigan laughed. "You been thinkin' too much, Clint. Layin' in bed, imaginin' things. That big goof is harmless. I think you'd better get moving again."

Clint smiled. "Tomorrow I ride out to my homestead."

Hannigan went to the door. "You talk about not likin' Sig. I ain't got no love for that Injun of yours. He'd sell out his best frien' for a shot of rotgut."

"What makes you think that?"

"Hell, he's just a renegade bum. Jumped his reservation and tryin' to live like a whiteman. You never can tell what one of them bucks will do, Clint."

Clint nodded.

"We've got everything set, huh?" Hannigan asked.

"All set, Nels."

Hannigan put a bony hand on the doorknob. "We'd better skip out after a few more raids, Clint.

Me, I've got what I need to start that Argentine spread."

"This one," Clint said, "and another — a big one."

"Sounds good. So long."

Hannigan strode downstairs. Slow Elk sat in the lobby. Hannigan said, "He's all yours, buck," and walked out. He bought a bottle in the saloon after killing three fast double shots. The whiskey burned his belly, bringing a good glow.

Marshal Snodgrass entered. "Soda water," he told the bartender. Then, to Hannigan, "Hear tell you farmers are meeting tonight?"

"You heard right."

"Going to move against Circle Y?" The question was bluntly to the point.

"Might."

"That'd mean war," Snodgrass said. "And that I won't tolerate, Hannigan."

"What about my burned-down spread? You stand for that. You afraid Wad Martin might get hurt? Mebbe kilt?"

"I stand for the law," Snodgrass said.

Hannigan laughed. "How about Sig Westby's two shot milkcows? Circle Y killed them. And the bullet holes in Westby's new water-tank? How about those, Lawman?"

"No witnesses saw Circle Y shoot those holes."

"How about Matt Harrison getting slugged?"

"Harrison didn't want to file a complaint. Had he registered one, I'd have served it."

Hannigan laughed. Because of the argument neither man had seen Jocko Smith and Wad Martin enter.

377

"Somethin' botherin' you, Hannigan?" Wad Martin asked harshly.

Hannigan spun. Automatically he went into a gunman's crouch. His long fingers were splayed over his holstered gun. Surprise grooved his ugly face.

"You walk light, Circle Y!" Hannigan said.

Wad Martin's eyes were narrowed. Jocko Smith had his right hand on his leathered gun.

"You mentioned Westby's cows," Martin said. "I understand he went out and roped two of my range-cows an' is milkin' them."

"Do you blame him?" Hannigan asked.

"That's cattle-stealin'," Martin said.

Hannigan laughed hoarsely, surprise now gone. "And how about my shack? You burned it down!"

"I never torched it. Neither did Jocko."

"Then who did?"

"I don't know. Maybe it accident'ly caught fire. But I gave no orders for it to be burned."

"Maybe Circle Y man went against your orders?"

"If one did — and I find out who he is — then God help him," Martin said.

Hannigan studied Marshal Snodgrass, then moved his eyes over to Smith and Martin. He wet his lips. "You three work together." He started for the door. "You're a bunch of damned liars, all of you!"

He had said too much. With two quick strides, Wad Martin was on him, hard fingers bunching the front of Hannigan's shirt. Dirty cloth tore.

"You calling me a liar?" Wad Martin gritted.

Quickly Marshal Snodgrass barged between the two men. He knocked down Martin's brawny hand. Martin now clutched the cloth torn from Hannigan's unwashed shirt.

378

"That's enough, Wad," Marshal Snodgrass ordered. "Make tracks out of town, Hannigan!"

Hannigan's whiskery lips sneered. He had said too much and he knew it. One of the worst things you could do on this range was question a man's honesty. Relief flooded him now that the marshal had moved in. He was safe again. Back came his old swagger and braggodicio.

"You'll pay for this, Martin," he said tersely. "Us farmers are meeting tonight and we might talk about what to do with Circle Y!"

"So I've heard," Wad Martin said, "and I might attend, Hannigan."

Hannigan said, "You ain't got the guts."

Martin laughed sardonically. He threw the piece of Hannigan's shirt to the floor. "So filthy it dirties a man's hand," he said. He went to the bar, Jocko Smith trailing him.

Hannigan left.


The farmers met in a grove of cottonwoods beside Beavertail Creek because there was no house large enough to hold the men, women and children.

Makeshift benches had been built. Matt circulated around keeping his ears open and his mouth shut. One thing was apparent: these sodmen were afraid. They were heavy-handed men of toil who wore ragged clothing, their women old before their time from back-breaking labour and from child bearing. Most of them had been mere share-croppers back East. Now they had land of their own and because of this land their lives were in danger.

Some mentioned Hannigan's fire. This fire had occurred about a week ago during the night. Hannigan had not been at home at the time. His few rods of fence had been ripped out. Nobody had seen Circle Y riders, though.

Two farmers were unmarried and they openly courted Jane who revelled in their rough attentions. To Matt, Jane acted as though she were a wanton, openly flirting with the men. Matt scowled and wondered what type of woman she was, then decided this was none of his business. His life, at this point, had no place for a woman. Maybe later when he got his farm fenced, his buildings erected, his land ploughed and in crops, but not now. He kept on moving around.

Much talk also centered on the fact that Jocko Smith had shot Clint. Others talked about the killing of Sig Westby's two Holsteins and the bullets put by Circle Y into the Westby's new water tank. Now Sig had deliberately stolen two of Wad Martin's heifers. Would Circle Y retaliate with red flaming guns? Many farmers wondered why Sig had stolen the cattle. By stealing the two cows Sig had placed the farmers in deeper danger? This stealing did not appeal to many of the farmers, Matt realized. They were mystified by Sig's audacity.

The deal mystified Matt, too.

Lemonade and cookies were served, but no whisky or beer. The lemonade was hot. Apparently no ice was available. Matt noticed Hannigan occasionally going off into the brush, a few farmers following him. Evidently Hannigan had a bottle or jug cached there.

Sig Westby ambled over, sat beside Matt, sighing loudly. "Got to get rid of some of this suet," he said, smiling.

Matt nodded.

"Been fat all my life," Westby said. "Ever since I was a little boy. Kids called me Porky. Sure had some fights over that name."

"My brother Clint's the leader of this bunch, huh?"

"Yes. Clint got them in here, you know. Ran ads in papers back East. Hit them three hundred bucks a family to locate them. He made some easy money." Westby smiled.

Clint always made easy money, Matt thought. Only reason Clint was not gambling steadily around Beavertail City was that there was no loose money floating around. He still couldn't imaging Clint becoming a farmer; farming was hard, back-breaking work — and Clint and physical labour had long been divorced.

Something was haywire here, Matt knew.

But, try as he had, he still could not see the answer. Maybe Clint had finally decided to work honestly for a living? Matt dug out his makings, almost smiling at this foolish thought.

"Slow Elk never come over with you, huh?" Westby asked.

"I asked him to but he said no dice." Matt grinned. "Maybe he stinks so much he figures he'd chase everybody out?"

"He and water do seem to be enemies," Westby joked.

Matt again wondered why Clint, who had hated

redskins all his life, tolerated Slow Elk, who stunk like a dead skunk. He could think of only two reasons: first, Slow Elk was free labour — just a few cents for a bottle once in a while and second, Clint could throw his weight around the Crow, treating him like a dog — which was typical of Clint Harrison. Clint had always tried to boss everybody around. He had tried it on him, Matt, when they had been kids in Texas, but when Matt had got big enough, he'd really beat Clint up — thereby stopping all domination for once and for all.

"Where did Slow Elk come from?" Matt asked. "We're miles from the Crow reservation."

"Don't know. Just bummed in, I guess. Got here about when my sister and I arrived, and we were the last of the farmers."

"You fall for one of Clint's ads, too?"

"No, we're the only ones who aren't here because of Clint's ads. I was working in Helena. Hauling ice in the summer. A couple of years ago I happened through this country — liked its looks — we saved a small jag of money, moved out here."

"I don't suppose you stand so high with Clint, seeing he never got three hundred bucks off you."

"Oh, I paid him a fee — like a sap."

Suddenly Nels Hannigan cried, "Hear ye, hear ye! Meeting is now coming to order."

Farmers and wives drifted to benches. One mother took the children down along Beavertail Creek to get them and their noise out of the way. Hannigan mounted a big stump.

"I'm going to sit beside Matt,' Jane said.

Her full thigh briefly brushed Matt's. Matt's

382

throat tightened.

"You're nice, Matt."

"You're not bad yourself," Matt said.

Matt glanced at Sig, who was studying Hannigan. A moment ago Sig's enormous eyes had been grinning. Now they were soulfully sad. Matt wondered at the sudden change.

Hannigan droned off charges against Circle Y: Clint shot, his own shack burned down, his fences pulled up, the shooting of Sig's water-tank, Sig's two shot Holsteins.

Hannigan's voice droned on. Dusk crept in to push aside day's heat. A slight wind stirred cottonwood leaves.

Matt glanced at Jane.

Their eyes met. Their eyes held. Jane's blue eyes were impish, alluring.

Matt's throat clogged again.

Matt was the first to look away. Jane smiled softly, white teeth flashing. Suddenly a boy ran from the creek screaming, "Circle Y — they're comin'!"

Matt sprung to his feet. Instinctively, his hand went to his gun. Surely the boy was joking?

Surely Martin and Circle Y would not dare ride to this meeting. The word Circle Y was a fighting-name to these farmers —

Matt stared.

But the boy was not crying wolf.

Circle Y was really coming. North across Beavertail Creek Matt saw the riders, Wad Martin leading them on a big blue roan. Behind Martin a pace rode Jocko Smith, white arm-sling plain in the dusk.

"What'll we do?" a woman screamed.

Matt hollered, "Stay where you are! Don't run! Circle Y is riding in openly, folks. Martin wants to palaver!"

Hannigan snarled, "Who are you to give orders, Harrison?" He had leaped from the stump, face twisted with rage. "I'm the boss of this crew." He shoved toward Matt.

Suddenly huge Sig Westby pushed his tonnage between Matt and Hannigan. Enormous hands grabbed Hannigan's shoulders, twisted him as though Hannigan were a toy, propelled him backwards where Hannigan stopped, staring at Sig, the fear of Sig's great muscles etched in his wide eyes.

"Matt's speakin' the truth," Sig gritted.

Nobody paid Hannigan any attention, now. All watched Circle Y riders break through Beavertail Creek's low brush. Automatically, Matt counted — four horsemen beside Martin and Smith, and one was Margaret Martin.

Jane said, "The bitch."

Matt glanced at her. Hate ripped her face, hardening her lips. Matt had a new insight into her character. She smiled much, joked — but underneath, he saw, lay dangerous emotions. When in rage, she would show this face to her husband — and Matt moved away a pace.

"Nobody reach for a gun," Sig Westby warned.

A woman screamed, fainted. Her husband caught her, laid her on the ground, paid her no more attention, his eyes riveted on Circle Y.

Matt spoke quietly to Sig. "Those all the men on Circle Y payroll? Only five, counting Martin?"

"Spring calf-roundup's been over for two weeks,"

Sig explained. "Martin laid off most of his crew after round up. No need to keep a bunch of men laying around idle. He'll hire again for fall beef gather."

Matt understood.

Martin reined in, Smith on his right, Margaret moving up to occupy her father's left. Margaret's eyes fell on Matt. She smiled. Matt smiled. Again, the thought hit him — here was a beautiful woman.

Wad Martin said, "We came for no trouble, folks. You'll notice we pack no six-shooters. Our holsters are empty. We have no Winchesters on our saddles. Our saddle-boots are empty, too."

Matt had already noticed this.

"What'd you come for, then?" Nels Hannigan growled.

Martin's eyes fell on Hannigan. "You spokesman for this group?"

"I am."

"Then keep a civil tongue in your head, please?"

Nels Hannigan's leathery face reddened. Behind Hannigan a woman snickered. Hannigan looked at her, eyes hard.

Sig asked, "Why did you come here, Mr. Martin?"

Martin looked at the big man. "We came here to present Circle Y's side of this thing. There are a number of points I want made clear."

"Such as what?" Sig asked.

"First, Circle Y never burned down Hannigan's spread. Circle Y never tore out Hannigan's fences."

"That's a lie," Hannigan challenged.

Wad Martin's eyes pulled to slits. "You're too free with your mouth, Hannigan. You called me a liar once before. If the marshal hadn't broken us apart, I'd have rammed that word down your gullet!"

"There's no marshal here," Hannigan reminded.

Martin put his weight on one stirrup preparatory to dismounting but his daughter reached over and grabbed his arm. "Don't fall for it, Dad. Use your head, not your temper."

Martin settled back solidly into saddle.

Matt looked at Jocko Smith. Smith was studying him coldly. Their eyes met, held, locked. Hairs bristled on Matt's neck. He knew that the next time he and Jocko Smith met it would be gunflame. Matt only hoped his gun would be the faster. If it were not, then he would indeed remain on this Beavertail range . . . six-feet under.

Smith smiled cynically.

Devils ripping, Matt winked at Smith. Surprise mashed Smith's face, making his eyes waver. Matt grinned, looked back at big Wad Martin. Then he decided Martin was too homely to waste eyesight on, so he looked at Margaret, catching her eye.

He winked at her.

Margaret openly winked back. Beside him Matt heard Jane mutter, "The damn' hussy," and this pleased Matt, who had difficulty keeping from grinning.

"What else is on your mind, Mr. Martin?" Sig asked.

"This is no farming country," Martin said tersely. "Too much dry wind, not enough rain — look at your headcrops. Grain sprouted, died two inches above ground."

"Next year'll be a good wet year," a farmer said.

"We're building a dam," another said. "Irrigation will make this valley bloom like a rose."

Martin smiled. "Next year, next year . . . and maybe the year after. But water's scarce as gold this year. And you've got barbwire around some of Circle Y's best watering-holes. My cattle have to hike miles to other water. The long walk drives fat off my steers. My cows threw poor calves — the calves can't walk too far."

"What do you aim to do then?" Hannigan asked.

"I'll lay it straight on the table. I'll buy each of you out for three hundred bucks each, what you paid in filing fees to that shyster Harrison. And you go?"

"And if we don't sell?" Hannigan sneered.

"Then Circle Y hits."

The words hung in the still air. Behind Matt a woman gasped. Another woman said, "Somebody kill him — now! Kill them all while they have no guns! Save my baby — my family —"

Sig Westby said angrily. "Stop that woman, somebody! Any man who lifts a gun, I shoot — and I mean that. These men are all unarmed. It took guts to ride in here without a weapon. More guts than lots of you ever had — or ever will have." He looked back at Martin. "Are those all your terms, Mr. Martin?"

"Yes."

"How long will you give before you hit?"

"One month, to the day."

"We can appeal to the law. We can go beyond Marshal Snodgrass. Snodgrass is honest and unbiased, but one lawman alone can't do it. We can ask Uncle

387

Sam for military aid."

"Think Uncle Sam would spend out soldiers?"

"It's been done."

Martin laughed quietly. "It would take six months at the least . . . if cavalry ever came. Letters would go back and forth, Washington big-moguls would meet, consider, talk — and do nothing."

"You're right," Sig said. "You got us."

"I've been losing cattle. Somebody is stealing them. There's nobody else on this grass but you grangers. If I ever catch one of you hazing a Circle Y beef, my orders are for my men to shoot you from horse without warning. Is that clear?"

"Clear," Sig said.

"That's all," Martin said crisply. He waved a hand. His riders turned, rode away — with Margaret in the rear. Farmers stood and watched, stunned and still. Only the slight wind was heard rustling cottonwood leaves.

Suddenly Hannigan blurted, "I'm downing me one of them!" and his hand went for his gun.

Matt's uppercut, coming from around Matt's boots, landed flush on Hannigan's blocky jaw with a smacking sound. Hannigan's arms flew up, throwing his gun wide. Hannigan walked backwards three paces, hit a tree trunk and sank down, lying unconscious on his side, mouth open with spittle drooling into the dust.

Sig grinned at Matt.

"You beat me to him," Sig Westby accused.


Next forenoon Clint Harrison, dressed and armed,

came out of the hotel. Across the street Matt and Sig were just dismounting. Clint swaggered over, gun tied low.

"Matt!"

Matt stopped. Sig stopped. Marshal Snodgrass, dozing in the shade of his office, looked up, siesta broken by Clint's rough word.

"Something on your mind?" Matt asked.

Clint stopped six feet away. His boots were anchored in the liquid street dust. Matt stood on the plank sidewalk's edge, eyes on his brother. Matt's heart beat jerkily.

"What's this I hear about you knocking down Nels Hannigan last night?" Clint asked.

"He's got too big a mouth," Matt said.

"You could be accused of the same."

Matt's face reddened. "I don't go for shooting unarmed men in the back," he said.

"Is this farmer — Circle Y trouble your business?"

"Yes, it is."

"How come?"

"I filed on a homestead down Beavertail from you. I came into town to put my letter to the Federal Land Agent in Malta in the mail, asking for filing papers." Cynicism touched Matt's voice. "You afraid you'll lose out on your three hundred buck graft?"

"Hannigan acted in my place. I appointed him chairman of that meeting. When you hit him, you hit me."

"You're breaking my heart."

From the corner of one eye Matt noticed Marshal Snodgrass hurrying to them, tugging his gun around to ride flatter and lower on his skinny hip.

"Get out, Matt! Make tracks!"

"You seem awful anxious to run me out, brother. You afraid I'll expose you for the black devil you are?"

Rage twisted Clint's lips. Clint's hand dropped to his gun. Sickness hit Matt, curdling his belly. He thought of his pioneer mother and father, now both under Texas sod. He knew then he could never draw against his brother.

"Clint, for God's sake, man!"

Marshal Snodgrass moved in between them. "You two are of the same flesh-and-blood," he said. "You move that gun up an inch, Clint Harrison, and I'm buffaloin' you cold right here in the street dust — and don't think I won't, bucko!"

Clint eyed the marshal. He looked at Sig Westby, also with his hand on weapon; Clint's cold eyes travelled to Matt.

"You got any truck on my homestead, Matt?"

"Not a thing. Hannigan told me you were coming home today. I packed everything I own in my bed-roll. It's tied behind my saddle."

"Good."

Clint wheeled sharply, and left.

Matt stood watching his brother leave, the sickness still churning. Clint crossed the vacant lot beside the hotel and went toward the alley.

"He's got his horse back by the alley," Sig Westby explained. "Stabled there."

Matt only nodded dully.

Marshal Snodgrass said, "I'll buy you boys a drink."

Sig smiled. "Now those are the words I love to hear!" he said.

They entered the saloon.

Nels Hannigan was the only customer. The thought came to Matt that Hannigan spent more time in Beavertail's saloon than he did on his homestead — and his homestead looked like it.

Hannigan had a bruise on his jaw. Had Matt known Hannigan had been in the bar he would not have entered. To his surprise, the gangling farmer stuck out his hand.

"Sorry about last night, Matt. You did right in sluggin' me. I lost my head."

Matt shook hands with him. Something was wrong here, Matt decided — Hannigan was not the type to forgive and forget. "We were all upset," Matt said. "Snort?"

"Don't mind if I do," Hannigan said.

The bartender poured three shots of whiskey, for Snodgrass called for soda-water. Hannigan threw out four-bits and got fifteen cents change. "Odd thing about last night," Hannigan said.

"What was that?" Matt asked.

"Our friend Westby here." Hannigan jabbed a long thumb toward Sig. "He runs in two of Martin's cows. Starts milkin' them. And Martin said not a word about it last night."

Matt had been thinking the same thing. He had mulled it over before going to sleep last night. The only reason he could think of was that Martin had forgotten to mention Westby running in two Circle Y cows.

"Martin's a friend of mine." Sig Westby joked.

He raised his glass high. "To Beavertail Basin."

"What's eating on Clint?" Hannigan asked. "I couldn't help but hear him eat you out on the street, Matt."

"My big brother just doesn't want me around," Matt said.

Hannigan shrugged. "Too bad. Brothers shouldn't fight. Blood against blood is bad."

Sig Westby ordered another round of drinks. Marshal Snodgrass dropped out. "My poor old belly can stand just so much soda," he explained. He left.

Matt thought of his bankroll. It was getting almight slim. After paying his filing fee for his homesteady he wouldn't have much left. Maybe he could rustle a job punching cows? He smiled at this thought. Circle Y was the only outfit on this grass. And Wad Martin would never hire him or any other farmer.

He decided this would be his last drink. A man with a small wallet shouldn't waste his money in whiskey. Suddenly he whirled to face the rear door, hand splayed over his holstered gun. Once again the stern voice of Jocko Smith had turned him swiftly.

Jocko Smith blocked the doorway. He was crouched and his right hand hung over his pistol. His long face was twisted, his eyes narrowed slits.

Hurriedly Hannigan and Sig Westby moved away from Matt, leaving him along facing Smith. Matt remembered Smith's cold eyes last night when Circle Y had ridden into the meeting of the farmers. Evidently Smith was not one to forgive or forget.

"You gunned me down," Smith said shortly. "An' now I'm paying you back, Harrison — and with interest! You've got a gun. So use it here and now —"

Smith had not noticed that Wad Martin had come in behind him — even now, Jocko Smith was pulling. Matt rolled to one side, gun rising — he put everything he owned into his draw but sick coldness told him Smith had him bested. Jocko Smith was lightning fast.

Smith shot once.

The bullet ploughed into the floor at Smith's own boots, shooting up splinters. Wad Martin had hammered a hard fist down on Smith's head from behind, sending him reeling.

Gun level, Matt held fire. Were he to shoot at Smith, he'd hit Martin. Wad Martin stepped ahead, kicked Smith in the wrist, sending Smith's .45 tumbling.

Sig Westby picked it up.

Smith was on one knee, holding his wrist. Grimacing with pain, he glared up at Wad Martin.

"This wasn't your fight, Wad!"

Martin spoke roughly. "I gave these farmers a month of grace, Jocko. I gave you and my other hands orders not to lift a gun against a farmer during that month unless the farmer lifts first, remember?"

"Harrison ain't no sod-buster!"

"You don't keep your ears open, Jocko. Otherwise you'd've heard that Matt Harrison has filed on a homestead."

Matt stood spraddle-legged, muscles tense, balancing his gun, watching, listening.

"What if Harrison pulls on me first?" Smith demanded.

"Then you can fire," Martin said.

Jocko Smith swore hotly.

"That's the way the wind blows," Martin said.

Sig handed Smith his gun. Smith holstered it. Matt crammed his .45 into leather.

"Drink?" Martin asked.

Matt had had enough booze for one day. He figured Sig Westby had enough, also. Hannigan he did not know about . . . nor did he care. And it was Hannigan who said, "Okay with me, Martin."

"Belly up," Wad Martin said.

Matt and Sig could not decline. To do so would be an insult to Wad Martin. Each man bought and then the slate was clean and Matt said, "Reckon we'd best amble on, huh, Sig?"

"Got chores to do. Cows to milk," Sig said.

Wad Martin said, "I hear you run in two of my range cows, Westby. I'm not movin' against you to get them back. I'm leavin' everything to tie in within a month . . . if you farmers haven't jerked stakes."

"That's real nice of you," Sig said cynically.

Sig and Matt left. Wad Martin toyed with his drink. He and Jocko Smith had ridden in for the mail for this was one of the days the stage brought in mail from Malta. Wad Martin was in a sour mood. He had borrowed twenty thousand last spring from the Malta bank. Now the bank was demanding partial repayment. And beef round up was some months away. And from the looks of the grass, burned to the roots, there'd be little beef on Circle Y steers come fall.

Also, Circle Y was losing cattle. Quite a few head, too. More than the farmers could ever eat.

Wad Martin wondered if a gang of organized rustlers was working his range. Galena needed beef — and lots of it. Galena was a new mining-town — a tent and shack town — in the Little Rocky Mountains. Gold had been hit there a year before in Discovery Creek. Wad Martin estimated that right now Galena held at least three thousand population.

A month back, unbeknown to anybody at Circle Y, Wad Martin had ridden to Galena, where he had talked to George Emerson, owner of the slaughterhouse. Emerson had told him that he, Emerson, always brought his beef-cattle from cowmen to the southwest, down in the Judith Gap country.

Martin had walked around the small slaughterhouse, looking for hides — he wanted to read the brands on these hides. But he had found no hides. Either Emerson sold cowhides immediately to tanners or he stored them in a hidden place.

Martin did not come out and ask Emerson where the hides were of slaughtered cattle. To do so would have put Emerson to believing that Circle Y thought Emerson was working with rustlers stealing Circle Y steers.

Wad Martin had learned but one thing — that Emerson was a shifty, shady character. Or so Wad Martin judged by the man's appearance, his failure to meet your eye when talking to you.

Martin killed his drink. "Well, we got the mail — so home for us, Jocko. I'm damned sorry I had to hammer you down. But you're actin' kinda nutty lately about Matt Harrison, I'd say."

"He shot me down."

"It was a fair fight. No, not quite fair — you caught

him off-guard. Let me tell you something, and you won't blow your bottle?"

"What is it?"

"You're a fast man with a gun, Smith. About as fast as anybody I've ever seen. But each time you've jumped Matt Harrison you've had the edge on him by coming in from behind. I say that if you face Matt face to face — not come in and surprise him — he can outdraw and outshoot you."

Smith scowled. "That's your opinion, not mine."

Wad Martin decided to waste no more breath on this arrogant, ignorant man. "We'd better head for home," he said.

They rode out the wagon trail leading from Beavertail City to Circle Y. Wad Martin looked about and liked what he saw. Montana's tumbling rangelands were on all sides — rolling hills and boulders and juniper and a few scrub pine. Overhead the blue deep sky was without clouds. Martin looked toward the east, and his mouth soured.

There he could see the shacks of the farmers sprinkled along the banks of almost dry Beavertail Creek. He gave his thoughts over to these horny handed men and women. The farmers claimed they would dam Beavertail Creek. They would run ditches below the dam and irrigate their fields. Martin knew full well what this meant. It meant the end of open range for Circle Y.

He could not allow this dam to be built. This land would raise good crops with irrigation water. With a dam built, other farmers would move in. Raw impatience pulled at the big cowman. But he had given these farmers one month. He would abide by his word. He only hoped that within a month these sodbusters would be gone. He figured that the wives would work on the men, for the children were in danger — and a good woman thought always first of her family's safety. But what if they did not move? There would be only one thing Circle Y could do and that was move in with black dynamite and roaring guns.

Wad Martin's blocky jaw tightened.

Dusk was creeping across the arid land when Martin and Smith rode into Circle Y. Sitting his horse momentarily before the big barn, Wad Martin let his gaze travel briefly over his holdings.

Circle Y was a proud brand. His father had run Circle Y in Texas, down around Laredo, years ago — starting the brand when a young man, just as he, Wad Martin, had been a stripling of sixteen when he had trailed in Circle Y cattle to Montana, some twenty four years before.

Wild morning-glories almost covered the long low log ranch-house. Every building was of Montana native pine logs. Many of them he had cut down himself when building his spread.

His father had said, "There's little open range left in Texas, Wad. Cut out two thousand head of Circle Y cows — take a few bulls along — and trailherd into Montana. Was I twenty years younger, I'd move north with you. But there's too much of me to leave behind, son."

Three years later, the father had died of cholera. Bankers had swooped in, stripped the Texas Circle Y bone-bare. Now only two graves bound Wad Martin to the Lone Star State.

Circle Y had its private graveyard on the slope back of the house. Here was buried Wad Martin's first wife. Her death had left no vacancy in his heart. She had been a Miles City dance-hall girl — and a first class bitch. His life with her had been living hell.

Now the hostler said, "You goin' set on that cayuse all night, Wad? Or do you want down so I can unsaddle him?"

Grinning, Wad swung aground.

Jocko Smith said, "So long, boss," and bow-legged toward the bunkhouse. Down by the black-smith shop somebody hammered a red hot horse-shoe, the sound metallic in the still Montana evening.

Martin walked toward the house, glancing occasionally at Jocko Smith. Martin had been on this Beaver-tail range but a few years when Jocko Smith, a shave-tail button, had ridden in on a leg-tired horse that packed the XIT brand, Texas biggest cow-outfit.

Between himself and Jocko was a fine thread of friendship, although that friendship became rough at times — as today when he'd kicked the pistol from Jocko's grip.

But Jocko was a good hand. Jocko knew cattle, range-conditions — he could handle roundup crews well.

There was, Martin realized, only one serious flaw in Jocko Smith's makeup: his terrible, ever-burning pride. Jocko let anger over-ride discretion. If Jocko continued the way he was going, either him or Matt Harrison would be dead. And, give Matt Harrison an even break and Matt's gun would kill Jocko Smith.

Matt was just too fast.

Martin crossed the wide flagstoned porch, boot-heels hammering. The heavy door burst open and a small boy came running to meet him. Martin swept him into his arms, looking at the boy's dark-skinned face. Martin hugged him, kissed the boy's cheek.

"Daddy, I've been waiting for you."

"Pretty soon, son, you'll be big enough to ride with daddy."

"Mama's cooking supper."

"Good."

Martin carried his son across the big living room with its soot-blacked huge fireplace and went through the archway leading to the kitchen. His wife was at the range, back toward Martin and his boy — evidently she had not heard them enter.

Martin looked at the squaw, his son warm and alive in his arms, and a great thickness entered his leathery throat. He had been south around the Little Big Horn, buying some cattle, and he had seen her in a Crow camp, and she, in turning, had seen him.

They had been married a week later at the Mission. And the little squaw — now Mrs. Wad Martin — had said to her father. "My husband pays no ponies for me. Those days are gone. I go to him of my own accord."

She'd never returned to her people, even for a visit.

With her coming, the life of rough Wad Martin had changed. The softening influence of a good woman — who soon became a mother — made great changes in Wad Martin.

Yes, and in Margaret, too.

Margaret had that same stiff beauty, that overbearing pride, that her mother had had. And with a new wife moving into Circle Y household — and a squaw, at that — Margaret had frozen into silence, stiff and uncompromising, although she and her father, even before the coming of the new wife, had never been very close.

Now the little squaw turned and seeing her husband and son, she smiled slowly, dark eyes lightening. For a moment Martin and his wife looked at each other, and a great sickness entered the cowman's soul.

He thought of Clint Harrison's farmers.

What if they would not move? What if they were on homesteads after the month had passed?

This, he knew, bothered his wife. He put his arms around her gently. She was small, womanly. She came to him, and he felt the imprint of her womanhood.

"I have great faith in you," she said.

Martin's throat clogged. "Thanks."

"You will see us through."

Martin thought. She's got more faith in me than I have in myself. That bothered him.

"Where's Margaret?"

"She's in her room. She's riding to Malta."

"Malta? Starting out this time of the day? She goin' ride all night?"

"She says it is cooler at night."

Martin nodded. He didn't like the idea of his daughter riding the long miles to Malta — all alone. The last few years Margaret had become completely unmanageable. He wanted her to go back East to school. This she would not do. She had spent her grammar and highschool years back in Chicago. In a girl's school.

Martin saw things from his daughter's viewpoint. Margaret was, in one way, a pariah on this range — almost without friends because of her position in the social scheme, because of the coldness of her character. He'd go to Margaret's room. Talk with her. Try to get her to go back to school. Even though Circle Y faced big bills, there'd be some for Margaret's education. Any sacrifice to get her away from loneliness and the constant silent strife between his daughter and his wife.

Margaret never bellyached to the squaw's face. Always she protested on the side, to him.

Wad Martin knew he had spoiled his daughter.

Margaret's room was empty. It was a disordered mess — boots in corners, riding-skirt over the unmade bed, cobwebs in corners. As a housekeeper, Margaret left much to be desired. She took after her mother in that respect. Wad Martin had seen only one woman lazier than his daughter; her dead mother.

He heard hoofs leaving.

He went to the living room and looked out the big window. Margaret was spurring a black out of the yard, dust kicking behind plunging hoofs. She sat saddle as though part of her bronc.

Martin's eyes narrowed.

Odd that his daughter would pull out this time of the day for the long ride to the county-seat. And once she got there, what would she do? Buy some pretties, he supposed. Margaret ran to gaudy things, as had her mother.

But still, there was something here — something

sinister — that plagued Wad Martin's thoughts, begging for life but as yet unborn. He tried to put a solid thumb on the thought; he couldn't. He felt a small hand slide into his. Instinctively his big fingers tightened.

"Mamma's got supper ready, daddy."

Cattle moved through the Montana night. They came off hogback ridges, spilled down brush-choked hills, horns back, running, jostling. And hazing them were savage, grim-lipped riders astraddle plunging cowhorses.

Circle Y cattle.

All steers.

No cows, no calves. No bulls, either. Two years ago Martin had shipped in some purebred Hereford bulls to breed up his Texas stock. He knew every bull by name. To steal a bull would be stealing a marker. Martin would miss him immediately.

And Buyer Emerson would not buy cows or calves. Emerson wanted steers — and steers only. And steers he would be getting. Long-legged, big-boned, Circle Y steers. Three-year-olds and four-year-olds with an occasional older steer that, somehow, had managed to escape fall beef-roundup.

They were a conglomeration of colours — some solid roans, solid bays, others brockle-faced, vari-coloured hides showing mixed breeding. But they were all heavy animals, big of bone, and, even with the drought, they still carried hard flesh.

Clint Harrison pulled in his horse savagely, setting the sweaty beast back on haunches. He sat saddle, bent slightly over the horn, one elbow on the saddle's fork, looking over sleeping Beavertail range.

Far to the east, a dim pinpoint of light, was a lamp in the shack of a farmer, the only lamp lit at this midnight hour. Clint wondered idly what farmer's shack held that light, and why that particular farmer was not in bed, cabin dark, at this late hour.

A horse crashed brush at Clint's right. Clint's .45 leaped into his hand, swiveled, covered the commotion. He figured the rider would be Nels Hannigan. Still, a man had to take precautions.

Now, he recognized the horseman. His .45 lifted, slapped into holster. Clint's eyes hardened.

"You ride like an idiot, Hannigan," he hissed. "I could hear you a quarter-mile away."

"Thick brush." Hannigan's voice was hoarse. "Lots of boulders. You ride noisy yourself, Harrison!"

Clint laughed drunkenly. He dug a bottle from his chap pocket. He drank noisily, handed the bottle to Hannigan, who merely raised it, pretended he was drinking, and passed it back.

"You're not much on the booze," Clint said.

Hannigan frowned. "Not at times like this."

Clint laughed again. "No danger, Hannigan. The world sleeps — only you and me and the females toil." His voice hardened. "You've got scruples lately, huh?"

"What'd you mean?"

"I told you to get rid of my brother. Shoot him down, leave his carcass for the buzzards — but you only sprinkle lead around him, not kill him."

"I thought I'd scare him out of Beavertail."

Clint drank again. He killed the bottle. He threw

403

it into the moonlight; somewhere it crashed, sound sharp. He dug back into his saddle-bag, came out with another pint, shoved it in his chap pocket.

"You oughta know as Harrisons better than that, Nels. A Harrison never runs. My grandfather on my father's side was captured by the Mexes at Santa Fe when Texans stormed that town. He made the march into Mexico. At Monclova they pulled the beans. Nine white beans to each black one — the man who pulled a black one was shot. My grandfather pulled a black one. Mexicans asked him to get on his knees when they blindfolded him. He told them to go to hell — a Texan bends his knee only to God. One bullet — right through his brain — but the old boy was standing, not kneeling."

Hannigan said nothing. He'd heard this before. Whenever Clint got deep, Clint always told this story.

Clint asked suddenly, "Where're the females?"

"Jane is hazin' across the canyon. Margaret is stationed a few miles south of Circle Y's home-ranch on guard."

"And Wad thinks his only daughter is in Malta!" Clint slapped his thigh, palm smacking leather chaps noisily. "How many head you figure will deliver to Emerson?"

"Around six hundred."

Clint did some quick arithmetic. Twenty five times six hundred was fifteen thousand. But the women figured they were getting only fifteen bucks a head. He'd tell them they collected only nine thousand. Cut nine thousand four ways and each had two thousand and two hundred and fifty bucks.

Cut the addition six thousand two ways, and he and Hannigan would come out of this with at least five thousand and two fifty. Clint knew his mental arithmetic was correct.

All his adult life, he'd dealt with figures. Across green-topped tables, cards sliding soundlessly — figures moving through his head, grouping, collecting, adding up truthfully.

Emerson would pay in gold. The old plan would be worked — Clint take all the money, each person come to him next day or later for his or her share. Never divide on the spot of payment. If this were done the women would get wise.

"Let's move cattle," Clint said suddenly.

They were bunching the steers on Widetop Mesa, a flat area of land flanked by high brush and scrub-pine. Once the herd was gathered it would be moved west, hitting Skeleton Canyon. Skeleton Canyon threaded its way to Calena, ending just below the boom mining town.

Clint figured the herd was gathered. He hazed Circle Y steers down the south slope. Jane took the north. Hannigan circled east to pick up drags. Already cattle were beginning to lumber west.

Clint Harrison worked with cold dispatch. His bullwhip whined, but he did not pop it; his bronc whirled, cut-off cattle. Already the lead steers were trotting up Skeleton Canyon.

Ten minutes later, Clint met Hannigan and Jane in the canyon. Jane rode her pinto and Harrison frowned. That gaudy horse was like a sign-board in the moonlight. When a man made a raid like this he should be astraddle a dark-coloured horse —

black, dark bay or sorrel.

But he said nothing. Later, when he gave her her cut, he'd jack her up about that pinto.

"Put 'em up the canyon!" Clint ordered.

Jane smiled at him. Her hat hung on her back by its throat-strap. Her blonde hair glistened.

"Hannigan, ride point," Clint ordered. "Jane an' me'll bring up the drag."

Hannigan spurred through the cattle and out of sight. Harrison leaned and kissed Jane lightly. Jane knew this man and his moods; right now, something bothered him.

"What is it, Clint?"

"I might be nuts, Jane, but I sure as heck think somebody else hazed cattle below you."

Jane's eyes showed fright. "Who would it be?"

"Margaret, I think."

"She's supposed to be watching Circle Y. So if any Martin men rode toward us, she could ride ahead and warn."

"Might be just my imagination."

"If she's behind us, I'll scratch her damn' eyes out myself! If she deserted her post, she put all of us in danger!"

"I'll drop back. I might be just imagining things, like I said. You drive cattle."

"I'll go with you."

Clint shook his head. "Somebody has to stay with the dogies, Jane. Otherwise they'll drift back. There's nobody behind us, I'm sure." He knew now he'd been a fool to confide in Jane. He was sure she was jealous of Margaret. He knew Jane would have no idea how far he had gone with Margaret. But Jane was a woman . . . and therefore eternally suspicious.

"Okay, Clint."

Jane rode ahead. She beat the steer's bony rumps with her doubled lariat. Clint dropped back into the canyon a hundred yards. He dismounted and hid his horse in the rocks. Here was a sandwash, very narrow. He figured the rider — if there were one — would ride down it. He was right. The rider came, horse walking. Clint saw it was Margaret. He lunged forward, dragged her from saddle, dumped her unceremoniously on the sand. Her horse shied, jumped, then stood, reins ground-tied.

Margaret recognized him immediately. She started to her feet, eyes angry — but he held her on her back. She stopped struggling. She looked at him, his eyes bored into hers. His eyes drank her dark face, her glistening black hair; under him, her ribs rose, fell.

"I should whip the hell out of you!" Clint gritted, "for leaving Circle Y. And I might do that little chore . . . yet."

"I don't want you alone with that Jane bitch!"

"She's Hannigan's woman." Clint lied from much practice. "She means nothing to me."

Margaret did not try to rise. She watched him, dark eyes swiveling. His hand made ventures. Margaret shivered delightfully. "I love you, Clint! Oh, lord, Clint —"

He treated her roughly. This, he knew, she liked. She responded, all woman, vibrant, living — and then both lay side by side in the sand, with Margaret murmuring endearments.

Clint had difficulty suppressing his smile. Both these females were fools — but what woman was not?

One more raid . . . and then no more Clint Harrison.

And neither Margaret or Jane would come with him. That he definitely would not allow. South America had women, too. Dark-haired, sloe-eyed, voluptuous females — and money would buy them, too.

Clint got to his feet, helping her up. "Now you ride outa here," he ordered. "Go to Sunken Springs line-camp. This time of the year your father has no riders that far out. Stay there until tomorrow morning. Then ride either into Circle Y or into Beavertail City. I'll have your cut waiting for you."

"Can't I move cattle with you?"

Clint shook his head. "Jane and Hannigan figure you're still at guard. When they saw you'd deserted your post —"

Clint's hands spread, fingers out.

"You're right, darling." Margaret kissed him warmly. She mounted. "See you tomorrow night in Beavertail."

"I'll have your cut."

Clint watched her ride away. Within a minute she was gone. He rode back to where Jane trailed drags. "My imagination," he said. "Nothing or nobody behind."

Cattle threaded up Skeleton Canyon. Gradually the rocky walls pinched together. Within fifteen miles the canyon was very narrow. Hannigan rode back.

"Emerson's at his usual spot in the canyon making his tally-count. He's got the usual two men with him."

"Good."

"You trust his count, Clint?"

"You've asked that before. Yes, I trust it. Why not? He's getting beef dirt-cheap. Each carcass will pay him over a hundred bucks slaughtered. Would he put a low count on to jip us a little? If he did, and we found out, no more steers from us — and would Emerson cut off his nose to spite his face? Use what little brains God gave you, Nels!"

Dust rose thickly. Hannigan, Jane and Harrison had bandanas tied over their noses. Finally the last steer lumbered past the count-point. Emerson slid down the slope, stopped.

"Seven hundred and eighty-six," Emerson said.

"I'll accept that," Clint said.

Emerson went to his horse. He took a buckskin sack from each saddle-pocket. "Each contains pay for four hundred steers," he said. "The way I figure you will owe me fourteen steers."

"Take them out of next tally," Clint said.

Emerson said, "Okay."

Already his men had the steers out of sight in a bend in the canyon. They would trail them the remaining twenty odd miles into Galena. Hannigan, Jane and Clint had done their job.

"When are you going to deliver another herd?" Emerson asked.

Clint laughed shortly. "You've got a lot of beef trotting up that canyon, man."

"Miners have big appetites," Emerson pointed out.

"Margaret or Jane will contact you," Clint assured. "Say about a week, maybe five days?"

"The sooner the better." Emerson swung into his

saddle and spurred away.

Jane said, "I'd better get into town. I told Sig I was going to spend the night with Jennie." Jennie was a friend of hers who ran the restaurant in Beavertail City.

"I'll ride with you," Hannigan said.

Clint nodded. "I'm heading for my shack."

Hannigan and Jane rode away into the night. Clint rode for his shack. He patted his saddlebags affectionately. He heard the satisfying tinkle in them and smiled broadly.

He uncorked his bottle, lifted it and emptied it. He heaved the empty flask aside hearing it break somewhere out in the night. He realized he was pretty drunk. He thought of his jumping Matt on Beavertail City's mainstreet. Sourness entered his mouth; his eyes hardened.

Matt had called his hand. Matt had been ready to fight him, his only brother — and Clint had not expected this. He had expected Matt to get angry, yes — and then leave Beavertail range. But the meeting had taught him one thing, and this was acid in his soul now.

He was afraid of Matt. Matt was big and tough and hard . . . and Matt had a fast gun. Smith had downed him, Clint, but Smith had not downed Matt. Matt had knocked Smith to the dust with a bullet.

Suddenly Clint Harrison hated his brother.

Bitter old memories lifted sourly, bubbling through the whiskey. He had made Matt's life living hell when Matt had been a boy. Then had come the day when Matt had been able to whip him.

It had been a savage, ugly fist-fight. Gradually,

410

Matt had gained the upper hand, fists working. Matt had given him a terrible beating. There had been hate before, but it had been under the surface — after that fist-whipping, that hate had zoomed upward and become visible.

Matt personified danger, too.

Clint realized he might make more than one more raid on Circle Y beef. This was a good profit-making deal — one of the best he'd ever stumbled on. And Matt could queer it.

One word from Matt that he, Clint, was an ex-convict, and all would be over. His stupid farmers — those he used as a Circle Y kicking-boy — would be against him. Marshal Snodgrass would then watch him night and day. Clint slowly shook his head.

His brother would have to go.

He dug out his Ingersoll. He could see the watch's dial clearly in the brilliant moonlight. There was still enough night left to ride to Matt's tent before daybreak, and kill Matt.

Clint spurred his horse viciously.

He rode hard, not sparing his tired horse, zigzagging around boulders, finally reaching the sagebrush flat country. Within minutes after that, his horse was was hidden in the southern brush and, rifle in hand, he approached Matt's tent, moving through Beavertail Creek's high buckbrush. He stopped, looked at the tent.

The new tent glistened in moonlight. Later on Montana's bitter sun would turn it an ugly gray. Something was wrong.

Matt's bay was gone.

Clint had expected to see the horse on picket

near the tent, but the bay was not in sight. Clint knew the animal was not in the brush, for he would have seen the bay on his route to kill his brother.

Matt was gone.

Openly, Clint walked to the tent, rifle in hand. Boldly, he entered — as he had suspected, the tent was unoccupied. Matt's bedroll was in a corner, a tight round cylinder.

Matt had not slept in this tent tonight.

Where was he?

Clint could only decide that Matt had ridden into Beavertail City. Evidently Matt had got tired of the homestead and its loneliness and had headed into the saloon.

Matt should be coming home soon, Clint reasoned drunkenly.

To get to their homesteads the farmers had to thread down a sandwash called Hogbelly Wash. Brush-choked hills flanked this draw. Clint tied his horse in boulders on the crest of a hill, then moved down rifle in hand, settling behind some sagebrush. He poked his Winchester out in front of him as he lay on his belly. Bottle beside him, he waited, drinking often.

Clint's drunken mind had worked correctly. Matt had gone to town about midnight, his sleep done. He had rolled up his bedroll through mere habit, pushing it into the corner.

He had shot peapool with Marshal Snodgrass and the bartender in Wad Martin's saloon. At three thirty the bartender locked up and Matt had headed for his homestead.

Now he rode slowly down Hogbelly Wash. Within

a few minutes dawn would come and now the long dimness of early morning held the rangelands. Up on the hill, Clint Harrison slowly lowered his cheek to the stock of his Winchester. Carefully, he took aim on Matt, now three hundred feet away. Carefully Clint squeezed the trigger.

The ugly snarl of the rifle smashed the morning's stillness. Matt's horse reared, neighed, went side-wise, and fell on his left side, legs flailing. Clint knew he had not hit the horse; even drunk, he was a better shot than that. His whiskey fogged mind told him Matt had deliberately jerked his rearing horse over.

Hastily Clint triggered another shot, saw sand spurt beyond the horse and his brother. Suddenly a bullet buzzed overhead. He realized Matt had jerked his own Winchester from the saddle boot. Fear hit Clint and made him run. Common sense told him that Matt could not see him because of the high and thick brush.

Suddenly something white hot burned across Clint's left forearm. Dimly he realized a random bullet from Matt's rifle had accidentally hit him. Clint thought, my luck's running muddy tonight. Matt should have been in his bunk in his tent an easy victim . . .

Now Clint was in saddle, rifle brandishing overhead. He whirled his horse with a savage bit, spurs digging the creature's flanks. He rode madly through the brush. Within a minute or two he was securely hidden in the timber along Beavertail creek. Here he drew rein and looked back. No rider followed him.

Clint wondered if Matt were dead or just lay

413

dying. He uncorked his bottle and drank deeply. His arm was bloody but gave him no pain. Maybe there was no pain because he had drunk so much? Anyway the bone in his arm was unbroken, he realized.

He rode to his homestead wondering if Slow Elk were in his bunk. He unsaddled his horse and turned him loose and went to the lean-to where Slow Elk had his bunk. Slow Elk lay with his back toward Clint. Because of the heat the Crow Lay naked, coppery skin glistening. Matt raised his rifle slowly. He should kill this buck. He was tired of this stinking redskin. Then logic came in and told him he was getting much free work from the Crow. Slowly his rifle went down again. He entered his cabin. He peeled off his shirt and looked at his arm.

Only a shallow groove marred his flesh, the blood already congealing. His shirt held two holes and the sleeve was bloody. Clint went to the cupboard and got a bottle of iodine. Teeth gritted in pain, he doused the wound with the red liquid. The iodine burned like fire but this left and the wound ceased throbbing.

He did not know that Slow Elk watched him. Between the cabin door and the lean to was a heavy gunnysack curtain. Through its slit the redskin watched unnoticed.

Slow Elk frowned. Where had Clint picked up this wound? Slow Elk had seen Clint but a few hours before working cattle on Widetop Mesa with Nels Hannigan and Jane Westby. Had there been trouble between the rustlers and George Emerson and his men?

Or was this really a bullet wound? Because of the

dim dawn Slow Elk could not clearly see Clint's arm. Maybe Clint's horse had fallen and Clint had gouged his arm against a boulder's sharp edge?

Slow Elk tiptoed back to his bunk and quietly resumed his old position. He would see Sig Westby this morning. He would plant some potatoes along Beavertail creek. Westby would see him there and come and talk to him. He would tell Sig about Clint's arm.


Dawn tiptoed across the Montana rangelands to light the higher peaks of the Little Rocky Mountains with glistening redness. Circle Y buildings are shifting bulks against the dusty soil when Matt Harrison rode into the ranch. The old hostler came from the barn rubbing his red eyes.

"Heard your horse cross the bridge," he said sleepily before recognizing Matt. Upon recognition the hostler's eyes became wide awake. "What the hell you mean by ridin' into Circle Y, farmer?"

"Where's Jocko Smith?"

"In his bunk, of course. Now what'd you want with Jocko?"

"My business," Matt dismounted.

"What happened to your saddle?" the old man queried. "The fork is all busted like somebody put a bullet through it!"

"That's why I want Jocko Smith." Matt towered over the oldster. "Where's the bunkhouse?"

"Maybe I won't tell you!"

Matt clamped a hammerlock on the hostler who cursed and struggled but Matt slammed him down

415

on his belly, his knees grinding into the bony back. "Now where is Smith?" he demanded.

"You're breakin' my arm! The bunkhouse — it's that buildin' over there, Harrison! My god, my arm!"

Matt got to his feet, the oldster following him upright. The hostler rubbed his shoulder gingerly.

"Smith ride out last night?" Matt asked.

"Nobody rode out. I sleep light, if I sleep at all."

Matt looked at the bunkhouse. The hostler looked at Matt. Matt's jaw was set, his eyes narrowed.

Without another word, Matt started for the bunkhouse. Matt's belly was sore. The bullet had hit the fork of his saddle. Its tremendous force had ripped the rawhide-covered wooden-fork as though dynamite had exploded inside of it, tipping his horse over.

Upon reaching the bunkhouse's open door, he glanced back. The hostler was scurrying toward Circle Y's ranch-house. Matt grinned, stepped into the the close confines of the bunkhouse.

Circle Y's crew slept. Because of the heat, most riders lay naked on sheets. The windows were closed and the place stunk of staleness — the smell of unwashed bodies, of breathing in a closed area.

Jocko Smith slept in the third bunk. He lay with his back to the aisle. He wore no clothing. He had kicked off his dirty sheet. Matt looked at him for a long moment.

Without warning, he slapped Smith on the rump.

The sound was a thunderclap. It brought Circle Y instantly awake, men leaping up in bunks. Smith came up as though dynamited. He sat up, hand instinctively going upward to his .45, holstered in the belt that hung from the nail in the wall.

Matt hacked Smith hard across the wrist. Smith's hand fell, limp, useless. Smith glared at him, wide awake, eyes showing not fear but surprise.

"What t'hell you want, Harrison?"

"Somebody shot at me from ambush about an hour ago," Matt gritted. "Shot low, hit my saddle's fork, blasted my bronc to earth. And you're the type dog who'd try murder, Smith!"

Smith's left arm was out of sling. Matt noticed it was merely bandaged. Smith raised that arm to his face, brushing away the last of sleep. He handled his wounded arm easily. Matt knew that once again Smith would be dangerous with both of his guns.

"I never left this spread last night," Smith said thickly. "You can ask the old hostler. He don't sleep nights. Or if he does, it's like a cat. Nothin' can move nights on this ranch without him knowin'."

"You could have sneaked off into the brush. Had your bronc cached out there. So the hostler wouldn't see you."

"My horse is on night-pasture. Look at him yourself. Look at all the Circle Y horses on pasture. Or in the barn. You'll find none with sweat on him."

Matt scowled.

Did Jocko Smith speak truth? Maybe Smith had not ambushed him? Then, if Smith had not, who had?

It had to be Smith.

Now a harsh voice cut in with, "What's goin' on here, Harrison?"

Matt whirled, hand on his gun. Wad Martin stood in the doorway, the hostler peeking around him.

417

Martin was barefooted. He wore only his trousers, gunbelt, and .45.

"Fool farmer claims I ambushed him," Smith said.

"Did you?" Wad Martin's voice was a harsh rasp.

"Never left my bunk after hittin' it, Wad."

A cowpuncher said, "Jocko's right, boss. This bad belly of mine kept me runnin' almost all night. Between that and Jocko's snorin' I got danged little shuteye. He snores like a man crowbarrin' rusty nails out of a hardwood plank!"

Another puncher laughed.

"That clears you, Jocko," Wad Martin said. "Old Smoky here says you never rode out, either." Martin swung hard eyes on Matt. "You got a lotta gall, Harrison. Ridin' in like this — bold as brass — and accusin' Circle Y!"

"If Smith didn't, who did?"

"How would I know! I know nothin' about you. For all Circle Y knows, you might be a longrider — an outlaw — some old grudge-holder might have come in, found you were located on Beavertail, then decided to blast you out of your saddle. Where'd it happen and when?"

Matt gave details.

He knew, now, he'd ridden off too fast, too hot-headed.

"Circle Y doesn't ambush, Harrison!" Wad Martin's thick voice was glacial ice. "I've ordered my men to fight fair and square . . . or not at all. And they follow my orders — or they got me to face. Three years ago one of my riders pulled a shady deal in town. Ask Jocko what happened to him?"

Smith said, "There's a graveyard down in town. Boothill. Only gunmen and low-down stiffs are planted there. Townspeople have a decent graveyard of their own. And this gink the boss's talkin' about is in Boothill."

Matt said slowly. "You're the only guy who'd want me out of the way, Smith. You got my apologies, man."

"Maybe I don't want 'em," Smith growled.

Wad Martin said, "Don't act like a punk schoolkid, Jocko. Harrison here admits he made a mistake. You were half-full of booze the times you jumped Harrison in town. You're lucky he didn't kill you."

Smith, sitting on his bunk's edge, said nothing. Wad Martin touched Matt's arm. "My wife'll have breakfast ready about now. Come up to the house and eat, huh?"

Matt studied him, then grinned. "Why not?" he said.

Martin looked at Jocko Smith. "You slide into your clothes and come along, too," he said.

Matt scowled.


That afternoon Slow Elk worked along Beavertail Creek. First he cleared a piece of land of brush and trees, then he started spading. The sun was hot. He discarded his dirty buckskin jacket and worked naked to the waist, sun glimmering on his copper-coloured skin.

Sig Westby did not come that day.

Clint Harrison headed for town that noon. "Might make it back by tonight or might lay over in town,"

Clint told the Crow. "What're spadin' this for —
a garden?"

"Potatoes. Water seeps underground from the
creek."

"Good idea."

Clint rode away.

Slow Elk worked slowly, punching his turning-
fork into the soil. The fact that Sig Westby did not
materialize out of the brush did not disturb him.
Sig could take care of himself, Slow Elk knew. And
the mining-town of Galena was a long ways off.
Eighty mile ride, coming and going.

Dusk came. Slow Elk thought, Sig will contact me
tomorrow. He rode downstream to Matt Harrison's
tent. Matt crouched over a small fire frying eggs in a
cast-iron skillet.

Matt's saddle lay on its side. "What happened to
the saddle?" Slow Elk asked.

Matt told him.

"Did you see the man who tried to kill you?"

Matt shook his head. "Too dark and too much
brush. I peppered rifle bullets around him but don't
think I hit him."

Slow Elk remembered Clint Harrison, bloody
sleeve rolled up, pouring iodine into a shallow wound
on his forearm, and Slow Elk wondered. Had Clint
waylaid his brother? That did not seem logical,
even though the Crow had a very low estimation
of Clint Harrison.

Clint and Matt were brothers.

"Maybe Jocko Smith?" Slow Elk ventured.

"Smith wasn't off Circle Y last night." Matt told
about riding into the Martin spread.

"Then who could it have been?"

Matt shrugged. "Danged if I'd know. I've racked my brain silly. The only conclusion I can come to is that somebody's mistaken me for somebody else — but who would those somebodys be?"

Slow Elk merely shrugged.

"How are the farmers taking Wad Martin's warning?" Matt asked.

Slow Elk gave a rather detailed report. Most of the farmers were fighting-mad. Matt judged that this anger somewhat surprised the Indian. It surprised him a little, too.

He'd expected the farmers to move out, especially those married ones with children whose wives would apply pressure on them. Slow Elk reported that only one farmer — and he an unmarried man — was talking about leaving.

"They've got lots of faith in your brother," Slow Elk said.

Matt grinned. "Good luck somebody has," he said.

"You're really going to stay, huh?"

Matt's jaw tightened. "You're danged tootin', Slow Elk. Nobody's trying to kill me from ambush and me riding off without settling it for once and for all!"

"Somebody sure must want to get rid of you, Matt. That makes two times you've been shot at from the brush.

Slow Elk liked this tough, resilient cowpuncher. Matt had a good smile, and seemed an all-around good fellow. Slow Elk thought, I'd hate to be in the boots of that ambusher.

"Gotta get back home and milk," the Crow said. "Clint rode to town about noon. Might not be back tonight, he said."

"He sure seems to like that jerkwater burg," Matt said. "From the looks of him I'd say he's drinking purty steady."

"He ain't enemies to the bottle. So long."

Clint did not come home that night. Slow Elk remembered this was payday at Circle Y. Clint was probably gambling in the saloon. He did not show up next forenoon, either — but Sig Westby did, coming out of the brush about two.

"Anybody but us around?" Sig asked.

"Clint's in town."

"Saw him in there an hour ago. Got a game running in the bar with Circle Y. Gradually cleaning the cowpokes, too."

"He's a good gambler."

"Things turned out just as expected in Galena," Sig said. "I was in that town when Emerson drove in the stolen Circle Y herd. He's pasturing the cattle west of town in a hidden valley. He started butchering them yesterday, working fast. A few days and all those Circle Y steers will be beef."

"What does he do with the hides?"

"I don't know. I never got into his slaughter house. He's got guards all around it. I guess he's dumping the hides into an old mine shaft. Sig hesitated momentarily. "Who rustled those Circle Y cattle, Slow Elk?"

"The same four. Clint, Hannigan, Jane and Margaret."

Sig's heavy face became sombre. Sadness moved

into his huge eyes. "Jane," he muttered, "Jane, and yet it doesn't surprise me, because of all the people in the world, I know Jane the best."

Slow Elk said nothing. He and Sig Westby were undercover agents for the Montana Territorial Stockman's Association. Wad Martin had written Association headquarters in Helena for help. The Association had sent in Sig Westby and Slow Elk. Slow Elk had worked for the Association since it had been started six years ago. Wad Martin was a charter member of the organization.

This was Sig Westby's first job for the Association. Jane Westby had no idea that her brother had homesteaded on Beavertail Creek merely as a blind for his work as an Association spy.

Now Sig said slowly. "Jane has been a wild and greedy girl all her life. Maybe she got the bad blood from our father. The old man abandoned my mother and Jane and I when I was only eight. That was back in Des Moines, Iowa."

The abandonment of children was something Slow Elk could not understand. Crow families hung together in face of all troubles. If the father were killed or died a natural death, his relatives took his children and wife to support.

Sig rubbed his huge jaw. "Actually my mother was no good, either. She hung around mining camps and saloons."

"Maybe you shouldn't talk about it?" Slow Elk said.

Sig grinned crookedly. "What difference does it make? A whoremaster shot and killed my mother in a house of ill fame in Leadville, Colorado. I was eighteen then, mucking in a mine. Finally Jane and I landed in Helena. Jane is like her mother . . . bad blood. I had to get her out of Helena before she became a —"

"Clint Harrison will raid Circle Y again in a few days." Slow Elk deliberately changed the subject. "We've got all the evidence we need. We'll have to tell Wad Martin and because of Margaret — well, it'll be tough."

"It'll be no picnic," Sig assured.

"Have you got any plans?"

"We'll have to tell Martin the truth, of course. He might be able to keep his daughter at home during Clint's next raid — or at least ship her out. But then again if Margaret fails to show up when they raid — what will Clint think?"

"He might get suspicious and call off the raid, sensing a trap." Slow Elk reasoned. "He might even get so suspicious that he skips the country."

Sig nodded grim agreement.

"Have you found out anything definite about Nels Hannigan?" Slow Elk asked.

"The head office reports that Hannigan and Clint Harrison were cell mates in the Texas pen. Hannigan was ousted on the promise he'd leave Texas and never return, just like Clint was turned free."

Slow Elk nodded thoughtfully.

"I just learned that today," Sig Westby informed. "Had a letter from the office waiting for me in town today. This thing is driving me crazy, friend."

Slow Elk's deep dark eyes showed compassion. "I know how you feel, friend. There might be shooting — and with your sister involved in this — but poor old Wad Martin has the same problem, Sig."

Sig nodded. "I'd better sneak into Circle Y tonight and have a talk with Wad."

"Wad should have threatened to get even with you for running in his two heifers," Slow Elk said. "Then the other farmers would think that Wad had it in for you."

"Wad said he forgot to mention those heifers when he and his men rode into the meeting, but he did jump me about it in the saloon, though."

Slow Elk rubbed his jaw. "Will Wad really tie into these farmers if they're not gone inside of a month?"

Sig grinned crookedly. "He still talks that way, Slow Elk. But he can't win and I think he knows it. The Association is strong but not so strong one of its members can get away with murder. I'll try to talk him out of it."

"There's room here both for cattle and farming."

Sig smiled. "Try telling that to Wad."

Slow Elk watched huge Sig amble into the brush. The Crow's dark eyes were sad.

But what would he — or anybody else — do?

Nothing.

He scratched himself; he itched. He could smell himself. He needed a bath.

This playing the role of a stupid, stinking renegade Indian was not so good . . .

He went to the cabin for a bar of soap. He stopped and looked again at the shirt that Clint Hannigan had worn night before last. Clint had washed it in the creek.

He had washed the blood from it. But he had not mended the two holes in the sleeve.

Slow Elk knew they were bullet-holes.

He had told Sig about Clint standing there, pouring iodine into the raw wound on his forearm. He and Sig had talked it over to some length, finally deciding that Clint had tried to ambush his brother, and one of Matt's bullets had by accident burned Clint.

There was no other explanation.

Slow Elk returned to the pothole of Beavertail Creek. He shed his dirty buckskins and waded out into the tepid water. He was lathering himself when Clint Harrison rode through the brush.

"Good lord, what's next?" Clint said. "You're finally takin' a bath, Injun!"

"I smelled myself." Once again Slow Elk spoke broken English.

Clint's eyes were bloodshot. Dark circles ringed his eyes. He turned his horse, rode to the cabin.

Slow Elk figured Clint would hit his bunk and sleep until night, despite the day's heat.

Slow Elk waded out of the pool. Naked, he lay on the dried grass, looking at the empty sky.

Many doubts plagued him.

The sun was very hot. Matt sleeved sweat from his forehead. Around him farmers worked.

They were starting Beavertail Dam. Here the river banks were two bluffs forty feet apart. Upstream was a wide meadow that would eventually constitute the lake behind the dam.

Slips and fresnoes, pulled by horses and mules, were moving dirt out of the bluffs to make abuttments. Matt had four mules on a fresno. The dirt being pulled out was being deposited below the dam site. It was hot, sweaty, tough work.

Matt's hands were getting blisters from handling the Johnson bar of the fresno. He had thought his hands tough from rope and branding-iron, for the Canadian cow-outfit he had worked for had just finished spring roundup before he had ridden south into Montana Territory.

This work, though, was tougher than saddlework.

He couldn't understand these farmers. Apparently they held no fear of Circle Y. Or, if they were afraid, they failed to show it. They toiled, joked, made bantering talk.

But yet there was an undertone — savage, strong. Matt found himself admiring these brawny men. And their women, too. Pioneer women with families, hard-workers, toiling from sunrise to sunset — women who, if a showdown came, would handle rifles, shotguns and pistols. And who, if necessary, would die beside their men and children.

For the first time the enormity of Wad Martin's task hit Matt with full force. These farmers would never move. Only death could take them off this range.

What would Circle Y do?

Would Circle Y hit, guns roaring? Would Wad Martin lead his men, rifle talking?

Matt knew one thing for sure: Wad Martin would never win. He had seen farmers — and their hated barbwire — come into Texas' Panhandle. Big cowmen there had fought farmers. The war that had followed was still being talked about down on the Staked Plains — the deadly Wire Cutters War. And the farmers had won. And they won not because they were better fighters than the cowmen, but because there were more of them. When one farmer got killed, five others took his place.

Cattlemen had seen the folly of their gunsmoke. Within a year, cowboys were stringing wire, side by side with farmers.

Wad Martin could never win.

But did Martin know this? Or was he too ignorant to read the handwriting? Matt sighed, hoping Martin was not.

"Lemonade, Matt?"

A little red-head spoke the words. She was the oldest daughter of Henry Lucas, a farmer from Indiana.

"Lemonade, Lettie! Now where in tarnation did you get a lemon out in this wilderness!"

Lettie smiled. Her worn housedress did not hide the ripeness of her young figure. Despite the fact she was barefooted — she loved the damp earth on her feet, she had told Clint — she looked neat and efficient, her glistening red hair a bun on her sun-tanned neck.

"Last time we were in Malta mama and I bought some," she said.

Matt liked her father and mother. Henry Lucas was a stocky, pipe-smoking man who said little and Martha Lucas was another red-head — well built and still girlish despite having carried six children.

Upon seeing Lettie and her mother together Matt

always thought of the old saying: If you want to see what the daughter will look like later on look at her mother.

If this old axiom were true, Lettie in beginning middle-age would be indeed a lovely woman.

Matt smiled. "Pour it out," he joked.

Lettie poured lemonade from a cracked enamel pitcher into a glass. She blushed suddenly.

"What's up?" Matt asked.

"They're all joking me, Matt. They say I'm chasing you. Dad is teasing the life out of me!"

"Hope he keeps it up," Matt said.

"After this, I'm going to stay away from you."

"You do and I'll come after you."

"Matt, how nice."

Matt drank his lemonade. It hit the spot. He handed his empty glass to Lettie who scrambled over the pile of earth to where the women worked in the shade of the cottonwood trees. Matt grabbed the Johnson bar of his fresno. "Get moving, you long eared jackasses," he ordered. He worked automatically, the fresno filling with loose earth, the mules wheeling to pull the earth away and on top of the pile, where Matt tripped the fresno of its contents.

Who had tried to kill him from ambush? He did not know. He wished that he knew. He had eliminated Jocko Smith and Circle Y. With Circle Y out of the range of suspicion then who had tried to kill him?

Had Clint tried? Matt's belly soured at this ugly thought, but he did not push cowardly ambush beyond his brother. Vindictive Clint Harrison loved to nurse grudges. Plainly he did not want Matt on this range. And why?

Matt shook his head. This was too much for him. Neither Clint or Nels Hannigan worked with the farmers. Slow Elk toiled instead of Clint and Hannigan had hired a man from Beavertail City to represent himself.

Where were Hannigan and Clint? Matt figured they were probably in Beavertail City in the saloon gambling or drinking. Noon came at last. Mules were watered and fed rough hay cut by a scythe from the rank grass growing along the creek. It was not good hay but better than nothing. Matt dozed under the cottonwoods with Slow Elk lying beside him. The Crow did not stink. Evidently he had recently bathed.

Matt asked, "What do you think these farmers'll do, Slow Elk?"

"I say they intend to fight Circle Y, Matt."

"These people won't run," Matt said. "It'll be up to Circle Y to give."

"Looks that way to me."

The farmers still seemed to have much faith in Clint. Slow Elk mentioned that a rumour said Clint was sending out for cavalry. Matt discounted this. Uncle Sam would not move before powdersmoke burned. U.S. horse-soldiers would not be alerted until open warfare broke loose — if then. Cavalry was busy rounding up remnants of Sitting Bull's Sioux over in eastern Montana and South Dakota.

"Wonder who t'heck ambushed me those two times," Matt said.

Slow Elk had no reply.

Noon ended, work began again. At four Clint and Hannigan rode up, Clint solid in saddle. The two walked over the excavation, talking. Matt swung his mules, grinning. Clint was in his element. Clint was the boss. Clint was happy.

"Never figured I'd see you handlin' a fresno with a bunch of red-necked farmers," Clint said.

Matt didn't like his brother's tone, but he merely said, "Time changes all things, you know."

"She sure made a change in you. What're you goin' do if Circle Y lives up to its promise — hits within a month?"

"Hit back," Matt said.

Clint scowled and walked to his horse, mounted, and he and Nels Hannigan rode east, moving down-slope toward the homesteads. Clint glanced at Slow Elk.

The Crow stood watching Clint and Hannigan. His eyes, Matt noticed, were sombre, almost bitter.

Matt wondered about those eyes.

Hannigan left Clint when they reached Hannigan's farm. "Gotta get some shut-eye, Clint. We tackle those Circle Y poker-players again tonight."

"Those boys know cards," Clint said sourly. "Especially that Jocko Smith. He should be a pro, not pushin' bulls around."

"I can't understand Smith," Hannigan said.

"He's got me stumped, too. Here him and me have our gunfight — he plugs me. He knows I'm after his hide. Yet he rides into town bold as brass and twice as high and plays poker with me."

"Only thing I can think of is that Wad Martin has ordered Smith to walk straight — no gunwork until the time has passed to hit the farmers. Then all hell will pop loose."

"I wonder."

Hannigan's dull eyes raked Clint's handsome face. "What'd you mean by that?"

"I mean just this — this game is almost done. Martin's got around ten thousand head of cattle, but when you lift almost a thousand a time — well, he's bound to miss cattle."

"One more raid, huh?"

"Just one more."

Hannigan wet a wind-cracked bottom lip. "And then what about the two females?"

"I don't follow you."

Hannigan laughed shortly. "The hell you don't! Which one you takin' with you — the black-haired one or the blonde?"

"Both," Clint joked.

"We better not wise them up that this is the last raid. They learn that and sure as shootin' they'll want to come with us."

"You just keep your big yap shut!"

Clint's words were cold, driving. Anger smashed Hannigan's leathery face, then died bfore logic.

"They'll never learn from me," Hannigan rode toward his tent. Clint continued on to his cabin. The thought came that he would burn down the biggest house of the farmers. That would be Henry Watson's house. Some one of these nights soon he'd sneak in come dark with a kerosene can sprinkle coal-oil around the house's foundation, touch a match to it and pull back into the dark.

He had to keep trouble boiling between these

farmers and Circle Y. You conquered by dividing.

He went to his cabin. He stared at the shirt with the bullet-hole through the sleeve. Suddenly he wadded it into the stove, touched a match to it. He should have done this immediately after ambushing Matt.

But what ice did it cut? Slow Elk might have seen the bullet-hole, might not have. And what was Slow Elk but a dirty low-down *renegado* Indian? Slow Elk personified no danger.

Clint frowned.

Things were too quiet. This was not the way he wanted it. He wanted turmoil. For with Circle Y and the farmers actively fighting, rustling could go on unnoticed. Circle Y and the sodbusters should be at each other's throat in a death struggle.

Clint's frown died. He smiled. He mounted his horse. Thirty minutes later he rode boldly into Circle Y.

Smoky, the hostler, stood before the barn, staring, disbelieving his watery eyes.

Clint rode toward the house, heart hammering.

He was stone sober. When gambling, he drank little — cards needed a clear head. Whiskey was good for your opponents, but not you — whiskey addled the logic of those against you.

A sudden thought hit him. He should ambush and kill Wad Martin. The blame would be instantly laid on the sodbusters.

With Margaret already in his net, he could step in and run Circle Y, with Wad Martin dead. He'd run off the squaw and her whelp. If they didn't flee, he'd kill them too.

This new thought held much meat. It warmed his blood. But, if he stepped into Circle Y, the spread would not hold him down. He'd sell it to the last stick of lumber and the last cow. And then, poke filled with gold, he'd pull out, leaving Margaret behind.

He dismounted lazily in front of the house, looping reins around the tooth-gnawed hitchrail. Carefully, he looked over the cow-outfit, eyes narrowed.

Old Smoky seemed to be the only human on the outfit. At least, the only one in sight.

No men moved around the blacksmith shop. Horses grazed on pasture. A few more saddlehorses stood in the corral switching flies. Old Smoky started toward the house with the shuffling slow gait of the aged. Clint grinned. The old reprobate was harmless.

Odd that no dogs were around, barking. Usually a cow-outfit had a collie or two. Then he remembered Margaret saying she owned a chihuahua. The watchdog had always jumped her miniature prune-hound. She had made her father get rid of the big dog.

Margaret came out of the house, carrying her dog. Her eyes were wide. "What're you doing here?" she asked quietly.

"Your father home?"

"No."

"Ridin' range?"

"He went to town for the mail."

Clint remembered then that this was one of the three days a week mail came in on the stage from Malta. The thought came that he could ambush Wad Martin on his way from town to the ranch.

"Where's Jocko Smith?"

"In town, I guess. I heard you boys had a big poker game in the saloon. Only place I know where he could be."

Clint glanced at the windows. He expected the squaw to be peeping out. But, if she were, he could not see her. He asked quietly, "How about the cattle? You and Jane workin'?"

"I've scouted good. Jane couldn't get away without raising suspicions. But northwest of here — around Alkali Flates — big steers, Clint."

Clint had scouted this country carefully. Now he placed Alkali Flats in his mind. It was on the farthermost northwest section of Circle Y's huge graze, about twenty miles away.

They could trail the stolen stock over the hills, thread the steers down into Skeleton Canyon, and Emerson could make his count from the same high cliff — and pay at the same spot.

"Best place we could pick," he said. "How many head?"

"That's what worries me. Only about four hundred."

"That's enough . . . for me."

"I got to get out of here!" Margaret's red lips hissed the words. One hand was at her throat. "Something's closing in, Clint."

"Nerves!" Clint's voice was low and heavy. "Control yourself, Margaret!"

Her hand fell. "With you beside me, Clint, I could do anything. There comes my father now. And it looks like Jocko Smith is with him. What're you going to see him about?"

"Stir up trouble. We got to get him fightin' farmers.

Then we can work in peace."

"Good idea. I'll help all I can."

"Work on him."

"I am. All the time, Clint."

"Good."

Wad Martin pulled in his big sorrel stud and asked, "What you doin' here, Harrison?"

Jocko Smith sat a blue roan, eyes on Clint. Smith said nothing. He just watched.

"I guess I should have brought Marshal Snodgrass with me," Clint said.

"There'll be no trouble unless you start it." Martin looked at Smith. "Hear that, Jocko?"

"I heard."

Clint told about the fictitious letter he'd sent to the C.O. at Assiniboine.

Martin merely nodded.

"I settled these farmers," Clint said, "and I'm their elected leader. I'll do all I can to defend them."

"Your job," Martin said.

"You jump on us and we'll fight till either Circle Y or us are down."

"I see."

"When word comes back I'll show the letter to Marshal Snodgrass who'll be under my orders to tell you what it contains."

"What if your request is turned down? You'll show that letter to Snodgrass, too?"

"It won't be rejected."

Martin asked, "That all you got to say, Harrison?"

"That's all."

Clint mounted, swung his horse to leave, but Martin stopped him with, "Who ambushed your brother?"

"What're you talkin' about?"

"Your brother rode into Circle Y t'other day sayin' somebody had just tried to kill him from the brush. He jumped Circle Y. Circle Y never tried to bushwhack him. I told him that."

"Then who did?"

"I don't know. I only know Circle Y didn't. There's more than one way to skin a cat, Harrison."

"Yeah . . . What are some of them?"

"You figure that out, Harrison."

Clint dug for information with, "I don't follow you, Martin."

Wad Martin laughed harshly. "Use what little brains you got, Harrison! Now ride out and stay out!"

Clint looked at Margaret. Her lovely face was impassive. His eyes went to Jocko Smith. Smith had a bland, impersonal face. Clint turned his horse and rode away at a running-walk.

An icy spot formed between his shoulder blades. He wanted to whip his horse to a run, crouch low over saddle. Only be sheer effort did he make his slow ride to the point in the creek where the trees hid him from Circle Y. It seemed as though he rode for a century.

What had he gained?

First, he'd talked to Margaret. He'd learned where the next rustling raid would be held.

Coldly, his mind catalogued points.

Secondly, he'd discovered that Wad Martin was suspicious of him. Wad figured that he, Clint, was deliberately stirring trouble among the farmers, blaming it on Circle Y.

Martin had almost come out and accused him of ambushing Matt. Wad Martin was a long way from being stupid.

Thirdly, for the first time he'd learned that, after the ambushing, Matt had trailed into Circle Y, accused Martin. Had Matt believed Martin's statement to the effect that Circle Y had not staged the ambushing?

A cold lump formed in Clint Harrison's guts.

He worked on the assumption Matt had believed Wad Martin. Then, where did that leave Matt?

Matt would come to but one conclusion: somebody other than Circle Y was out to kill him. Matt might have already come to the same conclusion that Wad Martin had apparently reached — that somebody in the farmer's ranks had ambushed Matt, to make him jump at Circle Y.

One thing stood out: Matt would have to die. For Matt, if he had believed Martin, might point the finger at him, Clint Harrison. Clint decided that around his brother he'd have to go easy.

When Clint reached the dam site the workers had knocked off for noon. Mules and horses grazed along the creek, still wearing harnesses. The farmers were gathered under the shade of cottonwoods, eating lunch. As Clint rode in he noticed Matt eating with the Lucas family. Matt sat crossleged beside Henry Lucas.

Lettie Lucas was in the act of refilling Matt's lemonade glass. She stood poised, holding the pitcher — a lovely bit of femininity outlined clearly, body magnificent.

Clint's throat tightened. He had tried to make time with Lettie. He'd got nothing but a polite cold shoulder. He would like to take Lettie — at least once — before he jerked stakes.

Usually women fell into his lap.

But not Lettie.

He pushed such thoughts from his mind, concentrating on his opening words, and soon he uttered them.

He sat his horse while he talked.

"As your elected leader, folks, I rode this morning to Circle Y, where I had a long talk with Wad Martin."

Men stopped eating. Women hushed children. All eyes were on him, and this pleased him.

"I told Circle Y I had written a letter to the Commanding Officer at the Assiniboine Reservation. In that letter I told about Martin's threat to wipe us out in thirty days."

"Twenty-six days now," a man interrupted.

Clint nodded, angry at the interruption. "All right, twenty-six days then, to be exact."

"What did Martin say?" Henry Lucas asked.

"He laughed at me. His big, loud horse-laugh. We almost went for our guns. But he had too many men around him — they'd've killed me."

Faces fell.

"We oughta ride in, wipe Circle Y from the earth!"

Nels Hannigan had ground out the words. Clint was surprised to see Hannigan in the group. Hannigan must not have hit the hay as he had said; instead, he had apparently ridden back to the dirt-camp.

Angry rumbling swept the gathering. Nerves were on edge despite the placidity of the faces. "That's what we oughta do," Hannigan growled, "Moonlight yet, and we could see to shoot good."

"God in Heaven," a woman wailed.

Clint held up his hand for quiet. "Stop that talk, Hannigan," he said sternly. "That would only lead to death, man. Foolish idea."

"Then what do we do?" Hannigan demanded. "Sit here like ducks on a pond waitin' for the shotguns to boom?"

"We wait until we hear from the military," Clint said crisply. "Uncle Sam settled this land. Our gover' ment will help us hold it. Troops will come in."

"I don't believe that," Hannigan said. "I know the military. I served in the cavalry in the Custer campaign — just a button."

This was a lie, but only Clint knew it.

"We wait," Clint snapped, dismounting.

Farmers got to their feet, preparatory to starting the afternoon labour. Clint walked over to Nels Hannigan. They were apart from the rest. Clint said very softly, "You're on the right track. Move among them, stir them up. Hell's fire, I sent no letter."

"I still say we should raid," Hannigan said sternly.

Clint grabbed Hannigan's shirt-front. He pulled the man close. He said distinctly, "Don't cause us no trouble, damn you!" He pushed Hannigan, releasing him.

Hannigan stood, fists hard. He eyed Clint. The camp watched, eyes missing nothing. Chick Lannigan pushed between them. "For Lord's sake, men! No fightin' among ourselves, please! Save your fightin' for Circle Y."

Hannigan stepped back, mumbling angrily, then wheeled and stalked toward the grazing stock, not looking back.

Clint said, "Thanks, Lannigan."

Lannigan said, "I gotta get to work."

Clint moved over to Matt, getting him alone. "Martin said you rode into Circle Y. You accused Circle Y of ambushin' you."

"What's it to you?"

"You know an' I know Circle Y shot from the brush. If Martin himself never used that rifle then a Circle Y man did — Jocko Smith, or some other Circle Y hand."

Matt said nothing.

"When Circle Y ambushed you it became my worry for two reasons. First, I'm the elected head of these farmers. Second, you're still my brother."

Matt watched him.

Clint's voice lowered. "Hell, Matt, I know — we never have got along very good, you an' me. But still, blood is thicker than water. You're still of the same flesh and blood as me. And I'd rest a lot easier if you'd take my first advice and ride out, brother."

Sardonic humour flecked Matt's blue eyes.

"I'll give it much thought," Matt said.

That evening after work Matt rode to Beavertail City. Clint was not gambling in the saloon as he'd expected. Clint had ridden away from the dam-site immediately after their talk.

Wad Martin and Jocko Smith came out of the Mercantile carrying two boxes of supplies. Matt happened to be walking past the Circle Y wagon when the two dumped the boxes in the rig.

Jocko Smith glared at Matt, but said nothing. Wad Martin wiped sweat and also was silent.

Matt did not speak to them.

Matt walked to the end of the street, turned the corner by the blacksmith shop, came to the alley and went down it, and then the low voice of Wad Martin came from a deserted shed.

Matt entered the old building.

Squatting backs to the wall, Matt and Wad Martin talked quietly. Once Martin snorted, "Gunfight! The lyin' bastard! We never at any times came close to guns."

"You think he really wrote the army?"

"I doubt it. The C.O. over at Assiniboine is an ol' time friend of mine. Durin' the Sittin' Bull trouble he quartered troops at Circle Y. I'm ridin' into Malta tonight. I can wire to Assiniboine from there."

"Good idea."

Wad Martin got to his feet.

Matt asked, "This rustlin' cattle. I'm working with those farmers. And for the life of me, Wad, I can't picture them as cattle-thieves. They claim you've lost no stock."

"Then why would I say I have?"

"To point the finger toward the farmers. That's what they say, Wad. They say you're claimin' to lose stock just to get them upset and have a reason for movin' against them."

Martin swore softly. "I wrote to the Stockman's Association in Helena. Asked them to send out a range-detective. He's never reported to me, if he is on this grass — and he might not be."

"Why say that?"

"The Association is terrible busy, Matt. Lotsa cow-stealin' goin' on all over the territory. Down in

442

the Judith Gap country, Angus MacDonald's Bar 5 has been almost rustled outa business. MacDonald hung six rustlers the other day, not waitin' for the law to step in." Martin chuckled mirthlessly. "Hope he never by accident strung up an Association detective."

Matt knew what Martin meant. Association men worked in with rustlers, helped them steal to get the goods on them — they played a dangerous, tough role. And one might have got hanged by mistake.

The disclosure that Martin had sent out for a range-detective put a new light on this situation to Matt Harrison. Martin had not told him this that day on Circle Y.

"I never needed no supplies," Martin said. "I jus' come to town on a hunch that you'd be here. Ride light, Matt. An' if somethin' breaks, come to me."

"I'll do that."

Wad Martin went to the door, glanced up and down the alley, saw it was empty, and left. Matt rolled a cigarette and inhaled deeply, thoughts busy.

Now who on Beavertail Range could possibly be the range-detective? Carefully, man by man, Matt reviewed everybody he knew on this grass, but got absolutely nowhere.

Angrily, he ground his cigarette dead.

Matt rode home after seeing Wad Martin. Ahead of him in the moonlight he saw the thin dust left by Circle Y's wagon. He followed the well-travelled wagon road, taking no shortcuts.

The irony of this hit him, making him smile.

He had ridden into Beavertail to say *hello* to his

brother. Wad Martin had slugged him from saddle. Now he and Martin were in cahoots. The world was a mixed-up affair.

He reached Beavertail Creek and left the road leading to Circle Y, turning east on the farm-road. This trail, though, occasionally twisted through cottonwood groves; he avoided these, riding south across the prairie.

The night was calm without wind. Only a few of the farmers held lights although the hour was early. This was only logical. These men and women had worked hard all day at the dam-site. And morning came early to weary bodies.

Matt's heart went out to them. They were good, strong people — they'd uprooted themselves from old ties and moved west into a wilderness, fighting to tame it. He realized they slept brokenly with the overshadowing threat of Circle Y slashing their dreams.

Suddenly, he tensed in leather. He'd glimpsed something move in the brush north about a hundred yards. Instantly his rifle was out of scabbard, to his shoulder roaring.

He shot four times, the rifle-reports making brittle crackings. He was off his horse, lying on his belly. His horse stood with reins down. He looked at the horse's ears. They were not pointed toward the grove. Slowly, Matt got to his feet, cramming new cartridges into the rifle's magazine.

He cocked his head, listening. No retreating hoof-beats, no scound — only the stillness of the silent Montana night.

Leading his horse, rifle under his arm, he walked

into the brush, stopped, stared at the mule-tail deer, lying dead in the short burned-down grass.

Matt shook his head slowly. His nerves were really on edge. He'd glimpsed movement, fired — and killed this buck deer. An ugly thought hit him, souring his belly.

What if this had been a farmer riding along — or somebody just going from a shack to the creek for water?

He would have killed an innocent person.

He was angry at himself for acting like a trigger-happy killer. He would have to keep a tighter rein on his nerves in the future. He looked around. The closest shack was that of Henry Lucas a quarter mile away. It had a light but nobody came out. Matt guessed that the Lucas family had not heard the shooting.

He cut the buck's throat, bled the carcass, tied it behind his saddle, and mounted. When he rode past the Lucas house he thought of Lettie. She was a beautiful, kind, sweet little woman but he would walk light around her . . . at least for the present. to make advances toward Lettie would be unfair to her for somebody was out to kill him.

Nels Hannigan's tent was dark. Matt could see no saddle horses around it nor on the pasture. He scowled. Where was Hannigan? In bed asleep? Matt had not seen him in Beavertail City. He shrugged and dismissed these thoughts.

Clint's shack also was dark. Maybe Clint had gone to bed early? And Slow Elk had also hit the sougans at an early hour. Clint had reason to be in bed. His poker game had run through two straight days and nights of gambing.

Matt glanced back at the buck deer. He could not eat all this venison before it spoiled. Slow Elk might like a bit of venison. Matt dismounted and pounded on Clint's door but got no reply. He pounded again and called twice but still no answer.

He saw three saddle horses on the pasture, but he did not know if any were missing for he did not know how many horses Clint and Slow Elk had. He twisted the door knob. The door was unlocked. He entered and thumbed a match to life.

The flaring light showed clearly the dirty shack — Clint's unmade but empty bed, dishes piled on the table, a bunch of unwashed pans on the cast iron stove. Clint went to the gunny sacking that made a door to Slow Elk's lean to. The Indian's bunk also was empty but the bed was made up and the room such as it was, was neat and clean. The match burned Matt's fingers. He dropped it and ground it dead with the sole of his boot, scowling as he rubbed his burnt thumb.

This was not logical. At least Slow Elk should have been home, for the Crow had worked all day under the boiling sun; he should be in bed sleeping the sleep of the tired. But he was not. And where had he ridden to at this hour?

Matt returned to his horse and rode toward the Westby farm. He would give the Westby's some venison. The Westby shack also had no lights.

Matt leaned forward in saddle, helloing the cabin. His voice died in the distance of the night but nobody came to the door nor was a light lit inside. Frowning, he dismounted and knocked on the door, but got no answer. He knocked three more times but still nobody came.

The door was unlocked, but he did not enter. He went instead to the barn. Jane's gaudy pinto was missing and so was Sig Westby's black gelding.

Again Matt frowned. This seemed to be the night he could not give away venison, he thought ironically. He rode home where he hung the buck by his hind legs in a cottonwood tree.

He gutted the buck, skinned him, folded the hide neatly over a limb, and then entered his shack undressing in the dark for bed. He would quarter the buck in the morning and distribute it among the farmers.

Sleep was slow in coming. For a long time he lay in the hot darkness thinking. It seemed odd that both Clint's shack and that of the Westby's should be unoccupied. He had seen neither Clint or Slow Elk or any of the Westby's in town.

Sleep came in and claimed him.


Clint Harrison met Margaret Martin the next night at their usual meeting place. This time Margaret did not run into his arms, though; Clint scowled.

"Something wrong?" he asked.

"I don't like this, Clint. I'm doing all the work alone. You and that Westby hussy spend the whole of yesterday down on that darned dam, leaving it for me to push cattle down on Alkali Flat."

Anger grabbed Clint but he held it. "There's one little thing you don't know, Margaret. Last night Jane and me worked cattle down toward the flat. You were home sleeping. At least you should have been. Then today Jane and me were at the site of the dam so nobody would get suspicious that we were in the saddle all night long!"

Margaret's dark eyes studied him and then she laughed lightly. "Once again I'm wrong as usual! I thought somebody had moved some of those steers closer to Alkali. I'm sorry, Clint. But my nerves — they're filed sharp, lover. I want to get out of here. Let's leave after this next raid? You and me together, Clint? Please."

Clint's breathing tightened. Last night in the brush Jane had put the same question to him and now he answered Margaret as he had answered Jane Westby.

"We've got something here that pays us good money, darling. I hate to ride off and leave it too soon. Let's make this raid and one more and then jerk stakes, huh?"

"I want to leave after the next raid," Margaret said. "I've got little to take — in fact, so little I could tie it behind my saddle."

"Let's make two more raids," Clint said.

"But there's danger, Clint, and we have enough money. I've found you at last. darling, and the thought of maybe losing you . . ." Her voice trembled.

Clint put an arm around her lovely shoulders. She laid her dark head on his chest, sobbing slightly. Clint waited patiently for her sobs to stop.

"We stage just two more," he said quietly, "and then we leave, honey. What do you say about Mexico City?"

Her sniffling stopped immediately. She stared up at him with parted lips and gleaming dark eyes.

"Oh, how I would love that! Lots of new dresses, swell cafes to dine in — you and me on the big boulevards! I've read about Mexico City. Clint, I can't believe it, sweetheart!"

"It can come true," Clint lied, "but first we have to work cattle, Margaret."

Margaret paused. "My father. I can't understand it, Clint. Last night, after Dad and Jocko Smith came back from town!"

"What happened?"

"They came home about nine and Dad immediately saddled a fresh horse and rode north toward Malta. I know. I trailed him ten miles."

Clint's heart jumped. "When did he come back?"

"Six this morning. And he rode in on a horse he had rented from the livery stable in Malta. He must have really pounded leather, for the horse he rode in on was lathered heavily."

Clint realized instantly the significance of Wad Martin's long ride to the county seat. From Malta Wad Martin could have wired the Commanding Office at Fort Assiniboine, for Malta had a railroad and a telegraph wire. From the Commanding Officer Martin could have learned that he, Clint Harrison, had not sent Fort Assiniboine a letter asking for cavalry help. Clint's blood chilled.

Silently he cursed himself for thinking up such a silly idea. But the plan had come on the spur of the moment and now it had apparently backfired. This left but one thing to do; get out and get out of the country fast.

"Let's work cattle," he grunted.

They mounted and pointed their horse toward

the northwest. Jane would not ride with them tonight. Clint realized he had made two other errors also. One error had occurred when he had had Nels Hannigan shoot at Matt. The other had happened when he had tried to ambush his brother. Clint knew his brother. Matt had the tough Harrison blood in his veins. Matt was angry now and anger to Matt was a slow and burning and driving thing. Matt was a bulldog; he had his teeth clamped on a problem. And Matt would solve that problem or die trying. Again coldness hit Clint's blood, chilling his belly. Tomorrow night this herd would have to be moved and sold to Emerson. He leaned over in saddle and told Margaret.

"By tomorrow night we'll have one half of the steers gathered," Margaret assured. "Alkali Flats has lots of big three and four year olds. What's the rush, Clint?"

Clint decided to keep his mouth shut. He might tip his hand by talking too much. Jane and Margaret would not ride on this last raid unless each accidentally muscled in somehow. He looked at the big moon. The calendar said this moon would last another week.

"You're right," he said. "There's no rush. This will prob'ly be our biggest raid. This is Tuesday, ain't it?"

"All day," Margaret said.

"We move stock Friday night."

They pushed on through the night, two dark dots moving across the silent frontier, and Clint let his thoughts range to finally settle on Matt. He did not know that even now Matt and Wad Martin and Jocko Smith were in the brush behind Matt's tent holding a meeting.

Wad Martin said, "Your brother lied. He sent no letter to the Commanding Officer at Fort Assiniboine."

"Maybe the letter hasn't had time to get there," Matt said. "I'm not trying to protect Clint. I'm just stating a fact."

Martin shook his head. "The mails can't be that slow. Clint claimed he sent out the letter the day the stage came out with the mail from Malta. The letter would reach Malta by the next morning and get thrown on the Great Northern train going west and be in Fort Assiniboine by the next day at least."

"Lying is nothing now for Clint," Matt said.

Martin asked, "Is Clint on his homestead now?"

Matt shook his head. "I just came from there and Clint's not there. Neither is his Indian."

Jocko Smith spoke for the first time. "Clint ain't in town. I just come from there."

"Him and his Injun are out rustlin' Circle Y beef," Wad Martin growled.

"We have no direct proof," Matt pointed out.

"Where else would they be?" Martin demanded.

Clint did not answer that. "I scouted Clint's shack last night, too," he said. "Both him and the Indian were gone. And the Westby shack was empty, too."

Martin shook his head. "I don't understand all of this," he admitted.

Jocko Smith cut in with, "Hell, boss, it's simple! Westby an' his sister are out rustlin' Circle Y beef, too!"

Matt said, "No direct proof on that, either. We're just letting our imaginations work for us, men."

"Where else would they be at night?" Martin said testily. "Where are the Westby's now?"

"They're in their cabin," Matt said. "Or at least they were a half hour ago. I know because I delivered some venison to them."

"That was half an hour ago," Martin said. "They could have both ridden out since then."

Matt got to his feet. "I'm going to have a long talk with that Westby guy," he said.

Martin grabbed Matt's arm. "That's my job!"

Matt studied him.

"They're stealin' *my* cattle," Martin pointed out.

Matt said quietly, "Take it easy, Martin. We're all in the air on this thing — nothin' certain. And we don't want to fly off the handle, jump wrong."

Martin dropped his hand.

"I'm only sure of one thing," Matt said, "and that is that these farmers ain't rustlin' your beef. I've been with them about a week now. I know them purty well. They're worried bad . . . but they'll fight. And they all claim, to a man and woman, that none of them is stealin' off Circle Y."

"I'm beginnin' to believe that," Martin said slowly.

"Westby knows something', I'm sure. He's gone from home too many nights. But I want to talk to Westby when his sister can't hear."

"Why?"

"Jane Westby's gone over Clint. Hell, a man with one eye can see that! Clint's got a way with females, believe you me. And if Clint is on this rustlin', and Jane finds out we suspect him —"

Martin nodded.

Jocko Smith nodded.

"Wait here," Matt said. "I might be gone a long time, but I'll bring back Westby."

Matt was hidden in Beavertail creek brush when Sig Westby came from his cabin at nine to get a handful of twigs for the morning fire. He was bending over picking twigs when Matt glided silently in from behind, his pistol burying itself in Westby's broad back. Westby stiffened as though shot.

"Matt Harrison, Westby. Sorry to do this but couldn't take any chances. We're holding a pow-wow beyond my tent."

Westby stood up. "Put your gun away, Matt. Who's the *we*?"

Matt holstered his weapon. "Jocko Smith, Wad Martin and me."

Westby turned slowly and faced Matt. "That will save me a ride to Circle Y," he said, and Matt wondered at his words. "My sister's asleep. Or anyway she should be."

"Check her," Matt ordered.

Westby went into the cabin. Soon the lamp there died and Westby returned, a huge ambling bulk in the night. "She's sound asleep," he said. "Let's go."

They walked to Matt's place with Matt leading his horse. He tried conversation with Sig Westby but got only grunts. Jocko Smith and Wad Martin awaited in the same place. Only then did Sig Westby talk.

"You men have this cattle rustling figured out correct," the gnome informed. "And I should know, men, because I'm a range detective from the Stockman's Association."

"Where are your credentials?" Martin asked.

Westby laughed hoarsely. "Do you pick me as an absolute idiot, Martin? I pack no credentials. If I did, and somebody discovered them, I'd be a dead duck inside an hour. You'll have to take my word or contact Association headquarters in Helena."

A short pause. "I'll trust you," Martin said. "Why haven't you reported to me? I was the one that sent for a detective?"

"For two reasons. First, we had to get proof. Second, if seen talkin' to you, suspicions might be roused."

"Who's the *we*?" Matt asked.

"The Crow. Slow Elk."

Martin grabbed a hoarse breath. Jocko Smith stared at the huge man's wide face. Matt quickly added things up mentally.

Slow Elk and the Westby's had come into this area about the same date. Slow Elk had immediately tied himself to Clint. Matt's belly roiled acid. Clint had overstepped this time.

Westby talked low-voiced. He and Slow Elk had scouted range. Clint Harrison was the boss of the rustlers. Nels Hannigan rode with Clint. "Tomorrow I was going to look you up, Martin," Westby said. "Slow Elk and I have all the evidence we need. You just beat me to the draw."

"Where do they sell my steers?" Martin's voice was hoarse.

"So far every deal has been made in Skeleton Canyon. A butcher from Galena buys the steers. His name is George Emerson."

"I scouted him," Martin said. "I rode to Galena. But found no Circle Y hides around."

"He disposes of all evidence immediately. I don't know how he does it, but he does. And he butchers right away, too."

"Who rides with Clint Harrison and Nels Hannigan?" Martin asked.

Westby said slowly. "My sister, for one."

Matt's breath froze. He had suspected this but had hoped his suspicions groundless. He felt sorry for this huge man. It had taken a lot of soul-searching. lots of guts, to make this statement.

"Good God," Martin breathed.

Jocko Smith asked, "Anybody else?"

Sig Westby's huge eyes were on Wad Martin. Sig said, "Yes, one more person — your daughter, Martin!"

Wad Martin's jowls sagged suddenly.

Clint Harrison pulled in his sweaty black bronc. He cocked his head, listening. Surrounding him was the pitch blackness of Montana's highlands, for the moon had yet to rise.

Wind sang in scrub cedar, a monotonous sound that made listening difficult. But somewhere, downslope, a bronc broke brush, moving up the hill on which Clint sat.

Tension sawed his nerves, making them taut. He knew that the rider had to be Nels Hannigan, for he and Hannigan had agreed upon this spot as a meeting place.

Still, this was a dangerous game — and a man had to watch all corners, night and day. And Clint Harrison's big .45 was in his hand, covering the approaching sounds.

Behind him, wings suddenly boomed loudly in the night. The harsh sound twisted Clint Harrison in saddle, boots braced solidly in stirrups, his pistol instantly wheeling to cover the roar. Suddenly he heard a death cry — sharp and blood chilling. Then he realized the booming sound had been made by an owl sweeping down on a cottontail rabbit. He heard huge wings rustle away but he could not see the owl.

Tension left him and his gun sagged in his fingers. Again there was but the sound of approaching hoofs. He sleeved his forehead, realizing he was sweating. But that was only logical for the night was stinkingly hot and the humidity high.

He thought of the farmers. They would be lying naked on their bunks with their beds close to the open windows. Clint grinned to himself. Fools, these farmers — all of them! Idiots, in fact.

A man would have to be crazy to become a farmer and fight this parched earth and break his back for a few lousy dollars a year. He had nothing but contempt for the farmers.

He thought of Beavertail dam. Would Circle Y allow the dam to be finished? He did not know; he did not care. He had gold and plenty of it. There would be this one raid and then no more. Everything he owned — even his money — was in the slim bedroll tied behind his saddle.

After getting paid tonight for this stolen herd he would tell the women that there would be one more raid and that tomorrow they should sneak in and he would pay them. But they would get no pay. By morning he and Nels Hannigan would be drifting toward the Gulf of Mexico and a tramp steamer for Argentina.

Now the rider loomed indistinctly in the darkness and Clint recognized Nels Hannigan's bony figure.

"This way," he said, holstering his gun. Hannigan drew rein. His horse breathed harshly, ribs rising and falling from his steep climb.

"Where's Margaret?" Hannigan asked.

Clint laughed. "I told her we would hit these cattle on Friday, and she's home sleeping, I suppose."

"We might need another rider. These steers are sort of ringy."

"We won't need another hand," Clint coldly pointed out. "These steers are already pretty well bunched."

"You're the boss," Hannigan said. "Where's Jane?"

"She's prob'ly working cattle down on the Flat. I worked at the dam this afternoon and she wasn't there. The big goof of a brother of hers wasn't there either — he was home, too. Therefore I couldn't ride in and talk to Jane." Clint scratched his jaw thoughtfully. "That brother of Jane's — Sig — I can't quite peg his place on this grass."

Hannigan scoffed. "Hell, Sig Westby is just a big dumb farmer, nothin' more."

"I hope you're right," Clint said. He turned his horse. "We'd better get off this rimrock and start working cattle because the morn'll be up soon."

"What'd we do with Jane after we get paid?"

Clint Harrison laughed sourly. "Use what little brains you've got under your Stetson, Hannigan! Things will be the same as usual. Jane will go home figuring I'll give her her cut tomorrow but when tomorrow comes Clint Harrison won't be around. And the same goes for Margaret."

Hannigan laughed sourly. "There'll be two mad young sagehens on this range tomorrow night this time," he said.

Clint asked, "Did you see Emerson?"

"Yeah. He'll be in Skeleton Canyon as usual. I wonder if me not working today at the dam caused any questions? It was a heck of a long ride to Galena and back in one day."

"I made an excuse for you," Clint said. "I told the Raymers you'd got a letter saying that your mother was seriously sick and you'd gone to Malta to wire your brother about her."

"My poor mother," Hannigan said. "She's been under Texas sod for only about thirty years now and now she's sick."

The moon was up by the time they reached Alkali Flats. Jane was hazing cattle downward where the herd was slowly forming itself on the wide mesa. Jane rode out of the brush on a sorrel horse. Clint had bawled her out about riding the showy pinto.

"Did you clear yourself at home?" Clint asked her.

Jane nodded. "Not hard at all. You see, Sig wasn't at home when I left. He rode into town right after eating supper. He said he intended to play cards and shoot pool in the saloon."

"Good," Clint said.

"Where's Margaret?" Jane asked.

"Home in bed, I guess. She and me chased cattle all last night. I'm dead on my boots from lack of sleep."

Jane's voice hardened, "I hope you did no more than chase steers," she said curtly.

Clint summoned a laugh. "Don't talk so silly, Jane. You're the woman for me and by this time you should know it and not talk so loco!"

Hannigan looked down at the steers to hide his smile. The steers were a black dot below on the clearing. "This herd is pretty well bunched," he said.

Clint spoke to Jane. "Why didn't Sig work on the dam today?"

"He said he wasn't feeling well and he stayed in bed all day. And I was glad, too. It gave me an excuse not to go to that damned dam! Besides I got some sleep, too."

"Start moving cattle," Clint ordered.

Soon wild steers crashed through the brush. Clint worked cattle automatically, dead tired in the saddle, his thoughts for some reason swinging to the Crow, Slow Elk. Slow Elk had worked only the morning shift on the dam. This afternoon the redskin had gone out hunting. When Clint had left the homestead Slow Elk had been occupied with salting down a blacktail buck deer he had shot.

Clint did not know that a few minutes after he had left the shack, Slow Elk had ridden out and met Matt in the brush. "I made a long ride today," the Crow told Matt. "I changed horses four times, roping range horses, and I rode them hard."

"Whad did you find out in Galena?"

"Emerson is low on beef. That means that these rustlers might move a herd tonight."

Matt nodded. "I met Jocko Smith along the hills about sundown. He and Wad Martin have been out ridin' all day and Jocko told me the cow thieves had quite a herd already gathered and that it looked like the cows were ready to be moved toward Galena."

459

"Herd in the same place?"

"Yep, it is. On Alkali Flats northwest of Circle Y."

"Sig Westby's hiding out in the brush behind Circle Y," Slow Elk said, "And I'd better get over there and warn him. I'll see you later, Matt."

"I'm riding with you," Matt said.

"Matt, what's the idea? These rustlers haven't been rustling your cattle. You're not a detective for the stockmen."

"I know I'm not," Matt said, "but remember this — I've been ambushed twice, and I almost got killed the last time. If that bullet had been two inches higher I'd've got shot in the guts."

"But what has that got to do with cow stealing?"

Matt grabbed the Crow by a wrist, finger digging the dark skin. "Slow Elk, you're not telling me all you know," he gritted. "You've scouted this range and I think you know who ambushed me! Come on, fella — talk!"

Matt's pressure tightened. Slow Elk studied Matt, thick lips sagging slightly.

"I've got my ideas about the man who shot at me that day when I was fencing," Matt said. "That was Nels Hannigan, I'm sure. He said he was hunting his work horses but he sneaked into the hills and used his rifle on me. But who shot the fork out of my saddle?"

"Matt, please —"

"Do you know, Slow Elk?"

Finally Slow Elk said, "Let go of my wrist, please." Matt released the man's arm. Slow Elk said slowly, "I guess I might just as well tell you, Matt, although I don't want to."

"Clint? My own brother?"

"I never saw the man who did the shooting, of course, but I was in my bunk when Clint came home that night. He thought I was sleeping. I saw him douse iodine on a break in the skin on one arm."

"My own brother." Matt's voice was hollow.

"Next morning I saw Clint's shirt he'd worn that night. Two holes in it, made by a bullet. Blood around the holes. Later on, he burned the shirt — and it was a good one, one he'd just bought."

Bitterness curled Matt's belly. But he had suspected this, all the time — therefore, in reality, this knowledge only confirmed.

"He's still your flesh and blood," Slow Elk said slowly. "You're not evil at heart, Matt. You couldn't kill your own brother."

Matt nodded. "No, but I could beat the hell out of him," he said, and swung up.

They rode toward Circle Y, neither speaking.

Sig Westby crouched in the high brush behind Circle Y buildings. The moon had just risen. Westby carried a Winchester .30-30 rifle. He looked at Matt, then at the Crow.

"You told Matt?" He spoke to Slow Elk, who nodded. Sig Westby's heavy face sagged. "I wish you hadn't."

"He had to," Matt said, "or I'd've killed him!"

"They'll move stock tonight, I'm sure. A big bunch of Circle Y's best steers are bunched on Alkali Flat."

Matt nodded.

"These men are killers, Matt. There'll be shootin'. And Clint is, after all, your brother."

"He *was*, you mean," Matt clipped.

461

Sig sighed loudly. "Margaret has been chasing out steers today. Worked until noon. Jocko Smith reported up to me an hour ago. Wad and Jocko saw her."

Matt realized he wasn't the only one tormented by a flesh-and-blood problem. Martin was in the same boat.

Sig asked, "Where's Jane?"

"You rode toward town," Slow Elk said. "A few minutes later — after you were out of sight — Jane left the homestead."

"Out in the hills shoving down stolen stock." Sig Westby's voice was a husky whisper.

Sig was in that boat, too.

"Margaret?" Matt asked.

Sig said, "Smith said she was sleeping like dead. Martin'll station the old mozo to see Margaret doesn't leave Circle Y. At least she won't be in the line of battle . . . like my sister . . ."

"They might not fight," Matt said. Then, to the Crow, "Slip down to Circle Y and alert Martin and Smith."

"Margaret might be up and around."

"Look in the corner of the living-room window. Martin and Smith promised to be in that room. If Margaret is there, don't tap — go to the second window on the east side."

Slow Elk nodded.

"That's Martin's bedroom," Sig said. "If Margaret is in the living-room, either Smith or Martin will be in that bedroom."

The Crow melted into the moonlight.

Matt asked quietly, "What're the odds, Sig?"

"Emerson will have two men. He usually does and

I think this will be no exception. Then there'll be Clint and Hannigan. And Jane."

"Who's riding with us from Circle Y?"

"Martin. Smith."

Five against six, Matt reasoned — but one of the six was a woman, and Sig probably meant to throttle her first, dragging her out of the battle. After this was over, Clint would either be dead or put away in prison for a long, long time — probably the rest of his life. Or Circle Y might hang Clint and Hannigan. They strung-up cowthieves on this range.

But he'd never let Smith and Martin string up Clint. Prison, yes — or death, but no hanging.

"We might have this figured all wrong," Matt said slowly. "They might not run beef tonight."

Sig nodded.

"Then what?"

"We got to catch them in the act," Sig Westby said. "The law reads that way, Matt."

Matt could only nod.

Within minutes, Slow Elk, Jocko Smith and Wad Martin came out of the brush, Smith and Martin leading dark-coloured horses. Margaret was sleeping like dead.

Martin said, "We ride to Skeleton Canyon?"

Sig said, "Yes."

"You're the stockman's detective," Wad Martin told Sig Westby, "and it's up to you to handle this affair."

Sig nodded. "Let's ride," he said.

463

Overhead the calm Montana moon rode in a cloudless sky. Under that moon cattle moved. The steers were bays, duns, sorrels, blacks. Some were splotched with black and gray and others red and gray. They were all steers. No calves, no cows, no bulls. They were three year olds and four year olds. They were big of bone and long of horn. They all bore the Circle Y brand.

Clint Harrison rode the drags on the north side, pointing cattle toward the upper reaches of the foothills. This was a wild herd and the cattle had reason for being afraid of man.

As calves they had been roped and branded and castrated. As steers they had been hounded during beef roundup and had been shunted aside until they had got old enough to ship to the railhead and be shipped to Chicago and the market. All their lives riders had handed out one thing to them — and that had been pain.

Now for almost a week riders had prodded them, cut them back from their home range, and pushed them toward Alkali Flats. Now they were all bunched on that mesa. Their sharp hoofs pounded the white crust of alkali and sent up a thin gray dust that hung listlessly in the moonlight. Clint Harrison pulled up his bronc, eyes on the herd in hungry appraisal. These cattle meant money . . . and lots of it.

Greed dried his throat, made his arteries pound. He glanced up at the moon. It should last until the cattle were in Skeleton Canyon and were the charges of George Emerson. He saw Jane move out of the hanging white dust and he rode closer to her and drew rein.

Jane smiled lovingly at him, strikingly beautiful in the moonlight, and this soured the belly of Clint Harrison. This tiny, lovely little blonde was a fool. Margaret Martin was a fool, too. All women were fools. They were meant to be used and then thrown aside.

Clint said, "You're lovely tonight, darling."

Jane smiled. "Thank you, sweetheart."

Nels Hannigan rode out of the night. He had a bandanna tied over his nose because of the dust. To Clint he looked like a highway man. Hannigan pulled down his mask.

"How many miles to Skeleton Canyon, Clint?" he asked.

Clint scowled. "I'd guess twelve miles."

Hannigan whirled his horse and turned back a steer that was quitting the herd. Clint's eyes momentarily rested on Hannigan's back.

Hannigan also had his money tied in his bedroll. Hannigan had a back and a man could put a bullet between Hannigan's shoulder blades. Or in the back of Hannigan's head. And then Hannigan would have no more money. Clint Harrison's hand itched for his gun but common sense held him back. The time to kill Hannigan was after this herd had been sold and when he and Hannigan were alone, their horses headed south.

They pushed the herd fast the first few miles to take the edge from the beeves. Steers rolled down coulees, climbed side-hills, sharp hoofs dragging on the parched soil.

Herd and riders entered the rough country. Now hills hid them from Beavertail Basin and the badlands were ahead. Once in those badlands they'd find an old trail and wind cattle along it, heading for grim Skeleton Canyon with its high, igneous walls.

Hannigan rode point, steers behind him. His job was to keep them from turning into a blind-coulee. Because cattle moved through a defile no flank-riders were needed; therefore Jane and Clint tailed the drags. Bullwhips were not used. Sometimes a bullwhip made a loud noise that could be heard a great distance.

Doubled lassos beat on bony backs.

Sweat coated Clint's forehead. He wheeled his horse with, "I'm droppin' back to scout."

Jane said scornfully, "Nobody tails us."

"Never know," Clint said.

He dropped back, found a dim trail leading up a cut-coulee. He put his bronc up it, hoofs scrambling. Puffing, straining against the saddle-cinch, the hard-breathing animal reached the summit. Here in the gigantic boulders Clint drew rein.

Eastward the land tumbled, savage and eroded, coulees leading down into Beavertail Basin, a moon-drenched land whose serenity was broken by dark clumps of brush and trees.

Because of the hill behind it, he could not see Circle Y ranch house, but carefully and slowly he ran his gaze over the territory — seeing no dark moving spots that would be riders.

Tension ran out of him, sagging his muscles. But still he watched, remaining on the hill for ten minutes before turning his horse down into the coulee again.

He spurred along the draw and, when he got to the herd, Jane was not in sight, and he frowned. He then heard hoofs behind him and whirled his horse, face angry.

"You scared me, damn it!"

Jane smiled through dust. "You're edgy, darling. I hid back there in the brush to make sure it was you, not somebody else. Put your gun away."

Clint holstered his .45. "You got brains, Jane. You'll do."

"To go all the way with, huh?"

"All the way," Clint lied.

"See anything?"

"Nothing but wilderness."

"Nobody's wise to us," Jane said.

She hammered a lagging steer over the rump with her catch-rope. The steer trotted into the herd, pushing his fellows aside.

"How long until Skeleton?" Jane asked.

Clint glanced at the moon. "About a hour."

They threaded Circle Y steers into Skeleton Canyon in less than that, the steers moving along the bottom of the huge defile. On each side were steep cliffs dotted with clumps of brush. Ahead three miles would be Emerson, stationed and counting.

Clint breathed deeply.

Soon the gold would be his.

Clint Harrison grinned.

Now two riders came plunging through the herd, riding against the stream, jostling the steers. Clint thought first that one was Hannigan, but they were the two Emerson hands.

"Boss says to move 'em faster," the tall one said.

Clint growled, "What's wrong with Emerson?"

"He wants them run through faster, he told me.

Sent us two back here to help you tail."

"Where's Hannigan?"

"Up with Emerson. Runnin' count with him."

Clint beat a steer with his lariat. "We'll move them faster," he said. "Anythin' to please his nibs."

Matt, Slow Elk, Sig and Circle Y held a brief conference back in the brush on the heights overlooking the point where Sig said Emerson always stationed himself to run his tally.

"Usually Hannigan or Clint ride lead," the gnome said. "Emerson usually has two men with him. That makes four men stationed on the bluff below."

"Sometimes the lead man rides back through the herd to help haze," Slow Elk said.

"We got to figure four at the count-point," Sig said. "That leaves only Harrison — or Hannigan — riding back with Jane."

Nobody spoke.

Sig said, "Slow Elk, take Smith and Matt with you. Station yourselves hidden in the brush on the canyon just opposite check point."

"You're the boss," the Crow said.

"Martin and me'll be back down-canyon about opposite the drags."

Matt understood. Sig figured his sister would be tailing beeves. He wanted to be close to her when trouble started.

"I'll go over it again," Sig said slowly. "We let about half the herd go by the count point. Then we break loose with rifles, stampede the herd west.

468

With most of them past the count point, they should run ahead, not back."

By stampeding the cattle up-canyon there'd be less danger of Jane being trampled to death, Matt knew.

"We can gather the stock after this is over," Sig said, "and point them back toward Beavertail."

Matt rubbed his jaw.

He and Slow Elk had swung northwest, after the riders had left Circle Y. He and the Crow had scouted and discovered the herd being moved. From a hill he had looked down on Clint working stolen beef.

Once sure beef was really moving, he and Slow Elk had rejoined Sig and Circle Y at Square Butte, and they had ridden to this point in a body, keeping in canyons to escape detection.

"Well," Sig said dryly, "here we go."

They left their saddle-horses in the boulders on top of the cliff. They pulled rifles from scabbards, crammed in shells, tugged six-guns into position.

Sig Westby and Wad Martin drifted away and became instantly lost in the shifting shadows. Matt and Slow Elk and Jocko Smith dropped over the lip of the canyon and started working their way downward, moving from brush clump to brush clump.

Matt glanced into the canyon below. Here the gorge was so narrow only two cows could pass abreast. It was an ideal spot to count cattle. Lying in the brush on his belly, Matt studied the scene below. He saw three saddled horses tied to a tree on the canyon's opposite wall. These would be the saddlers of Emerson and his two cow thieves.

He could see no trace of Emerson and his men.

Evidently they had hidden themselves in a motte of high brush. He looked about but saw no trace of Jocko Smith or Slow Elk. Crawling on all fours Matt descended to another bunch of buckbrush. His flesh tingled. If he were glimpsed from below a bullet might tear into his body.

He worked downward cautiously, carefully, seeing he loosened no boulders or rocks to tumble into the canyon as a warning. It took him a good twenty minutes of careful crawling to reach the base of the canyon where he stationed himself in an area of juniper about ten feet above the canyon's floor. Carefully he drew himself up into a sitting position. He held his rifle across his knees. He listened.

From down the canyon came the low sound of men speaking in quiet voices. He could not see the speakers. Again he looked about for the Indian and the foreman of Circle Y. Again he saw no sign of Smith or Slow Elk.

He waited with thumping heart. Time shuffled by on leaden boots. The period of waiting seemed never to end but finally his ear caught the cadence of faraway hoofs and then he heard the muted bawl of an angry Circle Y steer.

Now a rider spurred up the canyon to pull to a dust-raising halt at the point where the cattle would be counted. Because of the distance Matt could not see whether the rider was Clint or Hannigan. Three shadowy forms came from the brush. They would be Emerson and his two cowboys. After a while Matt saw two of the group climb the slope to the saddle horses and then these two loped down the canyon.

Matt did not like the way things had turned out. Now only two men were at the point where the cattle would be counted. Three cowpunchers would be driving the herd with only Wad Martin and Sig Westby to face them. Suddenly he heard a distant hiss from beside him. He swung his rifle, thinking a rattlesnake had made the sound, but then he saw Slow Elk lying on his belly ten feet away, and Matt's rifle drooped.

Slow Elk inched forward and halted at Matt's right. The Crow whispered, "Jocko Smith dropped back to help Wad Martin and Sig, Matt."

Matt nodded approval. By now the sounds of the approaching cattle were much stronger.

"Here comes the cows now," Slow Elk said.

The lead steers were moving around the bend in the canyon, their hoofs grinding rock and sand. Within a few feet they would be passing the point where they would be counted. Matt glanced up at the ridge and saw a dim form move to its lip, the cattle trotting underneath the man's view, dust rising in the thin moonlight.

Evidently the man on the ridge was Emerson. Even as Matt watched another form moved ahead and stood beside Emerson. This would be one of Emerson's cowboys, Matt reasoned.

Heart hammering, Matt studied this man, his eyes trying to pierce the uncertain moonlight, and he decided it was not Clint but Nels Hannigan, and his blood settled.

Hoof-sound was louder now. Slow Elk put his mouth close to Matt's ear, breath hot on Matt's cheek.

"Be sure to let more than half the herd go past the count point, Matt."

Matt nodded.

Cattle moved on, pushed faster now. Matt got to his haunches, sitting there, watching. Dust rose, reaching his nostrils. He liked the sight of cattle below. Always the sight of a cow-herd stirred him. He realized he was, at heart, a Texan, a cowman.

Harshness grabbed a muscle in his left thigh. Gingerly, he uncoiled his leg, stretched it. His eyes caught Slow Elk's. The Crow smiled softly. At that moment he liked the Indian very much.

No shooting had occurred at the drag of the herd. That told Matt that Smith, Hawkins and Sig Westby were going to move only after the rifles of Matt and Slow Elk boomed.

Cattle moved endlessly . . . or so it seemed to Matt. Finally, Slow Elk got to his feet, rifle raised.

"Pick a man," he said.

Matt got to his feet, blood yammering again. He did not like this; it bespoke too much of ambush. Then he remembered a bullet tearing his saddle's fork, spilling his bronc.

His jaw hardened.

"I'll take Emerson," Slow Elk breathed.

Emerson was on the right.

Matt raised his rifle to shoulder. He tried to find his sights but the moonlight was not that brilliant. He centred on the man whom he believed to be Nels Hannigan.

"All set?" Slow Elk asked.

"As much as I'll ever be."

"Shoot!"

Two rifles roared as one.

The canyon rattled with noise bouncing back from granite walls. For one long second everything stood still. Now the steers, wide-eyed and boogery, stampeded — the wrong direction.

Matt had expected them to run up-canyon, but they didn't. The lead animals whirled, horns clashing, and swung the herd around so it stampeded, tails high, horns battering, back down the canyon.

Matt's breath froze. He thought of Jane, hazing the steers — she'd be caught in the stampede.

Matt realized his bullet had missed Hannigan. Even now, Hannigan was zigzagging into the brush, heading for his horse on the mesa, Matt catching occasional glimpses of him as Hannigan moved from brush clump to brush clump.

He glanced at Emerson.

Slow Elk's bullet had missed, too. But Emerson, in his fear, ran the wrong direction, piling toward the lip of the cliff. Reaching it, he turned right, but he'd gone too close to the canyon. A rock slid under him, Emerson screamed. Then he was sliding down slope. Matt watched, throat tight.

It was a frozen tableau of horror. Emerson screamed again, tried to scramble up-slope, but gravel slid under him. Matt saw a steer hook Emerson, horn catching clothing, and Emerson slid under the grinding hoofs and out of sight.

"Hannigan!" Slow Elk yelled.

Matt swung his rifle toward Hannigan who barged into a clearing, not more than ten feet from his saddle-horse. Urgency hit Matt's trigger-finger — once in saddle, Hannigan would be gone.

Again, he and Slow Elk fired simultaneously.

Matt never knew which one hit Hannigan. Hannigan stopped as though he'd crashed into a stone wall. For a long moment, his body bent, then came rearing upward.

Hannigan said nothing. He stood poised against the moonlight for a moment, then broke and slid on his face, rifle slipping from his fingers. The rifle slid downward, caught on a bush.

Slow Elk said, "We need horses."

Already the last of the herd had passed back through the cut, leaving dim dust trailing behind. Matt ran down slope, skidding on a talus cone, rifle held high, Slow Elk pounding at his heels. They reached the canyon's bottom, ran across the sand, then hastily climbed to the mesa, slung legs over the horses of Emerson and Hannigan.

Matt swung into saddle, curbed his rearing mount. The stirrups were too short, but that made no nevermind.

"Shooting," he gritted. "Down canyon, Slow Elk."

"She must be a hell of a mixup, Matt." Slow Elk jabbed a thumb toward Hannigan's inert form. "He's dead. I checked."

Matt hollered, "Let's ride!"

Horse slid down onto the canyon's floor. Matt spurred his borrowed horse ahead with hard rowels, Slow Elk pounding on the bronc's heels. When they loped past the place where Emerson had fallen into the cattle, Matt looked down. What he saw made him shudder.

Emerson looked like a limp bag of old clothing. Sharp hoofs had hammered him into the sand. Matt and Slow Elk loped on, neither speaking. Dust hung in thick clouds. Matt coughed and spat and bent lower over his saddle. He could hear no shooting ahead but the hoofs of the stampeding cattle made too much noise, he knew.

Matt and Slow Elk came to the cattle, a bunch of running bovine backs. Matt tried to spur into the beeves but his horse bounced back, unable to make an entry.

Slow Elk hollered, "We can't ride through those cows, Matt. We'll just have to drift with them. No horse alive could beat his way into those tons of beef!"

Matt realized the Crow spoke the truth. All was dust and running, bawling cattle. Suddenly a rider appeared ahead in the dust. Matt realized he had reached the point where the Circle Y men and Sig Westby had been stationed. He heard Wad Martin holler, "Hold your fire, boys!" Only then did he recognize the rider as the owner of Circle Y.

Matt and Slow Elk reined in, horses rearing as they fought their bits. Now the dust had blown away and Matt saw Wad Martin's big face clearly. The face was strained, the eyes narrowed.

The last of the cattle thundered out of sight around a bend, and a gust of wind whipped in and cleared the dust away, and only then did Matt see the other riders.

Sig Westby was on his knees bending over the form of his sister. Matt stared.

475

Wad Hawkins laid his hand on Matt's arm. "She's dead," he said tonelessly.

"And my brother?"

Wad Hawkins waved down-canyon. "Down there — dead — in the sand."

Matt remembered Emerson's broken, hoof-hammered body. "Where's Jocko Smith?"

"Back on the slope. Your brother killed him."

Matt looked at Sig Westby. Sig had his huge hands over his face. His thick shoulders shook.

Matt asked quietly, "Tell me."

Martin talked slowly, shock of the night still on him. Sig had jumped Jane, hoping to drag her from leather, shield her with his huge body, but Clint had hollered, "So you sold us out, you bitch!" and shot, just as Sig's arms got around Jane.

"Jocko and I shot at Clint at the same time. I don't know which one of us hit him, but he went from horse. He fell to one knee, swung his rifle — and Jocko got it in the chest, dying instantly."

Matt's face was pale.

"What became of the two Emerson men?"

"They got out, someway. I think one was shot, but I'm not sure. I saw them both good. I'd recognize them anywhere. Snodgrass'll pick them up."

Slow Elk looked at Sig and Jane. Matt saw sorrow engraved on the wide, dark face.

"My cattle will drift back," Martin said. "We'd better get to work here. Slow Elk, will you ride up on the bluff and bring back our horses?"

The dead were tied to saddles.

Martin said, "With Jocko dead, Circle Y needs a

range-boss. You want the job, Matt?"

"I'm a farmer," Matt said.

Martin's face was serious. "I can't fight these farmers. No land in the world is worth a night like this, Matt."

Matt said nothing.

"I'll run cattle back in the rough country and feed winters on the meadows — cut some hay of my own and buy from the farmers. I'll locate cowpunchers on homesteads, buy their homestead entries — I'd like to buy yours first, Matt."

"I'll sell."

"You tell the farmers, Matt. And I'll see you ride into Circle Y in a day or so?"

"I'll be there."

"I'll send Margaret back east for good. I should have done it a long time ago. She's always been a thorn between me and my missus."

Matt remained silent.

Martin rode east leading the horse carrying Jocko Smith.

Slow Elk gathered the reins of the horses bearing Emerson, Hannigan and Clint Harrison.

"I'll take these to town for burial, Matt."

"Tell Marshal Snodgrass about the two Emerson men," Matt said.

Slow Elk rode southeast. Matt watched until his brother's body was out of sight and then walked over to Sig Westby.

"Can I help you, friend?"

Sig climbed ponderously to his feet, red eyes holding tears. "I tried to save her, Matt, but Clint shot too fast. He accused her of squealing — double-crossing him."

"Martin told me."

"This is a hell of a thing for a brother to say, Matt — but maybe it was for the best. She was wild at heart — she wanted men — she'd have gone the way of her mother. And I'd rather see her dead than in some saloon —"

Matt looked at Jane. Jane lay on her back, face drained, blood on her blouse, golden hair a shimmer. Hardness grabbed Matt's throat; silently he cursed fate.

Sig went to his horse and mounted, sitting behind the cantle on the saddle-skirts. "Hand her up to me, Matt? And gently, please! I'll bury her on our homestead. I'm keeping our farm."

Tenderly, Matt raised Jane into saddle ahead of her brother, who put a huge arm around her. Jane's head lolled. Sig kissed her on the cheek.

"I'm ready, Matt."

Matt swung into leather. They rode across country toward their farms. They rode slowly. The moon would last until they reached Beavertail Creek. Matt would get the farmers out of bed and tell them of Wad Martin's promise.

Farmers and sons would shout for joy. Wives and girls would dance and sing with glowing, happy eyes. Children would run and holler and wrestle and scream.

Matt thought of Lettie Lucas.

Lettie would smile up at him, eyes gay and dancing. Matt liked that thought. Lettie was lovely and clean and good.

478

And because Matt Harrison thought of Lettie, he found a great deep and solid happiness.